The Short Life

The Short Life

A Novel
by

Aharon Megged

Translated from the Hebrew by Miriam Arad

TAPLINGER PUBLISHING COMPANY
New York

First printing
First published in the United States in 1980 by
TAPLINGER PUBLISHING CO., INC.
New York, New York

Copyright © 1980 by Aharon Megged
Printed in the United States of America

Library of Congress Cataloging in Publication Data

Megged, Aharon, 1920-
   The short life : a novel.

   Translation of ha-Ḥayim ha-ḳetsarim.
   I. Title.
PZ4.M49Sh   [PJ5054.M352]   892.4'36   80-13001
ISBN 0-8008-7180-4

The lines on pp. 70, 71, 73, are from Tchernichovsky's poem "In
the Heat of the Noontide," from *Gems of Hebrew Verse*, translated by
Harry H. Fein. Reprinted courtesy of Branden Press, Inc., 21 Station
Street, Brookline Village, Boston, MA 02147

The realistic novel, based on a chronological, cause-and-effect narrative, has nothing more to say. It is a poor man's literature. Anyone attempting to go back today to the Flaubert or Tolstoi manner—out of ignorance, naivete, or incompetence—will turn his writing from an "imitation of reality" into an imitation of literature.

DR. ELISHEVA TAL-BLUMFELD

On the face of it, Yehoshua Tal, an insurance agent in his forties, ought to have been happy. Three hundred and twenty-seven clients, a spacious apartment, a car—if a small one for the time being—a handsome, accomplished wife, a tall pretty daughter whom it's a pleasure to be seen in the street with—

In the middle of his life—yes, you might say in the middle of his life—he discovered that things weren't going right with him somehow: the income tax people were after him, the kitchen sink was getting clogged again and again, his daughter was withdrawing . . .

And friends. He has no friends. On the face of it, people are fond of him, slap his back, smile—but friends, no. All at once, at the office, taking a call, waiting on the line for an answer, it may hit him: there's no one! Not one!—and ripples of that thought stay with him sometimes all day. His mind roves over the whole town, the whole country: no one. Who? Where? So many contacts—with companies, clients, bank clerks, assessors, garage owners, widows—and no one. A chill seizes him, panic: alone in midocean. Well, yes, Raphi Gilead, from childhood. But Raphi Gilead is in the Regular Army. Far away. A different crowd. Come to think of it, it had been like that even in childhood, at school: everybody fond of him, everybody fondly calling him Fatty—and no one.

Elisheva, of course. But Elisheva teaches at the university. And in the evening, nearly every evening, right after supper, him still at his coffee, she gets up—sometimes a peck on his cheek: "I know, Shuka, but what can I do? My bread and butter . . ."

Retires to the study, shuts the door. . . . Only at midnight, maybe after—how long can a man stay awake after a day of running around?—he may sleepily register the stirring of the bedsprings as she gets in.

And the dirty dishes piling up in the sink.

And her never once asking how's business. He could be running up debts. He could be losing clients, couldn't he, instead of gaining new ones? Accidents do happen. Road accidents, fires, people dying, natural deaths and unnatural. Just plain human decency, isn't it, to show some interest?

Or take Acropolis.

Eight months back, when he'd left his two partners and set up on his own. Right after he'd fixed the brass plate to the door on the second story:

ACROPOLIS
Yehoshua Tal—Insurance

He had sat down by the phone and, just for fun, to surprise her, had called home and said in a deep and sort of very respectable voice: "Hallo, this is Acropolis speaking." "Who?" she had asked, sounding annoyed at the interruption. "Acropolis!" he had repeated, laughter bubbling up inside him. "Wrong number," and she had hung up.

Well then!

And when she had at last graciously consented—just once, mind you, because he had accused her of indifference and she had realized he was hurt—to come and see the office, one afternoon between lectures, she had stood in the middle of the little room containing nothing but a desk, chairs, and two filing cabinets, and exclaimed:

"Acropolis! What unspeakable taste to call such a hole Acropolis! Why not Taj Mahal, for that matter? Or Notre Dame?"

"So what would you have called it?" he had asked, smiling, his large shape ensconced in his chair behind the desk, monarch whose realm is being disparaged.

"Rachel's Tomb at best!" Swinging her handbag in a curve across half the room. And she hadn't liked the calendar because it showed a large picture—ugly, according to her, cheap—of forests in snow. "Then buy another," she had said when he explained to her—patiently, restraining himself—how that was what he'd been sent by Canadian Manufacturers Life Insurance. And she had decided to fix the place up herself: to move—with her own two delicate hands—one of the filing cabinets to another corner so that the two of them wouldn't stand "symmetrically" like that, one on each side of the desk.

"But what's wrong with symmetry?" he had said, drawing her away from the cabinet, not caring where it stood but worried she might strain something shifting it.

"I can't explain. It's just wrong!"

So now the two cabinets stood end to end at one side of the desk. Handier, actually.

And since then—not once.

If she shuns Acropolis, he told himself, I'll shun the study. And swore he wouldn't set foot in the place, and stuck to his word. Almost.

That is, not counting the occasional visit when no one was at home; slipping in, glancing at the books piled on the learned desk, looking up at the three pillars of wisdom—three wallfuls of fat volumes, floor to ceiling, mostly in English—like a tourist standing before the ancient Acropolis pillars; picking some encyclopedia off a shelf, opening it, skimming a few lines, taking good care to put it back without leaving a trace, slipping out again.

As though he had never been.

For all that, he thought, Acropolis was a sound name, good taste or not. A name that inspired confidence, evinced solidity. Absolutely.

And then there was income tax.

Their nagging.

He who keeps such meticulous account of all profit and expense, who holds on to every receipt, files it away, he who conceals nothing—who *has* nothing to conceal, dammit!—finds his mailbox stuffed with notifications, warnings, summonses, nearly every week! So go and dig up your sixty-three bank account! And tell them how you came by each miserable sum! And sit there, accused, suspect, cross-examined by some little clerk—

What a world!
And now this business with Jeanette.

JEANETTE Levy. Five months now.
Maybe more.

"Twenty thousand?" she had said, sitting across from him at the office and looking straight in his eyes. With a resentful look, he thought. Or no, not resentful—impudent.

"That's what it says in the policy," he told her. "Why?"

"That what it says?"

"Here, look."

"Okay," she had said, her eyes fixed on him.

Hostile again, he thought, or maybe suspicious. The widow's shawl across her shoulders went well with her face. A strong face, the color of cinnamon.

Tal took the particulars. Name, father's name, place of birth.

"Malta!" he exclaimed, marveling. "Mean there are Jews in Malta?"

"Some," she said. "Were."

"From Spain," she added.

Spain. *Corrida.* Briefly he felt the hot Mediterranean breeze, saw a gypsy on high heels, red dress whirling. *Olé!*

"Yes, electrocuted at the harbor." Answering his questions steadily. "Touched a steel bar. On the spot."

She searched her small handbag for cigarettes. He had none to offer, apologized, "I don't smoke."

"Doesn't matter," she said.

"Malta," he said, and blushed, because her face was close to his and the fierce stare unflinching. "What did he do there, your father?"

"Trader. Carpets."

Doña Levy. Exiled princess. Young widow and mourning becomes her.

"So?" getting up, breasts jutting. "You'll let me know?"

And when she turned to leave and pranced to the door on

high heels, he saw that her thighs in the tight black skirt had an exciting life of their own, and their parting message held a note of provocation.

Or flippancy.

A week later he had driven to her house in Bat Yam to take her the check himself, had refused to come in, stood by the door, embarrassed, conscious of his hulk, offering the green check. She held the check open in both hands as though reading it—the child, a boy of five, lame, supporting himself against her hip— and when she thanked him her look was sort of soft, sort of moist.

"Me . . . just my duty . . ." he said, and marched back to the pavement, proud of himself for not lingering even a single unnecessary minute.

He had almost forgotten. Almost.

What if, after all, he'd wanted to, that is? . . . An insurance agent frequently has to deal with widows. Some of them young and willing. He has got something, he knows, that makes him attractive to them. Warm and fatherly, protective. The low warm voice. The laughter. He laughs easily, those bubbling belly laughs, shaking his body, infectious. In short, there's no lack of opportunity. Freudinger used to be full of stories on the subject, some of them true, mostly bluster. Like the famous milkman jokes. If he'd wanted! But the thing is to *resist* temptation.

A question of self-respect.

Though actually, well, three or four times over the years. Unimportant. Accidents. Silly. He'd long crossed them off. As though they never happened.

But a fortnight later she had phoned:

"Jeanette Levy. Of Bat Yam."

"Yes, I remember." Blushing; hadn't his heart told him?

"Sorry to bother you but . . . I just don't know what to *do* with all that money!"

And pronouncing that "what to *do*" with such a sensual drawl that the blood surged up hot in him suddenly, as though her breath had touched him. Or her knee, under the table.

"I . . ."

Only an insurance agent, he wanted to say.

"I know, Mr. . . ."

"Tal."

"It's not your job, I guess, but I got nobody to ask, so . . ."

And at that point she paused for a moment, and her pause contained a hint of intimacy, allurement; even impudence really, considering he was a virtual stranger to her.

"I thought like maybe you could help me . . ."

And another pause, expectant.

He pulled a handkerchief out of his pocket and wiped his forehead.

And when he replaced the receiver he thought: after all, a plain human obligation. What with that kid and all. And marveled at the way things turn out in this world, for hadn't he, the minute she had come into the office a fortnight back, as soon as he set eyes on her . . .

Ah, Malta! Spain!

The Mediterranean! Oriental carpets!

And he had taken a few hours off from his work each day, made the round of officials, went to the Municipality, the Trade Union, explained, pleaded, urged, his legs carrying the big bulk of him lightly, the heat and sweat not bothering him. Joyfully, with no thought of reward—hell, he'd only drop in at her place for a couple of minutes, between one office and the next!—he went about it. "Bergman, you'll do this for me!" he said at the Licensing Authority. He hadn't had such satisfaction in years!

Did Elisheva ever tell him anything of her university affairs? Well, then!

"How am I going to thank you!" Giving him her steady look, promising, explicit, when, a few weeks later, he had brought her the permit to open a stand on the beach.

"Oh, the pleasure's all mine!" Dropping his eyes and stroking the head of the little boy clinging to her skirt.

"I do hope we haven't seen the last of each other, Mr. Tal!" Her voice sang him on his way.

And getting into the car he was glad he had taken no reward. Not even an innocent thank-you kiss. She may name the stand after him if she likes, he laughed.

He drove away light of heart, flinging her name and looks to the wind, singing under his breath—

· 6 ·

"Señorita, señorita, you're a doll
La luna con el sol . . ."

And stopped once on the way, by a stand in Jaffa, emptied a glass of orange juice in one go—since it was hot and he was sweating—bought a bag of sunflower seeds, cracked a couple, and handed the rest to the first child who came along. "Go ahead, take it!" he said to the startled boy who didn't see what it was all about.

And even Ziona at the office wondered what had gotten into her boss that day. "Look, Ziona," he smiled at her when she put the mail on his desk, "that's not how you ought to do your hair: that tower thing on top, that's fine, suits you all right. But at the sides . . ." And *that* from a man who'd never even noticed what she looked like! Could he have been drinking?

But after a fortnight, maybe three weeks—

By accident, really.

"Listen, Shuka, I've got other things on my mind!" Elisheva had said that evening, when he charged her with failing to bring him the dentist's receipts he needed for his income tax returns. What does she mean, other things on her mind, he raged, when those people come up with demands for thousands and insist on receipts for every single expenditure. "So I lost them!" she said. "What can I do? I lost them!" "But it's not the first time!" he shouted. "It's coming to hundreds of pounds, and I've asked you again and again . . ." And when he went on at her she slammed the door of the study in his face and shut herself up in there, as usual.

So he in turn slammed the door—the front-door—and ran down the stairs.

And got into the car and drove south. To Jaffa, and on.

No, he told himself. It's beneath your dignity. And your position.

On account of which he parked the car at the end of the street, on the corner, and decided to see, just out of curiosity, whether there was a light in her window. It was after nine and she'd no doubt be asleep in any case.

But there *was* a light in the window, to his dismay, and he felt his knees go weak.

No, no one had seen him. The street of her sandy suburb was dark as far as the corner lamppost.

What folly all the same: a respectable man like him, married, father to a girl of sixteen and a half. Who's this Jeanette anyhow? Stretching his hand to the latch of the low gate in the fence.

But if he raised the latch it'd be bound to rattle, and the hinges would shriek through the evening stillness and announce his visit.

And since it was physically impossible to reach the front door without opening the gate first, he turned in his tracks.

Back by the car he noticed, a little way off, around the corner, an open shop, and though usually he did not smoke he went over and bought a pack of cigarettes.

He fancied that the little man with the pale, Diaspora-Jewish face was regarding him with suspicion, or at any rate with dislike, as he put the pack on the damp counter.

He walked back to the car, got into it, lighted a cigarette, and told himself: now let's think this over calmly and reasonably:

If you turn back after having come this far, it'll be an act of weakness, cowardice.

However, going in there will also be an act of weakness—a yielding to temptation.

On the other hand, why miss such an opportunity?

Though there *is* something improper about it.

Why, though?

While you sit here shilly-shallying the window's probably gone dark. She's gone to bed.

Considering which he inserted the key in the ignition.

Even so he stopped short of turning it and decided to see once and for all whether Jeanette had gone to sleep or not.

The window was alight. And as it would be humiliating to sneak back to the car yet again, he opened the gate—whose hinges did not creak after all—and walked as softly as possible up to the door. Head bowed he knocked twice, not hard but not too lightly either. Not as loud as the pounding of his heart anyway.

And was greatly alarmed to hear the tapping of bare feet on tiles and a voice asking, "Who is it?"

"Me, Tal," he said, his voice strangled.

"Who?"

It was all he could manage to repeat, louder: "Tal." But her, "Wait, coming!" sounded eager and the barefoot tapping held a joy and a readiness.

"Oh, Mr. Tal! Do come in." With a bright, inviting look. Yet also as though she had been expecting him, had been sure he would come, and that was a bit mortifying.

"I'm sorry about . . . such a late hour . . ."

"Oh, that's all right, I'm happy to see you." Taking his hand, and with her other hand drawing the neck of her dressing gown closer against her breasts.

"What'll you have? Tea? Coffee?" she asked, seating him on the sofa behind the table.

"No, thanks, nothing, I just dropped in for a . . ."

"Maybe some wine?" Delighted with her thoughts.

"All right, just a drop. I only came to hear how . . ."

And when she left to fetch the bottle he felt ill at ease, his body trapped between table and sofa and much too big for this room, and he was afraid the child might suddenly appear from the other room, or that there might be someone else there as well, and didn't it make him, Yehoshua Tal Insurance, Acropolis, husband of Dr. Elisheva Tal-Blumfeld, the university, look like a fool, to be here at such an hour. A cheap fool.

But Jeanette came and sat down close beside him on the sofa, and had a drink with him, and laughed a lot, and told him over and over how glad she was he had come, and before he knew it everything turned out to be very simple, much simpler than he'd imagined.

Although—a bit too simple. That is, when he opened his eyes and found himself next to her peacefully sleeping body— putting his shoes on, casting a glance at the wedding photograph on the buffet, she in a veil and the late Mr. Levy in a suit and clipped mustache, bold and confident, proudly sticking out his chest—he felt something of an insult at it all being taken so much for granted, so expected, so like the result of some mute agreement. . . . After all, it wasn't as if he . . .

But the second time it was even simpler: he was not afraid the hinges might creak, and his double knock on the door wasn't hesitant. And he brought chocolate for the child. And turned the photograph on the buffet to the wall when she left the room for a moment.

Afterward, things took on their own pace; about once a fortnight, say. Not more often, because he felt that wouldn't be in good taste, somehow; but not less either so as not to lose contact. He'd bring toys for the child: a car, a coloring book and crayons, key holders. Jeanette hung the Canadian Manufacturers Life Insurance calendar up in her kitchen. Snowed forests facing the white gas range.

She had a pleasant voice, a bit husky with smoking, sensual; and once she sang the current hit, "Talk to Me with Flowers, My Love," for him. He told himself it was a "cheap," a "sentimental" song, but driving home at night through the long empty streets, he told himself: So what? I *want* cheap, dammit! Why not? What the hell is wrong with that?

He told jokes that made Jeanette laugh and marvel at him. There would be almonds and pistachio nuts on the table and she would stick them between his lips. "Do come to the beach sometime." Cuddling up against him. "Why don't you come to the beach sometime? I'll serve you cold drinks free!" "Me?" he would laugh. With his big awkward shape, the thick arms, the flabby muscles, the burly head. "You've got a nice figure!" Rubbing his hairy chest.

At times he would think that if there was such a thing as divine justice, then he would surely be punished.

Even though this justice wasn't *seen* to be done: crooks, tricksters, traitors, whom you'd expect to pay the penalty, would be thriving, their victims pining to see them fall—and they thrive. The Divine Providence never intervening. Not as far as he could see.

Yet perhaps it *is* applied, this justice, to *certain* persons. To those who fear it. Like himself, for instance. And then, suddenly, it will hit you: the heart attack, meningitis, who knows, cancer. There is an all-seeing eye, in spite of everything.

If at least Elisheva would *suspect* something. But when he lets himself in late at night, on tiptoe, she is generally still closeted in her study. Believes him to have been kept by work. As a matter of fact, though—she never asks.

Five months now? Maybe more.

AND what amazes him even more—or is it only his imagination?—is that ever since this affair with Jeanette, women have begun to notice him. More and more so. In the street, at the office, on house calls when he comes to collect. Funny: does he emit some invisible rays or something? A mark on his brow?

Before a traffic light, say. He pulls up. One hand on the wheel, one elbow on the window frame. A girl passes, throws him a glance, he smiles at her—even if she won't return the smile, she'll return a glance. He sizes her up as she walks on, appraises her figure, her gait . . . The light changes and he must move. Nearly hits the car in front.

Or before a zebra crossing: brakes hard when he sees a pretty woman with her child, or her dog, waiting at the curb. Waves her on, the road is yours. She crosses, smiles her thanks, turns her head to see who this gallant knight might be. The gallant knight is already off.

Or he may raise his hand at her through the window without turning his eyes: the parting salute of the rider galloping over the skyline and still to be thought of with yearning for many a day.

Or take Ziona, with whom his relations are cool and formal as a rule. He calls her over to the desk, dictates a letter. The phone rings and he talks into it. She tilts the tip of her pencil against her underlip and watches him. No, not just curiously. Her lips are slightly parted, her knees crossed, one foot nursing the other ankle. Her look is quizzical, tentative, speculating. He pretends not to notice.

Or on the road, when he goes to collect dues in the villages of the south and picks up hitchhiking girls at crossroads. The ease with which he gets a conversation going surprises himself. Asking from where and whereto, and soon enough, often enough, discovering common acquaintances. "Nes-Ziona, born and bred," he announces proudly. No one remembers old Tal any longer, not even by his former name, Tolkovsky. At any rate, these young ones don't. But who doesn't know Blumfeld? Even Rehovot and Rishon-Lezion girls do. So he rakes up tales from the thirties and forties, when the British were in the land, the

Arabs, the riots, war; asks after old teachers, village-council secretaries, ageless cranks; takes a bar of chocolate out of the glove compartment and offers it; tunes the radio in on pop music. Sometimes he whistles some aria from *Carmen* or *The Barber of Seville*—off key, but so what? (Elisheva stops her ears when he whistles: "I'll never understand why it is precisely the people who can't stay in tune who are the loudest whistlers!") And it provides an opening for an exchange of views about operas, films. Once he had got a student. Dr. Tal-Blumfeld? Of course she knows her. She's a student of hers! "My wife," he had said in all modesty. "Oh," glancing at him, blushing, "I adore her! We all do." "Me too," he grinned. "No wonder," she smiled. And he had gone out of his way to drive her to her doorstep. "What's the name again?" he had asked, opening the door of the car for her. "Ariella. Weissman." He'd remember that, till to-night.

He wasn't the man to touch them, a hand or a knee, not he. Or turn off into some intriguing sidetrack between orange groves. Better the pleasure of knowing that if only you wanted, if only you made the slightest effort. It was something you could sense—by a glint in the eyes, a tone of voice, a way of sitting. Just give them a hint and they drop, ripe, right into your lap. They're all alike. Not all. Most, though. The moral climate.

The moral climate? Sometimes, alone in the car, he would ponder it: Is it the change in himself or in the moral climate? Because things didn't use to be like that, did they? And he hasn't grown any younger, or better-looking. Nor can you say he wears an aura of glittering opulence. The car's fairly modest. His dress, too. What is it then? Maybe just his age, his maturity, the confidence that his heavy shape inspires, the paternal warmth. The generosity. And maybe the readiness *is* all, maybe it gives off some secret rays that produce a counterreadiness. Like with animals. Like between electric poles. Moral climate?

Annabel. The very name would make his head swim a little, make him drunk, ring in his head with a clear silver chime. Hadn't she asked for it?

Annabel Shofman with the sapphire-blue sports car. Walking from the gate to the door of the villa, across the wide, rose-bordered lawn, he would rein himself in, walk softly not to disturb the castle stillness. Softly he would knock the lion's head against the bright vermilion door and Annabel would let him in. A green glint in her slanting eyes (provocative? sly?), a blue glint to the soft hair falling over her cheek. And the living room—huge, cool, dim, enchanted. Heavy drapes keeping the midday heat out. On the wall a painting in a heavy gilded frame, portrait of a femme fatale in a creamy dress reclining on a carpet of fallen leaves under a forest tree—an air of golden twilight.

"A Runge," said Annabel.

"Old?"

"A hundred and fifty years. More. And that's a Liebermann. You've heard of him," pointing to the portrait of a burgher in a white hat.

And a momentary fancy: not Herzliya, not the Mediterranean, not Israel—Vienna. A castle in Vienna. Early in the century, the previous century.

And Annabel would indicate an armchair and move, slender, willowy, to the built-in bar.

"With soda?"

"No, thanks," he would say, for all that he always wanted to say yes, thanks, and never knew why he didn't

And afterward she would fetch a checkbook and write down "IL.350." Every few weeks. An insurance premium for over half a million: the villa, the paintings, jewelry, two cars, life.

"My sister Margot's a ballet teacher and she's interested in a very special kind of insurance . . . the legs . . . that possible? . . . Do you think that's possible?

The legs. . . . All at once Tal felt himself borne skyward, aloft in a balloon. Insurance became an important profession, unusual, mysterious even. The legs. . . .

Once she said to him: "Would you insure flowers, Mr. Tal?"

"Flowers?" Laughing, thinking she was making fun of him.

"No, not live ones, of course. . . ." She laughed, too, and fetched a large, copper-bound album containing pressed flowers, a flower to a page. "A legacy from my grandmother. And I'm afraid they'll shrivel."

And as she turned the pages he identified most of them by name. Annabel looked at him sideways with a quizzical smile: "You mean you're a botanist as well?"

"No, no, just remember from childhood, from school. . . ."

Her look lingered on him in silence for another moment and then, abruptly, she shut the album and rose to return it to its place. And she had never referred to the insurance question again. Odd.

At night, at home, he would picture her sometimes as a savage huntress, whip in hand, and sometimes as a captive princess in an enchanted castle, waiting for the knight to set her free. Knight mounted on a small Fiat; he laughed at himself.

And yet . . .

What did Annabel do all day at home by herself? Shofman would be away on business, Shofman would often be abroad. They had no children. And he was at least twenty years older than she. Old and heavy and coughing. Maybe impotent. As like as not.

Hadn't she asked for it?

"Your keys, Mr. Tal!" Once, on the doorstep, jingling the bunch of keys which he had forgotten on her table.

"Oh, I'm sorry, of course." But even before he had reached her on his way back from the gate, she had thrown them to him in a high arc, with a light, graceful sweep of her arm, and he had caught them up in both hands. "Thank you," he had said, reddening, and felt as though this throw-and-catch act had been an intimate contact between the two of them, romantic, a secret password, message, hint, invitation.

Once, one morning, knocking on the door, he had got no response. He had turned to go, and just then had spotted her convertible approaching with a soft hum, a swift, soft hum, swan on a lake, with Annabel at the wheel, in a bikini, hair sparkling, skin smooth—

She had waved at him from the car, regally, like a duchess, like a fairy-tale nymph, and called, "A jiffy!"

With a swift soft hum she had parked the car, jumped out of it, and clack-clacked on her beach sandals to meet him.

"I'm sorry. I know we said ten."

"Never mind."

"The sea . . . so wonderful . . . nearly forgot." Hurrying in front of him.

· 14 ·

And as she leaned over slightly to insert the key in the door lock, his head swam again: the shapely, suntanned legs, the bare brown waist curving with such suppleness to the buttocks . . .

He'd insure those buttocks.

"I won't keep you. Just sit down a moment." She hurried— upright, smelling of sea and salt and early morning—into the next room.

Tal stood where he was. He had a brief vision of himself driving to the beach in the morning, leaping into the water, swimming out to her through the waves, he takes her hand, together they cross the breakers, swim far out, return, come up on the beach dripping water, laughing.

"All right like this?" Handing him the check and coming to stand by his side.

Tal stared at the check in his hand, aware of her naked, sun-and-sea-drenched shoulder touching his, her damp salty hair near his cheek. With a single sweep he could have crushed her salty lips against his if he dared, her jutting berries against his chest.

"Pretty name, Annabel," he said, flushed, not raising his eyes from her signature at the bottom of the check.

"Thank you." Laughing. "So is Tal."

"English? French?"

"Annabel? Oh, lots of languages! My parents back in Germany thought it would be so cosmopolitan, you know. You were born here, weren't you?"

"Yes. Nes-Ziona."

"Long time in insurance?"

"Fifteen years. Longer."

"Interesting?"

"Insurance?"

"Getting to know people, problems . . . rather personal ones even . . ." Gaily.

"Yes, in a way. . . . We in the business say that every person has three friends in whom he puts his faith: his doctor, his lawyer, and his insurance agent."

"In that case you're my only friend, Mr. Tal." Clapping her hands together and smiling at him with an air of boundless devotion. "I have no faith in my doctor, the lawyer is my husband's business, so there's only you."

"Always at your service."

"I know, Mr. Tal."

She saw him out. Leaving, he thought, I could have, of course. . . . Especially under the circumstances, the bikini, the nearness . . . But just *because* she has faith in you, just *because* you're sort of like a friend . . . It's common decency.

And a fortnight ago—

After she had handed him the check she had asked him to come with her, had taken him to the garage to show him some damage to the car. It had been quite minor, the front bumper slightly dented. They had been standing together deep inside the brick structure, dim and recessed, and Annabel had pointed at the damaged spot and told him how it had happened—a truck backing up and scraping her. Tal squatted to feel the bumper. She leaned over as well and passed her finger over it.

What had she done that for?

The hem of her dress brushing his face, her scent, the darkness, the whispering. He trembled.

When he straightened up he was flushed, burning. "Yes," he said, "yes."

There was only a narrow space left between car and wall and they stood there together, cramped. "Terribly hot. Aren't you hot, Mr. Tal?" Smiling, tossing her hair back. And when she had squeezed past him on her way out he had been dazzled: the full length of her body to his.

Walking to the gate he had reproved himself: she'd fairly been begging for it, hadn't she! It's what she took you in there for! And you . . .

But once out in the road he said: All the same, glad I didn't.

And he couldn't decide who it was he hadn't betrayed: Elisheva? Jeanette? His self-respect? As an agent?

The harsh noon light lashed his face, hurting, blinding.

In the car, the key in the ignition, he had paused a moment before turning it. Why Jeanette of all people? he had asked himself. Jeanette? Who's she?

Past the intersection he had pulled up to give a lift to a soldier. "As far as Arlosorov," he said.

ON May 17, 1966—four days before his forty-fifth birthday—Tal woke up feeling low, feeling quite miserable in fact: a kind of wishing not-to-be, to disappear, a sense of doom. . . . He tried to figure out why, what had happened? A bad dream? He made an effort to remember and couldn't. What then? A number of things adding up, very likely: one of his clients, Yanai, had had a bad motor accident; on the eighteenth, that is tomorrow, payment on the promissory note was due at the bank—250 pounds; on the radio last night there had been news of another border incident, one killed, two badly injured. . . . But no, none of these things could explain this gloom that had settled over him, clinging, sickening, like a film of sweat on a hot day. The time was ten to seven—at his right, fanned out over the pillow, covering her neck and shoulders, Elisheva's black hair, her arms hugging the twisted sheet like some precious treasure—and he told himself that as soon as he got up, this gloom would slide off him to the floor.

Beyond the window, in the Persian lilac, two birds were playing a skipping game up and down branches.

But when he did get up it didn't slide off. Doffing his pajamas, he stared unhappily at the bulge of wide hairy belly; no, no potbelly yet but still—taut as a drum. He stepped into his trousers, buckled the belt on its last hole to subdue the mutinous mound, and when he sat down on the edge of the bed and bent over to tie his laces, a thick fold of flesh bulged out, sandwiched between chest and knees. He'd take a butcher's knife and cut it off.

What, what then? What was this sick longing? This wish to die, yes, to die!

Suddenly it struck him: the telephone bill. At the office. Three hundred and eighty-five pounds! Damn that Ziona, the private conversations she holds in his absence! *That* it? No, not that.

Isn't a man entitled to a bit of sympathy from his wife? But Tal could do nothing except remark with bitterness upon Elisheva's singular genius for sleep: curled up, the sheet between her arms, hugging treasures of wisdom garnered last night, her behind stuck out at him.

An ideal behind, you must admit. With its perfect curves, its two cheeks, precious china bowl shining through the green gauzy nightdress.

He'd wake her up and tell her: Look, Elika . . . this morning . . . sort of feeling . . .

But she doesn't have to leave till nine.

A clatter of dishes from the kitchen: Avigayil.

"Good morning," she hailed him over her shoulder when he crossed the passage on his way to the bathroom.

"Good morning," he grunted. Those late homecomings every night. One o'clock! No, half past. And just you try and say a word. As if she'd listen!

When he stood by the mirror shaving, he noted again how unbeautiful he was: the sickly pallor of the round, too-broad face; the thinning hair, a drought-stricken field from brow to crown; and worst of all the eyes, the small brown eyes which now, lather-locked, were gazing back at him like the eyes of some deprived animal harboring an ancient sorrow. A reddish tinge began to seep through the white, and rinsing his face he saw the cut in the taut skin of his cheek.

Sticking his head under the tap—the blood mingling with the cold water and trickling pink over the back of his hand—he told himself: This business with Jeanette has got to stop. Unclean, undignified, and bound to come out. These furtive departures in the evening, coming home after midnight and sneaking on tiptoe the shortest way between the carefully opened front door and the bedroom, past Elisheva in her study . . .

And fraught with trouble, he told himself, dabbing his face with a towel and pinpointing it with a scatter of pink dots. And gazing back at his eyes in the mirror again he asked himself how he should go about it. That is to say, he might just fail to turn up, but then what if she'd phone him at Acropolis again, the way she already had once or twice before, and demand, in her coaxing voice which sends the blood into his face at once: "Gogo? You coming tonight?"

Gogo! The bloody cheek! And why "Gogo" when there isn't a *g* in his name to start with? A private, possessive pet-name, staking a claim, assuming rights over him, his family—all his orderly, respectable life—and pulling him to her, a puppy for her lap! No, he'd just not go there anymore. And he'd slam down the receiver.

No, replace it. Quietly.

"What did you shout for like that last night?" Avigayil, pouring coffee into her cup.

"Me?" startled.

"Uh-huh. Kind of roar, haa-a-a. Sounded like somebody was trying to kill you," she said, favoring him with a smile.

Had he been dreaming? "I don't remember. . . ."

But he did: a feeling of helplessness. Pursued. Strangled. Fighting for his life.

"When did you get home last night?"

"One. . . ." Curtly, not raising her eyes from the magazine folded lengthwise beside her cup.

"One!" he flared up.

Avigayil went on reading. Only after a minute, between lines: "*Mother* doesn't mind."

"Night after night. In the eleventh grade."

His glance, drooping to her breast, darkened: budding fruit of this tree he had nursed for sixteen years, to be plucked now by some stranger, gratis. Snatched. From *his* garden.

"Still, not such a bad student, you'll own." She turned a page and bent her head to inspect the picture.

And that imperturbability, amounting to contempt. Absolutely.

"It's ruining your health!"

"You're funny, Daddy." Removing her cup to the sink and awarding him, from the height of her tall stature, a very grown-up smile.

It's a lost battle. The rule of "Fridays only" had long lost force. But this going out every night, night after night, with whom? Where? And who knows what?! Isn't it up to a father at least to give warning? So that when a day of reckoning comes his warning will at least be on record?

"You giving me a lift?" Stopping, schoolbag in hand, in the kitchen doorway.

"No!" he shot out at her, in protest.

Wasted. "Bye," she said pleasantly and went.

He regretted it at once. And was afraid she'd be late. And rushed, penitent, to the window, to call her back, to wait, he'd take her, but just when he looked down at the pavement she, too, glanced up, and he hid himself at once, shamefaced.

He went back to the bedroom—the sheet had dropped to the foot of the bed, the ideal behind was turned up, her face buried in the pillow—pulled the zipper of his briefcase and inspected his office diary:

"Collect prem. Ehrlich. Claims Dept. Zion. Bank! Gen. History for A. Find out accident Mashbir. *'Isn't life too short to be a burden.'* See Ella. . . ."

Who's Ella? He raised his eyes to the window. The two birds were chattering in the foliage and for a moment he watched their play: one of them skipped onto the other's branch, and the other hopped promptly up to a higher one; the first bird sought it out again and the other flitted to a branch opposite, tucked its beak under its wing and seemed to go to sleep. Then suddenly they both flew up and away on an unknown journey beyond the rooftops. He threw another tentative glance at Elisheva. Still asleep. He shut his briefcase, wedged it under his arm, and left.

Halfway down the stairs he came to a stop: Yes, Ella Dvir. The colonel's wife. At ten thirty.

The little Fiat was dew drenched. And wiping the windshield he felt soothed. The car was submissive, obedient, responding to his motions like a faithful pet, and when he would caress her flanks, her back, her rounded behind, he'd feel a physical satisfaction. He shook out the rag, folded it, got in, and settled himself comfortably behind the wheel.

And then the last straw!

When he inserted the key in the ignition and tried to start, both indicator lights came on red but no sound came, not a whir, not a buzz. The starter was dead.

He tried a second time, and a third, and a fourth. Nothing.

The last straw, God, today of all days, on top of everything else: the telephone bill, Jeanette.

He dropped his head to the wheel and closed his eyes. He felt betrayed, forsaken in his hour of need. Elisheva asleep, the car paralyzed. And with a surge of anxiety he remembered: that was exactly what his dream had been about—him trying to start the car, struggling, and it paralyzed. It must have been then that he had uttered that slaughtered-animal roar, that "haa-a-a" Avigayil had heard on her side of the wall.

And when he turned the key once more, another thought occurred to him: maybe it was the other way around. Maybe not a betrayal but an expression of solidarity, of fellow feeling, of mute and humble sympathy for his suffering. Because he recalled it wasn't the first time the car had broken down just on a day when something in his life had. Like that time with Jeanette. But then it had been a protest, when she had stalled at night on the way home from Jeanette.

Somehow there was a kind of mysterious connection all the same.

He got out, raised the hood, stuck his head in, pulled at a wire here and there, tried tightening a bolt, loosening it—everything down there was such a tangle, as incomprehensible as some mathematical formula fraught with symbols. When he straightened up he was wet with sweat. He glanced up at the third-story window. No help. The street stared emptily back at him, already brewing with a noonday heat. His eyes blurred. Failure. All of life.

Azulai was approaching at a brisk pace, making for his Lark.

"What's up, Mr. Tal? Anything wrong?"

"The starter," said Shuka, "Stone dead."

Azulai peered into the engine's bowels, groped about inside, jiggled some pin, got grease on his fingers, and ordered Shuka to get in behind the wheel and try to start.

"Again! Once again!" he called at him from the nether regions. Nothing happened.

"Well?" asked Shuka, standing beside Azulai again and faintly hoping for some magic formula.

"Your battery," said Azulai wiping grease off his fingers, "guess it's empty. We'll try pushing; maybe she'll start."

Maybe. Shuka got back in behind the wheel without much confidence, put her into gear, stepped on the accelerator. Azulai began pushing her down the street. The miracle happened: after a splutter or two the car started and sped on its way, easily, eagerly.

· 21 ·

Stopping for a light, waiting for it to change, he felt so depressed that he decided not to go on his errands today and to hell with it all, he'd go where the car took him.

And crossing the intersection he decided to go to his mother. He had a sudden urgent need to see her.

H E found her bright and radiant and, it seemed to Shuka, in the grip of some excitement. Her blond head was sprouting a luxuriant crop of pins and curlers, row upon row. "Shuka!" she exclaimed, surprised by his unexpected visit, and when Shuka assured her that nothing out of the way had happened, that he had just looked in to see how she was as she hadn't called for several days, she told him to go into the kitchen and get himself some coffee while she did her hair. On her way to the bathroom she pulled out a pin and one doll curl dropped playfully over her forehead.

Shuka did not go to the kitchen but to the living room, wading through the pool of sun on the immaculate floor. A pleasant warmth began to seep through his limbs. He'd gladly stretch out on the sofa here, nod off, sleep his fill, sleep for hours and hours on end, and when he woke up his mother would bring him clear chicken broth with grains of rice floating on top, whole and shining grains of rice, also a succulent chicken's leg with baked potatoes and mashed carrots, and afterward he'd go to sleep again. . . .

"How's Avigayil?" his mother called from the bathroom.

"As usual."

"Is coming to see Grandmother too much for her?"

"She's busy."

"Exams?"

"*And* a boyfriend."

"And a what?"

"A boyfriend!"

"Congratulations!"

Tamara Tolkovsky hadn't set foot in their house for the past six or seven years. When Avigayil, at ten, had contracted pneumonia, she had accused Elisheva of being more concerned with her university career than with her household, the care for her daughter's health included. Ever since then she hadn't referred to her by name but called her "Oxford." ("Oxford doesn't feed you, no wonder you're so pale.") And whenever she got Elisheva on the phone she'd say nothing but, "May I talk to my son?" In this eternal feud Shuka would stick up for his wife when faced with his mother, and for his mother when with his wife. One way or another he floundered between the two of them, suffering the worse because it was all so hopeless.

"Remember Hoshea Hurwitz, Shuka? The one who had a grove near ours and pulled it all up in the war? He's dead. Killed in a road accident. Sonia dropped in at the shop yesterday: Hoshea Hurwitz. Who'd have believed it? Such a strong person! Got shot at by Arabs three times: in twenty-nine and thirty-six, in Jaffa. . . . And now—a road accident. Sixty-eight he was. Still—"

Sitting on the sofa Shuka felt the tension go out of him. The sun slanting in from the balcony seemed to remove this room from the city pale and bring in a distant summer of wide spaces, till he could picture bees humming among the bright downy blobs of acacia hedges. The furniture and bric-a-brac, moved here whole and intact from their house in the village years ago, had preserved his childhood for him. The silver trinket on the sideboard—a carriage harnessed to a team of silver steeds—gleamed with a memory of Russian affluence from before his birth, conjured up tales of Boris Godunov and Russalka and Ludmilla told by his grandmother; the green velvet tablecloth with a fringed tassel at each corner of the big table reminded him of tranquil evenings, with the soft bubble and suck of the ancient oil-lamp and the croaking of frogs in the irrigation ditches outside and his mother knitting and chattering, knitting and chattering; and the silky tufts of the rushes in the long-stemmed vase told of bare feet on the banks of a wadi shrinking to a trickle on its way to the sea. He had "got lost" there once, in this wadi among the dunes, when he was eight or nine. Not lost, but the other kids had gone home and left him behind on purpose, because he was fat, and awkward, and funny. The slimy weeds in the wadi bed among a tangle of rushes and tickle grass and spikenard had fascinated him and, squatting on his heels, he had watched the tadpoles wriggling through the weeds and water lilies, had tried to fish them out with a stick, and when he had looked up the others were gone. His voice had lost itself among the dunes, and night was falling fast, and the terror of jackals, yes, the jackals—oh, the howl of jackals!—had stifled his throat, and tears had welled up in his eyes at such wickedness, such perfidy, such low-down trickery, and his feet had foundered in the shifty sand, he was floundering, drowning, and the stars out already, and from far, far away he had heard his father's voice. . . .

"Ready in a jiffy, Shuka! But you didn't take any coffee."

His father's face looked at him from the photograph on the sideboard, a shriveled face, the grim, bristly mustache in the middle, and the eyes—harsh and bitter as wild almonds. He was standing in the shade of a leafy citrus tree, one hand holding the reins of the tall white donkey on whose back he would do the round of orchards, farmyards, stables. With his crumpled, open-necked shirt, draggled sleeves, loose khaki trousers, he did not look like a veterinarian but rather like a hard-up day laborer. Stubborn and proud he had been, and versed in suffering, and such too had been the Hebrew he spoke—stubborn and proud and refusing to yield to new coinage.

His father had wanted him to be a veterinarian, of course, for Shuka loved animals and had a kind heart, and Nahum Tolkovsky, who was a patriot, also thought the profession would be of service to the country and, in due time, to the Jewish state-to-be. But Shuka did not excel at school and became a bank teller, and later, with the help of Elisheva's father, an insurance company clerk, and only much later an independent agent. What would his father have thought of that? His face looked out of the photograph not with reproof but with regret, bitter regret, disappointment. Six months after Shuka had married Elisheva Blumfeld, he had died of a heart attack.

And Mother, in the best years of her life, still full of bounce, had not taken very long to recover, had picked up the goods and chattels, collected the savings and the money brought in from the sale of the house and orchard, moved to town and bought a small perfumery, hygienic as a pharmacy, a kind of private shrine with herself as combination priestess, fortune-teller and privy councillor to girls, wives, widows, a steady set of the faithful.

"I need your blessing, Shuka." She came tripping into the room, painted, primped.

"What for?"

"Do me up first though." Turning her back to him.

Shuka rose and fumbled with the hook-and-eye affair at the back of her neck. The ringlets of shining platinum blond hair tickled his hands, the friction of silk against amber seemed to draw sparks of electricity.

Tamara moved off a little and turned on her heel.

"Like my dress?" putting one foot forward, fashion model on a stage.

"Not bad."

The dress was, as always, capriciously defiant of any fashion whatever, much as the hairdo was daringly defiant of her age: a print of green vine leaves on orange, the leaves climbing up and down her figure. How young she is, lots younger than her sixty-five years, thought Shuka, marveling at the peachy complexion, the snub nose in the face with hardly a telltale crease, and the full figure, marred only by the too-thin, spindly legs. He felt flattered by her looks, and grinned.

"Twenty-three pounds, a bargain. And now you'll have coffee with me. I'm sure you haven't had breakfast either. Sit down, I'll bring it in here."

It was after nine and he ought to be going. The square of sunlight had reached the table, kindled the stately vase and made it shimmer. There was something festive about the room, a Sabbath air, like then, at the house in the village, a week after his father's death, when he hadn't felt any pain but only a kind of pleasurable relief, sort of like having a soft dressing put on a wound. Outside, the avocado leaves had matured to a glowing green, and the floor, half awash with sun, had radiated eternal peace, sent from Eden, Father's last rest; and his mother, who had not worn mourning, quietly preparing him a meal. As a child, in summer vacations, he had sprawled on those tiles with their colorful geometrical pattern and played chuck stones. His mother sitting in a chair, sorting lentils in the dip of her lap between her knees. Want to help, Shuka? she had asked gently. And he had crept close to her and, his belt touching the hem of her dress, had sat on his knees quietly for a long time, picking the dross out of the little mound of lentils.

"What'd you say if I got married, Shuka, eh?" She placed a cup of coffee and the sugar bowl before him, sent him an amused smile, and left for the kitchen again at once.

For a moment Shuka thought he had misheard, or misunderstood. Was she joking? Sounding him out? Was that the blessing she'd asked for? All of a sudden a wave of depression swept over him, as in the morning, and his whole being wanted to protest: She's gone mad, mad!

"Well?" Smiling as she entered with a second cup and sat down across from him. "I guess you're thinking: She's gone mad, my old mother has, eh?"

"I don't know," he whispered dully.

"Oh, but it can't be all that much of a surprise for you!" Encouraging him, laying her moist palm on his thick, hairy arm. "After all Sasha has been coming here nearly every evening for the past two years. He's an old friend!"

Sasha, Alexander Dushkin, was an engineer, retired, about seventy but with a well-built, athletic figure still and small, clever, twinkling eyes. He treated Shuka with a benign affection, rather as if Shuka were the big faithful dog of his friend Tamara's, and Shuka responded with due consideration. Now Shuka's only thought was: This house is going to be barred to me. Forever. It'll never be the same again.

"Get married?" Helpless in the face of the inexorable.

"Why not, after all, Shuka? I asked myself the same thing. At your age, I told myself, what'll people say! But why not? I'm still young, aren't I?" her voice gay, and truly young.

"Yes," he said with a wan smile.

"And Sasha's so kind to me, and so generous, and such a good friend, so undemanding. . . . It was *his* idea, you know?"

Shuka kept silent. A *fait accompli,* he realized, gazing at her in despair.

"And he came out with it so . . . naturally." With a rather theatrical wave of her hand. "So I just laughed! Just laughed at first, you know, and then I said to myself, Really, why not? As long as we're meeting every day anyway, and going out together, visiting people, going to concerts, so we might as well get married."

Her voice rang too loud, shattering the morning peace and all the glass and crystal trinkets in the room.

"When?" Faintly.

"But I said to Sasha: I've got to have my son's blessing. Yes."

"Oh!"

"See, Shuka? It's a topsy-turvy world! You didn't ask me for *my* blessing, but I *am* asking yours!"

"Didn't I?"

"But I didn't give it!" she laughed, but less airily, with a note of the ancient grudge in her voice.

"Father did!" He smiled.

"Father *gave in.* Childhood love . . . an old flame . . ."

Even at school. The seventh or eighth grade, not taking his eyes off her rippling black hair three rows in front, or her hand shooting up at every question; or during breaks, following her with his eyes, bitterly resentful at being ignored, at her scornful, offhand manner when, with fluttering heart, he had approached her for help with some homework problem; or evenings, at home, when he would weave spells and concoct magic formulas to capture her heart, like combing his hair in seven strokes and at each stroke whispering her name. . . .

"And Father had his principles: never interfere. Though he was quite well aware of his highness the Baron Blumfeld's sentiments toward the obscure veterinarian Nahum Tolkovsky."

The eminence of the seventy-five-acre citrus grove, the building supplies store on main street, a share in the Halva'a Vehisachon Bank, a share in the Migdal Insurance Company; a vassalry of Arabs, men and women, in grove and household; all the same, one evening Yirmiyahu Blumfeld had entered the house, offered a steady hand to the grim veterinarian, and even before sitting down had said, "Well, I hear your Yehoshua wants a title deed to my girl. . . ." "They say the price of real estate has gone down since the war. . . ." Tamara had retorted to defend her honor. "Oh, no, not with me," Blumfeld had said, easing himself and all his formidable assets into a chair. "So you're selling, are you?" "Nobody asked," said Blumfeld, laughing, "though frankly, I *was* a bit surprised. . . ."

So was Shuka. He had already been a bank teller then, and Elisheva was back from university in England, and one day in the summer vacation, she standing at the cashier's counter, he perched behind the latticed window, bear in a cage, counting out bills, she had watched his fingers smilingly and said, "Hard to believe you're so quick." "Why?" Blushing. "You never used to be." And she had reminded him how in high school, in games of hit, the ball would invariably find his big body. He laughed, a warm heavy laugh, and was surprised she should have noticed, let alone remembered, and a few days later, going for a stroll together in the evening, and straying beyond the village, between the heavily scented acacia hedges, he had been surprised even more when she had pressed herself against him as though seeking protection, and fragile as she was, seemingly nothing but abstract intellect, she had caught like tinder and had abandoned herself to him with an eagerness he had never expected of her.

"Oh, what's that got to do with it. You know perfectly well that Elisheva never cared a damn about money or anything. . . ."

"For all of which she didn't forget to register the apartment in *her* name!"

"Not she, not she!" he cried for the hundredth time since their marriage, and felt the blood boil up in him again, "Her father! Her father bought it and *he* registered it!"

"But she didn't say no. . . ." Smiling sweetly.

"She never even *knew* about it!" he yelled.

"You're such an innocent, Shuka!" Her look pitying him, a backward child.

"That'll do!" He rose and fished the keys of the car out of his pocket.

"In your heart you know I'm right," she pronounced, with that finality with which she always scored up the results of the game.

"You've been right for the past twenty years," he muttered on his way to the door.

"If I could at least be sure that you. . ."

But he was already on the staircase.

The telephone bill, the car, and now Mother getting married, he told himself as he started the engine.

Tнis business with Jeanette has got to end. Definitely. For good! Tal was telling himself as he climbed the worn gray steps to his office, Acropolis.

"A fire," said Ziona without interrupting the swift pecking of her fingers at the keys and shifting the carriage of her typewriter to a new line, "Werblovsky and Company."

"Last night?"

"Now. Ten minutes." Pulling the sheet out and feeling for a paper clip, "Zion people called to say."

"Where is it?"

"Dunno. You're supposed to know." Clipping the two sheets together.

Sack her!

And bad news—always producing it with a show of indifference. Or gloating. And on top of that, the smudge of lipstick overrunning her lips, vulgar.

"Look it up, will you please?"

"Yes, Mr. Tal." Without a glance at him, mincing over to the cabinet, taking out a file, turning pages, and after a minute, replacing it, her back to him: "Giv'at Herzl. No number."

Four hundred thousand. Maybe half a million.

"They called from Hamashbir. Want to know about a claim by Schenker, or Mencker." Sitting down again behind her typewriter.

"Yes, I know. Anything else?"

"Somebody wanting to talk to you." Inserting a new sheet. "I didn't know when you'd be in, said to try again around noon, maybe you'd turn up by then."

Sack her.

"I'll be back in an hour or so, if anybody asks." He turned to go.

"Do I say anything if Hamashbir calls again, Mr. Tal?" she called after him in a little-girl voice.

"That I'll be back in an hour, I said!" Emphatically.

And went down to the car and sped southward. Reaching the commercial district he could see the smoke clouds from afar. A fire engine pursued him with a wail, brushed him aside; he stopped to let it pass, then drove on and parked the car not far from the site of the fire, in a side street, among trucks and tricycles.

Thick black smoke was belching from the large shed of Werblovsky & Co.'s carpentry workshop, licking at the corrugated tin roof and billowing upward in fat gushes. Little tongues of flame flickered inside and waved as though choking in their own smoke. The firemen were training their jets in on two sides but seemed only to be fanning the flames, for the smoke thickened with each jet, boiling over and seething up like steam. Policemen were shooing away children and moving the crowd of onlookers back to the main road, where a traffic jam had built up, cars hooting in a variety of voices like a chorus of whining protest.

Tal spotted Goldberg from Zion, Jacobson the assessor, and another person, one of the owners presumably, standing together at one end of the site and watching the flames. He crossed the street, past the policemen, and joined them.

"How did it happen?" he asked.

None of them seemed anxious to reply.

"Short circuit, I guess," said Jacobson at last, not looking at him.

"What the hell are they doing?" yelled Goldberg suddenly, advancing a step, "Can't they at least locate it, the bloody idiots! Just look at them!"

The fire had taken hold of the timber in the yard and in an instant a forest of roaring red flames shot up on every side. Brandishing his briefcase Goldberg swept up to the firemen, but only got as far as the policemen, who stopped him. Cries of protest and alarm came from men at the next-door workshops. The short fellow with the hat who stood near Jacobson was watching it all, pale and silent.

Now the jets were aiming for the limits of the yard, encircling it. Two more fire engines arrived, men leaped off, bustled about with hoses, pushed bystanders out of the way and began to play their powerful jets upon the center of the shed. New waves of smoke towered up inside and forced their way out.

"How much are they insured for?" Jacobson asked.

"Half a million, I think," said Tal.

"It'll all go," said Jacobson.

Then he turned to the hatted man, seized his elbow, and took him aside. The two of them moved off in the direction of the street.

Tal wiped the sweat off his forehead, his throat, his neck. It was stifling, a dry eastern desert wind, and the fire blowing hot in front. The sweat dribbled into his eyes, stinging them. The tall column of smoke widened at the top, fanned out like a black sail and cast a shadow over the yard. Sparks flew, fell and went out. The burning wood crackled merrily, a thousand gamboling crickets frying in a giant pan.

Looking up he saw, at the tip of a flickering tongue of flame, the flickering figure of his mother, dancing, with her doll curls, her snub nose, her soft round arms, dressed in a long green affair cut deep in front and revealing the cleft of her breasts. Occasionally the smoke would blur her smiling face, but she went on dancing, her thin legs one with the tongue of flame, swaying and bobbing with it, and it was a ridiculous and pitiable performance, in sight of all this crowd, in the heart of town. No, he'd never forgive her. At sixty-five. He felt a lump in his throat. Never. If she'd done it ten years ago. And who with! Standing under the canopy. A ring. Wineglass. The Seven Benedictions. Family. Maybe a veil, too. Here comes the bride. To bury himself, bury himself in the dust. Why the hell couldn't she have gone on the way she was! That house barred. No more!

"It's the boss hisself done it."

Tal turned his head, saw a swarthy, gleaming face on his left and fat lips grinning under a flourshing black mustache.

"It's him hisself fixed his place! Short circuit, hell! There never been no short circuit here!" snickered the fellow. The sleeves of his shirt were rolled up to the elbows of his burly arms.

"How do you know?" Tal asked carelessly.

"He was broke, that's all!"

"You . . . work at this place?"

"Nearby. I know the guy."

"Rubbish," said Tal curtly.

The fire was beginning to lose ground, the timber that fed it being rapidly consumed.

"One match! You go prove it afterward. Wood all over the place!"

Tal waited for another moment, then turned his back on the man. He could never stomach those onlookers who went throwing around dark suggestions, inciting. Near a lamppost he saw Goldberg talking to three policemen, Goldberg flushed and exasperated. Coming nearer Tal heard one officer say, "All right, I heard you, so what do you want? Want us to piss on it? We're writing a report, the rest you can argue out in court." "At nine twenty-five!" Goldberg shouted after them as they walked away from him. "Not good enough to answer you even!" and, paying no attention to Tal, he scurried to overtake the little man with the hat who was marching with bowed shoulders toward the nearby store.

The roof of the shed which, by some miracle had not caved in, was wreathed in a white steam now, a sizzling, curling vapor. Twisted, squashed, water-sloshed machines loomed through the smoke inside. Utter ruin.

To grow avocado, thought Tal. Counting out money behind the bars, in his cage at the bank—sixteen, eighteen years back—he used to contemplate the idea: he'd grow avocado. A close tropical plantation, cool, dense foliage. Dry dust on the leaves in summer, and in winter sparkling, dripping. Luxuriant grass, clouds of insects, hush. A house with spacious rooms and tiles cool under bare feet. A small garage down below. An estate. Sabbath going out in the car—the wife, the three kids—visiting aunts and uncles in nearby villages. The water had defeated the fire but what remained? Coals and ashes.

"You from the insurance company, aren't you?"

That Oriental fellow again with his shining copper face.

"No."

"Have one." Flicking a cigarette out of the pack in his hand.

"Thanks. Don't smoke."

"You *are* the agent, though?"

What does he want, that pest?

"Yes."

"Big loss for the company."

Tal didn't feel like saying anything.

"Look, the men were all there at nine. There's taps there and all. If it'd been a short circuit . . ."

"What's it got to do with you anyway?"

"I'm not saying it has," said the fellow sweetly, his small eyes twinkling in their fleshy sockets, "People stand, watch, everybody's got his views. . . ."

"Keep 'em to yourself." Tal dismissed him and moved off.

"You needn't get mad at me, mister. . . ." He heard the voice behind him.

Even from afar he already spotted the white sheet of paper, folded over and stuck to the windshield of his car. He couldn't believe that really—oh, no, oh, damn and blast. Arriving he pulled the ticket out of the wiper's grip, glanced at it—illegal parking—tore it over and over and scattered the bits to the wind, dammit.

On his way to the office the shining Oriental face kept coming to his mind. Who was he? What the hell did he want? Did he know him from someplace? Had the man been trying to trap him into something? Rubbish!

E RECT, brisk, a yellow summer suit on her slim, ungirdled figure, Dr. Tal-Blumfeld—lecturer in Comparative Lit., and in this, the final term, giving a seminar on "Reality and Fantasy from Gogol to Joyce"—walked from the bus stop to the campus, a distance of 210 paces.

Integritas, consonantia, claritas. In order to extract the full significance of reality, the true essence of being, the emphasis has shifted—as we have been noticing in the works of Hamsun, Gide, and Mann, and to a much greater extent, Proust—from objective description. . . .

Did I get my change? She stopped and opened the clasp of her handbag: a confusion of comb, lipstick, crumpled receipts, bills,

· 33 ·

coins, and fingered three sparkling coins. I wouldn't know how much anyway, a trifling sum—and walked on, high heels clicking on the hard dry asphalt.

From objective, or purely subjective description of external events, to the complete exhaustion of a random moment. Ah, to *teach* Joyce instead of lecturing *about* him! *Ulysses* itself would require a year at least! Didn't I tell Koch? Instead of a narrative moving in time, in a chronological sequence, with its orderly introduction of characters and their conflicts, as in *Madame Bovary* . . .

What *were* they building here? She lingered briefly beside the tumult of a cement mixer chewing a cud of gravel, sand and water, spitting out a mushy gray porridge poured into wheelbarrows trundling along a rickety trail of planks. A standards institute or something. "Measure-and-size/Measure-and-size." And she looked up in awe once more at the wonderful creature of a crane, rearing tall and dinosaurian beside the scaffolding of the structure nearby, reaching out day by day toward the blue sky, "Out-of-nothingness/A-town-shall-rise." And there's a measure of beauty in these high-rise apartment buildings soaring upward all around as far as the eye could see with such a primal, virile vigor, all that grumbling about the violation of nature regardless.

Integritas, consonantia, claritas. She walked on, a light breeze ruffling her hair, and the two large earrings, circles of yellow plastic, swinging in rhythm with her step. The stream of consciousness: narrative breaking up into minute and would-be random processes within a multileveled Time—personal and environmental—without dramatic situations, without analyses of the characters' conduct and motivation, so that the reader does not tend to ask whether so-and-so should have acted in such and such a manner or not. Bloom, for instance, at eight o'clock in the morning, 7 Eccles Street, making his wife's morning tea, going to the butcher's to buy kidneys. Not chaos, no.

It's like a Mediterranean oasis in the desert of cold, gloomy, Dublin drabness suddenly to encounter familiar Hebrew phrases, albeit in Latin script—compatriots met in the street of a strange town—in the pages of *Ulysses*: orange groves and melon fields north of Jaffa. A model farm at Kinnereth on the lakeshore of Tiberias. *Shema Israel.* Next year in Jerusalem. Had Joyce really learned Hebrew, as Sylvia Beach says? Nevertheless, mistakes: "Agendath Netaim" instead of Agudath Netaim. The *u* turned upside down? Or: *Schorach ani wenowwach benoith Hierushaloim.* In a distorted Ashkenazi pronunciation, probably overheard from religious Jews. Agendath Netaim. . . . She chuckled to herself.

Daddy used to have a Panama once, colonial, like South African planters. Don't see those hats anymore now.

A mistake to compare Bloom to Jesus as Richard Ellmann does. Ellmann? Yes. Not Jesus—Paul. A Jewish evangelist in exile, wandering cosmopolitan in a heathen world. Dublin.

(A morning of snow in London, forty-seven. She was a university student. Russell Square pure as a fairy tale, a Christmas card with the snow over everything, perched like a miracle of equilibrium on the long bare fingers of trees. On her way to the British Museum library, dropping into an antiquarian's, place filled with knights' helmets, shields, brass candelabra, graceful double-barreled pistols, old Scottish frocks, pictures of proud lonely castles looming out of the mist. And there, in the inner room, in the books-and-maps section, she stumbles on a frayed little book in a worn leather binding, 1657, *The Headless Fenian* by Glen O'Brien, opens at the first page, reads the first lines, and her eyes light up: 1657! Before Swift! Two hundred and fifty years before Gogol, before Kafka! She buys it for £4, hurries to the library and there, in the narcotic yellow light—where if she shuts her eyes she seems to be spinning on a merry-go-round in a world of books—she swallows the story in a sitting, and when she closes the book she is elated, limp and elated, flushed with pleasure, as after lovemaking. And next day, in class, at a lecture on Joyce, she asks good-looking, blue-eyed, gentle Patrick O'Donovan, "Ever heard of Glen O'Brien?" and no, he never has, no one has ever heard of this Irish writer. The professors included. Her own private secret.)

Ireland, an old sow eating her farrow. Exercise: Walpurgis Night in Goethe's *Faust* and in the Circe episode in *Ulysses.* Image of the sow as whore, since Homer, yes, since Homer!

Next exercise: Walpurgis Night in Mann's *Magic Mountain.* Note how here, here, too, during the ball at the sanatorium everybody is trying to draw a pig and Hans Castorp confronts his beloved by means of the pencil she lends him—a phallic symbol, obviously!—for him to draw a pig with. Only after that we get his confession about the body, about—

Casting pearls before the swine. Except for Hadassah Hermon. Excellent remark that, about the Hebrew association in Bloom's answer to Zoe when he trips on the steps of the brothel: the just man falls seven times.

And in the distance, at left, they have boarded up another square and someone is digging there with a shovel, and the sand is strewn from the shovel as through a sieve, rustles, settling, and sinks—

She felt a wave of nostalgia for Tel Aviv of long ago, with its white silica brick houses and white brick fences in front, with the large grains of building sand like innocent eyes, sea salt, water-washed eyes gazing out of the dry hardened mass, and those capitals crowning gate pillars, shaped like wide, concrete flowerpots, knop and flower, knop and flower, and palm fronds waving out of them green and long-fingered, and the Venetian shutters, the big Mediterranean, Greece, Italy, Alexandria, and the sand, silk-soft, deep and whispering sighing sinking—

Still, it's a question whether stream of consciousness or interior monologue can be used for simpleminded characters.

Like Shuka, say.

That is, it can, but the question is whether it would be relevant, whether it would go very far to explain, to explore. Perhaps in this case, straightforward narrative, plot—

"One morning," an opening sentence framed itself in her mind, "Yehoshua Tal, a fairly well-to-do insurance salesman, woke up . . ."

Heavens, nearly forgot: this Friday! Haven't bought anything yet. His birthday, dear Yehoshua, happy birthday to you. Forty-five, middle of life. Eighteen years together. Petty squabbles notwithstanding. With a sigh she recalled Patrick, heavenly Patrick O'Donovan. Even today, even today, still a twinge. And back from England then, all you wanted was peace, peace and quiet.

What's pricking and twisting there at the sole of her foot? She bent to grope a finger in the curve of her shoe and extracted a tiny piece of grit.

Bear, a warm and kindly bear, Shuka. There was a perfect and upright man in the land . . . Eighteen years and not a slip. What makes you so sure? Always in for surprises in such matters. Everybody knows except his wife, as they say. Nonsense!

Remember to invite Julius!

The artist, like the God of creation, remaining beyond his handiwork, invisible, indifferent, paring his nails.

Breathing hard, drops of sweat welling up on her forehead, she climbed the palatial steps leading to the wide gleaming lobby. A stream of youth swept past her: book-laden, bag-laden, girls with highly spiritual makeups, young men keeping the world at bay behind a shield of spectacles, sloggers filled with grim zeal, cheerful scholars, glowering scholars, acolytes in jeans, tousled, like ice skaters. For an instant the entire lobby seemed a skating rink, gay and dizzying. Good morning Dr. Tal-Blumfeld, good morning, Doctor, hi, hullo. Phrases flashed at her from the bulletin board: Torah portions *Emor, Balak*, Introduction to Apocalyptic Thought. Room for one near university, please phone. Students registered for examination in Christian Mysticism. Dr. Navon's lecture postponed.

"Good morning, Doctor": Hadassah Hermon, bespectacled, stooping, eyes alight with humble and unassuaged hunger for knowledge.

"Good morning. Well?"

"Yes, I read it." With the delight of a successful treasure hunter, "I asked myself why Bloom happens *almost* to meet Stephen three times and yet every time the meeting fails to come off. At the editorial office, at the library . . ."

With long sensitive feelers she moves over the letters in the Book of Mysteries. Think she's writing on the sly?

"How would *you* explain it, Hadassah?"

"I thought . . . perhaps another analogue with Telemachus and Odysseus, the first meeting at the swineherd's . . ."

"Yes yes yes." Affection flowing from the frank look of the teacher to the humble one of the disciple.

There is a secret bond between them, an unspoken dialogue in the classroom, over the heads of the others. But Hadassah will lower her eyes, will not venture.

"Do you do any writing yourself? The honest truth."

"No. A bit. No, not really." Smiling as she reddens, "See you in class, then, Doctor."

At the department office, a worried and woeful Dr. Warshavsky was studying a circular handed him by Miss Bloch. The sun lit up his wreath of white hair topped by a black skullcap. Against the square of window, polished ficus branches and a strip of sky, his profile was a facsimile of an Aristotelian scholar, laurel wreath and all. Ancient lines scored his brow.

"Two calls for you," said Miss Bloch, shifting the carriage of her typewriter to a new line without looking up at her, "one from your husband and one from some literary editor."

"My husband?" Elisheva's voice rang loud in the sunlit room. She opened her handbag, took out a packet of red-and-gold Royals and a silver lighter, lighted a cigarette with nervous fingers, and inhaled deeply.

"Have a look at this." Dr. Warshavsky passed her the circular with a contemptuous grimace.

Rabbi Stanley S. Segal, professor of Ancient Jewish Literature at the Jewish Theological Seminary, N.Y., associate professor of Comparative Religion at Columbia University, author of *Jews in Modern Affluent Society, Menorah and Christmas Tree, Scriptural Sources in the Writing of Eusebius,* and others, member of the Long Island Academic Institute for the Research of Community Culture, will be guest lecturer at a seminar on "Martyrology and Messianism in the Midrash and Early Christian Writing" during the first term of the coming academic year.

Dr. Tal-Blumfeld turned a questioning look at Dr. Warshavsky.

"In the talmudic tractate *Toharot,* said Dr. Warshavsky in a voice thick with phlegm, a pained smile at the corners of his mouth, "it says that a scholar who receives an ignoramus within his house defiles it as far as his arm's extent."

"Ignoramus?" said Elisheva, raising her eyebrows.

"I read an article of his in the *Jewish Quarterly Review,* something called 'Apocrypha and Pseudo-Apocrypha in the Literature of the Second Temple Period.' The man doesn't even know

Hebrew. Not to mention the absolute bosh he comes up with, like the influence of the Assyrian texts on Ecclesiastes. He may be a high priest at his theological seminary in New York, but in the Talmud it says: Better a bastard scholar than an ignorant high priest. Stanley Ass Segal!" He gave a brief snort and left the room.

"We didn't get paid this month, did we?" said Elisheva.

Upset at Dr. Warshavsky's annoyance, Miss Bloch hammered away aggressively at the typewriter.

"In July. And June's salary in September." With a cold, keeping-my-distance glance at her.

"Give me a line to my room, please."

"Yes, Doctor."

Out in the narrow corridor, a wall on either side, Julius Gertner stood in her path, lanky and long-limbed as primeval man, his brow a bay of wisdom lapping at his skull, narrow slanting eyes smiling cleverly behind rimless spectacles.

"Thou hadst a goodly dream last night," he told her, clasping her hand warmly in both of his.

"How do you know?" With a flutter of her eyelids.

"By the light of thine countenance."

"Thank you, Julius."

"Rumors afloat that our dean is moving to Jerusalem."

"Crisis?"

"Comme toujours."

"Frankly, Julius, I couldn't care less. I do my job, whatever the powers that be."

"Me likewise," laughed Gertner from his heights.

"We're having some people over Friday evening. Will you come too?" She raised a hopeful look at him.

"With pleasure. Any special reason?"

"Do you need one?"

Julius smiled fondly down at her.

"I had an uncle in Breslau, one of the Wissenschaft des Judentums people, who was rather fond of the bottle. Whenever he sat down to work he would put a bottle of cognac on his desk and ask himself: What excuse do I have today? One evening I dropped in—the bottle is on the desk as usual but his glass is still empty. Well, Julius, he says to me, what excuse do I have tonight? I'm not starting on a new chapter nor ending one, I haven't come up with any discovery, and today is just an ordinary weekday. Then he took out some lexicon and discovered happily that according to tradition it was the birthday of Confucius!" Julius chuckled.

"Well, this time it's my husband's. Forty-five."

"Forty-five!" Julius put on a sorrowful expression as if mourning the loss of youth. "He always seemed much younger to me!"

"Oh, *tempus fugit!*"

" 'If time mock thee, trust it not, or it will dance with glee for having thee deceived'!" quoted the professor of medieval philosophy at a singsong.

Mephisto—his eyes. Tricky devil. Hairy horse legs, cloven foot. Let him provide a something pole/ And not be frightened of the hole.

Alone in her bright room Elisheva crushed her cigarette in the ashtray, crumbled the ash, lifted the telephone receiver and dialed. "Acropolis?" she said. "Mr. Tal, please." It's been ages since he called here, she was thinking anxiously; think anything's happened?

With a little skip she seated herself on top of the desk, crossed her legs and waited, the receiver at her ear. Julius, Julius, swinging one long, shapely leg, that I knew the secret of your power.

And you should see those girls of twenty at a lecture of his: fascinated, spellbound, dreamy-eyed, gazing at him in openmouthed adoration! And he himself: the confident voice completely under control, modulated at will, his mind seemingly on nothing but spiritual matters. . . . Ah, Julius, the power of intellectual virility.

Especially combined with that air of subtle European polish, a German scholar's courteousness, Wissenschaft des Judentums wit, and the unobtrusive confidence, the allusive humor, the talent for creating an atmosphere, like that time at his place, the light of the green antique oil lamp, the gilded bindings, and Biedermeier furniture and he in a deep leather armchair, emitting flashes of erudition spiced here and there with a pointed anecdote aimed at someone or other, its malice well concealed, or with a joke, never smutty, of course, though come to think of it, yes, oh, yes.

"Shuka, I hear you called. Anything wrong?"

"No, nothing, I just wanted to tell you. . . . I saw Mother this morning. . . ."

"I can't hear you!"

"I said I saw Mother this morning. . . . Imagine, she informs me, bang, like that, that she's . . . getting married!"

"What?!" she shouted.

"I couldn't believe it. I just couldn't believe it. With Dushkin. . . ."

The old painted sow. Right out of her mind.

With her free hand she groped about behind her, found the cigarettes, extracted one halfway.

Don't react.

"You sound cut up, Shuka."

"Imagine, at her age . . ."

"What did you say to her?" Raising the cigarette to her mouth, crooking a shoulder and giving herself a light. A puff of smoke drifted into the beam of sunlight.

"What could I say?"

"Congratulations."

"I just can't take it in."

"That you're going to get a father?"

No answer. What do *you* care, anyway?

"When's the wedding?"

"Aren't you amazed?"

"We'll talk about it. I've asked some people over, for Friday. Remember?"

"I'm not much in the mood for it."

"Oh, nonsense! When are you coming home today?"

"Four, five."

"I'll be in before you. So long, Shuka."

She let out her breath with a little sigh. Odd how today of all days the image of Patrick O'Donovan kept recurring to her. The fine blond hair falling over his forehead, the almond-soap smell. Where would he be now? A father of five?

Standing by the open window, blowing smoke into the air

outside, she tried to picture it: A woman of sixty-five, fed and pampered, and still going strong in the marital bed.

Behold, our bed of love is green . . . and his fruit sweet to my taste. . . . Detaching herself from the window and gathering her books from the desk in one sweep. Five minutes to go. She leafed through her pad for a last glance at her notes: Bloom and Stephen in Night Nocturnal Town v. Virgil and Dante in purgatory. Stream of consciousness as a musical score in which the notes . . .

The telephone, shrill, annoying.

"For you."

"Yes."

"Dr. Tal-Blumfeld?"

"Speaking."

"This is Amnon Brosh. About your article . . ."

"But I sent it to you!"

"Yes, I got it. It's just that . . ."

"It doesn't suit you. So send it back, that's all!"

"No, it's not that. I think your subject's very important . . ."

"Well, then?"

"It's just that I'm afraid the readers . . . that it's going to be too difficult . . ."

"Difficult?" she shouted.

"No . . ." Intimidated. "I needn't tell you . . ."

Oh, the fool!

"Look here, Mr. Brosh, you don't know me and I don't know you and you needn't feel any obligations toward me. All you have to do is to just put the stuff in an envelope . . ."

"No, look, after all I solicited it, and of course I'd very much like to . . . It's hard to discuss all this on the phone . . ."

"Till what time are you staying there?"

"Till half past two, three."

"I'll be there at two twenty. Good-bye."

The Philistine! Slamming down the receiver she grabbed her books and went to the lecture hall.

AT five minutes past two, right after her second lecture, Elisheva ordered a taxi, and at twenty-five past she arrived at the editorial offices. The girl at Information gave her Brosh's room number and she breezed up to the second floor.

"Mr. Brosh? Tal-Blumfeld." Shaking his hand with her strong, slim fingers.

"I'm so sorry you had to . . ."

Younger than I thought, she noted. "Oh, that's all right! May I sit down?"

"Please, of course." Indicating a chair and sitting down himself.

"I'm listening." Crossing her legs and taking the packet of cigarettes out of her handbag. "Smoke?"

"No, thanks. I feel rather bad about this whole business . . ."

Lighting her cigarette, she squinted at him out of the corner of her eye: quite good-looking. Intelligent as well?

"Let's forget it, Mr. Brosh. What was it you didn't like?"

"It's not that I didn't like it," he said with a faint smile. "It's just that I'm afraid it's too . . . academic, if you can put it like that. . . ."

"For your readers."

"Naturally."

"And that's bad."

"It's too good."

"Should I take that as a compliment?"

"I'm sure you don't need . . ."

"No, no, I would just like to understand why an article that is too good, as you say, isn't suitable for a literary supplement. I only ask because I'm curious. I'm sure you realize I'm not in search of pegs to hang my articles on. I hardly ever publish at all, as a matter of fact. But since you asked, urged . . . Why, by the way, did you apply to me to begin with?"

"I'd heard from students . . ."

"Oh, students! They don't even understand what I'm talking about altogether! Yes, yes, don't laugh, it's quite true!"

"In that case, imagine readers without any academic training . . ."

"Look, Mr. Brosh, I am not writing for 'readers' "—with a sweeping gesture to indicate some abstract generalization—"I am writing for five, three, one reader. Maybe just for you. . . ." Laughing across at him.

Brosh went pink, smiling back into her face. "I, at any rate, found it extremely interesting. . . ."

"Well, then!" she teased. His face was too near, but behind the momentary embarrassment its features were pleasing: the square firm chin, and for contrast—something elegiac and yearning about the eyes and brow.

"Consider," he ventured again, "how many people do you think have read Simone Weil? I suppose that in Hebrew . . ."

Through the cigarette smoke her eyes detected—among the tumble of manuscripts overflowing from a file on his desk—the pages of her own crowded typescript and the two-line title: "The Waiting-for-God Motif in Three Literary Works of the Mid-century."

"One of my aims, Mr. Brosh . . ." She felt an itch to call him Amnon, but decided it was too early, "is to awaken curiosity. Both in my listeners and in your readers. If I have achieved that you ought to be content."

He was, for the moment. But glancing down at her manuscript, he felt rather unnerved again by the awkward patch of bibliographical notes and references—twenty-three in all and none of them in Hebrew.

"To be frank," he said, raising his eyes, "I had hoped you would write on a subject nearer home, something from Hebrew literature."

"If you'd said that to me at the start I'd have told you right away: No!"

"May I ask why not?" Brosh really wanted to know.

"Because I'm not interested. Look, can you name me three Hebrew prose works that are worth writing about? Agnon, sure. Who else?"

"Depends on your approach. . . ."

"The local scene and all that? Doesn't interest me. One could, of course: Israeli society, fluctuations, values, and what have you. Not me. *La Condition humaine.* That's what interests me in literature. All the rest is journalism, or sociological treatise, or gossip. I'm sorry, but that's about all I find in what's being written in this country today."

"You might say the same about most of what is being written everywhere in the world today, don't you think?"

"But I'm not concerned with the average! The average is the concern of statisticians, or newspapers! I hope you won't count that against me, h'm?" She smiled again, chummily.

"If that's so, we're down to just five or six works in a generation," said Brosh, maintaining the distance between man-in-office and visitor.

"Maybe. Though I think that actually, both *Homo Faber* and *Herzog*, and to a certain extent Dürrenmatt, and Henry Miller as well, are all concerned with the *Condition humaine*."

"Henry Miller?"

"Yes! *Sexus*. The human condition. Definitely."

"I should have thought that belonged to what you call gossip . . ."

"Oh!" Elisheva got to her feet impatiently and began pacing up and down before the desk. "In that case Apuleius too, and Petronius, and Boccaccio, Rabelais . . . why not Homer, for that matter?" She stopped in front of him, throwing her hands wide.

"I don't see the connection exactly. . . ." The big yellow earrings dangling from her ears struck him as rather peculiar: a kind of joke, kind of *parody* of cheap taste. "Henry Miller? . . . A long list of erotic adventures, as good as a catalog . . ."

"Quite. But why are you prepared to accept a long list of battles, of military adventures repeated over and over in different variations as literature, as *classics*, and not a list of erotic adventures which also repeat themselves in different variations? Is it just because in war . . ." She flashed one look at him, sizing him up, and decided: No, not his kind of jargon. "It's really odd, you know—leaning over the desk to rub her cigarette out in the ashtray, the edge of her jacket touching his arm—"acts of brutality, murder, the massacre of women and children—that we accept, that we study and teach, but when we're offered tales of pleasure we feel we're being fooled, or corrupted. . . . Yet war corrupts worse than sex, wouldn't you say?"

Brosh was looking at her with a smile of wonder and curiosity as at some legendary bird that had suddenly alighted in his room. All of her—gestures, speech, earrings—struck him as a jest, albeit a scholarly jest.

"Homer," he teased, "Homer isn't just military adventures. . . . You've got Destiny there, Mystery . . ."

"Ever read Miller's *World of Sex*?" Leaning over to him, both hands on the desk. She felt a sudden urge to stick her finger into the little dimple on his handsome chin.

"No." The laughter welling up in him.

"Well, that is just what he talks of there: Mystery! Man on his own in the silence and loneliness, facing the mystery of the world. Sex is like a deity, he says, an omnipresent reality confronting man as an enigma. He, Miller, likens it to a mythological monster carrying the world on its back, and himself to Jonah in the Whale, the great Womb whose mysteries he explores. Miller's works, Mr. Brosh, are pessimistic frolics, a perpetual striving to solve a riddle that is insoluble! He describes hundreds, thousands of copulations, not in order to titillate the reader—he's neither a fool nor a charlatan, mind you—but in an endless search to solve the riddle, the *ding an sich,* the very essence of being! And why through sex? Because that is the myth of our times, just as war was the myth of the ancients, or romantic love the myth of the age of chivalry! Why this fear of sex?"

Brosh couldn't suppress his laughter. Wiping his lips, he said, "I just don't see the point of all those endless repetitions. They bore me."

"Quite. And Dante doesn't bore you? All those endless repetitions of sins and punishments, from one circle to the next, one canto to the next, one horror scene to the next! Or *Candide*! Or large chunks of *Don Quixote*! Because you're not going to tell me that descriptions of hell wrapped up in Christian morality afford you greater pleasure than the descriptions of erotic experiences in *Tropic of Cancer* or *Tropic of Capricorn*! Those are the picaresque novels of our time! And of course you get repetition, it's inevitable. *And* exaggeration, *and* apotheosis, *and* humor— as in *any* picaresque novel! Who is this hero wandering from woman to woman, from bed to bed, who conquers and fails to find happiness—who if not the Odysseus of our times who has lost his cultural heritage and who tries to find himself by means of sexual contact, which in a world drained empty of love is the sole human contact still?"

Brosh was utterly fascinated now, following her with his eyes—her gesticulating hands, her walk as she moved from desk to cupboard, cupboard to chair, as she drew near him as though to back him up against the wall, drew away, completely at her ease. It was all an "academic ballet" as he privately called it. And he had already made up his mind too: I'm going to publish that article come what may. This Friday. Lock, stock, and barrel, twenty-three footnotes and all.

"De Sade! But De Sade calls his *Justine* a philosophical novel, aimed at exposing the sham of conceptions about good and evil, and showing that suffering may redeem the pure but ravaged and violated soul and put it back on the right path! And that in 1791! Today, a hundred and fifty years after De Sade, with innocence completely corrupted by civilization, what wonder that man turns back to the most primitive, the most atavistic, biological myth and finds, *just* in that . . .

"I've worn you out." She dropped tiredly on the chair. "Well, give me my manuscript and we'll say good-bye, and no hard feelings, h'm?"

"Leave it with me for the time being," said Brosh, taking hold of the pages on his desk. "I'd like to go over it again, if you don't mind."

"You needn't feel any obligation toward me. Really, I mean it. And I won't be the least bit hurt if you *don't* print it."

Rising, she lingered for a moment to light herself another cigarette. Only after blowing out the smoke, her eyes on him, she put out her hand and said, "I'm glad to have made your acquaintance, Mr. Brosh." With an open look, with satisfaction.

"Taxi! Taxi!" Out in the street, waving her hand, she ran to overtake the taxi which had pulled up a little way in front.

ARMED with a green plastic bucket containing a broom, a dustpan, and an assortment of rags, his wooden-soled slippers loud in the silence of the stairwell, Shuka Tal came down on Friday afternoon at five o'clock to give his car a washing. When he reached the pavement he saw Azulai, in sandals, shorts, and vest, already playing the hose in great squirts over his white Lark, four cars away from his own. Azulai's spotless white vest pointed up the tan of his muscular arms, and Shuka grinned to himself as always at the funny black fleece growing on Azulai's upper arms in straggly, scrambly patches. He put his bucket down by the fence, set the doors and windows of the car open, picked up the broom and the dustpan, and squatting on his haunches began to sweep the floor of the car. The rubber mats were covered in a fine gray dust and he raked it out of cracks and corners, from under the seats, from as far down as he could reach, heaped it up, swept it into the dustpan and spilled it in the road beside the wheels. Raking, he noticed that the front mats were growing tattered, were even showing tears here and there and would need to be changed for new ones. That would be some 70 or 80 pounds again, he reckoned, and decided to put it off for a couple of months, till he got paid by the companies. With a worried frown it occurred to him that Avivi was getting badly behind with his payments. Avivi of all people.

"Good afternoon, Mr. Tal. Keeping up the good work, I see. Every Friday, like clockwork." Pincus stopping beside him on his way home.

"Yes," said Shuka, straightening up, broom and dustpan stuck out like the arms of a scarecrow at either side of his body, "you neglect her even one week, she makes you pay for it."

"Me, I haven't got the patience. How much does a washing cost? So you're out *another* three pounds."

"I like doing it," Shuka grinned.

"You know what it says: The work of the righteous is done for him by others," and he waved himself on his way.

Now it was the turn of the fittings. He stripped the seats of their covers, shook them out, flapping and thumping in the twilight air till the dust flew, spread them on top of the clipped hedge, took his bucket to the tap, filled it with water, carried it back and chose a soft rag to polish the knobs, frames, panels, wheel, windowpanes—dip and scrub and dry, scrub and dip and dry. The water in the bucket clouded and the fittings grew bright and sparkling. The thought of the "birthday party" Elisheva had prepared for him tonight was getting him down. He detested birthdays, and even worse the guests who would be coming, lecturers, professors, his wife's crowd who, on her orders, must not be made to mingle with lesser fish. He knew he was in for some hours of protracted misery, a whole evening of it, till the last of them would be gone. Every time one of those came to the house he would manage to be out on business, or would shut himself up in a room and go over his accounts. Tonight he would have to put up with it, though. At noon he had driven Elisheva around the shops and she had bought cakes, herring, a big spread. What for? Yet there was something else nagging at him too and he couldn't remember what. Like an unpaid debt preying on one's mind. He had quite a few things on his mind, come to think: his mother, the phone bills, the leaking kitchen drain. And today, coming home, he had found a summons from income tax too, asking him to come and clear up some points in his annual declaration. The thought made his blood boil: why the hell couldn't they get off his back, he who like a conscientious schoolboy took care to enter every incoming penny, every expense, who had never concealed a thing! But no, it wasn't that. Not that.

Avigayil. Yes. The relations between them which had gone hopelessly wrong. Her silences at meals. Her withdrawal. He'd been telling himself that he must, absolutely *must* have a talk with her, a frank, straightforward talk, try and get her to speak her mind. But he puts it off from day to day, has been putting it off for a year. And it gets harder and harder. He watches the distance between them growing, watches it with his own eyes and for all that doesn't lift a finger to stop it. The spirit is willing but the flesh is paralyzed, as it were. Tears well up in him sometimes, thinking of it. Like today, when she brought him a bunch of roses for his birthday and before he could even kiss her for it she had gone to her room and shut the door. Couldn't he at least this once have knocked on her door, gone in, sat on the bed, yes, taken the first step, the *first step*, sat on the bed, by her side, and said, Look, I'm your father . . .

A ball started rolling between the two pavements, and galloping feet: "Shoot it!"

Shuka emerged from the car and exclaimed angrily, "How many times have I told you kids not to play football here!"

"We got as much right to this street as you!" A cheeky little brat bouncing the ball at his feet.

"You've got an empty lot right over there, why don't you go there?"

"You go there yourself!" a towheaded urchin piped up from across the street.

"Come and see what you've done!" he called to the one with the ball.

"What've we done?" And hugging the ball to his chest he came shambling over at his ease.

"Come on, come on." Shuka went at him, grabbed his hand, and propelled him to the car. "Look," he pointed at a dent in the hood.

"That isn't us," said the boy, feeling the dent with his fingers. "Anybody can see this wasn't done by a ball anyhow."

"Not a ball, eh? And what if I saw you throw it at the car with my own eyes?"

"Never"—appraising the dent with an expert's squint—"with a Simca maybe, but not a Fiat. Body of a Fiat's tough enough to not get hurt by a football."

"It's Ronny there kicked it. Everybody seen him!" the urchin shrilled from a safe distance.

"You are not going to play here!" declared Azulai in his authoritative voice and converged on the ball owner, "Off with you! Beat it! Or do you want me to take this ball away from you?"

"Just you dare!" the boy fired a last volley in retreat.

The two victors watched the rout of the enemy, smiling.

"I say, why don't you buy yourself a hose?" Azulai asked Shuka. "Spares you a lot of work. I get the job done in fifteen minutes flat."

"Guess I don't set much store by it," said Shuka.

He couldn't explain to Azulai how it was precisely because of that, because washing her with a hose was such a quick, slapdash job, that he preferred the bucket.

"Your paint wears well, though. Mine's already starting to fade," said Azulai, passing his hand over the smooth top of his neighbor's car.

"That's it, you got to take care of her. Like a horse. You give her food, drink, keep her clean—she stays faithful to you."

"You wash her with detergent or kerosene or what?"

"Never!" Shuka advised him. "Soap, kerosene—those eat away at your paint! I know many people make that mistake, in a year or two she starts peeling. Water, just water."

He loved this hour of a Friday afternoon, the fellowship of car owners here and there along the street, giving their pets the weekly grooming, wandering over to a neighbor for consultation, exchange of opinions.

"Mine needs a new paint job, but who's got three hundred and fifty pounds?" said Azulai.

"Expensive affair, a car."

"The upkeep! The least repair—fifty, a hundred pounds. Fairly gets you. Last week I drop in at the garage to get the carburetor cleaned—how much do you figure I paid?"

"Seventeen pounds."

"Forty-eight!"

"How's that? Adjusting's six, overhaul and assembly another eleven—it's in the price list."

"I dare say, but what if while they were about it they found the filter was worn out, the oil pump needing fixing, and the plugs and all. It's like the dentist. You go to him with a toothache, he tells you you got another two cavities in back and one at each side. Better not go at all."

"As long as you're healthy," Shuka consoled him.

"You're right, what's money, after all?" agreed Azulai in parting and went back to his car.

Shuka carried the bucket to the tap, changed the water, returned to the car, rolled up the windows, and shut the doors from without. Then he dipped the big woolen rag in water and with a broad sweep of his arm whisked it across the top of the car.

But before going on with it, he decided he'd tackle Azulai once more. He left the car, water dribbling down its windows, and warily approached the Lark.

"Happened to think over what we talked about?" he ventured cautiously.

"The insurance?" said Azulai, interrupting his window mopping. "No, I intend to live a good while yet!"

"Bless you," Shuka laughed, "till a hundred and twenty! But like I explained, it's a kind of savings too."

"Look, Tal, if I have fifty pounds a month to spare I'd sooner put them in the bank and earn some dividend on them."

"But work it out for yourself: two hundred pounds'll get you at most—at *most,* I say!—fifty pounds profit a year, and you still have to pay income tax on that. Now, if you insure your life for thirty thousand pounds, and if then, heaven forbid . . ."

"Do me a favor and don't go on . . ."

"None of us is immune to misfortune . . ."

"Look, old man, I've a theory about it: misfortune's like a sleeping dog, I say. You walk around it, watch it—it ends waking up and jumping you. Better keep out of its sight, if you see what I mean."

"An ostrich theory, if you don't mind."

"Give a man a bit of peace!" hooted Azulai.

"That's just what I want: to give you peace, no worries . . ."

"Believe you me, I've got plenty to worry about."

"Think about the wife, the kids . . ."

"What the hell, I'm fit as a fiddle!" said Azulai with a guffaw.

"So be fit with thirty thousand pounds more, why not?"

"Oh, no! That's just the way to stop being fit! Every month, the day the premium's due, I'll be thinking of death! What's the use of that?"

"Usually it's the other way around, when a man *doesn't* know what'll happen to his family . . . how his family'll manage. . . ."

"You're wasting your breath, Tal. You won't talk me into it. You come back when you can get me an insurance against death." And Azulai resumed his window mopping.

Disappointed, Shuka walked back to his car, dipped the rag in water and swept it over the top again till the water ran down in streams along the entire width of the shoulder. He was blaming himself: it's a mistake to talk about "misfortune." It sort of rattles them, scares them off. Better talk about a long life, till ripe old age and all, and about the tidy sum a fellow can count on in his declining years. He'd slipped up on that more than once before, and he'd still not learned from experience. Actually he's right, Azulai: better not think. What for? After you're dead . . .

Ziva Lotan, the "queen of the street," appeared round the corner. He saw her approaching—tall, queenly, the straight blond hair falling to her shoulders. He knew she would stop by him. She always graces him with a greeting and a few courtesies. Tal pretended not to have seen her and attacked the car with zeal.

"Hi, Mr. Tal." Stopping beside him.

"Hi, Ziva." Turning to her, surprised, rag in hand.

"Washing her, huh?"

"All in a day's work."

"I always notice your car, Mr. Tal. The brightest of the whole lot."

"Thank you. Once a week. Got to."

"How's business?"

"Fine, fine." Beaming at her. A bold mouth she has, unpainted, appetizing as a ripe plum.

"I read about lots of traffic accidents these days, isn't it terrible!"

"Yes, wild driving, careless . . ."

"What can you do? As many people killed as in a war!"

"Better not think. And you? I saw your picture on a cover. Great!"

"Oh, a terrible picture!"

"I was really proud! Girl on our street!"

"Don't remind me."

"I expect you'll be picked Bathing Beauty of the Year again!"

"I've had enough. And I'm going away anyhow."

"Abroad?"

"England. Not for long. A year."

"Going to study?"

"Stay with relatives. But I guess I'll study too. Public relations. I'm awfully keen on that."

"Splendid!"

"See you, Mr. Tal."

"Bye."

Tal watched her go: the thighs alive, vibrant, the give-and-take of buttocks. Briefly he raised his glance to the third-floor windows.

Then he poured the bucket out over the entire body of the car, returned to the tap, filled it, poured it out again, puddles forming beside the wheels.

Taking the felt rag and starting to mop up the water, drying, wringing, wiping the back, shoulders, sides—he dreamed of meeting Ziva Lotan in London, in the street—Fancy meeting you here!—embracing her in full view of the street. . . . What are you doing here, Mr. Tal? A world congress of insurance agents, between one session and the next, and who do I see! What a funny coincidence, two people from the same street . . . Coincidence, Ziva? No, no, I always dreamed that sometime, somehow . . . Exactly. All alone? And he invites her to a bar, no, to an expensive restaurant, and at the table, chatting, comparing notes, laughing. . . . Actually, ever since . . . Yes, ever since . . . Afterward, renting a car, a shining black Ford, driving north, to Scotland, to the green hills, the lakes. At night—a hotel. A single room . . .

A single room?

Tal cast another brief glance up at his window.

The rag seemed to be moving of its own accord now, smoothly, as though anointing, over the top with its lovely curve, the rounded flanks, the back, lightly sweeping the windows, polishing. The body took on a noble sapphire-blue sheen—this quiet, submissive body, mutely grateful.

The sun had dropped below the rooftops and in the west a crimson conflagration subsided in the space between two houses. Tal collected his tools and turned to go in. At the gate he stopped for a last look at the car: she was handsome, cleansed for the Sabbath, arising from her bath in a soft glow. He could see Azulai's Lark beyond the top of the fence, its owner gone. Slowly he drew near, bent and peered inside: leather seats. But cracked and worn. Badly worn. And the backs dull, lackluster.

● ● ● THE curve conveys vitality. Look at the harp, for instance. Or the blade of a sickle. A gondola. Now take modern architecture—all straight lines and right angles. It's dull, it induces a psychosis of conformity, and that isn't even the worst of it. My point is that it shows positive evidence of degeneration!"

Tal was sitting on the couch, elbows on knees, fingers around a glass—which he had just refilled for the fourth or fifth time—and threw a sidelong glance at Dr. Hadar. The curve conveys vitality, does it? He laughed to himself. And how about the curve of a middle-aged man's belly, eh? Does that, too, convey vitality? Or maybe just the opposite? Consider, Dr. Hadar!

And he looked at the man's small, tight potbelly with a touch of glee, and at the curves of the chin on the pampered, pasty face, and at the two red spots spreading across the full cheeks, and at the big round spectacles.

Their voices seemed to come to him from a little distance, seemed to float in a warm, vaguely festive cloud: they were discussing the new buildings going up at the university. . . . Or no, not the buildings, that is, but modern architecture in general. And when Meir Shapira, the high-school teacher, was telling them about buildings he had seen on his trip to Europe—dropping names like Courvoisier, Sagrada-Familia, Barcelona, Marseilles, Gaudi or something—he noticed two things: one, that the man's Hebrew was too grammatical, too pedantic despite his relative youth; and two, that while speaking he helped himself to the tenth or twelfth sandwich of the evening. And that's bad, he reflected, bad, because his figure's too flabby as it is. Definitely.

Very Important People! Passing his eyes from Dr. Hadar to Dr. Hofmann, from Dr. Hofmann to Professor Julius Gertner. . . .

But who was that emerging from the kitchen if not Elisheva, bearing a fresh tray of sandwiches, thin slices all dainty and garnished, a whole blooming kitchen garden.

"As a matter of fact," she announced, "as a matter of fact we're building ourselves cubes just like the Romans used to build for their lowest class of soldiers, and the Egyptians for their slaves"—lowering the tray to the table—"simple geometric formulae expressed in military idiom. Don't you agree, Julius?"

Why Julius? Why not Shuka? Hofmann? Shapira?

Well, Julius, and what do you have to say to that? Tal fixed him with his smile, a smile that had been glued to his face from the moment the first guest had shown up and that, to tell the truth, was beginning to hurt slightly, beginning to feel like the imprint of a slap in the face. Roman cubes?

"The Egyptians?" Gertner's drawl.

Julius Gertner was sitting upright on his chair, thumbs stuck in his trouser belt. He conferred a weary, an oh-so-weary and indulgent smile upon Elisheva.

"But look," Dr. Hofmann, lecturer in economics, twirling a glass in his fingers, "there's a world of difference between one cube and another. I should say that a low cube, for example, with an oblong inner space, would create a more, say, democratic atmosphere than a tall and narrow one. . . ."

What drivel! Shuka snorted to himself. Every schoolboy knows that a cube can be neither oblong nor narrow, because it's a *regular* shape! And that from a professor!

"And what I think is," came from Ariella, Shapira the teacher's wife, "is that what our architects are bringing here from abroad is not the achievements of world architecture but quite the contrary—its shortcomings!"

Right you are, thought Shuka, but why say it in such a loud, ringing voice as though we were out in the open instead of inside a room? Then it occurred to him that as a matter of fact he, too, might contribute something to the discussion if he had a mind to, like, say, how he hadn't cared for the plans of that famous German—Brazilian?—architect, whose model for a town in the Negev he had seen some time ago; but he didn't have a mind to. Besides, he couldn't for the life of him recall the name of that architect. Bodenheimer?

Bodenheimer?

But there, Professor Julius Gertner was talking now. Telling something. Taking his time about it too. Drawling. And everybody attentive. Telling a Rabbi Nahman of Bratzlav story, the "Lamp of Flaws." Very interesting: A man had sent his son abroad to learn a craft and the son had come back and said he had learned to make a hanging lamp. . . .

Tal gazed into his glass and thought: If I tilt it to the right, the drink'll spill on my pants; if, on the other hand, I should tilt it to the left, the drink'll *also* spill on my pants. And considering that was the case he emptied the glass into his mouth in one gulp.

And poured himself a fifth glass, or maybe a sixth.

And decided he was overdoing it a bit. And what bothered him, too, was not being able to recall the name of the young woman sitting on a chair to his right. The one who hadn't touched any of the food offered her, and had kept silent all evening like himself, and whose face wore a melancholy but rapt smile reflecting some inner fire—to which her flaming cheeks bore witness as well. All he remembered was that she was a poetess. And divorced. Divorced? Uh-huh, divorced.

"But, Dr. Hofmann, what has the style of public building in the Western world been for the last thousand years if not a collection of *phallic symbols?*" he suddenly heard his wife declare. "What else are the Gothic spires, the mosques, the towers, the skyscrapers, even our own water towers, or those gas towers with balloons on top you see in Europe—what if not phallic symbols? Everything sticking bolt upright. . . ."

And even though—amid the laughter her words provoked—he did consider it slightly vulgar to talk like that in company—be it even the company of highbrows—Shuka admired her courage. And found her view both astute and interesting, and truly funny. Mosques, for instance, with their ledged minarets. . . .

"And it wasn't by any means always like that. The pyramids, for example, aren't phallic symbols. Neither are the Babylonian or the Greek temples. . . ."

"If we were to introduce the feminine principle the way you want," said Julius Gertner with an affectionate smile at Elisheva, "then we ought to go back to holes and caves. . . ."

"Well, and why not, Julius?" said Elisheva, refusing to join in the general laughter. "Why not go back to the soft, rounded, indrawn shapes. . . . I could think of worse things for this extrovert civilization of ours!"

And when Dr. Hofmann began to discourse, gravely and elaborately, on experiments in the direction suggested by Elisheva, of "sculpted structures, low and rounded like Arab mud huts," in the south of Spain, the work of a young architect by name of André Block, Shuka took another sip of his drink, blurring the rest of the speech, and said to himself that if he'd only make a slight effort, just a very slight effort, he could come out with something much cleverer than anything said here this evening. He would say, for instance:

that the most noble thing in the world is not-to-be.

Uh-huh. Not-to-be. Like an empty sky. Like water. Not-to-be. Something very wonderful.

And when he woke briefly from this joyous sense of fusion with the not-being—everything around him drifting in a warm haze, a ring-around of preposterous faces intent on some comical ceremony, each of them performing his or her part on cue—he was surprised to hear them talking of other things, while he hadn't even even noticed the conversation taking a turn. Somone now mentioned "hippies," and someone else was talking about a philosopher called William James who over fifty years ago had already noted the effect of drugs upon the "cosmic and mystic experiences" of Christian saints, dervishes, Sufis, Buddhists, to whom God had been revealed after a dose of chloroform, or hashish, or nitrous oxide, and it was all old hat—

"And the Cabalists?" Shapira's wife cried, again in too loud a voice.

And he couldn't for the life of him understand what Cabalists had to do with it, and wondered how an uneducated woman like her had the nerve to speak out loud like that; and heard the name William James invoked again; and when Meir Shapira was telling—again in very pedantic phraseology as though lecturing to students—how William James writes that sobriety contracts the field of consciousness and emphasizes the *naysaying* to experience, whereas intoxication expands consciousness and stimulates the yea-saying urge, he wanted to shout that no, wrong, utterly wrong, except that just then Julius Gertner said—

"Now I know why the hippies yell yea-yea!"

Which produced an outburst of laughter. And he laughed,

too, though aware of something about Gertner that aroused his dislike, yet unable to define just what it was. His mock modesty? Or the confidence of the ironically smiling eyes, the confidence that whatever he said was invariably subtle and profound? Or the faint, hardly visible twitch of a muscle in his left cheek?

"But you are right about the Cabalists," he said. "It is told of the saintly Isaac Luria, for instance, that he would eat of the plants of the desert: weeds and thistles. Marijuana, obviously."

And even before the laughter had died down he added, "In which case perhaps the *clippot,* the "husks" of Cabalistic lore, are nothing but the husks of morning-glory seeds, which I believe are used in the production of LSD! So maybe we could call hippies 'clippies' in Hebrew."

And that, thought Tal, really *was* witty; but when Elisheva got up to go to the kitchen for fresh supplies he followed her, threading his way between table and guests and marveling at himself for stepping so lightly and steadily without veering left or right, and entering the kitchen he told her, "The party's going great, and this Gertner really is a smart fellow!" "Yes," she said, removing the meat pie from the oven, "but you're drinking too much, Shuka"; and when she left the kitchen with the tray he poured himself another glass from the bottle on the drainboard, gulped it swiftly as though slipping one over on himself, and wiping his mouth with his hand ("Bitter!" with a shudder of distaste) had a marvelous feeling of freedom and told himself that now he was capable of anything, absolutely *anything,* and that he wasn't responsible anymore for anything, absolutely *nothing;* wherefore, a sly grin on his face, he tiptoed softly out of the kitchen and toward the front door, opened it absolutely quietly, shut it behind him without a sound, and escaped down the stairs.

And still no one had said a word, not a word all evening, about the article that had appeared in today's paper, Elisheva thought in distress amid the general acclaim of her meat pie. Impossible that no one had read it! Or was it so bad? Or so trivial that it didn't call for comment? Was Julius waiting to say something in private? "Have one of these, they're good." She knelt with her tray before Dinah Lev, who hadn't touched anything all evening. "No, thank you," said Dinah, the melancholy smile not leaving her face. "Some sherry, then?" "No, thank you."

"As a matter of fact, I don't believe any religion ever maintained that ecstatic conditions could be induced by artificial stimulants," she said, in order to tie a thread which had snapped in her absence. "The Christian saints were clear-sighted enough at any rate." Putting it to Julius in the form of a question.

"One can hardly talk of Christian saints as a *class*," Julius supplied. "Christian hagiography recognizes different categories of saints and martyrs. Some were canonized for their missionary work, like Boniface, or the Venerable Bede, or Becket. Others, like Augustine or Aquinas, for their theological writings. And then there were the visionaries, those who experienced ecstatic conditions, as you say—Gregory of Tours, Joan of Arc, or Saint Gertrude who heard a voice in church call her from on high, *sanctus sanctus sanctus*, and felt the Holy Son bend down and kiss her as a lover.... The female saints, at least, all belonged to the last category...." He laughed.

"St. Thérèse de Lisieux as well?"

"Without a doubt! She was a rather sickly girl with masochistic tendencies, and when she writes about her love for Jesus ... Look, she even made up an invitation for her wedding with him, complete with all the trappings: God on the groom's side, Mary on the bride's, hereby invite you to the Spiritual Marriage of their August Son Jesus Christ with little Thérèse Martin, on such and such day at such and such place. ... Oh, without a doubt!"

"I didn't know ..." A flush of excitement crept over Elisheva's face, as at the approach of danger.

"Which reminds me," said Julius, raising a finger at her, and she realized with beating heart that the hoped-for and dreaded moment had arrived, "I don't think I can agree with the honors you heap upon Simone Weil as having had divine revelation, as if she were some latter-day saint. ..."

"I didn't say she was a saint!" she protested and felt her eyes blur, while at the same time catching the murmur to her right and Meir Shapira explaining to his wife that the point at issue was an article in today's paper.

"Simone Weil didn't know the first thing about Judaism!"

Julius enlightened Elisheva. "Judaism as far as she was concerned was the Old Testament, with at best a smattering of Maimonides. But it's obvious she was perfectly unfamiliar with the Midrash, with Cabala, with Hasidism, or with Albo's *Principles!* What she says about Judaism is sheer rubbish—that it's a racial, totalitarian creed with no concern for the individual and without love or grace! The kind of rubbish you can trace back to the self-hatred of an apostate—*and* an ignoramus!"

"I didn't touch on that side of her . . ." she apologized, flustered, wilting before his disapproval. "I only dealt with the moment of 'Attente de Dieu' in her philosophy, with her rejection of God as consolation, as a kind of insurance against disaster. . . ."

"And that, too, you will find in Judaism, as Buber pointed out long ago. . . ." But seeing her so crestfallen he added with a gracious smile, "Though what you say about the affinity between her conception and Beckett's *Godot* and Camus's *Fall* is an interesting point. It had never occurred to me, in fact."

"Yes, that was excellent!" Meir Shapira chimed in, and took another slice of meat pie.

And somewhat cheered by that, and by the others' agreement, and so as not to let the conversation flag, she gave an account of her meeting with Amnon Brosh, and of how reluctant he had been at first to print her article because it was too "academic."

"He's quite a pleasant young man, though," she said. "I just happened to hear yesterday that he himself writes too. Read anything, anyone?"

"Oh, yes, he's already had two books published," said Shapira, "one of short stories, and another just a few months ago."

"Any good?"

"Fairish . . ."

"I liked it very much," Dinah Lev put in, for the first time that evening; and everyone turned to her, in relief and affection, and wishing her to go on.

"What's it about?" asked Elisheva, pleased that her guest—and protégée—had at last come out of her shell.

"It's called, *Ravens There Were None,*" said Dinah, her low voice rippling gentle and solitary in the room. "It's about a man who has withdrawn from the world and put up a small road inn at a lonely spot in the Negev on the road to Eilat, and after a year the road is shifted and he loses his means of support—it's sort of as if a river had altered course and left the field dry—and the man decides to stay where he is anyway and tries to grow things. . . . The point isn't the story itself though, but the beauty of the landscape descriptions, and of the relations that grow up between the man and the desert. . . . It's a novella, really, a lyric novella."

"Sounds very interesting," said Elisheva.

And it was only then that she became aware of Shuka's prolonged absence from the room. She rose and hurried out to the kitchen, from the kitchen to the bathroom, the bedroom, Avigayil's room, the study—oh, the big baby! The big silly baby! Where had he run to? His mother's apron? What had he taken offense at? It was his own fault, not opening his mouth all evening except to pour his big body full of that poisonous stuff! And what am I going to tell them now? And why does he do this to me on an evening like this? . . .

And when she came back the talk had switched to Ben-Gurion, his retiring to the Negev at the time, his complex personality, and Julius was giving them some Midrashic explication of the verse "Away, get thee down," said by God to Moses in Sinai. Sitting down beside Dinah Lev, she whispered to her: "Yehoshua didn't feel well. He's been having stomach trouble for some time. Had to go and lie down." "I was noticing him," said Dinah, "keeping silent, and you feel he's got more insight than any of them." "He shouldn't drink," whispered Elisheva. "What's the name of that book you mentioned?"

"*Ravens There Were None.*"

"Yes."

And she made a mental note of it.

T HIS business with Jeanette must stop, must stop once and for all, Shuka was drumming into himself as he started the car and sped it on its way to Jeanette's. The circle of guests was reeling around him as a huge, colorful

Ferris wheel, faces merging, blurring, and the road rushing toward him—ashimmer with the headlights of oncoming cars and with flashing neon messages—as on a collision course. The night air was hot, too hot to sober him up, and he turned on his inner braking mechanism: think of the road, only of the road, nothing but the road; and admired himself immensely for his masterly driving, pulling up before every red light, shifting gears faultlessly, not once missing a turn, a hairbreadth between himself and the flank of a car streaking past, but not touching, not grazing, not crashing, and speeding onward, and Julius Gertner can go jump in the lake—

Oscar Niemeier! With a triumphant shout the name of the German—Brazilian?—architect he had been racking his brains for all evening came back to him. Oscar Niemeier! He laughed. Him and his showy, highfalutin plans for putting up towers in the desert, as though Beer Sheva or Arad were Pithom and Raamses or Brasília; what does he know, this Niemeier fellow, about the sand, the dry wadis, the Nabataeans, Abdeh, the copper mines, the Pillars of Solomon, the heat, the eastern wind, the scorching heat, the wind—

He couldn't stop the Ferris wheel, and out of the reeling colors his eyes caught flickers—of Gertner's face, of the poetess, Gertner, the poetess, he could have gotten together with her, why hadn't he, the two of them whispering together, if only he could think of her name! When was it she had first come to the house, some evening, the sad smile on her face, nice not stuck-up—Me, I'm to see Elisheva, she at home?—and afterward closeted for hours and hours in the study, whispering, and Elisheva's voice ringing out once beyond the door: But you *mustn't* see him!

Phallic symbols! He chuckled aloud as the spire of the Sheikh-Hassan Mosque loomed up before him, and braked hard with a shriek of tires and nearly fell over. Without switching off the engine he got out of the car and stood in the road looking up admiringly at the mosque and its minaret, and measured its height and saw a kind of deathly pallor in the arc of its windows and on its brow, and a wild and primitive and pagan fierceness in its virility thrusting upward at the moon, the moon ringed by a hazy nimbus, the sad and lonely moon. Phallic symbols indeed! He smiled and crossed to the stone fence of the mosque, pulled down the zipper of his pants, and made water against the wall, relieving his bursting bladder. Beautiful are thy nights, Canaan, a beautiful Canaan night, hot and beautiful—he looked up at the pale forlorn moon and felt a wave of compassion, for it, for this desolate desert land preyed on by jackals; which now, under this moonlight wandering over mosque and ruins and bare open spaces appeared to him as in days of old, with an Arab horseman roaming the white sands and himself a child. With a twitch of his shoulder he shrugged off compassion and returned to the car, humming impatiently, waiting for him.

Ought to buy something. Sweets, Turkish delight, cashew nuts, almonds and raisins. He slowed down. But the shops in Jaffa were shuttered and barred, the streets empty, only a couple of loiterers here and there, defying the headlights of passing cars. Oh, city of lewdness and sin lurking in dark alleys! If the sea rose and flooded, and cleansed! This business must stop once and for all, by God!

Nearly eleven! his watch showed as he drew up at the street corner. But his legs carried him lightly to her house, as though he were weightless, and he gave three knocks on the door and leaned his head against the doorpost and waited what seemed a long time, the wheel spinning and spinning behind his closed eyelids.

"Gogo!"

Tal grinned: her eyes wide with surprise, breasts gleaming through the lace of the blue dressing gown. "Yes, it's me, Zizi. . . . Woke you up, did I?"

"Aren't you a one for surprises! On a Friday!? You never come to see me on a Friday!"

"Yes, Zizi, Friday . . . Why not Friday?" Putting his arm around her neck to draw her inside.

"No, Gogo," she whispered and shut the door behind her. "The kid's a bit fidgety, keeps waking up. We better not go in."

Tal tried to stop the wheel of his brain and get a grip on himself: "He ill?"

"Dunno what's wrong with him. Nods off, wakes up. . . . Let's just drive around a bit. It's hot out."

"To the sea. Let's go to the sea, huh?" As a secret in her ear.

"You've been drinking, Gogo!" Rebuking him. "Bad boy, Gogo!"

"Just a bit, Zizi."

"Since when you calling me Zizi?" she said with a giggle.

"Since tonight!" He kissed her cheek. "Don't you like it?"

"Sure! So what's made you come like that?" Lifting moist eyes up at him, amused.

"I missed you. . . ."

"Don't you lie to me, Gogo!" Pinching his middle hard. "Your wife kicked you out, eh?"

Tal shut her mouth with a kiss.

"Had a fight, eh?" Sticking a fist in his belly.

Tal choked her off with another kiss.

"You've drunk a *lot,* not a *bit!*" Slapping his chin, "Where are you coming from now?"

"Far, far away . . ."

"Far away where?"

"Barcelona . . ."

"Stop fooling, Gogo! You been at a bar! You been with a girl! Tell me honest!" Giving him a shove with her hip.

"You aren't jealous, Zizi. . . ."

"I'd kill you if I found you'd been going out with other girls!" She pinched his arm.

Tal crushed her against his chest, promised her with a kiss that there was no one else, no one but her.

"Where're my keys?" He fumbled in his pocket.

Found them. In the left pocket.

"I still owe you twenty pounds, Gogo!" said Jeanette getting into the car.

"What's twenty pounds! I'm rich, Zizi!" He started the car.

"No, no, I'm gonna give it back. There's somebody owes me money, that Hungarian I told you about. . . ."

Tal took in a gush of quick warm patter: That Hungarian, him of the deck chairs, who buys cigarettes from her on credit and tries to cheat her on the bill. "Every week he thinks he'll fix me, that . . ."

"I'll wring his neck!" said Tal. "One day I'll come to the beach, and I'll catch him by the throat . . ."

"Tough guy, Gogo!" Jeanette giggled, "Yes, and that blouse you bought me," rubbing her arm against his, "such a cute blouse."

"You wearing it?"

"You come to the beach and see! I bought slacks to go with it too. You'll see what a fit they are. . . ."

Tal could see her in his mind's eye, serving drinks, in her honey-sunny blouse, brown arms bare to the salty sea breeze, the young gallants of the beach in minuscule bathing trunks crowding round the stand, rippling their muscles, joking with her coveting . . .

"The lifeguard, you hear, every half hour he comes for a drink of orange juice. My, ain't you drinking a lot? I say to him. I see you, he says, all got up in orange, I get thirsty! You figure I'm an ad, I say. So he gives me a look like . . ."

Tal put his hand on her knee and made it crawl up her warm thigh, delighted to discover she had nothing on under her gown.

"Cut it out!" she giggled, squirming, "I can't talk when you're doing that!" And pressed his hand against her crotch.

Tal stopped and cut off the engine, crouched over her, pulled at the gown, buried his face between the two hot summery pomegranates and didn't know which of them to eat up first.

"Not like this, Gogo!" Jeanette panted. "Not in here . . ."

The sand was dry and soft, and Jeanette's bare feet sank into it. Tal was carrying her slippers, and his own shoes grew heavier with each step.

"Look at that moon!" Jeanette stood still at the top of the dunes and turned her face upward.

Tal glanced at the moon and saw nothing of particular interest about it. It was surrounded by a tired, hazy nimbus. Jeanette's face, on the other hand, was bathed in a dreamy light, and her hair—dazzling magic. He kissed her mouth, pulled her to him, and behind her back the slippers dropped out of his hand.

"My slippers," whispered Jeanette.

Tal bent and picked them up.

"Do you love me, Gogo?" asked Jeanette, hugging his middle.

Tipsy as he was, Tal remembered that if he said yes it would be a betrayal. Only then would it be a real betrayal. And he stopped her mouth with his.

"No, say it!" Jeanette pushed his face away. "I want you to say you love me!"

For a moment his head cleared and he hated her: she'd not make him!

· 66 ·

"Come on, Gogo, say it!" Lightly slapping his cheek.

Tal grabbed her hand and crooned the line of a song in her ear: "I love your sa-han-dals . . ." and pulled her after him, running and floundering, running and floundering down the dune.

At its foot he dropped into the sand with her.

Devouring, soaring, heaving with the waves, seesaw with the rhythmic surge of the sea.

And becalmed, eyes closed, he saw Julius Gertner, sitting in the armchair, raising a finger at him: There *is* retribution! There *is* retribution!

And when he opened his eyes he saw that the moon had seen, a witness in the sky.

The last time, he said, tearing through the long, empty, jaundiced streets on his way home.

Passing the mosque he stopped suddenly with a screech. There had been something fishy there: Why hadn't she let him come in? The child ill, she had said, wakes up. But in that case, how could she have left him alone? She ought to have said not today, or let him in and asked him to be quiet. Why had she shut the door so quickly? Could there have been somebody in there with her? He killed the engine.

Now, sober, he could retrace every move: he had stood by the door waiting quite a long time. Too long, it now seemed. Had he heard whispering on the other side? He couldn't remember. And later, the surprise on her face, and a hint of alarm. Alarm? Maybe not. A forced note in her voice, though, not quite natural, false. In her laughter.

Rubbish! He started the car again and drove on, recalling how she had pressed his hand against her thigh in the car, and how she had given herself there, on the sand, as always, eagerly, as always. More. And her good-bye kiss. And the warm smile in her eyes.

A bit peculiar though, how she'd said, "Don't give a girl such surprises, Gogo. . . ."

It'd be the biggest joke if you, Mr. Tal, started getting jealous at this point in the game. Yeah, get obsessed by it maybe, too. Showing up unexpectedly, peering in at the window, listening at the door . . .Or mornings at the beach, spying on her to see with which one of the young dripping he-men . . .

The windows up there at the third story were dark. Tal got out of the car, locked it, turned his trouser cuffs and shook out the sand, wiped his shoes thoroughly on the mat and climbed the stairs, two by two, softly. If Elisheva was awake he'd tell her he'd spent his time at a bar, drinking, yes, drinking, till now. Next time *he* was going to make up the list of invitations! Phallic symbols! He stood by the door, composed his breathing, stuck a hand into his back pocket.

The punishment! Blood rushing to his face.

The wallet. With the keys, the papers, driver's license, insurance, receipts, thirty pounds.

Shaken, he tumbled down the stairs—breaking all the rules of caution—opened the car door, bent inside, feeling the seats, thumping them, joggling—

He went down on all fours—like a dog, a scavenging dog!—pawing the floor under the seats, around the gearshift, back of the pedals, the brake—

Straightening up and looking at his grimy palms, he wanted to cry. Gogo! . . .

Yes, the punishment.

There, on the sand, under the moon. Incriminating evidence. There! says the policeman and places the wallet before the judge.

He got in, sat, started. God! The whole long, blasted road!

And once again the night-black streets streaking backward, the empty doorways, alluring blank alleys, lampposts flashing past, a lone prostitute, a solitary straggler, a solitary hurrier. And what if it's not there?

Or if he's stopped by a policeman. For speeding. Without papers, insurance. Or—a sudden accident!

Or, in the morning, tomorrow, day after: Elisheva alone at home, the honest finder appears, hands it over: found this, on the beach. Saw by the address on the driver's license . . .

The end.

He stopped the car near the dunes. This isn't the spot. Or is it? He got out, started up the dune, floundering, again floundering at each step. Look what a moon! . . . No trace of footsteps. Going down, at a run. But where? Big, sprawling, swishing sea, and the same arcs of wave prints the whole length of it, lapping, foaming, soaking in, retreating, and at left the same gentle curves of soft sand, innocent, without a trace.

A desert.

Tal wandered, got lost in it, in the spaces of sea and water everywhere. He went south, then north, took the shade of a hollow for wallet, strip of driftwood for wallet, litter, lumber; dropped on his knees, groping, sifting, got up and searched with his eyes: not a sign. Where had it been?

He sat down on the sand at the foot of the dune. From this point, the way he had sat with Jeanette before, after, her hand on his shoulder, it would be easier to remember.

The gentle slap-slap of the waves, rows of surf, the endless streak of moonlight. Let's go back, Gogo, it's late. . . .

And it struck him: the cinder of a burned-out bonfire ahead! About four paces ahead and to the right! Yes.

Now, systematically: comb the length of the beach for cinder. There!

And right beyond, four paces from the dross and ashes.

Black on white.

For all to see.

Witness.

Miracle.

It was half past two by the time he reached his own gate once more. The soles of his shoes were sticky with tar and he broke off a branch from the hedge and scraped at it. Then he went up, cautiously turned the key in the lock, tiptoed into the bedroom and slipped out of his clothes. She wasn't asleep: her breathing irregular, and when he got into the bed she turned her back to him.

The last time, he swore.

Wide-eyed in the dark room, he saw Gertner again. He'd ask for a meeting, go to his house, confess: Terribly degrading, Mr. Gertner . . . this deceit . . . this betrayal of faith . . . . Professor Gertner smiles: Happens every day . . . greater men than you . . . greater in wisdom and virtue . . . human frailty . . . No, Mr. Gertner, you don't understand . . . it's not that, not that . . .

*H*IGH *in the midst of the sky stood the*
Thammuz sun, scorching and blazing.

Marts were no longer frequented, the roads and the streets were
vacant;

None dared to go in the blistering heat 'bout his mission or
business.

All their heads suddenly turned . . .

But Avigayil gave up in despair. Almost as soon as she had sat
down to read, the shouting match between study and bedroom,
back and forth past the closed door of her room, had started,
shattering the lines of the poem. What had happened last night?
Had he really gone off in the middle of the party—how silly!—
and run out of the house? Drunk? "So you'd better put up with
it, Shuka! Put up with it once and for all that that's my kind of
crowd whether you like it or not! And if you get a morbid
pleasure out of fancying that it's snobbishness . . ." Why "*morbid*
pleasure"?

And not her footsteps marching to the kitchen, and a bellig-
erent rattling of aluminum pots in the kitchen cupboard, and had
she said "insurance salesmen"? "So you're ashamed of me being
in insurance!" Daddy's muffled voice from his lair as from a
dungeon. "I'm not ashamed! I've told you so a million times and
you go back to that banal refrain just so you can . . ." And the
psychological dissections of his character, his behavior, his having stuck himself "in some idiotic foxhole where he's the
would-be simple fellow fighting some fancied aristocracy out to
get him," and how he nurses a "mutinous bitterness, as compen-
sation for . . ." Don't let her go on, don't let her! She can't hit
under the belt like that. Flesh of her flesh, and it isn't fair, no.
When a person can't defend himself—

Stooped, as his custom diurnal, his neck wrapped about with a
kerchief.
Placed were his hands in the sleeves of his glistening velvety
caftan,
The right hand placed in the left sleeve . . .

"It's enough to drive one crazy! Not say a word, slip out of the house like a thief. The disgrace! Me not even knowing how to excuse such . . . such infantile behavior!"

And the neighbors! With the abuse flying out of the open windows into pricked-up ears: and mind you, such an educated family too, those from the third floor, university people . . . . The tragic elements in Tchernihovsky's poem "In the Heat of the Noontide": the destiny of a Jewish child in the Diaspora who, drawn to nature, is misunderstood by his surroundings . . . .

"And to drink like a fish! Fog up your brains so as to escape all responsibility, avoid any mental effort . . ."

And now—about some girl who had been sitting all by herself beside him and had waited for him to pay her some attention, while he had just sat there and not said a word, not a word.

"And just tell me how come that a man of forty-five shouldn't be capable of communicating with another person, not even with a young girl, a lonely young girl!"

Well, so what? So what, Mother? Isn't it better like that than the other way around, like Gideon's father, a prominent attorney who keeps a mistress, and his mother fading away at home? Is that what you'd rather? Or maybe you would? But why doesn't he answer, say: Yes, that's the way I am, shy, timid, girls scare me. . . . Oh, to shake that clumsy father out of his sluggishness—

Man is thus wont to indulge in superfluous exaggerations;
Some exaggerate things, others minimize them and belittle.
Soon came relief to my sorrows, although I must not speak falsely:
Navels fell off in due time . . .

"And what gaucherie, not to be able to invent something, some excuse, to say you don't feel well, for instance, or at least to let *me* know. . . . Where as a matter of fact *did* you run off to?"

Don't answer, Daddy, don't answer.

Duly they crawled on all fours and duly they walked firm and
*   steady.*
All went to cheder, then entered business, as God had commanded
*   . . .*

Ah, God, not that! She closed her eyes hearing her mother

· 71 ·

fling it at him, how it'd have been typical of him, perfectly typical, to make straight for under the broad wings of "Mother Goose." Because now everything would blow up. And sure enough—bang! The door of the bedroom, followed at once by her storming up to it, throwing it open—"Why do you bristle up like that as soon as I just mention her!" Doesn't she know? Is it news to her? And those hints, what does she mean, about how Grandmother doesn't need his protection any longer because now she's got someone else. That engineer? "That perverse union, holy trinity of mother and son and immaculate spirit!"

And now a great, gaping astonishment, a kind of hollowness in her stomach, hearing her mother talk of Grandmother setting him against her about an affair she'd had in England . . .

"Must you? With her in her room? Now? So she'll hear?" Daddy's furious, piercing whisper, nearing the door.

But she doesn't care whether I hear, and she goes on, and on.

What had happened there, in England, before her own time? An English lover? An English love? On the campus of a London university? A tale trumped up by Grandmother out of spite or jealousy? Those secrets that I'll never know, never be told. What's at the root of their relationship, hers and Daddy's. Who courted whom, and why? There, back at the village, on that brown farmstead of Blumfeld's, surrounded by dense orchards, mysteries of leafy shadow, running veins of water channels and pump pounding away in the distance. Compare the yearning of Velveleh-Dunce for nature and for the company of the village boys with that of the child in Bialik's "Behind the Fence" for Marinka, and show in what way both poets express the national aspiration of Russian Jewry of the period.

"And her snoopy, prying looks whenever she came here to 'lend a hand with the housework,' as she called it. A complete one-woman espionage network—that's what your mother was!"

And now he's seething and it's going to burst! Crash!

"I can just see it, the charming idyll of Mum and her darling sonny boy sitting down to a glass of Russian tea and honey cake, and confabulating about the dangerous virus eating away at the pink and comfortable body of the dear little animal family! Winnie-the-Pooh and Mamma Pig, tiddely pom, tiddely pom!"

No answer.

Madness came over the child. For instance? He'd dream in the
  daytime,
Choose a forsaken corner, and big were his eyes with amazement.
Fond of the garden was he, when it darkened at night and grew
  silent.
Rise would be early to gaze at the sun . . .

"And anyway, what was that about coming up and going down
and coming back again an hour later? Scared I'd still be awake
and you'd have to face the enemy? A man who sits on top of the
Acropolis ought to have a little more guts!"

And she, bewildered, didn't understand why just at this point
he had to slam the door so hard! Because of the "Acropolis"?
And what is Mother doing, what is she doing?

Because now she heard her quick steps moving toward the
bedroom—"If that's the way you want it, all right, but for
good!"—going in, picking up things, out, and like a whirlwind to
the study, and back again, and collecting—the bedclothes?—and
past her door, and banging her own, and the echo loud through
the whole house, and silence.

Tears burned her eyelids. To run away, away, to the kibbutz, to
Eilat, abroad, anywhere but here! Now there would be silence,
days and days of it, strained to snapping point between the two
rooms, Mother sleeping in one, Daddy in the other, and herself
on the thin tightrope between them. May it do them good, this
silence, until the collapse!

An educated family!

She closed book and notebook, wiped away tears, got up and
left the house, she, too, slamming the door hard.

E LISHEVA bought a copy of
Ravens There Were None in the morning, at the first bookstore,
shut herself up in the study and read it through in two hours,
sustained by eight cigarettes and two cups of coffee. When she
reached page 35, the description of Hava's visit at Jonathan's
hermit's retreat and the agonized night between them in the
desert loneliness—she felt she had to stop because she so much

wanted to go on. She put the book facedown on the arm of the easy chair, went to the kitchen and made herself a cup of coffee. Afterward, sipping, she was able to slow down the pace of her reading somewhat. She made the second cup somewhere about page 80, at the end of the long tense description of the dog's dying throes. When she finished she stayed in her chair for a long moment, sitting still with her head in her hand. Then she rose and began pacing the room, taking out books and replacing them. She had to admit to herself that the story had moved, but also slightly irritated her, she knew not why. She opened the book again at random and the lines sprang to her eyes:

"A wilderness of flintstone. And the flaming edge of light piercing his eyes, sun spreading like wildfire through the this-tles. The partridge, startled, flew up with a loud beating of wings and he saw it, dust gray, the crescent of throat cutting through the fiery haze as it fled, the echo of a scream trailing behind. But the lizard, old, gnarled, scaled, stayed rigid, clinging grim and desperate to the cracked earth, an aura of deathly intrigue surrounding it. The faint hum of the truck could be heard coming from the north. Late. His watch showed ten thirty."

Jean Giono? Hamsun? Frishwin? Julius would have smiled and said, "Blut und Boden." Among the most corruptive or Nietzschean effects on literature. Heathenish pantheism. Anti-Kantian denial of reason, of civilization. Man isolated from society. And yet this book had stirred something in her, if not in the region of the heart then in the bowels. A kind of churning she refused to countenance. And it was nothing at all like any of them, not Giono, not Hamsun! And that ending! She opened the book at the final page:

"The yellow and tattered dust-cloud smothered the shack, the two idle fuel pumps clawing at the rutted concrete, then moved east, thick, turbid, wailing, driving along loose stalks, whipping up two scraps of newspaper—kites saved from a fire, last letters to God about a raging holocaust; and as he stood there alone beside the half-sunken milestone, the empty pail in his hand—"

Magnificent, to end a book with an unfinished sentence! Leaves you openmouthed, wondering, hungry, amazed and yet thrilled, a kind of application of the "open-circle" theory, too flagrant though, wasn't it, or maybe not, maybe the inevitable consequence of the endless-cycle idea, or of the acknowledgment that there is no solution. Something pure about it, cleansing. What's bothering that fellow Brosh? However brief our life—she remembered her Proust—it is only when we suffer that our mind brings the infinite world into our field of vision, whereas we never see it through our window at moments of calm and happiness. . . . And for all that, something was missing here, something very basic whose lack made you uneasy. She thought it over and her vague intuitive resistance began to form itself into definitions: words, phrases. And on an impulse she decided to call him, right away, because if not now—never—and grabbed the phonebook and flipped its pages, found the number of the editorial office and dialed.

"Mr. Brosh? Tal-Blumfeld speaking. . . ."

He sounded pleased, said he was glad she had called because he wanted to admit he had been wrong: the article had been well received, enthusiastically in fact.

The compliment, however flattering, put her out. She decided nevertheless to go on with it.

"I've read your novel," she said. "I'd like to write about it. On your page. Not praises though. At least, not *only*."

She could tell from the silence at the other end how taken aback he was. A kind of sudden sinking. Bad blunder.

"It's very interesting of course"—trying to put some cheer into her voice—"I read it in one sitting, as a matter of fact, but . . ."

"Go ahead, write. . . ." His voice dispirited. Numb fly in spider's web. Well, what did you expect the poor guy to say?

"Don't get me wrong . . ." She tried again, but how to mend matters now? "When I say 'not only,' I don't mean to belittle it. Not at all. It's just that there's something . . ." Oh, you're only getting yourself deeper in! "Actually it's hard to discuss on the phone. Maybe we could meet, if you would . . ."

"Be glad to." But he wasn't, had said it reluctantly, dully.

"When?"

"Could you come to the office?"

"To the office?" Piqued.

"Or wherever you like. . . ."

Café Shor. And in the evening. And already she pictured the two of them in a small, intimate room, the table between them, two drinks on it, and the conversation a card game: a card on the table, then another, and a fan of them hiding the face, revealing, hiding, revealing.

"See you Thursday then, half past eight."

And replacing the receiver she felt her cheeks burn. And had to unclasp her bra, so hot she was.

And asked herself whether she wasn't starting out on some dangerous adventure.

Adventure? Ha! Younger than me by maybe ten years!

And she felt an urgent need to talk—at once, this minute!—to Dinah Lev.

"Dinah? Elisheva."

"Oh, you!" Dinah believed there was a telepathic link between them, and when she said that right this minute she had been going to phone, Elisheva wasn't surprised. It seemed almost a matter of course.

"I've read *Ravens There Were None.*"

"Have you?" rejoiced Dinah. "Well?"

"Interesting . . ." she said, with approval but without warmth.

"Weren't you moved by it?" said Dinah, disappointed, her conviction shaken a little by weightier judgment.

"Yes and no. But we'll talk it over," she added quickly. "Listen," she breathed into the receiver, "do you know him, Amnon Brosh?"

"Sort of. No, not really. I've met him once or twice, that's all."

"I wonder what his biography could be."

"Why?"

"To know what makes him tick, what makes him such an escapist. Is he married? A bachelor?"

"Divorced, I think. Some painful story. I don't know much though."

For a moment Elisheva withdrew into silence. In a flash long ravines yawned before her eyes, branching out into dim, deep creeks filled with mystery, harboring surprises, so intriguing! But she only asked Dinah how she had been.

"I felt so much like a chat with you," crooned Dinah.

"Then come.Come over now."

"But you're so busy. I couldn't disturb you." In a little-girl voice. As so often.

"Do come! I don't feel like working anyway. Let's have us a little party, h'm?"

"Sure?"

"Come on. I'm expecting you!"

And already the "little party" spirit had caught her, and she rose and hurried back to the study to tidy up. She swept students' notebooks into the lowest drawer of the desk, returned Coleridge's *Biographia Literaria* with due respect to its place on the shelf at left, stuffed Matthew Arnold—must still look up a few things there—among the pile crammed on top of the big *Oxford*, and her page of notes—

She glanced at it briefly:

"The preoccupation with the minutest details of Julien Sorel's life could only have proceeded from an anthropocentric awareness in Stendhal and in his age. The question to be asked is what bearing the anecdote can have in an age when the very comprehensibility of the world lies in doubt, and its so-called destiny can no longer be identified with the rise and fall of individuals, families—"

She pushed the slightly crumpled page into the middle drawer. The continuous present in which there is no retreat for the memory! Folding the bed sheets and thrusting them into a compartment of the chest containing a surreptitious hoard of cream jars, bundles of letters, a small whiskey flask, and sanitary napkins. A little party! Her mind reverted happily to the start— so accidental and yet so inevitable!—of the curious relationship between herself and Dinah, the great difference in age notwithstanding! How—only three months ago—she had asked permission to attend a lecture of hers—yes, on Stendhal—and afterward had come over to thank her, and walking to the bus with her she had expressed such original opinions—confused and original—about the pointlessness of psychologizing in literature, about the "lack of order" in human behavior, which is mysterious, "biological," and not subject to any logic or reason. And after the third meeting Elisheva had already known everything about her: childhood in the village of Merhavia, in the stillness humming like grasshoppers in mown maize, between the Hill of Moreh and Mount Gilboa, a dreamy girl leaving the farmyard—cows squelching the mud, chicks scurrying under the mushroom top of the brooder, urns of milk and jars of yoghurt—to "go out into the world": to study painting at the Bezalel Academy; and there, in Jerusalem—"moss-worn Jerusalem where I felt like a captive princess in a castle, like Byron in Chillon"—she had begun to write poetry and given up painting; and there she met that Party politician, Yehuda Ullman, for whom she had been "a kind of alibi, to prove to himself he had some lyrical streak in him somewhere too, a need for the higher things in life so to say, the other side of his extrovert coin. . . . But he was lying to himself, Elisheva, lying all the way! A woman *can't* be an alibi!" "And what was he to you, Dinah?" "To me?" Dinah laughed and told her how as a child she used to go for walks by herself at dusk, cross the fragrant pine grove, and from the shelter of the trees peer out at the old yard of Merhavia the kibbutz. The smell of fresh bread would be wafted at her from the kibbutz bakery, and their dining hall would be alive with the bustle of active, purposeful men and women, and she had imagined that the world was *there*, in that rushing stream where the future was shaped, the whole destiny of this land, and she herself but a bit of weed by the roadside. And perhaps it was due to that old feeling of envy that she had been drawn so strongly to the men of action, the string pullers, "to give me a sense of being *inside*, not looking on from without." A childish illusion that had burst like a balloon after two years of marriage and turned into a crumpled bit of ragged, shapeless rubber! And for all that—thought Elisheva—Dinah had remained a girl of seventeen, and whenever they met, the two of them—silly, wasn't it?—they were like a couple of schoolgirls together. . . .

Dinah appeared with five tall irises in her hand. "Oh, you shouldn't have!" Elisheva reproaching her for spending the little money she had. "And you look marvelous today!" Admiring a new skirt Dinah was wearing, wide, bell-shaped, a bright orange color. "You'll never guess how much I paid for it! Twelve pounds!" "Twelve pounds!" marveled Elisheva, and while she arranged the flowers in a vase on the study desk, Dinah told her how such a bargain had come her way, in a little shop on

Nahalat-Binyamin, and how its flaw—no flaw to her: faded rings along the edge which only gave it an added touch—had made them let it go cheap. "And I bet the boys whistle at you in the street!" Elisheva flattered her. "Whistle? Strings of them behind me. Me and the Pied Piper!" And when her glance fell on *Ravens There Were None,* she said, "Now tell me what you think of it, everything!" But Elisheva did not have the slightest wish to discuss the book. "Know what let's do?" she said animatedly. "Let's run up some real delicacy in the kitchen, h'm?"

"Yes! Let's!" cried Dinah, and gave her an adoring look. She considered Elisheva the most beautiful, wisest woman she had ever known.

And like conspirators off on an illicit adventure they went to the kitchen.

"What'll we make? How about a pie? An apple pie?"

"No, too heavy? Crepes?"

"Dumplings? Russian dumplings, you like that?"

"How about cheese turnovers?"

"How about angel food cake?"

"But that's such a lot of work, Elisheva!"

"Right, we'll make it cheese turnovers then. And you sit down over there and tell me what's new."

"You forget I'm a born cook."

"So you'll take a little breather, child."

"Yes, teacher."

Elisheva was a poor housewife: absentminded, impatient, preparing meals casually and at irregular hours, which always annoyed Shuka. But sometimes, in a playful mood, she would be inspired. Now her hands went about their work gladly: mixing flour with eggs and milk, mixing cream cheese with sugar and butter, putting a frying pan on and pouring batter in. The smell of gas at such a moment reminded her of far-off days, in England. Patrick O'Donovan, where was he now?

Dinah was telling her about a letter she had received that morning from her twelve-year-old brother. Such a sweet funny letter! About him and Daddy going to mow alfalfa in the late afternoon, and suddenly seeing three Red Indians with bows and arrows before them. He had gone to meet them with his sickle at the ready, but they didn't even string their bows! The one of them named Lapwing-of-the-Silver-Ring took a baby lapwing out from under his cloak and handed it to him. The one called Yakulus-Yakulus took a field mouse out of his quiver and it flew off in the air. And the third one, Morning-Star-Golden-Glory, sounded a sort of glorious trumpet flourish from his mouth, "like a glorious burst of sun rising over the mountains of Gilead." Then all at once they had all disappeared, and the sun went down.

"He reads a lot, h'm?"

"It's his kind of humor! He's pulling my leg, making up those stories and pretending to believe them himself!"

"Showing off?"

"It's more a trick to get stories out of me in return. I ought to show you our correspondence sometime: it's story for story. Maybe I'll publish them someday. With illustrations. For children I *can* draw," she laughed.

The pan sizzled and spread a good smell in the kitchen, and Elisheva smeared the flat cakes with the cheese filling, folded them up and turned them over. And when Dinah went on talking about her brother and her parents, Elisheva felt a twinge of remorse, a sense of squandering herself, wasting her offerings on alien altars. The house cold and empty, just she and her books. No husband, no daughter. So much warmth in the world in which she had no part. Would she ever have been capable of talking about her family the way Dinah did about hers—with such affection, with such a fondness for intimate details, objects, the small day-to-day events in the life of each one of them? With such a sense of belonging? The study, the bedroom, Avigayil's room—each an island to itself. Three or four times a day a little boat sets out with supplies from here to there. . . .

But when they sat facing each other across the table, the cups of coffee and the cheese turnovers brown and gold between them—the sunlit fields vanished to make place for shady groves. Dinah went back to Yehuda Ullman, and Elisheva loved these soft trips along narrow twisting paths rich with secret recesses. Last night, after ten, Dinah said, he had showed up again, unexpectedly, not letting her know beforehand, not apologizing; and what vexed her most: how utterly he had taken it for granted that she'd receive him, so much so that it had never even occurred to him there might be a need to sound her out first, to find out how things were standing between them. Nor had he shown the least interest in her doings, let alone her feelings. He had sat and talked of some bickering within the Party and of his own part in it. And next morning, after he'd left—such a degrading sense of not having been yourself but someone you didn't want to be! A kind of coming apart that has a touch of dying about it!

"Did you go to bed with him?"

"Of course. And the odd thing is that I wasn't revolted or anything. I even enjoyed it. Maybe an aftermath of old habit. Like time blurring sort of, if you know what I mean."

"Making yourself forget."

"I had this feeling of him coming back from his trips, meetings, all that mixed-up business of his, and needing rest, a sailor home from the sea."

"Doesn't he have other women?"

"I suppose he has. So has a sailor, in every port," she laughed.

The sailor image seemed so much romantic poppycock to Elisheva. Though she had never met this Ullman fellow, the picture she had formed of him from Dinah's stories was quite the reverse of romantic: an ambitious young cad, sneering at emotion, ready to trample flowers on his way, Dinah being one of them.

"Out of compassion, then?"

"Oh, no. I never felt sorry for him in my life! Only because I have this adolescent tendency to find the good in people even where it doesn't exist. Really, it's so funny. . . ." She buried her laughing face in her hands.

"What's so funny?" asked Elisheva, smiling.

"A scream!" Uncovering her face. "He came in last night and said he was famished . . . and I was so moved by that . . ." She stopped and laughed again. "All of a sudden—a human touch. A man is hungry. Asks me to fry him an egg. It can bowl me over, a thing like that."

"Yes, I can see."

"No, but he isn't human. Know the kind of people I detest most? Those who aren't capable of getting hurt. And that's him. He knows what failure is, but not what hurt feelings are. A kind of obtuseness. If they'd kick his chair from under him he'd fly into a rage, but if they spat in his face he'd just smile. To think that after all that happened between us before we parted he can come, just like that. . . . There are things I'm ashamed to tell you, ashamed for *his* sake. . . ."

Elisheva didn't press her, knowing she would tell anyway.

"Six months back, when I told him I couldn't live with him anymore, well, it did something to him, of course. But not really, not deeply, the way that makes you shrink and grow silent, or cry, or just for one day at least not feel able to cope, to get up and go to work at eight in the morning, but . . . More as though he'd got an order to pay a big sum in income tax, or an order of attachment on the apartment. A kind of prosaic matter-of-fact failure like that. And then . . ." she blushed and faltered for a moment, "he wrote to my father, behind my back. Told him that *he* had decided to leave *me*, so sorry and all that, but he'd found out I'd been unfaithful. . . ."

"Incredible!"

"And all the time, I don't know since when, he had been carrying on an affair with one of the typists from the Party pool! And after we'd already fixed a date for the divorce he brought her home—to show me. . . . What an evening! I had to act the betrayed wife who isn't supposed to know, serve coffee, make small talk. . . . And later he left me and went 'to see her home.' And didn't come back of course till the following afternoon. . . ."

"And after all that, you . . ."

"I know. It's degrading. It's awful. But only the morning after. Oh, dear, what a feeling! I took a shower."

"And if he comes again? Hungry for a fried egg?" And in the same instant the question grated on her ears. A kind of phony preaching, aware as she was that what she felt wasn't disgust, or disapproval, but on the contrary, a kind of envy; that's how one ought to live, a life full of complications, full of twists and turns and inner contradictions. And riches.

"I don't know. I've found that being a woman on your own is sort of perverse. And perverseness doesn't fit in with having principles. I expect I'd go to bed with him again. And hate myself for it again."

And yet—an innocence that nothing could defile! Elisheva

looked at her. A "zoological" innocence, she thought, noting the village-girl face, the wide mouth, the thick hair falling away from a parting in the middle. Only the green eyes with their flashes of wit adding spice to the somewhat phlegmatic drawl that marks the Jezreel Valley villagers.

"Don't be cross with me, Elisheva."

"Me?" With a nervous laugh that sounded shrill to her ears.

"I mean, well, I write. And I get satisfaction out of it, I'll say that. But actually . . . actually all I really want . . ." She stopped.

"Don't say: to milk the cows. . . ."

"No. But a home, a devoted husband. A peaceful life. Cooking meals. Five children. It's wonderful! *You* know what it's like."

"I've only one daughter, and I don't see much of her either."

"He's wonderful, your husband. Such a full serenity, full of confidence and integrity. Someone to trust to the end of your life. And even after . . . In our village, you know, in the graveyard, lying there two by two: Sarah and Moshe, Itzhak and Bronca . . . I always used to be filled with a sort of awe. In winter, with red and yellow wild flowers growing among the tombstones. Such a sort of . . . natural happiness. The way God created them. I'm talking rubbish, aren't I?"

"Life is short. One must make the most of the possibilities it offers," Elisheva heard herself say to herself.

"Yes, but a peaceful homelife opens up many possibilities too, in another direction, maybe a more profound one. I don't have to tell you . . ."

What do you know, Dinah! What do you know about how I reached out for Shuka like someone searching for shelter after a storm! Leaning against a thick tree-trunk, to rest, rest. . . .

"Weren't you ever unfaithful to him? When you were married?"

"Yes, once. But it was awful."

Elisheva waited.

"We were at a party. All of a sudden he disappeared on me. . . . It's sort of terribly humiliating to search for a husband in a crowd, with eyes following your progress, looking forward to a scandal. So I stayed where I was and tried hard to look gay. I guess you don't know the kind of effort it takes, keeping your reflexes in check. Needs all you have. I hardly caught what the man sitting next to me was saying. . . . You become very sharp-eyed at times like that, and of course I discovered who *else* had left. . . . And this fellow by my side . . . talking on and on. . . ."

Elisheva felt a stab of the old pain: Patrick O'Donovan, London. Her mind went back to that gray morning when she had found the slinky, thin-lipped, green-eyed actress in his room. He hadn't been the least put out when she entered, and the girl had stayed where she was, sitting on the couch, smoking, her bare feet stuck out in front of her. "Patrick and I got engaged last night. At the theater bar of all places," she had said quietly, smiling eyes squinting against the smoke. "Laurel, my director, performed the rites." It was raining outside, and she felt the London sky subsiding on top of her, not all at once but with a slow, burying heaviness as in a nightmare. Patrick had crossed to the table and poured whiskey into three teacups, and she had heard the gas stove rustle as though it were eating straw. Going out, to the rain, to the red bus approaching like a trained animal, she knew she had left her youth behind her forever.

". . . And I didn't object when he came up with me. I was in the kind of state where you tell yourself: Who cares, who cares what happens, what's the difference, everything's gone to pieces anyway . . . kind of suicide mood. . . . I let him turn off the light, undress me . . ." Dinah shut her eyes.

Notes from a distant radio floated into the silence of the kitchen, and Elisheva discerned Brahms' First.

"And?"

"Nothing. He got up, dressed, mumbled his apologies, and left."

"Yes."

"And then . . . that's when you really want to die. Such a sort of impure pain, full of shame, shame for yourself, for this man, this stranger, for the double failure, the pointless sacrifice, which isn't . . ."

"Did you ever meet him again?"

"I wouldn't know him if I did. When I think of it and try to recall his face I can't for the life of me! Sometimes I think—if I'd meet him I'd apologize to *him*."

When Elisheva was washing the dishes in the sink she told Dinah about her first lover, before her marriage with Shuka, before Patrick O'Donovan, when she had been a student in Jerusalem. Also a sad story.

FIVE TWENTY! Tal noted with dismay as he opened his eyes.

The third morning running that he had woken so early. And the fourth night alone in bed. Half of it wasteland.

And fuzzy rags of nightmare: accidents, collisions. Once running over Avigayil and wanting to scream, but being petrified.

To lie like that for an hour and a half, awake, and once more hear—

The single trilling note of a bulbul in flight, through the large empty dome of morning.

Then the sudden silence.

Then the busy twitter of a whole teeming chorus, dabbling in the foliage, diligent.

And the harsh metallic clang of dustbins, dragged out, scraping worn pavement.

The gurgle of water down the throat of the toilet bowl next door.

The time signal, six beeps pecking at the air from the neighbors' radio.

Followed by the morning Psalms—

An hour and a half!

No, he'd get up. The meeting at the packinghouse of the Shenkmann-Meller-Abramsky orchards was at eight, so he'd take the car and cruise around. Better than tossing about here on the white sheets, shrouds.

And to think of her sound asleep in that room, and going to stay that way till eight, nine! Amazing how that languid, fragile body of hers is never the least ruffled by the jolts of her perpetual fitfulness! Had she ever been ill even? Yes, teeth. Cavities.

("Frightful toothache, Shuka, frightful!" Sitting with one hand against a burning cheek. And when he had driven her to Dr. Mintzer and followed her into the clinic he had heard the piercing yell from the torture chamber as the bore went to work. A real yell of pain. And that night, he remembered, he had taken her, and with great relish.)

Putting on his trousers he was thinking how all his life he wasn't doing what he wanted to. Forty-five. Halfway through!

To grow avocado.

Or bees.

He had considered bees once. To move, top to toe in white overalls, like a diver, through the buzzing, through the light-blue hives, in a field of sun and flowers.

The walls of the passage gleamed dully in the morning light. A trace of sleepers' breath in the air. Avigayil's door shut, study door shut. No one awake, no one cares.

He shaved, went to the kitchen, opened the refrigerator. A draft of green chill. And the unwashed dishes in the sink!

He tiptoed to the study door, bent to peer through the keyhole: curled up in a sheet. Knees, blank arm, wisp of hair on cheek. Repose. No one cares.

Her calm, after all that had been, all that was, the aloneness, the dreams!

He went back to his room, seized a piece of paper and wrote in large letters:

"You can sleep where you like, do what you like, but you can't shirk your duties as *mother!* The fridge is empty. And I'm not supposed to take care of the dirty laundry either!

"And I'll be much obliged if you leave me the dentist's receipts!!!"

Page in hand he strode back to the study, pushed the note through the crack under the door, went to pick up his briefcase, and left the house.

At nine, at ten, she'd discover the message on the floor.

Traffic was still sparse: an early taxi rushing by, a truck bearing a covered load, a desultory bicycle. Hushed streets and heavy-lidded apartment houses. Only when he reached the outskirts—joined the swift stream hurrying southward, spurting, stopping, accelerating, slowing down, speeding up again in a solitary race—did the morning paleness dissolve, the morning teem under a swelling sun.

At the lights of the coastal road intersection he decided to go to the garage for lubrication. He'd gain half an hour.

"Shlomo!" Mula Mintz summoned a mechanic. "Get that Chevy off and put up this Fiat. He comes first with me." Fat, red-faced, Mula got in behind the wheel, listened to the engine, checked the gears, inquired after the battery, remembered that the oil pump had sprung a leak, knew the car as a vet knows the pedigree of all his cows by heart. "You look a bit under the weather today, Shuka," wiping his hands after lowering the hood. "Didn't sleep well, eh? Run out of fuel. . . . Never mind, happens to the best, that does." Shuka grinned.

He felt, as always, slightly embarrassed to see his Fiat hoisted up on the ramp. As though her skirts were being pulled up before his eyes. Before strangers. Worse when the mechanic placed the slop pail under her belly, unscrewed her navel, and a thin muddy flow drained out of her, straight down, then wavering to a dribble, a drip, and a final drop. It was a bit like the way he used to feel years ago, with Elisheva pregnant and the doctor examining her, blouse hoisted to chin, and himself, useless, embarrassed, waiting impatiently to retrieve his charge. The mechanic swung the long hose off its hook in the ceiling and injected lubricant into the wheel joints. The floor smelled of fuel and oil, and the compressor hissed and snorted.

"Long time no see," said the mechanic.

"You weren't here last time, about a month ago."

"Reserve duty." He was screwing the navel back into place over his head, "Jordan Valley. Bloody furnace."

"Clashes, eh?"

"Potshots. From Tawafik. No big deal."

"Tractor shot up, I read."

"Tractor, hell. They're like bloody rats: stick out a nose, you let fly at them, they run to hide. Dug in they are like you never seen. Except what? They're chicken!"

The Fiat descended slowly on the subsiding shaft, settled down on all fours and was herself again, decent, proper.

"Which oil you want?"

"Let's have the Special."

The mechanic fetched two cans, punched their tops, and poured their contents into the oil pan—pure, mellow, amber.

Tal served as quartermaster in the Reserves. Handing out equipment, munitions, stretchers, keeping lists. Custodian in a teeming, noisy household of men, applying for his services, joking at his meticulousness, calling out for him, Shuka, a thousand times a day. He had his meals in the officers' mess, dispatching two or three main courses at a time, the butt of affectionate banter. Three happy weeks a year, far from offices, clients' flats, bank accounts. The curved tin roofs of the old British barracks glinted to his eyes for an instant, scorching in the summer heat.

"Ought to give 'em the works, those fucking bastards. Heard what they did to our POWs?"

"Yeah, terrible."

"Whipping the soles of their feet, hanging 'em up by the balls. The bloody swine. Smash 'em once good, they'd scuttle on all fours to Damascus."

"That'd be war, though."

"War, hell!" Unscrewing the battery covers and pouring distilled water into the cells. Screwing them back, he added, "And what d'you figure you got now? Not a war? You ought to be at Tel-Katzir. Shooting every day, mines, the kids living in shelters. A hell of a life they got up there."

"And the Egyptians? . . ."

"Gonna meddle? Trust Nasser. Smart guy that. Knows what's good for him." He lowered the hood.

"Not so easy," said Tal. He paid, took the receipt, and put a pound's tip into the hands being wiped off on the cotton rag.

"But the Kinneret—gold!" Slipping the pound into his shirt pocket. "Lovely bit of lake!"

Southward, the flow of traffic even. Dunes, filling stations. Road skirted by dense citrus groves, clumps of tall eucalyptus trees like officers huddling over a map. By the time he reached the village main street, laborers, single and in groups, were already going off to work. Kerchiefed maids, Yemenites with baskets. Shops raising shutters, unbolting—Leibowitz, Kovalsky, Tambour Paints, Gil Restaurant, End-of-Season Sale, the drivers' banter, Katz & Sons, Building Materials, Lieber Always First. Shostak returning from synagoge, black phylactery bag under one arm. Old Azriel on his donkey, as of old. Arieli, Labor Council secretary, briefcase tucked under the armpit of his handless stump, at the entrance of Histadrut House, as early in the morning as that. Friedman the contractor, at the corner of Herzl, morose, bitter, surrounded by plasterers. Schneider, the crazy "Jewish labor" fanatic, handing out copies of *Davar*. Rabbi Shechter. God abounding in mercy. Earth on Father's grave. Could that be Blumfeld, over there?

He nearly hit the car in front. No, not him. Heart missed a beat at the squeal of brakes.

He cruised along the street, reached its end, turned off into a mud track, parked in the shade of dusty cypresses, got out. Only seven twenty. In the distance at the other side of the field—the thick dark mass of the Shenkmann-Meller-Abramsky orchards, the gray-tiled roof of the old packinghouse, walls of Arab limestone.

He walked along the margin of the track, dewy weeds brushing his shoes, wetting his trouser cuffs, squashing succulent undergrowth: couch grass, tickle grass, thistle, bindweed, goosefoot, mallow, all the dormant names awakening in his mind as he crushed them one by one. The field trips with the botany teacher, Shlomo Eitan, to observe modes of propagation: capsules, cells, winglike tufts, like this groundsel here. Chickweed, foxtails. This tickle grass has a panicle inflorescence, this quaker a spadiceous one. Quaker? No, not quaker—quaking grass. Silver campanula. Good years, back then, at school.

Even though—

The teasing: Shukả Fatbelly. And Elisheva—indifferent. And the crying fits behind the latrines. And the mediocre grades. Except in botany and math.

A briar? This one here with the round blue inflorescence. No, a globe thistle.

A cricket shot up before his feet and hopped the short flight to a mallow leaf.

Summer, and the thistles already yellow. And the oats golden. The entire cereal genus.

The tall cynara—scaly, succulent.

Going out Saturday afternoons to the heath behind the football field, scout's knife in hand, felling it—it topples like a giant. You peel the bast, tear off long strips of fiber, and the moist heart, sweet-sour to suck.

Or jujube berries, zizyphus. You climb the branches, pick the pale yellow balls, soft in the mouth, sweetish, till you come to the hard stone, setting your teeth on edge.

Tal stopped and glanced at a water tower white on the horizon, saw Elisheva waking up, finding his message on the floor, picking it up, tearing it through with an angry scowl.

Or an indulgent smile.

Another hour before she'd wake up.

A squirting cucumber in front of him. He put out a foot to flatten the swollen, hairy fruit. It burst disappointingly, with a dull plop, no squirt of juice.

Such a morning—a schoolboy in the summer vacation. At four, half past, before sunrise, before it grows hot, going out to gather peas with the hired hands, boys and young women, the pods still cool and firm and dewy, squatting on a sack, pulling and stripping and dropping into another openmouthed sack that fills up from plant to plant, row to row, now and then snapping a pod with a pinch of fingers and slipping a string of pearly seeds into your mouth. About sixteen *grush* a day it would come to, paid by the weight of your sacks. Helping Father. A thirty-pound debt at Grozensky's grocery, a debt of seventy or a hundred at the bank. Working from five to ten, till the sun grows hot and the pods turn limp and flabby. And the girls, gossip and giggle, tucking the hems of their dresses in between their legs so nothing'd show.

Even then.

When? Thirty-six?

"They will not frighten us, our enemies!"

And that song about the five who "went forth the ho-omeland to build." The sun quite high already. "And di-hidn't come back."

Two majestic parkinsonias stood still and solemn by the orchard gate—brides for fairy-tale princes. Chinese or Indian: a canopy of boughs reaching out and bowing down, a veil of delicate silky tendrils sowing glory, the butterfly flowers dripping to the ground to spread a velvety carpet of withered insects. Beyond them lay the shaded thickness of the orchard, last dewdrops trembling on its leaves. Only a quarter to eight, and Tal bypassed the packinghouse and turned in among the rows, trampling nettles, papyrus, purslane. Fleshy, sappy purslane nettles, many-legged, starry-eyed, pulled up by the roots, lumps of dry earth and all, wild vegetable for anyone to pick and make into a cool refreshing summer soup. The rhythmic swish of a sprinkler came from somewhere deep inside the trees, squirting water in tightly compressed bursts. Gone were the old concrete runnels, mouths stopped with sodden crumbling sacks, and the water flowing in long ditches, bearing straw and stubble on their oily scum, and beatles swept to the eddying water in the saucers dug around each tree.

A quarter to eight, and Tal sat down on a stray packing case and felt a great slumping weariness come over him. His eyes closed and he saw days of glory: Elisheva in her pregnancy, in the seventh month, frail and languid and snuggly, leaning on his arm on their evening strolls to the eucalyptus grove. The cool smell of the leaves and the springy moss underfoot. Frail and languid. Brownish patches on her face. Himself going gladly about the housework, an apron tied around his waist. The peace. Or the time she taught high school, Avigayil five already, school-girls coming to the house, please, Teacher, please, miss, and you part of the whole stirring round of terms, holidays, parties, grades, parent meetings. The salary. The quarrel with the Head. Even later, actually, the first few years at the university. The trip that summer, to Jerusalem—

Don't remind yourself—

What had it been that time, in Jerusalem, Katamon, among the lordly Arab houses, when she had suddenly been seized by a terrible fit of depression and had sat down on a stone fence and buried her face and not answered questions and afterward her eyes had been wet with tears?

Yehuda Dolav. Stored in the dark past, before, before. You'd never have known of his existence except for that accidental, purely accidental discovery of an old letter—broad firm script, a long and involved apology, not candid, no, about not having come to some meeting at Café Pa'amon because of some mysterious affairs—underground affairs? Yes, he'd been a member of the extremist IZL—and ending with that poor joke about only death releasing him from duty to his country, but never from love.

Oh, Shuka, not worth talking about. I was just a child. Yes, I loved him, so what? It's so unimportant now!

But it *was* important! It *was!*

Had he nodded off?

Maybe a minute or so.

Seems like the day halfway gone. Life halfway.

Zucker, round-shouldered, hollow-chested, did not recognize him for an instant through his misted spectacles. "Ah, Tal! Yes, the half-yearly installment. How much? Forty-five hundred, isn't it? Sit down, sit down." He lifted two files out of the cupboard, Workers Insurance, Property Insurance, put them on the table and leafed through the big shiny policies, the flimsy receipts. The old packinghouse, long since gone out of use, breathed emptiness. The floor covered in white dust, a pile of rotting mats in a corner, the obsolete well fenced in by railing. The "office" was distinguished from the rest of it by a screen of wire netting. "I've been reading an article by your wife. Didn't quite get it all, but a fine piece of writing, interesting." He jotted down some figures on a scrap of paper.

"You go in for that sort of thing?" Tal grinned, a faint blush creeping up his cheeks.

"I saw the name, Blumfeld, made me read it," Zucker went on with his calculations, his old-man's mustache yellow with tobacco, the jacket hanging loosely on his clotheshorse frame. "Besides, my girl attends her lectures, so I take a bit of interest . . ."

"Your girl taking literature?"

"Philosophy, but on account of your wife a bit of literature too. Interesting article. In January, I see, we paid twenty-seven hundred."

"Yes, that was the last premium, and the agreement says twenty-seven hundred and forty-five hundred."

"Insurance's better business than citrus growing these days," he grumbled without lifting his eyes from the page.

"Always been."

"So it has, come to think."

"Prices were high this year."

"A leaking barrel. Taxes, taxes, and more taxes."

"Same everywhere."

Zucker rose and replaced one file, sat down, pulled the tin cigarette box over, drew one out, broke it in two, and lighted one half.

"So it's seeking God, it is, eh?" Giving Tal a tired look.

Tal blinked, not understanding.

"The article, I mean," Zucker smiled. "Read it with interest. Except, I asked myself what it's got to do with us. I mean, this God-seeking isn't new. In Russia, too, and then, too, in the middle of the century. Past century, that is. Gogol, Dostoevski. But you know what Belinski wrote to Gogol?—and he admired him enormously, mind you!—You talk about God, about redemption, mysticism, asceticism—but what about Russia? What about the oppressed peasants—is *God* going to save them? Know what I mean?"

"The article was about ... Western writing ..." said Tal, vainly trying to recall names.

"And then Chernyshevski wrote his *What Is to Be Done?* and that caused a great stir! Because the question in Russia then was what to do, and not what to think, or whether to believe in God or not! And how about us today, eh?"

To grow bees, thought Tal.

"Because you see, analyzing literature, that's all very well, that's what a university is for, but our question is what to do. The national question, I mean. A small country, Arabs all around, and everybody always ready to sell the Jews for a barrel of oil. So the question is whether in literature ... Oh, well, that's not what you came for."

He opened a drawer and took out a checkbook.

To grow bees.

"Will three for fifteen hundred each suit you?"

"Yes, all right."

"July, August, and September." Writing in the dates. "But decidedly interesting. It's true that Blumfeld wanted his girl to be a lawyer, but if this is what she's good at, then why not?"

"Yes, the students admire her at lot, yes."

"That's one." Stamping the check and tearing it out and starting on the next. "You know, when Jabotinsky wrote his *Samson*. Think it was for the sake of art? It was for the sake of our national resurrection! And it had effect! . . . I hear Blumfeld's going to England. That so?"

Tal gaped. "I hadn't heard." In a low voice.

"I may be wrong. . . ." Tearing out the two checks.

"It's been some weeks since we saw him." Opening his receipt book.

"They say he's going to enlist investors. For some factory, at Ashdod. Plastics. May be only a rumor though. . . ."

"Guess we'll know soon enough." Handing Zucker the receipts.

"Where does one find these books she writes about?" Zucker rose and put out his hand. "I've looked for them. Are they available in Hebrew?"

"Haven't read them myself," said Tal, laughing.

Zucker regarded him with a sad smile, as if he saw it all, penetrated beyond the four walls of his home.

"Give her my regards. And my girl Berenika's."

Blumfeld to England. And she hadn't said a word.

Instead of heading for the highway Tal turned into a narrow cobbled road, potholed and sprouting thistles and making the car lurch and tremble, no doubt damaging the chassis as well to judge by the scraping noises. In the field at left, men were loading a cart with big shiny turnips. A burst pipe was spurting thin, forceful water jets, recklessly spraying the weeds among which two bee-eaters were screeching. In the distance, against the slope of the limestone hill, he could make out the sky-blue hives of Erich Jacobi, and he thought: make some inquiries anyway.

His father used to send him to borrow books from Erich Jacobi, fat German volumes with glossy pages and splendid colored pictures of butterflies and insects. Jacobi would wrap the book in a newspaper, carefully folding it around the edges, and say, "But to bringen it back like you gotten it. No flies und no *schmutz*." And Shuka would sign a piece of paper as pledge. "He's a misanthrope, Nahum," said Tamara, "and I don't see why it's necessary." "To begin with, pedantry isn't the same as misanthropy," said Nahum. "And besides, I give *him* advice without asking to be paid for it either." Shuka used to think that Erich must hate children, because he never smiled, and because when Shuka asked to look at the instruments in his library—a barometer, compasses, all kinds of clocks—he had told him, "That's nothing for you." Tall and skinny he was, and myopic, and he used to wear funny clothes, like a boy scout's or a mountaineer's: short pants, making his knees stick out comically on the spindly legs. In the morning he would leave the house on his bicycle, a deerskin rucksack strapped to his shoulders. Village rumor had it that he had taken in a fat, stupid Ekron girl, and that on the first morning, when he found she couldn't boil him a three-minute egg the way he liked, he had taken her to the hives with him and set the bees on her, and she had run all the way back to her parents' home at Ekron. He had brought one swarm with a handpicked queen from Germany in a glass cell, and here, on the slope of the hill, he had settled them in, bred and multiplied them by "scientific" methods. In high school, the teacher would take the agriculture class to the hives for observation, everybody would put on masks, and while Jacobi explained, in grudging monosyllables, how to tell the difference between queen and worker, Shuka would bend his head over the open hive. The humming commotion of bees straggling blindly over the honeycombs and hanging in bunches at the tips would engross and thrill him. He would watch the idle overgrown males as they trudged stolidly among the workers carrying beads of pollen in their mouths, and visualize their bitter fate—to be the murdered victims of ruthlessly austere females. The savage fucking in bridal flight through the golden air and the fall of the ripped dismembered body of the chosen male. The buzzing, bustling fuss of the throng of bees—crawling druggedly in and out of cell after cell with mechanical zeal, stirring and swarming, fluttering wings, crouching and defiling—would cast a spell over him in the heat of the summer in a field humming with thistles.

Propolis—he remembered. The name of that stuff they excrete to seal up the wax cells with.

And the queen bee lays two thousand eggs a day. Or three thousand.

Make some inquiries anyway: how much the initial invest-ment'd come to, where to obtain swarms and queens, how much the yearly turnover, the market price for honey.

A centrifugal tapping device.

When he left the car at the end of the cobbled road petering out into sand, he saw Erich Jacobi come out of his tool shed in the distance, wearing his mask and carrying smoke bellows in his hand. About a hundred paces to the hives, over the path cutting through a field with little suns of thistle flowers, and a quarter of the way there, seeing Jacobi interrupt his work for a moment to look at the visitor, Tal raised his hand in greeting. The beekeeper made no response and went back to his bellows. Shortsighted, Tal recalled, and went on, taking long strides. The radiance of the field filled him with gladness. And maybe not just inquire, he thought, maybe strike a deal, buy.

He felt only a dull blow against his forehead, not even a sting, and right after that Jacobi's voice calling through the shimmer-ing summer air: "No to come near! Bees not quiet now!" He stopped and smiled: the man hadn't recognized him apparently, his warning was meant for strangers. "It's me! Tal!" he called, "Tolkovsky!" and strode on toward the beekeeper, who stayed silent. All of a sudden the swarm was on Shuka, a crown of thorns to his head, round and round, and already one had caught in his thinning hair, on his skull, and a sharp swift sting, on his cheek, under the left eye, and another on his wrist, a blood sucking, and a third, a stinging burn, a touch of fire on his neck, and he turned and fled across the field, running, running, frightened, pursued, to his car.

And sitting behind the wheel he felt swollen all over, and a dry vicious heat throbbing through his body. The left eye sunk in a burning pad, nearly blinded.

ELISHEVA had difficulties deciding what to wear. She stood before the open closet, finger on lips and pondered: The black? The brown Italian? The flowered bell-skirt? Yes, but which blouse to go with it? You know you hate the salmon!

"Aesthetics and cosmetics are for the boudoir," she recalled with a smile.

In the end she resolved: the plainest. Yes, the plainest, the white polka dot. No coquetry, please. With the black handbag. And after putting it on she applied lipstick standing, two brief smears, and left.

In the street she nearly burst out laughing at the memory of Shuka's swollen face. Bees! Where on earth had he found bees? Had he gone to insure some beekeeper against getting stung? Gone to collect honey, the bear? *La dolce vita!* She had been on the verge of asking him this morning, but no, let him sulk, let *him* break this stupid silence! And those messages under the door. Yesterday, today—"I'll be much obliged!"—A proper Molière farce! Yes, Monsieur Jordain, I'll leave you your receipts!

Café Shor was a fifteen-minute walk and she did not want to arrive early. Better six or seven minutes late. She stopped, therefore, at the window of a bookstore: *Michelangelo, Daily Life in Ancient Egypt,* Buber's *Face of Man, Message of the Dead Sea Scrolls, Exodus,* two of them, *Poetry of Rising Africa, The Joy of Music, Sex Life in Middle Age, Treasury of Jewish Epigrams, Comedies of Aristophanes,* Velázquez, *The Bible in Art, Organic Chemistry,* Amichai: *Poems, Riches of Rock* by Ariella Gavish . . .

Amnon Brosh? Nowhere.

And Buber she hadn't read, except *I and Thou,* in English. Didn't trust him. Suspicion of moralizing pose under guise of theological abstractions. Not theological, but like God's privy councillor who wants to court favor with the infidels, too. Or the other way around. You should have said that to Julius!

He'd only laugh: Elisheva, my dear, don't you know that God was created by those whom the devil didn't smile on? Think of Augustine!

Oh, Mephisto! And how persuasive when you stand up there and preach the Gospel!

Those handbooks, sex in middle age, bedroom recipes for the million. Take a fresh male, put him in a heated bed, sprinkle a few kisses, add a spice of whisper, mince . . . The tyranny of the orgasm, as Mary McCarthy says.

Eight thirty-five!

And now she must hurry.

The first she saw of Brosh was his back. He sat leafing through a magazine, legs crossed. An angular profile, determined, and yet an air of weariness. How young!

When he rose to meet her, the magazine slipped to the floor and both of them bent to pick it up at the same time, and when they shook hands they were flushed and laughing.

"Coffee?"

"Yes, please," she said with animation. A bit overdone.

"And cake?"

"Oh, no! . . . All right, then, yes."

And while the waiter took their order Brosh asked about her work at the university, and Elisheva told him: She isn't happy about the curriculum, and as far as Comparative Lit. is concerned, they only offer the most generalized stuff, and the students are a *tabula rasa,* aren't familiar with the essential classics. . . For instance? For instance, the *Odyssey,* or Rabelais, Chaucer, Goethe, Defoe, Stendhal, not even Tolstoi and Dostoevski. One has to start from scratch, because high school doesn't prepare them at all. Who of them ever heard of Scott, Melville, Henry James? She has a feeling she's teaching botany to people who never saw a tree, flowers, never enjoyed the sight and smell . . .

Yes, botany . . . the question though—said Brosh—is whether treating literary works as phenomena, as objects for observation and scientific analysis, doesn't reduce them all to the same rank. Because you can find the same measure of scientific interest in a cedar as in a piece of moss. . . .

By all means!—Elisheva pounced happily—A piece of moss *is* just as interesting as a cedar, isn't it? And not less pretty either, don't you think?

No, he must have got his metaphor wrong. What he meant was . . . You might just as well take the cheapest pop song and "analyze" it in all earnest, discover its rhythmic pattern, verbal associations, write whole dissertations about it, and lose all sense of proportion. . . .

No, she doesn't count herself one of the New Criticism school. What interests her is—as she's told him before—human values. She sees literature as part of civilization and of man's spiritual dilemmas in the context of his time. Aesthetics as ethos. Naturally the first step is to examine the inner meaning of a given work, its rhythms. . . . Has he read Emil Steiger?

No, he doesn't read much literary criticism at all.

Well, Steiger says you must first be captured by a literary work and only afterward try and capture *it*. It's a *sine qua non*. And you can only be captured by it through empathy. . . .

The coffee was growing cold. Neither of them had touched it. Elisheva was dissatisfied: No, that wasn't what she had wished to talk to him about. Nor about his book either, as a matter of fact. There's a kind of "sick beauty" about him, a pale cloud. Tonio Kröger, though not the Northern type. And beneath his calm—a nervousness, suppressed. Whom had he divorced? Why? If he'd divorced me I'd have died.

"So I understand you didn't experience any empathy with my book. . . ."

"Oh, but I did! I couldn't put it down, actually. . . ."

"But?"

"Yes, but . . ."

Elisheva looked at him and suddenly burst out laughing, covering her face with both hands. What is the matter with you, Dr. Tal-Blumfeld, married and mother of a grown daughter, and behaving like a teenager! Tears of laughter came into her eyes and she took a handkerchief out of her bag and wiped them.

Brosh smiled.

"I'm laughing," she apologized, "at how I sit here to 'criticize' your book as though . . ."

"I'm listening," he said, echoing her own words to him when she had come to his office.

"All right," she began, overcoming her hesitation. "Well, first there's the matter of the name . . ."

"Yes, yes, I know, the name's no good, you're perfectly right," he hurried to forstall her.

"*Ravens There Were None* evokes Elijah, a man escaping to the desert with a sense of divine mission, whereas your hero . . ."

"Yes, quite."

There, this nervousness under the calm veneer.

"Secondly . . ." She hesitated, very reluctant to carry on with it. "You know, Ruskin wrote somewhere: 'Go to the author to get at *his* meaning, not to find yours.' "

"That's what you read books for. . . ."

"Then I'll ask you the way Ruskin would: Tell me what you like and I'll tell you . . ."

"What books?"

"Yes, every writer has some model before his eyes. . . ."

"I like Shtiebel editions," he laughed.

Elisheva laughed too. She knew just what he meant. To kiss him—so precisely did she know what he meant. What was the point of going on with "analyses" now?

"*Niels Lyhne, Thaïs, The Growth of the Soil?*"

"Yes, all of them! And they once published a wonderful anthology called *An Offering,* and there was one story there that made an unforgettable impression on me: 'Tiel the Railway Guard.' "

"Hauptmann. Yes. Frankly, I'd expected something like that. . . ."

"You take me for a romantic."

"No, it isn't that. It's that there's something of a nineteenth-century flavor about your story, or maybe early twentieth. Maybe that's what troubled me really."

"But it's a good story, isn't it?" he said jokingly.

"Yes, yes!" she laughed. Eyes gray as the sea, flickers of light in them.

"But?"

"What I said: the *Zeitgeist!*"

"The theme?"

"The theme is loneliness, of course. And loneliness, like love, has always been written about and always will. Yet . . . Kafka wrote differently about loneliness from Dostoevski, and Camus differently from Kafka, and Robbe-Grillet differently from Camus. There's a kind of process of devaluation on in these concepts, which expresses itself in a shift in the writer's point of view. A contemporary writer looks at 'eternal' values with a certain irony, because he is aware of their relativity in a world where absolutes are a dead letter, and which isn't anthropocentric any longer besides. Whereas your attitude, I'd say, is one of 'tragic identification,' of ritual solemnity. Loneliness for you is a kind of 'heroic weakness.' Like suicide in the last century or the one before last. And that sounds a bit . . . naive in this day and age. . . ."

"You're putting it very well!" said Brosh with a responsive smile.

"I see you've a touch of irony in you after all!" she laughed.

"No, I mean it. I think you're right!"

"You could always say: That's the way I am and that's the way I write, and I don't care a straw for the *Zeitgeist*—and you'll have me where you want me."

"Ah, but that wouldn't have any objective value."

Elisheva watched his eyes as she sipped her cold coffee.

"Of course I didn't miss the latent symbols in your story." Putting down her cup. "The gas station by the *side* of the road in the desert, adjoining and yet detached, and the gasoline running out of it as blood from an open vein; and the living on supplies that come from a great way off; the trucks traveling past and never stopping; the dog wailing in the desert like the voice of the libido; and, of course, the retreat of the road, its betrayal as it were, and the station left behind, cut off, idle, abandoned by Life. . . . You do have some marvelous descriptive passages. . . . Do you know Cesare Pavese?"

"No, haven't read him."

"There's an affinity. He also has this kind of loneliness moving toward self-destruction, and the same fatalistic attitude toward love, which is bound to end in suicide. I'll give you an example: When you write about Hava's visit and describe this night with both of you in the room . . ."

"Both of *us?*" exclaimed Brosh.

"Oh, I'm sorry . . ." Burying her blushing face in her hands. "Such a commonplace tendency to identify the hero with the author. . . . Well, then . . . when you describe how she is lying on the bed and Jonathan on the floor by the wall, in the dark, you write: 'A quiver-winged cricket crashed to the floor, crept to the foot of the bed' . . ."

"What a fantastic memory you have! Me, I couldn't quote a single sentence of mine by heart."

"Yes, I've a good memory. Well, first of all your use of alliteration here is misplaced, because it diverts the reader's attention from the main issue at a very tense moment. Secondly, and more important, you describe how the cricket crawls onto the bed, inches toward her, and then—she screams, leaps naked to the floor, and Jonathan gets up, goes to her, sees the cricket, picks it up in his hand, throws it out of the window, and goes back to his corner. Then comes her agony, her passion in the face of his aloofness. It's a very dramatic scene, very powerful in itself, but it belongs in the context of a different period . . . something like . . ."

"Dostoevski?"

"Or Tolstoi's *Father Sergei*. To present a situation like that in such a highly dramatized fashion is to depict the erotic relationship in a way that is utterly divorced from our own *Weltanschauung*. It might have been appropriate in an age of humanistic idealism, when the individual was ranked highest on the scale of values, but it is out of tune in an age which regards man as *homo absurdus*. . . . If you had adopted a certain . . . ironic stance, or maintained a measure of detachment, or if you'd even drawn a picture of pure sexual hunger per se, which would have offered some grotesque aspect . . ."

"I'd have thought loneliness is very much part of our world today . . . the communication crisis and all that. . . ."

"Yes, definitely! But . . . how shall I put it? You invest loneliness with an aura of 'nobility,' yes, nobility, that's the word. And that is what creates this sense of anachronism. You won't find anything like it in Camus's *Etranger*, and certainly not in Kafka, who stripped his stories of all emotion. You can't afford to go back on their tracks. . . ."

"But forward—to what?"

"To new forms. Forms that will express a skepticism, a present without illusions. . . ."

And that will have to do for you. Definitely.

"Yes." Smiling.

But in his heart mocking you: Look at her sitting there mouthing all kinds of questionable theories presently in vogue. What makes you so sure anyway? Just so many words.

"Do you often do this, telling writers what you think of them?"

"Me?" she laughed. "This is the first time. No, the second. Some months ago a poet sent me a book of his and asked for my opinion. I put it somewhere and forgot about it. A couple of weeks later he called up to ask. I apologized and said I hadn't read it yet, and promised that if he'd call back in a week I'd tell him. I don't quite remember what happened, I was busy, or the whole thing just slipped my mind again. . . . Anyway, when he called again I was so embarrassed and I felt so guilty that without thinking I heaped such praises on him as I never praised anything I ever read. . . . Right after that I sat down and read it. Absolute trash!"

"We've got sins in common then," Brosh smiled. "As an editor I'm familiar with that kind of thing."

And at once it all became very intimate. Not at cross-purposes. "Sins in common . . ." Something welled up from deep inside her.

"When did you write this story?" she asked softly.

"After I separated from my wife," he said, amazingly matter-of-fact.

Don't ask any more questions. Up and on your way now, to Matthew Arnold waiting on your desk.

"Were you born here?" She swallowed, choked a little, put a hand to her throat and gave a little cough.

"In the Old City. My father was a rabbi. Ephraim Burstein."

A kind of unmasking. And now she saw him in a new light: one of those Cabalist mystics, hot-blooded, struggling against temptation. And that would account for the ascetic pallor of his cheeks.

"You grew up there?" she whispered.

"Till the fall of the Jewish Quarter in forty-seven. And after we left there I left the straight and narrow as well. . . ."

"Where did you acquire all that natural science? Names of plants, thorns, reptiles . . ."

"Out of books," he grinned. "I used to read natural history books, geography . . . Then also, when I was in the underground, the Stern Group, at sixteen, we did some field training."

Yehuda Dolav, in Jerusalem. Don't.

Ah, charmed world of wonder and mystery, and so far away. Life is running out. She glanced about her at the small, rosy café. A young couple were whispering together at a nearby table, her head in the crook of his arm. Behind her she heard: "You don't

understand! It isn't *him,* it's his *parents* . . . So I said to him, if
you're such a spineless . . ."

"Well, I've already been taking up too much of your time."
Picking up her handbag.

"I love not working," he said.

Nevertheless they rose, and after paying he offered to see her
home.

On the way she found out he had worked as a diamond
polisher, together with his three brothers who were older than
he; that he had studied history at the university, but had given it
up because "there's order in history, one thing follows another,
while with me things aren't as neat as that, they're all mixed up,"
which made her laugh; and she liked him for saying he had
never been south of Beer Sheva in his life and didn't know the
Negev at all, he just saw it in his imagination and wouldn't go
there because he was afraid of a disappointment; and he was
altogether a city man at heart and was fond of the four walls of
his room and didn't go out much.

In the street the treetops rustled with some obscure nighttime
activity. The road was short, too short. To walk like this for
hours, walk till the dawn would rise blue, and unveil the staring
houses. When had it been, in Jerusalem? Oh, aching youth!

"You're a solitary, in fact," she said.

"I have contacts . . . people drop in at the office. . . . And if
they don't, I carry on a dialogue with them through their
writing. . . . And I used to be married, five years. . . ."

"But as you said, you separated."

"She was too healthy for me," he joked, "a very positive kind
of person, really. . . ."

Elisheva felt self-consciously heavy beside him, felt as though
she were limping, or walking with a stoop. Was her bag that
heavy?

"Did you get good reviews?"

"Reviews?" Laughing. "I received a few letters. One of them
was unsigned, and its writer informed me that the 'black
widow'—a kind of poisonous spider—is not indigenous to the
southern Negev. That didn't give me peace. A grave error. And
I was sure that the black widow, which usually lives under stones

and in ruins, had *got* to be there. I asked a naturalist who knows the country well and he assured me I was right. I'm still looking for a way to refute that hairsplitter to his face. I've thought: Maybe put a notice in the paper . . ."

"The truth is that when I read about the black widow I only thought of it as a symbol."

"A symbol?" Brosh laughed.

Climbing the stairs, Elisheva felt the afterglow of a "good talk." And coming in she did not go to the study but to the bedroom. She undressed in the dark, got into bed, and pressed close against her husband, felt his swollen face and kissed it. Shuka couldn't believe it, imagined a marvelous dream. Afterward a radiant field of flowers shining before him, marigolds and daisies, marigolds and daisies.

NEXT day, when before setting out to the university Elisheva rang up Brosh at the paper to ask whether he could recommend some good anthology of modern Hebrew stories, he answered with a cold, "No, I don't know," and it was as though they had never met last night, as though that conversation between them, so intimate and frank, had never been. She carried on for a few tentative phrases, in case he hadn't understood, hadn't recognized her voice, but his replies were brusque, impatient.

Elisheva replaced the receiver and couldn't understand it. She couldn't get to her feet either. She was overcome by a sense of humiliation that could only be redeemed by some act of revenge. To expose him, revile him.

She wanted to tell someone. Now, at once.

Not Dinah, no.

There's something malicious about him, she thought, a sadistic streak. You could see it even in his novel: that whole scene where he lets this Hava—who has come from such a distance, in a truck, on a blazing hot summer day—suffer torments on that bed without going near her, without granting her one word of kindness. And the way he . . . yes, *he* . . . picks that cricket off her naked body, between thumb and finger, like a flea off a dog, like some bloody botanist. . . . The sick fancy of a sadist!

And he hadn't even gone very far out of his way to conceal his identity: Amnon—Jonathan.

And you—with such trustfulness . . .

How wrong you can be about people. . . .

With an effort she made herself get up and go the university, to a lecture about Virginia Woolf.

CROSS, loathing the whole world, no, loathing herself, her very being, Elisheva Tal-Blumfeld came out of the auditorium and went down to her office, her heels on the stairs and along the corridor an exasperated click. Blah, sheer blah—she dismissed the lecture about Virginia Woolf—the worse for having been so erudite, poured forth with such evident ease, with such a flaunting of male, know-all ex cathedra authority. And this whole bloody place altogether, echoing under your feet, clickety-clickety blah-blah. "Degrading!" the English word came to her mind, the morning's insult rankling, haunting, a bitter taste in her mouth all through the lecture, a devil bobbing up between the lecturer's words, seeping into his would-be measured, would-be sane phrases about the simultaneity of states of consciousness in *The Voyage Out* and *To the Lighthouse*, about the mixing and matching of times, about the point of view—

Yes, Miss Bloch, I've resigned. Surprised, are you? Maybe they *were* satisfied with me, but *I* wasn't. Isn't that enough? No, not to Jerusalem University. I'll finish the year of course.

To England?

The afternoon sun filled her room with a brazen merciless glare. A jerk at the cord made the plastic blind tumble down, and now, caged in by bars of shadow, she could sit and indulge in her loathing. "No, I don't know." "No, I'm sorry." "I can't remember offhand." Good God, how does a person have the gall to put up such a vicious show of indifference toward one who only last night! Only last night! To humiliate! Deliberately! To show you you're nothing to him but a second-rate creature (Matthew Arnold, she recalled: The critical urges are secondary to the creative urges. Secondary, huh? And Novalis? Alfred Kerr? Sainte-Beuve? Benedetto Croce? And who is Amnon Brosh?); that you're a puffed-up creature, inflated with book learning, and with emotionalism, yes, emotionalism too, getting caught like a bird in a snare of artless candor, and bursting at a prick, collapsing with nothing left of you but a ragged bundle of nerves—

God!

"Black blood," black blood—boiling up in her as she wallowed in her degradation. Black blood blinding vision.

Calm down, will you? It's his form of self-defense.

Against what?

Against your invasion of his bastion. He sensed danger, rolled up and stuck out his spines, cut himself off.

Do me a favor, h'm?

No, whichever way she looked at it, she couldn't find any excuse for him, any justification. And remembering that frosty voice again, dry, distant, repudiating, reaching her from the fortress of his literary editor's room, the telephone his shield, the expression of his face invisible; remembering how softly she herself had addressed him, with what low-voiced intimacy, and how she had gone on asking, a second and a third time, so diffidently, so almost self-effacingly, even after the first shock, like an anxious girl dreading her mentor's rebuke—

(And what is he, after all? What if not a lame duck trying to hobble onto the literary scene and just managing to spawn one pretty-pretty story garnished with a lot of purple patches!)

She knew she would only be able to purge the "black blood" by some act of retaliation. Now, at once, while her passion was hot. Eye for eye, sting for sting. To break his pride, to make him know his place and behave with a little more modesty, less presumption, conceit—

Revenge is sweet, and in the afternoon stillness, between bars of light and shadow, she spun the golden fleece.

Not outright. No, keep the sting well hidden. It'll only hurt the more.

And send it to a different paper. That's another insult he'll have to swallow.

And already she envisaged the neat even lines of typescript on blank pages:

THE PROBLEM OF HARMONY AND HISTORICAL TIME

"In his essay on Goethe, Emil Steiger speaks of the harmony of a literary work as the criterion by which to judge its merit. This harmony—"

And maybe just to *his* paper, to put him to the test. If he'd print it—the devil, and if not—the deep blue sea.

"This harmony, he says, corresponds to the Heideggerian concept of time as an 'inner meaning' expressed through the unity of the musical rhythm, with which the reader can identify empathically and to which he submits."

Or he may invite you to the office and tell you, like last time: Yes, extremely profound, shows vast erudition, but not for our readers. . . .

Not for your readers, Mr. Brosh?

"But even Goethe himself in his conversations with Eckermann pointed out the relation between various harmonies and historical time. Making the distinction between the classic and the romantic, and pronouncing the classic 'healthy' and the romantic 'sickly,' weak, morbid—"

Is all this relevant? To the point?

Wait a bit. Patience.

"—he touched on a problem that has occupied literary criticism ever since, namely, that of the viewpoint adopted by the writer toward the world of reality he treats of. The substance of the great revolution that has come over Western literature since the beginning of this century is the writer's renunciation of his ability to judge the world—not excluding his own characters—objectively and from without. As Robbe-Grillet observes in his essay on the *nouveau roman*: Any significance ascribed to . . . reality isn't our private property . . . The 'novel of character' is a thing of the past. . . . It follows that a contemporary reader will naturally suspect—if not dismiss—a story that opens in the Stendhal manner, say, with something like: 'On the morning of

April 5, when Yehoshua Tal, a successful insurance salesman, woke up' . . ."

Shuka—faintly amused—Why him of all people? Funny, his turning up here out of the blue. Pang of conscience? But let's get on with it, skip the preliminaries, get to the point:

"In connection with this inappropriate and regressive revival of a would-be objective world, with an omniscient writer as it were the patron of his characters, it might be of interest to consider the example of a recently published Hebrew novella which is not without merit: *Ravens There Were None*, by Amnon Brosh."

The flutter accompanying this explicit naming of the name immobilized her for a long moment. A sinking. A faintness in the region of the waist, as during her period. His profile in the rosy light of the café. His ascetic pallor, spiritual, romantic, yes, romantic. Stirring up such a wave of yearning. How, for the love of God, how could he?

"If we strip it of all its frills, all the studs and spangles of its scenic descriptions (which, I believe, suffer from excessive ornamentation, for all of the writer's evident—too evident!— straining after meticulous observation), we shall be left with a rather pedestrian story"—

Pedestrian?

"—embellished with an obvious symbolism whose authenticity is somewhat suspect"—

Are you sure?

"—whose authenticity calls forth some doubts, seeing that the writer's attitude toward his characters is borrowed from the literature of a different age. It follows that this attitude is synthetic and pseudoliterary"—

Signed and sealed. Pronounced guilty in public, black on white in so many thousand copies. Pilloried. Yes, in so many words: pseudoliterary!

"—Since it would be unthinkable that the story of Jonathan's loneliness and his rejection of the love offered him could be totally cut off from all circumstance of historical time, and occur solely within the context of an eternal 'Nature' existing as an asocial entity (even Pope in his *Essay on Criticism* pointed out that

· 109 ·

nature has social implications;—a salient feature of romantic literature, which at once raises the question"—

Which at once raises the question, Dr. Blumfeld, whether you are really going to write all that. Whether you'd dare. Whether you'd let your intellectual honesty be warped by vulgar passion and reduce yourself to a level of crass vindictiveness.

Well, then, forget it. A fancy. Like other fancies that present themselves to you from time to time, about imaginary encounters, in imaginary circumstances, that will never be.

Oh, God, what are you left with, then? The university walls, the gleaming corridors, lectures on Virginia Woolf. About the dog Flush writing the Brownings' biography. About the dogs of Gogol, Chekhov, Kafka. Rigmarole.

Forget about him. Just forget. An episode. Not even. A chance encounter, a freak.

Yet the blood welling up into her face again because of her inability to get even, wipe out the insult! Because you've got to do something. *Got* to. If you could—

Julius?

She called up Julius on the extension and asked if he could spare her a little while. And when he said he'd come up right away she panicked and wished she hadn't and in the same instant recalled a dream she had had that night and in which a sentence had repeated itself over and over, distinctly, in English—"The horse is the artist, the horse is the artist"—and then she remembered there *had* been a horse there, a white, handsome, rather wild stallion that had kept rearing up on its hind legs as though to jump her. For some reason she hadn't been frightened though, but pleased with the sight of him, had even laughed and told herself, "The Wild West."

"What can I do for you, my girl?" Julius Gertner sat down across from her, the weary smile, loving or mocking, a glint in his glasses.

Elisheva smiled up into his eyes. "I need a confessor." Placing her hands on the table.

"Me?" Gertner laughed.

"I have no one else."

Gertner laughed again and folded his hands over his crossed knees. "A Catholic once asked a Jew"—his leisurely drawl—

"Why don't you Jews have a confessing priest? You sin just as we do, after all. The Jew said, We only confess before God. The Gentile said, Yes, but you don't get any answers! The answers, said the Jew, those we know ourselves. Confess, my child, the answers you know."

"Ex post facto," said Elisheva, "I need an answer now."

"That urgent?"

"The devil tempts, Julius. Sorely!"

"You only just discovered that?"

"He's giving me a bad time."

Julius's smile lingered on her face. " 'It is not good that man should be alone,' " he quoted.

"That's why I wanted to see you."

"No, that isn't what I meant," he laughed. "The Kotsker Rebbe once interpreted that verse as: 'It is not good that man should be without temptation.' What is bothering you? The sixth sin?"

"Not even that. No, it's such a trifle really that I'm ashamed . . . The way trifles can make life a misery though, Julius! . . ."

Julius's look, in the short pause she made, said he understood, understood oh, so well.

"Imagine, I happened to make someone's acquaintance. . . . We sat and talked about all kind of things, with a feeling of mutual understanding . . . of rapport even. . . ."

Elisheva broke off. The image of that scene, of the two of them sitting in the café, filled her for a moment with unbearable sadness.

"A few days later . . . It's silly, really, telling you about it. . . . I . . . come across him in the street, I greet him, pleased, you know, and he walks past me . . . as though he didn't know who I was! I felt so hurt, felt such a raging fury come over me!"

"Perhaps he really didn't remember you," said Gertner with a frown.

"He did, he did all right! And even if not—I greeted him didn't I? Even a stranger would acknowledge . . . But that isn't the point. The point is that ever since then I find myself thinking of him, brooding, plotting revenge, poison, murder. . . ."

"The number of people we kill in our imagination!"

"And it's so degrading, Julius! Degrading that this person whom I . . . whom I hardly even know . . . can obsess me like

that, get under my skin, invade my privacy. . . . I catch him
butting in on my thoughts even in the middle of a lesson. . . .
And what's even worse is the way I plot revenge, have the most
vulgar fantasies. . . . Can you understand that?"

"*Superbia, invidia, irae!*" said Professor Gertner. "The three
capital sins! If I were a Catholic priest I'd tell you: Seek that man
and when you find him, ask his forgiveness. But since I'm a Jew,
and not alone, not without temptation, I mean, and with a not
inconsiderable aptitude of my own for those three outrageous
sins, I say to you what I say to myself: To thy books! To thy
books, Elisheva."

"And you find it helps?"

"My dear," said Julius, "if I had time to spare for my tempta-
tions . . . Starve 'em, it is written, that thou mayst eat."

They chuckled wickedly together over that, while the recol-
lection of the tales concerning Julius that had done the rounds at
various times flashed through her mind. Charm covers up for
many sins, she thought.

"At least you taught me some Jewish lore," she grinned.

"What did you expect from an old reprobate like me? To
preach repentance and atonement at you? Morality is an idea, as
far as I'm concerned; a subject for research, for teaching. You
have a clear-cut division in this matter: some consider how to
practice it, and some how to elucidate. We—you and I—belong
to the second category. . . ."

"How frightening!"

"Frightening?"

"It's as though you said: There are those who live life and
those who observe it, and we belong to the observers. . . . You
make me feel ancient!"

From the remoteness of his age, a fatherly smile appeared on
Julius's face. "Erasmus in one of his Colloquies tells of a conversation between four old men who meet on the coach to Antwerp.
Each of them wonders how the others have managed to attain
such great age, and they proceed to tell one another their life
stories. One is the man of virtue who walked the straight path
and never looked right or left. The second is the libertine who
lived for pleasure and was the slave of his desires. The third
committed every kind of perfidy to gain his ends. The fourth

was endowed with wealth and wisdom and had been free to observe the world from above. And all and one they reached ripe old age, those who 'lived life' as much as those who 'observed' it. To thy books, Elisheva, to thy books," and he put out a hand and placed it over hers.

A feeling of warmth and ease settled over her. Under this wing she would be shielded from harm. Balm on her wound. She reproached herself for not having told him the whole truth.

"The silliest part of it," she said, "is that that man who made me feel so awful . . ."

A light knock on the door. His big hulk—oh, God! her heart sank. How? What on earth? Why? Filling the doorway, bear broken out of the zoo.

"Sorry . . . I'm interrupting . . ." Yehoshua Tal apologized.

"Not at all, not at all." Julius Gertner rose and extended his hand. "Sit down, I was just about to go back to my room. I've been telling your wife a nice little story by Erasmus of Rotterdam about four old men who each attained ripe old age in a different way. You tell it to him, Elisheva. A man dealing in life insurance may profit by it. Are you, too, haunted by the thought of your passing years, Mr. Tal?"

"My years? . . . No, I don't think so . . ." Tal grinned, his eyes pleading for Elisheva's help.

Why now? Why must he do this to me? She couldn't forgive him.

"There now! That's something we have in common! . . . And the beauty of the story is"—turning to Elisheva—"and that's where you glimpse the artist in Erasmus, by no means inferior to the philosopher, mind you, is that he concludes it with the coachmen debating whether to throw the old men into the mire! Ever read anything by Erasmus?"

"Very little," said Elisheva absently.

"A great artist! . . . You ought to read his *Praise of Folly*. Among the cornerstones of world literature. . . . Do you read English, Mr. Tal?"

"I get the drift . . ."

"Then you read it, too, *The Praise of Folly*. You'll like it. I'll let Elisheva have it, and you read it. It's the fools who make the world go round, says Erasmus, and that is a profound truth which no fool could have said. Which goes to show that we need a few sages around as well, if only to tell us the truth about fools, eh? I wonder why he hasn't been translated into Hebrew. Though as a matter of fact, hardly any of the medieval classics have been. They've been plagiarized, though, especially during the Age of Enlightenment. Solomon Rubin wrote a *Eulogy on Fools*, and the whole bunch of Odessa intelligentsia applauded as though he'd come up with something new. Perhaps he was never translated so the original wouldn't come to light.... Oh, well ..." He grinned, took his leave, went.

"I was passing and they said at the office you'd finished your lecture.... Thought I'd take you home...." Shuka tried to placate Elisheva. "Interrupted, did I?"

"No, you didn't." Elisheva picked up her books.

Silently they went out, crossed the corridor—sharp and pointed steps, heavy and hesitant steps. The keys in his hand jingled softly in the silence.

"You ought to talk to Avigayil," he said after starting the car.

"What about?" Roused from her reveries.

"I'm just coming from the school. Had a talk with her teacher."

"So you weren't just 'passing' ..." she said, her smile trying to take the edge off her words.

"Went out of my way a bit...." And turning to look at her. "Anything wrong?"

"No, nothing...."

"Looks as if you're angry with me for saving you a bus trip. I'm very sorry!"

"What did the teacher say?"

Tal didn't answer.

"I asked what did he say!"

"Never mind."

"Hurt your feelings?" she smiled. "I was just surprised. You never come to pick me up.... I thought you'd have given me a call first...."

You're only confounding the issue. It's not his fault you're in this mess.

"I'll know better next time. Thanks."

"What did he say?" In a conciliatory tone now, and laying a hand on his shoulder. But his body remained stiff.

Reluctantly Shuka told her about the teacher's complaints: she had failed the last math test. A bad grade in physics. Getting behind in lit and Scriptures, though she used to be among the brightest in her class. She's grown careless, doesn't do her homework, can't be bothered. A history paper which she should have submitted a month ago . . .

The bee that Julius had silenced for a while back there started up its buzzing again. Your wounded pride. *Superbia*. You should have hit back on the spot: So sorry for troubling you, Mister Editor! and slammed the receiver. Or: Saving your grace, Mister Writer! But the shock of it, leaving you dumb. Hit-and-run tactics! What was it had stung him? A few critical remarks? The fellow's hypocrisy: pretending he's so broad-minded, so modest, so ready to listen and defer. . . . And such frankness, too, opening your heart to someone you don't even know and without any reservations. And the moment you turn your back—like the true coward. At night in bed he had thought: How dare she! A hair of his head! Don't let her get away with it! Yes, Mister Writer, and not the first hair either. *Ira* has thrown other writers before you to the lions. We'll yet see the day when you, hat in hand . . .

"Though I'm not surprised, the way she carries on . . . gets home every night after midnight . . . her mind's on other things . . ."

Elisheva chased the bee off, tried hard to attend to what her husband was saying.

"Talk to her. Call her and talk to her. I'll finish up here," Shuka whispered at Elisheva, who stood by the sink washing the dishes after supper.

Elisheva said nothing, finished the dishes, and, blaming herself for having neglected her household duties, her mother's duties—for months now!—she knocked on the door of Avigayil's room, entered, and said, "Come, I want to talk to you." Avigayil closed her book unhurriedly, stood up from the bed, and trailed behind her mother to the living room. Elisheva shut the door behind them, and Shuka, who had lain in wait in the corridor, felt gratified, almost triumphant. He approached the door on tiptoe, eavesdropped briefly, then decided he'd better take himself off, out of sight, give them a chance. He'd get the results from Elisheva when it was all over. Easy in mind, filled with a sense that order had been restored, he shut himself up in the bedroom.

"You know Daddy went to see your teacher today, don't you?" Elisheva put a note of severity into her voice.

Avigayil sat facing her, head tilted, sweep of hair falling over half her face, and listened with a thin, hardly discernible smile.

All this solemn formality, the ceremony of the "I want to talk to you," and closing the door and sitting in armchairs facing one another—Elisheva realized how ridiculous, how absolutely ridiculous, this must look to her daughter. A put-on performance, the acting corny. She had noticed the thin smile.

"I hear you've failed in math. And in physics. Well, the sciences never were your strongest point"—trying to adopt a more natural, easier, "chummier" way of speaking—"though I'm sure that with a slight effort you could have made it a Seven or a Six. But what I can't for the life of me understand is why you should fall behind in the humanities! In lit? You, with your sense of language, your insight . . . Whom are you studying at the moment? Shneour? Mendele? That so hard? It's all Hebrew, isn't it? You do understand the text, it's just a matter of devoting a little thought . . ."

Talking, she could read her daughter's mind: How long can this possibly last? Another ten minutes? Fifteen? Let her have her say.

And she can reel it off by heart, whatever you say, whatever you're going to. With her sensitive ear she catches how, in the final analysis, you do not care all that much.

"And you could have called on me for help. I'm at home every day, after all, and literature isn't quite beyond me. I know I'm busy, but I'm not so busy that I couldn't spare you half an hour or an hour now and then. You're stuck with something—why not come and ask? Or before an exam . . ."

And in Avigayil's eyes, fixed upon her in patient attention, she could read the answer: Don't lie, Mother. Did you ever once ask what I'm learning? Ever show any interest? Did you ever go to a school meeting? Did you ever even see any of my teachers at all? What do you know about me?

"I'm not too familiar with Hebrew literature, I grant you. But the problems are the same, and analyzing a text is analyzing a text. What was your last exam about?"

"Feierberg's *Whither?*. I got an Eight."

"But your teacher says you're behind all the same."

"Because he expects more of me," she said laconically.

"And with good reason. I don't see why you shouldn't get a Nine in lit. *Whither?* . . . What's so difficult about that?"

"I'm not interested."

"Not interested in what?"

"In any of it. Just not interested," she said emphatically, by way of summing up many things that had been left unsaid.

Elisheva searched her daughter's face, only now really seeing her. It seemed years since she had. A rich world, and sealed, hidden from you, you who never even ventured to catch a glimpse of it. Fruit ripening slowly in this enclosed garden and you do not know and do not feel. Out of reach. It's not so long since you yourself . . .

"What *does* interest you?"

Avigayil gave a shrug.

Too late, too late. You should have asked a long, long time ago, and not like this. What a senseless attempt to unlock a delicate heart with a crude and rusted key!

"Look, Avigayil," she resumed in the matter-of-fact tone, extracting a cigarette from the pack on the table and lighting it, "you're not a child anymore . . ."

"May I?" Avigayil's hand going for the cigarettes.

Elisheva was taken aback. All at once the full sense of her daughter's surreptitious, unsuspected maturity dawned on her, as though in a flash the child had turned young woman. Her mother's sense of duty urged her to refuse, but refusing would only be added proof of her blindness. She moved the pack across.

"Thanks." Avigayil took out a cigarette, flicked the lighter with practiced hand.

"You know your future is at stake . . ."

But while talking—about grades, reports, the necessity to

conform to accepted regulations even if one doesn't agree with them—she felt she was reciting a piece. What triteness! Wouldn't it be better to put a stop to this ridiculous mother-to-daughter, teacher-to-pupil farce and say: Look here, Avigayil, you're quite grown up, maybe just as grown up as I am, so do as you wish, it's not for me to lay down the law to you. . . .

Avigayil blew a cloud of smoke up in the air. Seasoned veteran. And when the smoke of both their cigarettes mingled—woman to woman—Elisheva said:

"You have someone . . ."

Avigayil nodded.

"In love with him?" Elisheva with an understanding, expectant smile.

Avigayil closed her mouth on the smoke and, nodding her head in affirmation again, put a hand to her lips to stifle a brief cough.

Woman to woman. Elisheva was aware of a powerful temptation to ask her about her feelings, her experience, to tell her of her own. To converse, talk as woman to woman. A note of envy crept into her heart and she hurried to suppress it.

"Interferes of course . . . with schoolwork, I mean . . ." she said.

"Maybe. . . ."

A silence. Uneasy, hard to keep up and hard to end. What more can you say to her?

"All I ask, Gilly, is that I won't have occasion to tell you again what you yourself know as well."

Avigayil kept silent. The sweep of hair falling over half her face, shrouding her, her secret enclave, against her mother.

"Can I go now?" Squashing the cigarette in the ashtray.

She waited for another moment, then rose and went out. Erect. Proud.

Elisheva covered her face in her hands. This crushed feeling. The pressure on her heart. Wouldn't it lift then?

WHEN he had withdrawn into the bedroom—full of confidence in the outcome of the session taking place in the other room—Shuka's glance fell upon the Hebrew book lying on Elisheva's bedside table, underneath two English ones. He opened it, and when he began to read became absorbed at once and couldn't lay it down. The fierce light, expanses of flintstone, the wild scenery of mountain and crater and desert! And the rhythm, the dragging, monotonous rhythm, tight with a sort of choked-back grief! That's it, exactly! What he had been waiting for! And this lonely man, shunning life's tumult! His face was flushed with excitement.

When he heard Avigayil come out of the living room and enter her own, he stopped, went to Elisheva, was satisfied with what she told him, returned to the bedroom, and resumed his reading. Late at night, with Elisheva still in the study, he finished. He undressed, lay down, switched the light off, and couldn't sleep: the harsh light glancing off the barren mountains flashed before his eyes. And that meeting with the driver of the last truck to travel the road, when he, Jonathan, already knows that from now on he is going to be cut off. . . . The brief conversation between them, single words, short, seemingly ir- relevant phrases—about the price of fuel, about the camel ambling in the distance, about the brackish water—nothing could convey the sense of desolation better than that. . . . If he could meet this writer, thank him . . . Something told him there must be an affinity between them.

In the morning, dressing, he said, indicating the book, "A marvelous story!"

Elisheva started, blushed, as though caught in the act.

"Been reading it?" she said stiffly.

"In one go! Marvelous. Don't you think so?"

"Not bad."

"Not bad? He's a great writer, that man!"

"Great?" she said doubtfully.

"Yes, great!"

She felt something twist inside her. Those praises, and the encroachment, the unexpected encroachment upon the privacy of her pain. Like yesterday, when he had suddenly butted in upon her talk with Julius. Everything is wide open, you have nothing of your own, nothing to yourself.

"Just what's so wonderful about it?"

"All of it! The landscape description . . . But that isn't the main thing. He's got such an understanding of people! Such insight! . . . It's . . . it's moving!"

From her bed, Elisheva smiled up at him: so open and naive! Oh, my dear, it's not your fault, it's not your fault really that I'm like that. . . .

"Do you know him?"

"Who?"

"The writer."

"No. I mean, hardly. I gave him an article once. He's a literary editor."

"That last article?"

"Yes."

"What's he like?"

"In what way?"

"As a person."

"Intelligent. Bit spineless, though, I'd say. . . ."

"Very young?"

"Thirty-five, six . . ."

"And you didn't like the book?"

"I didn't say that. It's all right."

"All right!" he said derisively. "Know what I think? I think that what with being so busy with literature you've lost your sense of taste. You don't recognize beauty when you see it. Plain beauty! . . ."

You may be right, too, she answered him in her mind.

"No, Acropolis is the name of the agency," he gave a little laugh, went red. "I won't take up much of your time. Ten, twenty minutes . . ."

"But . . . to be frank, I . . . I'm not interested in insurance. . . ." He heard the voice falter, as though careful not to offend, but not to commit itself either.

"Maybe I'll manage to convince you . . . and if not . . . I wanted to have a few words with you about something else as well. . . ."

"To do with the paper?"

"Not exactly. Something personal in a way, I guess. . . ."

"Right. . . . Only I don't quite see when . . . Just let me have a look . . ."

And realizing he was about to be put off, for who knew how long, as some nobody, some nuisance of a salesman to be got rid of with an excuse, Tal gave in and said quickly:

"I expect you know my wife, Tal-Blumfeld . . ."

"Yes, of course! I didn't know you were . . ." He could hear the change in manner, the voice agreeable now, responsive.

And though glad the gate had opened at his sesame, he regretted having with his own mouth, in an instant, wrecked his plan, irrevocably. On his way to the office he had thought: I must meet this man, tell him what I felt reading his book. There is some bond between us. Maybe friendship, eventually. And without Elisheva's knowledge. Something of my own in which she'll have no share, just like *she* has . . . And now, with one hasty word . . .

"When?" asked Brosh.

"Even today, if you could. . . ."

"Say twelve?"

"Be at your office at twelve."

Brosh's greeting was effusive, a bit overdone, Shuka thought, a bit nervous even. He rose, offered this chair, that chair, asked whether he would have coffee, asked after Elisheva. . . . "A first-rate article that was," he said, "tough but first-rate." And he extolled her sound scholarship and her "original, very personal taste." Afterward he was prepared to listen. Tal pulled brochures and charts out of his briefcase, placed them on the desk and said:

"Before I begin I'd like to thank you for your book *Ravens There Were None*. I read it. Only last night, as a matter of fact. In one go. I was very impressed."

"Thank you," said Brosh demurely.

"It hardly ever happens to me that when I read a book I feel as though . . . as though it expressed *me*, personally."

"I'm glad to hear that," he said quietly, and looking up at him added, "In what way?"

"In the way it, uh . . . reveals things that you wouldn't even admit to yourself. . . . You see, I was born in a village, grew up

· 121 ·

there . . . and this feeling of a man falling in with nature . . .
Falling in isn't the word . . . *living* with nature, with no other
people about, in absolute seclusion, and against this background
. . . By the way, your descriptions of the Negev, with the heat,
and the dryness, and the thirst . . ."

"Not too detailed?"

"No! It's just the details that count. It's what makes it so
beautiful. You feel the landscape as if it were a living creature,
breathing, always *there*. . . . You must have spent some time there
yourself, the Negev. . . ."

"No, never. Just Jerusalem. Tel Aviv."

"In that case it's pure genius! . . . But that's not the point.
What I wanted to say was, about your hero, how against the
background of this scenery, this . . . this loneliness, he discovers
himself, gets to know himself more and more every day. . . ."

"Some people say that that's, you know, out of time . . ." he
said with a smile.

"What time?"

"Ours. Israel, 1966."

"But that's just what makes the story so good. That it's univer-
sal, if that's the word. That it concerns the problems of Man, *as*
Man, wherever he is. I mean, like the relations between
Jonathan and that dog. . . . Or the meeting with Hava at night,
when he . . ."

Things wouldn't quite come off. He became a bit muddled
about various episodes, mainly because Brosh didn't encourage
him with further questions and appeared a bit absent altogether.

They didn't come off either when he turned to the matter of
insurance. He passed his finger down columns of figures and
showed Brosh how, at his age, it would amount to no more than
25 pounds a month, which after thirty years would accumulate
into quite a tidy sum, linked to the cost-of-living index and free
of income tax. But he could do better than that: to make it easier
for him, he said, he might be able to draw him up a combination
of half comprehensive and half risk policy, which would cost him
a mere 15 pounds a month—a pittance!—and nevertheless get
him all the benefits of a regular policy. Brosh, who had been
following Tal's finger up and down the lists of figures and had

listened to his explanations in silence, said when Tal finished that he had never given the matter any thought because . . . "That's just it!" Tal cut in with the aplomb of one who knows what is coming next: "Most people are like that! Don't think of tomorrow, out of some kind of superstition, some fear that . . ." "No, not out of fear," Brosh smiled, "it's just that . . . I could never bother . . ." "Exactly!" said Tal. "That's exactly why I've come to you with this offer. You're a writer, and as a writer you need a great deal of free time, and especially peace of mind. It's what I thought after I read your book. You ought to be free of cares—material, financial cares. . . ." But at this point somebody called up Brosh on the extension, and he apologized and said he had to go down to the press for a few minutes, because this was makeup day and he had to give the men some instructions. And when he came back he embarked at once on, "Look, Mr. Tal, I'm not married and I have no children . . ." "But you must have other relations," said Tal, "and maybe some dependents as well. . . ." Yes, Brosh admitted, he had his mother to support, but . . . and here their conversation was interrupted again by the telephone, and Brosh answered and talked to someone about a poem to appear, and when he replaced the receiver he said, "Well, I'll think it over. Let me keep these brochures. Will it be all right if I get in touch with you in a few days?" "Sure, sure," said Tal and stuffed his papers back into his briefcase. "Just believe me that when I try to persuade you it's only because I know that you haven't got the time to think of these things yourself, so someone like me must do the thinking for you!"

And seeing Tal out, Brosh's warmth and courtesies were, again, a bit overdone.

One week later, during supper, the telephone rang and Elisheva got up to answer it.

"May I speak to Mr. Tal, please?" she heard.

The pounding of her heart on recognizing the voice right away . . .

"Who wants him?" Fighting giddiness.

"Amnon Brosh."

Her body shook.

"For you," she flung at Shuka in the kitchen. And was unable to control her trembling: The insult! Rubbing it in! Not even to introduce himself by name! Doesn't know you! God in heaven!

Shuka picked up the receiver, and hearing the caller's name cried happily, "Yes!"

"Sorry I took so long . . ."

"That's all right! Quite all right! Well, did some thinking?"

"Yes, I did. . . ."

"Well, and?"

"Could I see you?" said Brosh uncertainly.

"With pleasure! Anytime you say!"

The other hesitated again.

"Well, you see, it's a bit inconvenient at the office . . ." he said.

"Anywhere you like! Maybe . . . maybe you'd like to drop in on us here?"

And regretted it at once, and hoped he'd refuse. Another of those blasted slips.

"Yes . . . all right . . . when?"

"Tomorrow night?"

"Nine? Half past?"

"What did he want?" Elisheva asked with an agitated look at him.

"Business . . ." answered Shuka casually and sat down at the kitchen table.

"You and him?" Trying to hold back the impending explosion.

"Insurance. . . ." Shuka, with a smile.

"You—offered—to insure—him?"

Shuka was alarmed at her voice—the voice of a ghost roused by some fearful crime committed under its very eyes—and by the sight of her white face.

"Why not?" he asked weakly.

"You . . . you must be *out* of your *mind!* . . ."

And she ran out of the kitchen and collapsed on a chair in the living room. Like a landslide coming down on her. Everything slipping, crumbling, everything spinning in a giant wheel which was going to hit her, inevitably.

On tiptoe, as though afraid to rouse a beast from it lair, Shuka entered the room.

"What's wrong? I don't understand what's wrong?"

Elisheva hid her face in her hands. The wheel going around and around: the image of him at their meeting in the office, the image of him at the café, of him a moment ago, sitting in his room—where is that?—and telephoning here. To this house—without introducing himself to me!

The brutality of it! The heel—

"Tell me at least what it's about, I don't understand a thing. . . ." Shuka sat on the edge of the couch, little boy caught misbehaving.

The heel! Not even to say Hullo, good evening, not even that! Deliberately, in cold blood! To show that you don't exist as far as he's concerned. She felt utterly crushed.

"What did he say?" Uncovering her face.

"Nothing special . . . wanted to see me, that's all. . . ."

"When?"

"He'll come here tomorrow night. . . ."

"*Here?!*" Crying out. "*To this house?!*"

Shuka was alarmed anew by her white face, by the eyes popping out of her head as if in dread, shock, as if at some imminent disaster.

"But I don't understand . . ." he stuttered, utterly at loss.

"I'll have you know I . . ." Her lips trembled.

But all of a sudden she jumped up, rushed to the bedroom, grabbed the telephone directory and feverishly started turning its pages.

Shuka hurried to snatch his brand out of the fire.

"What are you doing?"

"You keep out of it now!" Flipping the pages back and forth.

"You can't do that. . . ." He tried to pull the book out of her hands.

"Leave me alone!" Warding him off with an elbow.

"Listen to me a minute. . . . I don't know what you have against him . . . but you can't call off a date I arranged. . . . You don't have to be there if you don't want to. . . ."

"He is not going to come here." Still turning pages, the letters swarming like ants before her eyes.

And all at once she stopped and closed the book.

"What've you got against him?" asked Shuka, seeing the storm abate.

Elisheva looked at him. "Fools rush in where angels fear to tread," the English phrase ran through her head.

"I want you to know," she said slowly, "that no matter what, I won't have you offering life insurance, or *any* insurance, to people with whom I have a professional relationship of any kind whatsoever."

"Professional relations?" Shuka grinned.

"Precisely, and even if it's a writer, or a literary editor to whom I may submit articles on occasion."

"Ashamed?"

"I'm not going to explain." Rising.

Shuka wanted to protest, to announce he'd not give in to such nonsense, but decided to put it off for some other time.

"A grown-up daughter," said Brosh sitting down on the couch opposite Tal; "how old?"

"Seventeen soon. In September."

"Looks very inaccessible."

"Oh, yes. Even to us."

"Does she write?"

"Maybe . . . maybe in secret . . . who knows?"

"Reads a lot in any case."

"Always. Swallows books. She read through yours in three hours. That's why she was so bent on seeing you when you came. Adores you!"

"She's lovely. Lovely face. Such dignity about her . . . a reticent dignity!"

"Has it from her mother. . . ."

"Yes, there's a resemblance. . . ."

Tal felt ill at ease, because Brosh was sitting stiffly upright—"as though he'd swallowed a broomstick"—not leaning against the back of the couch. He was dressed in a shining, long-sleeved white shirt, rather like some dainty exquisite from another age. On his knees lay a book he had brought with him, and he was holding onto it with both hands.

"After we met I thought that, you know . . . must be quite a fascinating occupation really, life insurance."

"Yes, in a way . . ."

"You meet a great many different people, hear life stories . . ." he said animatedly.

"If you had the time someday . . . I could tell you enough to fill ten books!"

"You learn their attitude toward life, death, the way they respond. . . . There must be some who blanch when you come to them with the suggestion. . . ."

"Oh, yes. Lots of them. They're frightened, protest, don't want to hear of it. You've got to disarm them, soothe, plead, explain you're not going to bring death any nearer that way. . . ."

"You must be quite a psychologist!" Brosh laughed.

"Absolutely. I had a case once, man of fifty-seven who shut the door in my face. I just managed to leave my card. Next day he rings me up, apologizes, asks me to call on him. I tell him look, Mr. Teneh, I don't want you to feel as though anyone were twisting your arm. Such a thing must be undertaken of one's own free will, so think it over for a week, and when you've made up your mind give me a call. Two days later he shows up at the office, just like that. It bothered him, you see. . . . Anyway, he sits down and says: Look, I've a sick wife and two kids in high school. Anything might happen. Who knows what tomorrow may bring? I've decided I'd better not put it off. . . . All of a sudden it seemed terribly urgent to him. Some fear had got hold of him. Afraid to lose another day. I explained the various alternatives, we figured it out and agreed on a policy of seventy-five thousand. I said I'd prepare the papers and mail them to him. He shook my hand, thanked me, and left. I heard his steps going down the stairs, and then a couple of minutes later come up again, and there he's back in the office! Terribly sorry, he says, I've thought it over again, and no, I've decided against. Sorry about all that trouble you went to. . . ."

"Fear working the other way! The idea that just by committing himself . . ."

"Exactly! But wait till you hear the end: a couple of weeks later I see a death notice in the paper . . ."

"Him!"

"Heart attack! I felt such a shiver down my back. . . . Felt as though I . . ."

"Were to blame somehow! . . . Terrible!"

"That's how I felt. As though I'd hastened on his death. . . ."

"Yes . . . There's a story like that in the Talmud, about a man sitting on his doorstep and people passing by and telling him: how pale you are, how ill you look . . . so often that he really begins to feel ill, and gets sick and dies. Yes, actually you deal in matters of life and death. . . ."

"I do sometimes feel like that . . . that it's like I keep account books of lives and deaths. . . ."

"Like God!" Brosh grinned.

"God's middleman," said Tal, chuckling.

"Very good!" Brosh beamed at him, "It really is a bit like that. . . ."

"And you're witness to misfortune, accidents, tragedies . . . Always sort of rubbing up against death. . . ."

"Yes, rubbing up against death," Brosh repeated as though storing up a memorable phrase.

"And then, of course, after every such tragedy you still have dealings with the family, relatives . . ."

"Yes, I suppose that's the hardest part—*after* . . . And then you must really feel like some middleman trading in lives. You come to a mourning household with a check for twenty, thirty thousand in your briefcase . . . the price of a life. . . ."

That's it! Just the kind of conversation he had been hoping to have! For years he hadn't had such a chance to talk to someone who listened, understood. . . . His heart had told him, even while reading the novel . . .

"I'm just thinking of another case I had: a young couple, thirty, thirty-five, who'd left the kibbutz. A healthy young fellow, getting a kick out of life, worked as a tractor driver for Mekorot. When I offered them a policy they treated it as a joke, of course, like any young Israeli couple. . . ."

Elisheva was shut up in the study, straining to catch the slightest sound beyond the door. She had heard the bell, the front door open and close, his greetings, polite murmurs, Shuka's, Avigayil's, had heard Avigayil say in reply to something she hadn't caught, "Yes, Mother's a severe critic." Had he dared mention her? Call her by name? Afterward the living-room door had slid shut and the house grown mute. The hidden presence hard by, here, behind the wall. Beyond this cell where you have buried yourself to cut him dead. Buried *yourself.* An enemy within thy gate. A choking gall. Be steadfast in your vow, fettered, barred among your books. Nothing can redeem the offense. "The novel redeems the fictional by lending it the credentials of a realistic structure," she wrote, applying herself to the open book before her. "The realism of the novel can be explained in two ways: one is to regard the novel as an empirical genre, inasmuch as it creates a new world ruled by an inner logic of its own, while at the same time striving to persuade the reader that its fictional experience bears a likeness to that of the reader's factual experience of life; the other is—"

A heart-to-heart chat, there, on the other side of the wall. To insure his life. Twenty, thirty thousand, the price set on them? Two hundred thousand the price of my humiliation. Many waters cannot quench. Had he come to Canossa?

"—historical, explaining the novel in sociological, cultural, and ideological terms. Thus its realism becomes the expression of society's communal urge to proclaim that Truth is its inalienable asset. Yet the manifestations of that truth, as they were molded by nineteenth-century literature—"

An endless bargaining. The premium. The conditions. A thousand for thee and two hundred for the keeper of my vineyard. Literature in the study, realism in the living room. To come to my house, sit here behind the wall—

"—were pure conventions, imitations of manners, emotions and elements of human experience which anyone could compare to his own by applying his knowledge of people, places—"

A unique opportunity: to go in, offer a cold, distant greeting, serve coffee, and leave at once. Eye for eye. Brace yourself and do it!

Fool not to have thought of that before.

She closed her book and got up.

With a light knock on the door she entered the living room, nodded at him with a sealed expression on her face, said:

"What will you have? Tea? Coffee?"

Brosh rose to his feet.

"I've brought the book you asked for. I'm sorry that when you called me I had nothing to say. . . . I had some people in the office, couldn't think of anything . . ."

Ah, the magic wand of one simple sentence turning night to day. In an instant lightening the whole load, scattering the clouds of stifling passion that had darkened her mind until—

"Thank you. . . ." Suppressing a sigh of relief as she took the book from his hand, opened it to hide her eyes from him, and dropped into an armchair.

Oh, the crushing weight you have lifted from my heart! The crushing weight!

"Your husband has suggested I take out life insurance." Resuming his seat on the couch. "I was taken aback a bit at first: me and life insurance? . . . The idea never occurred to me! Then I said to myself: Why not? Actually, everyone . . ."

"When I called on you at your office I could see you didn't understand a word I was saying," Shuka laughed. "You just looked at those rows of figures . . ."

"I'm not very strong on figures. . . . But I trust you. You tell me for what sum to insure, for what period, how much to pay . . . I'll do whatever you say."

Elisheva was leafing through the book in her lap, afraid to raise her eyes, to shatter the charmed moment.

"I haven't read any of these," she ventured, turning pages. "I'm really a complete ignoramus as far as modern Hebrew literature goes."

"Two or three good stories. As for the rest . . . I haven't read them," said Brosh, smiling. "I don't read much on the whole. A few of the older writers that I'm fond of."

Shtiebel editions, Elisheva smiled to herself. That's how I like you: little confessions, self-deprecating, something of a pose but very endearing.

"That many Israeli writers! How many of them here? Some twenty!" Leafing backward and forward through the book.

"I don't read much either. No time," said Shuka. "Evenings included."

"Read Yizhar. You'll like him!" said Brosh.

"Him I *have* read! Years ago! *Hirbet Hiz'ah, The Prisoner, Midnight Convoy*. You remind me of him a bit. . . ."

Elisheva looked at him askance.

"I mean, in landscape descriptions. . . ."

"Yes, I've been told so before."

"No comparison," Elisheva mumbled into her book.

"I used to know Yizhar personally. From childhood. In the village. He's from Rehovot, you know. One of the Smilanskys."

"You from Rehovot yourself?"

"Nes-Ziona. Elisheva and me," with a smile at her, "we went to school together."

"Funny how people still write like that in this day and age . . ." said Elisheva musingly, her eyes on the book. "Here, listen to this opening:

" 'After six years in the regular army, Major Amos Ramati, an artillery company commander and a strong and healthy male, felt weary and bored to death. Everything seemed flat and routine: the camp barracks, the wretched eucalyptus grove, the bare rickety desk in the company office, even the secret affair— lasting for about a year now and known to most of the men— which he was carrying on with his secretary. On the night following the conclusion of the field exercises, coming home and sitting down to supper with his wife, he said while spooning his soup and without glancing up at her: "Why, as a matter of fact, don't you take the Pill?" ' "

The three of them burst out laughing together, and Elisheva reddened.

"Very nice," said Brosh.

"Well, there's some humor in that last sentence of course," she conceded to Brosh, "but the style . . ."

"No, there's more to it than just humor. I happen to have read that story. I remember it. That question he asks—while he's eating, and after he's been away from home a long time—that's very good. . . . A kind of oblique ray lighting up a whole situation . . . the routine of his relations with his wife, an attempt . . . an unconscious attempt to break out of it, make a fresh start. . . . And at the same time . . . it reveals certain aspects of this man's personality—an insensitivity, egoism . . . and also a certain guilt feeling. . . ."

"I'm not denying that. It's a good sentence, sheds light on a situation, as you say, but . . . that opening! 'After six years in the regular army, Major Amos Ramati . . . felt . . .' Flat and routine, as the man says. Trite. Doesn't reveal anything new in the way of a literary personality."

"Me, I'd be tempted to read the whole story after such a sentence," Shuka laughed.

"It's so similar to countless other openings," she said to Brosh. "It actually reminds me . . . almost word for word . . . let me think . . ." Rubbing her forehead. "Yes, a Chekhov story that opens something like this: 'After Wanda—or maybe Anda—a charming young woman, left the hospital, she found herself in a situation she had never experienced before,' et cetera et cetera. The same rhythm, same cadence, much the same choice of words, only the names different. . . ."

"Chekhov?" said Brosh doubtfully.

"The rhythm, I mean."

"Yes . . ." he said, unconvinced.

"And the rhythm is the man. The literary man. And when I find a writer imitating someone else's rhythm . . ."

"Then it's fake."

"Definitely."

"Still. Still, Chekhov is wine of quite a different brand."

"Certainly! But . . ." looking at him, "when I was in Scotland I was told how the vessel, too, determines the taste of the wine. Whisky is kept in barrels of a particular type of white oak to give it its special taste. . . ."

"Shall I make coffee?" asked Shuka, and without waiting for an answer rose and went to the kitchen.

"You were in Scotland?"

"Didn't I tell you I studied in England?"

"Oxford?"

"London. Two cram-full years."

"Where did you stay?"

"Do you know London?"

"Boswell's. From his diary. Where did you stay? Covent Garden? Chelsea? Kensington? Westminster?"

"I see you know the map. No, Bloomsbury." And she told him about the long days at the British Museum library. The dazzling yellow light. Herself floating in space above pages of close print. Squeezed in a corner in the pillared pantheon of a great empire.

"Ah, Bloomsbury, that's *this* age. I used to dream of being in

· 132 ·

London—of the eighteenth century, Garrick, Goldsmith, Johnson . . ."

"In London the centuries aren't dead. They live side by side in mutual respect."

"But Johnson's dead. I envy those who picked crumbs from his table in the City pubs."

"Drank with him! Bottles and bottles of French port!"

"Not Scotch whisky?"

"Scotch? Not likely. Not with his opinion of Scotsmen!"

"Yes . . . 'The noblest prospect that a Scotchman ever sees is the high road that leads him to London.' H'm?"

"Yes . . . " with a sigh of nostalgia, "the noblest prospect that *I* ever saw was—the road to Dublin."

"Number seven Eccles Street?"

"I see you've read a lot more besides Shtiebels!"

"Not a lot. *Ulysses* I just skimmed through a few pages here and there. Didn't understand it."

"A few pages? The last chapter alone has forty-five!"

"Yes," he laughed, reddening, "*that* I did read, like all the Philistines. Under the table, though."

"For fear of the teacher?"

"The rabbi."

"Even today?"

"Yes. . . . Hard to get weaned."

"In that case I'll have to read your book again."

"Biographical illumination?"

"M'm . . ."

"Don't forget that every story is an alibi, too."

"I'll take it into account."

"And every critic a voyeur."

"That's putting tags . . . You could just call it curiosity."

Shuka entered with coffee on a tray. Placing a cup before Elisheva he said, "You mentioned rhythm, style . . . but how about the contents? The idea? I suppose this writer must have some new idea."

"Writers, Shuka, don't have new ideas," said Elisheva. "Whatever they 'discover' has been discovered long before by philosophers, psychologists, even sociologists—and they go about it in a much sounder way, too."

"When I read a good story I always find there's an idea in it."

"Not a new one though."

"Yes, sometimes. . . ."

"Tolstoi?" said Brosh.

"Tolstoi?" said Elisheva, surprised it should come from him. "When Tolstoi opened *Anna Karenina* with that famous sentence of his—'Happy families are all alike; every unhappy family is unhappy in its own way' . . ."

"Happy families are all alike?" said Shuka with a laugh, turning to Brosh.

"Uh-huh, the opposite is equally valid," Brosh agreed.

"In my experience . . . it's just the *unhappy* families, mourning . . ."

"It's a generalization, of course, oversimplified. But the wording was so brilliant that everybody took it for gospel. A profound revelation! No serious writer would dare write such a sentence today. A contemporary writer searching for novelty won't presume to make psychological or sociological discoveries. He turns to new forms, to . . ."

"Turns?" said Brosh.

Elisheva searched his face briefly. "How would you put it?"

"Behaves," he laughed. "When a writer writes—it's his way of behaving. . . ."

"Granted," she said after a moment of consideration. "Anyway . . ." She had lost the thread and started leafing through the book again.

"Your coffee's getting cold," Shuka told her.

"Here's another opening." Raising her glance to Brosh, then reading from the page:

" 'That Friday was an ordinary Friday in the kibbutz. The time was five in the afternoon, the heatwave hadn't spent itself yet and a warm wind was whisking leaves across the lawn and drying the hair of girls coming out of the shower. Dinah stood on the porch looking out at the road, the hand of her five-year-old son in her own. Late as it was, the dust cloud heralding the approach of the bus from a great distance failed to appear' . . . et cetera et cetera."

"What's wrong with that?" Shuka looked from Elisheva to Brosh.

"Nothing. Except that it's old and hackneyed and that it bores you still."

"Maybe something unusual is going to happen in that story," said Shuka, sipping at his coffee, "and maybe it's something interesting."

"Well, of course, after they start out by telling you how this Friday was 'an ordinary Friday,' you realize you're being prepared for something 'extraordinary.' And for all that—how 'ordinary'!"

"In what way?" said Brosh.

"Want me to talk shop? After office hours?"

"Don't you ever do a bit of free lancing?"

"Never. Freemasoning perhaps," she said with a laugh.

"I can't quite see you armed with a chisel."

"Rather with a lance?"

"Women have subtler tools than that!"

"Yes, I do sometimes use my feelers."

"I'm asking nicely."

In the end she complied and explained that in stories by, say, Maupassant, O. Henry, Chekhov, the writer prepares his reader for some dramatic development, some fascinating "revelation" about human nature, by means of a sharp twist of events, or by an unusual kind of plot. The writer will, so to say, "fool" the reader and tell him: You imagine everything is plain sailing, just the ordinary and familiar stuff, but you'll be surprised to find it isn't so but quite the opposite, and not at all as you believed it to be. And in more modern stories the "fooling" of the reader might work just the other way: the reader expects some astounding, sensational development, and the writer shows him that everything is ordinary, but that it is precisely this "ordinariness" that reveals life to be much more "complex" or "profound" than the reader had thought. In all of these cases the writer considers himself smarter than the reader and possessed of greater "wisdom" about human nature, or about life in general, and he goes about imparting this "wisdom" by means of an "illuminating" situation or event. The contemporary writer, though, should realize that he isn't any smarter than his reader and that he can't tell him anything he doesn't know already. All he can do is describe the "known," but in such a way that it "projects his own original, unique personality." And it is that, his *personality,* which points up the *Condition humaine*—which is the only thing we are looking for in literature today.

"So now you see why I like Borges and don't like Graham Greene," she added with a little laugh to alleviate the effect of her learned lecture.

"Borges?' said Brosh.

"I'm sure you've read him. The Argentinian . . ."

"Ah, yes. Only I thought it was pronounced 'Borjes.' But . . . if it were just the projection of a writer's personality I was interested in I could make do with one story by Maupassant. I read ten, twenty of his stories because I was interested in their contents!"

Shuka nodded in utter agreement.

"Mozart's symphonies have no 'contents' and you still don't make do with listening to just one of them. You want to hear more and more—if you like his 'melody,' that is, his artistic personality."

"But in a Maupassant story I want to know what happens with the pearl necklace, whether it was real or imitation."

"Or in a Brosh story I want to know what happened with Jonathan in the end," said Shuka hotly. "Whether he stayed in the desert or went back to town or . . . Why can't one be in love with the hero instead of with his author!"

Elisheva gave a forbearing smile, but at the same time felt a faint blush creep into her cheeks.

"Certainly," she said, "but if it weren't for the 'melody' of the story, its rhythm . . . I'll give you an example." Turning to Brosh. "We mentioned Chekhov. Maybe you remember his story *The Candlestick*: Someone is given a candlestick in return for some favor. The present doesn't please its recipient and he wants to get rid of it, so he gives it as a present to someone else, who gives it to a third, and so on till it ends up with the original owner, who gives it to the first man again. Now this is a joke, and a rather old one at that—there must be hundreds like it in existence. Why does this story, nevertheless, hold so much charm for us?"

"It's *how* you tell a joke that counts," Shuka laughed.

"Precisely! In other words: what we mainly care about isn't the 'what' but the 'how.' "

"It's both!" Shuka exclaimed.

Elisheva remained silent for a moment, then said, "Cocteau put it beautifully when he said, 'The style is the soul, and unfortunately the soul assumes a bodily shape.' *Unfortunately*, mind you! El Greco's madonnas don't interest me in the least as human beings. What does interest me about them, what fascinates me, are the colors, the light, the air of mystery . . . In short, El Greco himself!"

"Only it's fortunate for us that, unlike God, the madonnas are made of flesh and blood," laughed Brosh.

Elisheva settled herself to hear him develop this idea, but instead Brosh said to her, "Do you know that Arab village at the foot of the Temple Mount? Silwan it's called. When I was a child there lived an Arab there who used to deliver our milk. And sometimes when he would miss a day I would be sent down there to fetch it. Well, we weren't, of course, allowed to enter a church. Even *passing* a church we were supposed to look the other way. But down below St. Stephen's Gate there is a very beautiful Russian Church, Maria Magdalena, and in front of it the Church of All Nations. And coming back I always used to go out of my way to pass it, just so as to get a furtive peep at the painting in front over the portico. Jesus, the Apostles, all in bright gay colors. Such a contrast to the gray and ocher of the hills and the city wall. And there was a picture of a madonna there—might have been Mary—in a purple veil. Very chaste. All saints are always very sad, or very grave, never smiling. I decided that this was Hannah, the mother of Samuel. I was sure of it. And that she was so sad because Peninnah had children and she hadn't. I was in love with her. Even today, when I read the chapter about Hannah praying at Shiloh, I see that madonna before me. . . ."
He laughed.

Elisheva waited for a conclusion, a point.

"Your mentioning madonnas reminded me," he apologized, then added thoughtfully, "Fortunately the written sentence does have content."

"And rhythm."

"The mystic union. But that's Cabala. . . ."

"Did you study Cabala?" asked Shuka.

"I used to have an uncle, shriveled as a raisin. He'd fast five days a week and sleep on a bed of boards, and on his *left* side, in order to punish the evil instinct, which dwells on the left side of one's body. As a result he had red weals all along the ribs. . . ."

"And you got so furious when you heard he was coming. . . . Why *did* you get so furious, really?" said Shukas as they were undressing.

"You're right. I was silly." Putting her dress on a hanger.

"What did you have against him?"

"Never mind. Some old argument."

"He respects you, you know. Even if he doesn't always agree with you."

"You think so?"

"Didn't you notice?"

Naked she approached him. "I'm sorry. About last night." She kissed him and pressed herself against his body. "I was wicked. Awfully wicked." She closed her eyes.

Shuka gathered her to him. She was young, and hot, all on fire. Like in their first days.

ELISHEVA craved something spicy, or salty, something to tickle, entice, and didn't know what. The glass showcase of the delicatessen contained a dozen kinds of cheese, smoked and pickled herring, Polish sausage, Hungarian salami, enormous black Greek olives and smaller green ones stuffed with pimento, pickled cucumbers, pickled eggplant—but nothing seemed to answer quite. Safad cheese maybe? she deliberated. But no, that wasn't exactly what she had set her heart on either. "What's that over there?" she asked, pointing at a brightly colored can on one of the shelves. "Liver paste," said Mrs. Malkin, "French, Delicious." "No," dismissing it. "And this?"

Pointing to a jar of pickles floating in their brine. "Not kosher," Mrs. Malkin smiled. "Oysters in vinegar. Wonderful with a drink. Vermouth, vodka." Elisheva hesitated. What she craved had to be something exciting, heady and exciting! She could taste the memory of something like that on her tongue, a distant, elusive memory, just out of reach. She had felt the craving for it all morning. "Try one?" suggested Mrs. Malkin helpfully. She uncovered a slightly depleted jar, fished an oyster out with a toothpick and offered it to Elisheva. "Yes . . ." Exploring the taste on her tongue, "Ye-es . . ." Letting the delicacy linger and dissolve, "Good!" "Anything else?" Mrs. Malkin asked.

"Elisheva! In the middle of the day!" Rachel Romano with a shopping bag, radiant, brimming with energy as always.

"I suddenly felt like something . . . spicy. . . ." Elisheva swallowed.

"So school's out, I take it!"

"Nearly. Just the exams. Another fortnight."

"You look marvelous!" With warm approval.

"Thanks. So do you!"

Elisheva liked Rachel Romano unreservedly: her complete affirmation of life. The thick, shoulder-length black hair parted on one side gave her a youthful look, while the weariness in the brown eyes, betraying a hint of her age, appeared to Elisheva as the "ancient," "aristocratic" weariness of one descending from an unbroken lineage of four generations in the country. Seeing her in the street, strong, long-legged, she would think: a lady, to the manner born! And would envy her the elemental vitality of her body. And what endeared her to Elisheva most was that her wealth and beauty had not made her mean: she was generous and openhearted, and her vivacity was infectious.

"Going away anywhere? Abroad?" Rachel asked.

"Wish I could! No, I spend my holidays in my private castle. . . ."

"Traveling on the wings of the spirit, like they say. . . ."

"To rather unexciting landscapes. . . ."

"Me—I packed my husband off to Geneva, and I'm taking the two girls to Nahariyya next week, a hotel holiday."

Rachel Romano had four daughters: one of them married,

one a student of architecture at the Haifa Technion, the two youngest, eight and twelve, still at home.

"Why didn't you join him?"

"Oh, no! Not with him running about on business. I had quite enough of that last year, in Zurich! Had to literally hunt for cavaliers to take me to a concert or a café. . . ."

"Could be quite fun. . . ."

"Not when your husband's around," she laughed. "And besides, the Swiss male . . ."

A flash of woman-of-the-world irony appeared in her romantic eyes, woman of the wide, wide world.

"M'm, stale."

"What's wrong with Nahariyya anyway? Lying on the beach, getting a tan, playing with the girls . . . But all the bother beforehand, the shopping. Went over my rags today and saw I don't even have a plain, button-down affair to wear to the beach."

"Me, I suppose the last time I bought myself a new dress was a year ago."

"Then come along," she said gaily. "Let's go shopping together."

Elisheva was startled, yet the idea appealed to her all of a sudden.

"Let's! When?"

"Now! I'll just buy a few things here, drop them off at home, and we'll go."

Walking beside Rachel in the street, Elisheva discovered that she was really quite fond of Tel Aviv. She decided that the white of the houses wasn't at all neutral, as it was commonly considered to be, but a wonderful complement to the blue of the sky, the green of the trees along the pavement, and the golden sunlight, and that it contained an element of sand and sea. And there was beauty in the flat roofs, too, in the way they took the full light, with nothing between housetop and airy space. And she marveled at the town as a whole, as though seeing it again after a long absence: so open, unpretentious, cheerful, so Israeli —blue-and-white Israeli.

Rachel was telling her about the wedding of her niece, Ofra

Moyal, a fortnight ago at the Holyland Hotel in Jerusalem. A long and involved affair: Ofra had been in love with a law student of some obscure family from Ramat-Gan or Ramat-Yitzhak, and her parents had objected to the match. Firstly, because they had made some investigations and found the boy had no future, and secondly, because the Moyals, who had just bought themselves into the Swiss-Israel bank, wanted her to marry a young man of the Saharow clan, the Saharovs having considerable investments in Switzerland. The result had been tears, tantrums, runnings away from home, threats, and the paterfamilias had had a heart attack. "And that's what broke her. And let me tell you, she'll be happier with him. You may say my ideas are old-fashioned, but I believe in solid relationships, based on suitability and security and . . . yes, common material interests as well, and I'm not ashamed to say so. People don't make the distinction between loving and falling in love, you know. Falling in love is a big passion, but it burns itself out like a fuse, while love is something on a low flame, but surer and more lasting, and nursed over the years—by mutual understanding and adjustment and sharing. . . . Do you think I was in love with Shaltiel before I married him? He's my cousin. We played marbles together as kids. But we've been married for twenty-seven years now and—touch wood."

Listening to her story—with all its details, drawn with vivid imagery and humor: how the Moyal clan had flocked from every part of the country to call the wayward girl to order, and how after some weeks they had put her on a ship to Naples with her mother, and there, on board ship, had contrived a meeting between her and the bridegroom-elect, who had happened to be there with his own mother—Elisheva reflected that, as a matter of fact, she herself belonged, at least by birth, to this same breed of established and propertied families. Her mother had been connected on one side with the Diskins and on the other with the Stampfers, and the latter were connected by marriage to the Meyhuas clan. . . . The threads might even tie up somewhere with Rachel Romano herself. . . . Academic career and marriage —"marrying down" as her father would say—with Tolkovsky had taken her beyond the pale. She did not regret it, but was forced to admit to herself that the sounds of the prominent names and the descriptions of the brilliant salons evoked a touch of nostalgia.

"Didn't Saharov's girl marry someone of the Meyhuas crowd?" . . . In an attempt to gain a foothold in Rachel's stories.

"Which Saharov? The Saharovs are such a tree that you don't see the trunk for the branches. Yehoyakim?"

"The girl Tamara. Or maybe Dikla?"

"Dikla Saharov? You're behind, my dear, way behind!" Rachel laughed. "She *was* married to Amos Meyhuas! Hadn't you heard they were divorced over a year ago? It was in all the papers. The whole country was in a tizzy."

Elisheva never read *Woman's* or *This World*, and even in the daily paper she would only glance cursorily over the front-page news. She suddenly found herself quite out of touch with the march of events.

"And I don't blame him either!" said Rachel. "You had to be blind not to see that that marriage was going on the rocks. Dikla's a disturbed sort of person, you know, quite unbalanced. She's got a kind heart, I'll say that for her, but the mess she makes of everything! The smallest incident, things anyone else'd hardly take notice of, she'll make up into a huge mountain. When Amos was away in Teheran she all of a sudden started carrying on, and quite flagrantly, too, you know. One evening she was seen at Frederica, the next at the Sheraton. . . ."

Rachel knew the salesgirls by name, and when they entered the store they hurried over to her at once. "No, we'll see to my friend here first," she said. "Come and meet her: Dr. Tal-Blumfeld, lecturer at the university, and these are Rica, Violet. . . . Listen, I want you to find her a dress that'll make people sit up and take notice. She's very modest, and she doesn't do justice to her beauty, and all mankind suffers in result." Elisheva laughed. "You're the first who calls me modest," she whispered. "Maybe among your brainy crowd, I wouldn't know," said Rachel in her warm, rich voice, "but when I see you through my window sometimes, going to work, coming home, I think to myself: Such a good-looking and intelligent woman, and how little she knows what's due to herself. It's positively wicked. A sin against nature!" A cocktail dress? Evening gown? inquired Violet. Elisheva hesitated, surveying the racks. She knew what she really wanted: something sexy, tight-fitting, loud even. Instead she said, "Something simple for every day, and which I can wear for the evening, too." Rachel sent her a look of despair. "Let me pick you something, okay?" she said, and took down a lemon dress with flowered embroidery and lacy ruffs around the neck and wrists. Elisheva inspected the dress over her arm and turned to the mirror to try it against her figure. Rachel was exchanging smiles and whispers with the salesgirls. "I'll try it on," said Elisheva and moved to one of the dressing rooms.

"Like it?" said Rachel when Elisheva came back in the lemon dress. "Too wide, a bit childish, I think." "Of course," Rachel laughed. "This isn't your thing at all. I just wanted you to see what you *shouldn't* wear." And she passed her a dress which she had kept ready at hand: a purple sleeveless affair with straight shoulder straps and a narrow waist. "Not too loud?" said Elisheva doubtfully. "Try it on, try it on!" Rachel urged.

When she reappeared in it the two salegirls gave cries of admiration. "How?" Rachel's eyes asked. "Not too short?" "With *your* legs?!" "Short is *in*," said Violet. "Look, darling," said Rachel, "you want to know what your color is? Wine! Wine with a deep décolleté! You've got a light complexion, big black eyes, black hair—and that's just the type can afford to wear wine. And you've got a bust—wow!—and it'd be a sin to hide it. The open door beckons to the thief, like they say, but we've seen thieves force locks. It all depends on the doorkeeper. I meant to suggest a wine-red but I knew you'd stone me, so I compromised and gave you this purple, just so long as you get the idea." "Yes, nice . . ." said Elisheva, relishing the sight of herself in the mirror as much as Rachel's words. "And now that I look at you," said Rachel, watching her, "I remember I've a dress at home that'll fit you to a T." "Oh, no, I couldn't think of it." "My dear, I've got a wardrobe that's enough to rig out a whole gala concert. Don't you worry, I'm not going to miss it. Come up to my place on the way home anyhow. No harm in looking!"

For herself, Rachel chose a cheap simple dress: white with horizontal blue stripes and the same narrow shoulder straps. She was quick to make up her mind, and though it was the only dress she tried on, it suited her olive skin and tall figure perfectly.

"You don't look a day over thirty in that," Elisheva told her. "I play tennis, darling!" said Rachel.

When Rachel opened her wardrobe at home which took up the whole of one wall, it revealed the riotousness of an Oriental bazaar, the chic of French salons, and the theatrical display of Italian nobility. Pages of Proust came to Elisheva's mind. Something very gorgeous, not quite without a comic note in the mad profusion of it all. The wardrobe reflected not Rachel's personality but her wealth and the tradition of a heterogeneous family. "How many of these do you figure I wear?" she said with a trace of ennui in her voice. "Five, six, no more. It's a museum. And like any museum—tiresome!" And shifting dresses about she gave Elisheva the pedigree of a few of them: inherited from this and that aunt, a silver anniversary present, a present brought back by her husband from a trip to Paris . . . Casually she drew out a dark-blue velvet dress with silver buttons and handed it to Elisheva. "See if it fits. I wore it about twice all told. A glass of sherry?" And she left the room without giving Elisheva time to protest. Alone, changing into it, she felt herself yielding to a stronger will than her own, and wondered at her contrary behavior. You've changed, she told herself, weakened.

"My hunch was right!" Rachel stopped in the doorway with the tray and glasses in her hand. "It just wants taking in the hem an inch or two. But apart from that—*magnifique!*"

"No, no. Thanks a lot, Rachel, but I couldn't really."

"Don't you like it?"

"I love it! But I just never have occasion to wear this sort of dress."

"Dresses create their own occasions, my dear." Approaching and offering her a glass. "A woman who owns a party dress sees to it that she'll have a party. That's how it is!"

"For people who care for that sort of thing. I'm afraid I'm not a great partygoer really."

"But you can wear this to a concert, too, to the theater . . ."

"I dress very simply for those occasions. Thanks a lot, though."

"Look, darling, I wrote this dress off the moment the idea occurred to me. I'm superstitious in these matters. Take it and hang it in your closet or do what you like with it. Maybe if you ever have a lover . . ."

"No time for such things in a job like mine. . . ." Elisheva took a sip of her sherry.

"Oh, Lord, the stories I could tell you about university professors!"

"Men."

"Don't you believe it. Only angels in heaven don't sin, and even then only because they're sexless."

"Not the Jewish ones."

"Who? Gabriel? Raphael? Those aren't angels! Those are ministers—the Minister of War, Minister of Health . . . but flesh-and-blood people? Show me the man who is without sin . . . We've tasted of the Tree of Knowledge, haven't we? Well, then. The more you know the more you sin!"

Elisheva laughed. "I'm supposed to stick to certain standards, you know."

"No, no, I wasn't referring to you," smiling at her. "I respect fidelity. I practice it myself, what's more. Even though"—and again the flash of irony in her eyes, giving her that *mondaine* look—"we all have our frailties . . . you have to make allowances . . . and it won't do any harm to sometimes turn a blind eye. . . ."

"Yes, that's true. . . ."

"Look, Shaltiel and me, we've already celebrated our silver anniversary and—thank God. But he travels a lot, I travel. . . . Think I don't know he has a little slip now and then? . . . And I'm not made of iron either. . . . So what? We never even discuss it. We both realize these things happen because we're only human. That's the whole secret of our success! Want me to give you the recipe?" she laughed.

"M'm, excellent sherry." Elisheva took another sip. "What brand?"

"Plain Israeli. My theory is that we've been given our life in order to enjoy it. But enjoy it without abandoning your self-respect, your dignity. Do things you won't be ashamed of after. Not to yourself and not to those you care for. What I really detest is the underhanded business, sneakiness, deceit—that's what I call betraying. It looks marvelous on you, this dress."

"Really, Rachel, I won't know what to do with it. . . ."

"It's yours. Not another word. Wear it in good health. On occasion!"

"I don't know how to thank you. . . ."

"Don't. I get all the thanks I want from seeing a perfect job. A woman is an object of art and it makes me sad to see an object of art that isn't displayed to advantage."

Walking home with the two dresses in her bag, she knew she would never wear the velvet but was nonetheless filled with a kind of excitement to picture herself in it. Like a prize kept in store for her, maybe in some future incarnation.

TO grow bees! thought Shuka. He was doing his best to keep up a cheerful grin but the sadness, the sadness seeped through his body and rose to his throat. In the light shining from the spangles of the old chandelier, dripping on the men's suits, the rustling dresses, the bottles, the tiered wedding cake, he felt like a bloated, blown-up bag.

"Cheer up, Daddy!" Avigayil pinched his arm, but her smile meeting his frozen grimace retreated, puzzled.

"Oxford couldn't come, of course. Too busy!" Tamara Tolkovsky darted a look at him, passing and stopping by his side. The dotted veil draped round the shoulders of the white silk dress reminded him of a picture of Desdemona in the old Russian Shakespeare.

"I told you: she has a lecturer's conference tonight. In Jerusalem."

It was the second time this evening. And now in Avigayil's presence, to incite her!

"I thought August was their holiday. Must have been wrong. Excuse me."

"I told you: a lecturers' convention. She couldn't stay away."

"I see. And shall I tell you something? I'm not sorry."

"Must you? Right now?!" Trying to stifle his anger.

For the second time. And the first had been right before the ceremony, in the rabbinate courtyard. And even before she had wiped off the sneer, her face had assumed its festive expression as she lifted her veil to sip the wine—the cup of poison—cheek by jowl with that black scarecrow with his stuck-out chest, shriveled tree.

Like a bloody waiter with that bow tie, stamping on the glass with his shoe. Mazal tov!

"But you're a good girl, Gilly. So what do you think of your old grandma: gone crazy?"

"Not at all. A second youth." Avigayil smiled down from her height.

"Your turn soon, eh?" Squeezing her hand.

"Not that soon. . . ."

"Tut-tut. Know how old I was when your father was born? Nineteen! Remember, Shuka?"

"The army didn't take one at eighteen in your time!"

"So in my time there were other things. You've got a boyfriend already, haven't you? Shuka, you told me she had a boyfriend!"

"I did not."

"All right. So you didn't! Come on, Gilly, come and help your old grandma with the guests. Fine world, I must say, where the bride has to serve her own guests. Yes, yes, I'm a bride today, my dear son!" And with a wink at Shuka and a gay, coquettish gesture, she turned on her heel, pulling Avigayil with her.

You can kiss me you know where!

"Unbelievable how young she looks, that mother of yours!" Shulamith Margolis, Boaz Margolis's mother, following Tamara's progress with a good-hearted smile.

"Yes, always." Shuka thrust a hand into his pocket and fingered his keys.

"And Dushkin—such a personality, ever so dignified."

"What's Boaz doing these days?" he asked. His glance caught Dushkin talking to Amikam Shtupler beside the long table, his skeletal hands gesticulating nervously. Old fox.

"Boaz is in Africa. Building. So well thought of. They had a baby two months ago. A Congolese baby." Laughing.

"Congratulations! Their third, isn't it?"

"Two boys and now—a girl!" Her brassy voice rang out. Big matron. Shuka thought how as a child he used to love the brown

Italian face with its infectious vitality. "And your Avigayil—a princessa! Such a big girl already!"

"Yes, nearly seventeen." He saw Dushkin pouring vodka into Shtupler's glass, his burned-out eyes lighting up as he spoke, a flicker from the embers. Discussing the market? Politics?

"A brilliant student, I'm sure, like her mother. Haven't seen Elisheva in ages."

"She had to go to a lecturers' conference tonight, in Jerusalem. . . ."

"We do hear about her though. Every so often. That time she went to England—in forty-five, was it?—I said to Blumfeld: Elisheva's a brain, you mark my words, and when she gets back . . . Excuse me," and Shulamith Margolis hurried toward the voice calling her from the other end of the room.

The scarecrow in tails and bow tie and shining silk handkerchief peeping from breast pocket approached together with fat Shtupler the hippopotamus.

"Begin? That Pole never knew the first thing about honor and distinction!" Dushkin was saying as they halted close to Shuka. *"Omnia serviliter pro dominatione.* Do you know what the crucial moment was? When Jabotinsky tore up his delegate's card at the Seventeenth Zionist Congress and forced Weizmann to step down! That's when! And who remembers Jabotinsky today? The young generation don't even know his name! But what *he* said in thirty-one, everybody's saying in sixty-six! That's the great paradox! Think anyone'd have the guts to talk against private capital the way Katzenelson and Shertok did then?"

"But we've all of us, Dushkin," Hippo raised his slow, wrinkled eyelids, "we've all of us resigned ourselves to the existing borders."

"Because we're all of us, if you'll excuse me, a birch going to rot beneath a socialist poultice, to quote Uri Zvi Greenberg! A gang of petty shopkeepers who've sold the Wailing Wall, the Temple Mount, Hebron, the Jordan not least . . ."

"West Bank and East," Shuka snorted to himself.

And he pictured the Betar, Brownshirts, left-right-left, marching through the village street, grim-faced, inspiring terror. Blue insignia, green insignia, a high-breasted girl with a whistle. Splendor. Terror.

Raise high the banner, Alexander Dushkin, and march! "The River Jordan has two banks, ta-ra-ra-boom!"

"Gilly. A knife. From the kitchen. The big one." Tamara called over the heads of the crowd.

And the Jewish labor militants mounting guard before the gates of Blumfeld's orange grove: Don't deprive the Jewish laborer of his right to work! Down with Blumfeld!

Whole Bedouin clans descending on his grove, milling about the trees, collecting in the pools of shade under the close citrus foliage. Damp earth scored by hoes. Hollows between bare roots and ants scattering in the fierce smell rising from the depths of earthen tunnels.

Blumfeld. Tobacco scraps at the corners of his pale tight mouth, and the triangle of mustache yellow with nicotine, cigarettes held between limp, fidgety fingers. He had called in the police, British cops with batons—to break them!

Poor Father, turning in his grave under the rotting leaves.

Whom do you know here? Shtupler, Sverdlov from Discount Bank, Shulamith Margolis—

Some excuse: a lecturers' conference! Only found out about it yesterday, had she?

"Remember what Oved Ben-Ami wrote when they hanged the two British sergeants in Netanya? A dastardly crime! An infamous crime! That's what! And where did he end up? Begging crumbs from Sapir's cake! Kingpin of Ashdod Harbor! Millions from the *shnorrer!* But at the Acre jailbreak . . ."

"Sasha! You back in the thirties again?" Tamara bearing the wedding cake cut into thick wedges on a silver platter high over the heads of the guests.

"We've reached the late forties already, Tamarinka." With a patting hand on the bridal veil.

She under his banner. Blue-white.

Father, embittered, grumbling in the yard: To break, huh! Who they figure they're going to break? The branch we're *all* of us sitting on!

And had contributed two pounds to the Jewish Labor Fund. As good as two hundred today.

Down with Blumfeld! Shuka laughed sourly to himself.

How it had broken the miser's heart when his daughter

announced she was going to marry that beggar Tolkovsky's son! A veterinarian. No land, no chattels. And how he'd bloody well closed his fist and not given a penny.

Except for the apartment.

Which he'd registered in *her* name.

Seated in the deep leather armchair—a portrait of the Baron Rothschild on one wall of the sunlit parlor, an embroidered Herzl on tapestry, the famous rail-leaning visionary Herzl pose—in his white colonial suit, pale, wooden hands dangling loosely over his knees, and quietly, gracious-lord-of-the-manor-to-poor-farmhand: And how are you going to support her?

"No, thanks."

"The cake's kosher, Shuka, I promise."

"Thanks, no."

"Even people in mourning eat. Afraid it'll stick in your throat?"

"No." With a defiant look at his mother.

"A great lot of wrong I've done you. All these years." Troubled tears in her eyes.

Mazal tov, mazal tov, as the apple-cheeked rabbi had said stuffing a fat bank note in his pocket. After the kiss, under the canopy, herself in raptures!

"There's only one Party, Shtupler. All the rest are nothing but a pack of yes-men and crumb pickers. The almighty ruling Party! And if you ask me when the Nationalist camp will get on its feet again, I'll tell you. What we need is not a hundred politicians, but one single prophet, someone who'd tell us, in Tchernichovsky's words: Climb the hill and charge the ramparts. . . ."

And fixed him up with a job, the Baron Blumfeld had, with Migdal Insurance. A hundred and fifty a month. Big deal!

"Oof, I'm ready to drop." Avigayil pausing beside him with a tray of sandwiches. "My head's swimming."

"We'll soon go."

"And everybody feels it's his bounden duty to compliment me on Mother's account."

"And not on your own?"

"That, too. Thanks. I don't know anyone here. Do you?"

"Four or five. The rest must be friends of the, ahem, groom."

"Oh, Daddy, stop it! What's he done to you?"

"I don't care for him," he whispered emphatically.

"But he's nice. Such a gentleman, kissing the ladies' hands, joking . . . He's good for her."

"She can have him."

"You're funny, Daddy. You talk as if you were jealous or something."

"Jealous?" Shuka laughed. "Ho-ho!"

"Pure Polish vodka seventy-two!" Dushkin thrust a glass into Shuka's hand and filled it from the bottle. "A purely anti-Semitic brew. The Poles have their own brand of savageness, you know—brutal, crude, medieval. They're vicious! Vicious Catholics! And their vodka is the essence of it."

"And Russian vodka?"

"Oh, that's something else again. Something else entirely. A Russian *improves* with drink. Turns merry, buoyant, lyrical, carried away. They've taught our Hasids a thing or two."

"Are you from a Hasidic family?"

"Me? I'm emancipated! An emancipated nationalist!" Dushkin giggled. "I don't care for Hasids. They lack dignity. But can they drink! With drink, you know, there are two possibilities—you either turn into a hog, or your spirit soars. You don't much fancy the stuff, do you?"

"Not much."

"It'd do you good though!" Stabbing a finger in his chest. "You're too reserved, full of sad thoughts, who knows what. . . . You've got to be opener, freer! . . ."

Yes, Papa, as you say, Papa. I promise. . . .

"Look at your mother, at her age . . ."

"And you. At your age."

"Yes, yes! Life is short! You see two old fogies like us . . . making fools of themselves, you think. . . . Know what one shrewd Englishman said? 'Second marriage is the triumph of hope over experience'!" Laughing.

"Hope you're not wishing it on *me!*"

"Second marriage?" He looked at him quizzically, laughed.

"Yehoshua Tolkovsky!" Sverdlov laid a heavy arm across Shuka's shoulders. "Yehoshua Tolkovsky," turning to Dushkin, "used to be a cashier with us, let's see, maybe twenty years back. First-rate cashier, too: quick, polite, and never an error in accounts. Two years! Till the Blumfeld girl came and grabbed him!"

"Europa!" said Dushkin with a roguish twinkle in his eye.

"Europa?" asked Shuka.

"Mythological associations." Dushkin grinned, raising his glass. "Your health!"

"How's business, Tal?" said Sverdlov. "Heard of our new insurance scheme? Savings-plus. Index-linked."

"Yes, saw it."

"Tax free!"

"Ten thousand."

"Quite something, eh?"

"Doesn't worry me. . . ." With a cheerless smile.

"Now *you* are a banker, Sverdlov, a businessman," said Dushkin, "so maybe you can explain to me how this government squares an austerity budget with boosting investments. They say—immigration, attracting foreign capital, which is all very well . . ."

"Know how many've *left* this country over the past six months? . . ."

"Who's for coffee?" Tamara called out.

Second marriage. Shuka wound his way between groups of people standing about, reached the passage, went into the bathroom, and locked the door.

Europa! He frowned into the mirror. Greek story? A dark cloud rested on the face in the mirror. No smile could dispel it. Wash it under this tap and it won't come off. A lasting curse.

On the glass shelf under the mirror he noticed a razor, shaving brush, smeary shaving stick. The triumph of hope over experience.

He took hold of the brush and crushed its grizzled stubble against the enamel basin, swept it over the inside, round and round—Dush-kin, Dush-kin—smearing, swiping. Limp brush. Flabby limb. Triumph of hope.

He turned to the toilet bowl, lowered his trousers, and sat. Europa. Europe and you. A sea between, you alone, and no one. London, forty-six. English students in rooms, fair-haired, tall, athletic, uncircumcised. A tumble between lectures. And nights, no doubt, she'd spread her legs in some cheap hotel. Not hotel. Rooms. Hers, theirs. You'll never find out what, who. More than twenty years. Fine Oriental custom that, to display sheet with virgin's blood on bridal night. The nakedness of thy mother. Shalt not uncover. Jeanette. Cheap affair. Good thing's finished.

He strained, head in hands, but to no effect. Just wind. Windbag. Gilly, where's your father got to? He heard beyond the door, and the handle turned twice. To sit like this, an hour, two, not to come out till all the guests are gone. Safe refuge. Like then. Like then.

Not anymore. Not with this limp, gray shaving brush on the shelf. House barred. Forever. Expelled.

From beyong the wall came the brassy voice of Mrs. Margolis jollying the guests into song: "Bear the ba-ha-nner to Zi-on, the banner of Ju-hu-hu-dah—"

I N the waning afternoon light, soft on the bustling main street of Ramleh, majestic on the sky-lancing pines of Sha'ar Hagai; in an easy flow of conversation with only brief lulls for a tentative probe into the other's mind—about Fellini's *8½*, about *Last Year at Marienbad,* about the metaphysical quality of Pinter's plays (how we understand each other, she thought, even in hints!)—the trip to Jerusalem passed in a surprisingly short time. Rising, she gave him a smile that bespoke a great measure of affection but a touch of mockery as well. Child, she wanted to say, child, why so careful all the way not to touch me with elbow or knee. But in answer to his questioning glance she smoothed her dress and said, "Pins and needles behind from sitting so long." And as she made her way through the aisle she took pains not to brush against him, not as long as he was all that particular. After getting off the bus she stopped on the pavement and gazed at some point on the southern skyline as one arriving in a foreign town. Brosh waited. "Under the spell?" he said. "What are those houses over there?" Keeping her eyes on them. "Beit Jallah," he said. "Ah, of course, Beit Jallah," she said, and still remained motionless, as though lost in admiration. Standing as though lost in admiration like that, she waited for him to say, Let's go, or to suggest a place to go to, or whatever; because when she had suggested their going to Jerusalem together the day before he had said yes, with pleasure, and he'd show her some nooks and crannies of the town where he was born and grew up. (A warm flush had swept her body when he said "nooks and crannies," and for a moment she felt giddy.) But now he was standing beside her speechless, helpless. "Those are the broadcasting station antennae there," he said at last. "Yes, yes." Smiling at him and blinking, "A strange town . . . looks different to me every time . . . As though discovering it anew. . . ." "Yes, so many-sided," and he went on staring at the horizon. Yes, indeed, how right you are, and how originally you put it! she said to herself and wondered how all the spirit had gone out of him the moment they had left the bus, after having talked so well, so freely, all the way, and last night, too, at the café. . . . Or had he suddenly lost his nerve for the adventure? Bitten off more than you can chew, my boy? . . . With a toss of her head she dismissed both her train of thought and the skyline and said, "All right. I'm ready to go. On foot. For hours. I don't care how far!" "Shall we go to Abu Tor?" he suggested. "Wherever you say!" she declared vivaciously. "I'm with you." "How about a wide circuit, through Romema, Mekor-Baruch, Meah She'arim . . ." "Lovely. Whatever you say. Even if it's all night."

But once they began to walk through the uncrowded streets, she realized how ill at ease he was. He skipped from one side to another—now she found him walking at her right, now at her left, and once she thought she had lost him altogether and found he had got himself entangled with some passersby and was hurrying to overtake her. She laughed, joked, tried to act the giggling teenager-in-love with lighthearted chatter, but only managed to embarrass him the more. After they had walked some distance and he still hadn't regained his composure, she told herself: Now it's one of two—you either pull him into some dark doorway hereabouts and crush your body against his with a kiss that'll leave him gasping, or you grab the first taxi that comes along and get back to Tel Aviv. She stopped with her back against a wall, took hold of his wrist, raised her eyes to his, and felt an urgent desire to say: Look, Amnon, let's stop this game and enter the first hotel we come to, I can't keep this up forever.... But seeing the rebuff in his eyes, as though he anticipated what she might say, she smiled and said slowly, deliberately, "You really love this town, don't you?" Brosh smiled. "You have beautiful eyes," he said. Yet searching his she found affection in them, but no desire, and felt like hitting him. And since she couldn't hit him she tried to stir some life into him. "Let's go to Silwan, h'm?" Her eyes shone moist and her voice betrayed a sad yearning. Brosh laughed. "Of course I love this town," he said. "Jealously!" And as they walked on she only half heard what he was saying. He was saying that a man's birthplace is like a mother—hence the Biblical "city and mother"—and that the Old City, with its bowels of blind alleys, its gory markets, its warmth, dimness, was like a mother's womb which after one leaves it one goes out into the cold and longs all one's life, both in love and resentment, to come back to. . . . She only half heard, and didn't care for the simile, was irked by it. "I always thought Zion was a virgin!" she interrupted. *"Was,"* laughing, "before she was deflowered." "And then what?" "Then she became debauched. . . ." "So you've an Oedipus complex!" "Why?" "Because you're jealous, you said so!" "Maybe it's because she has a Moslem for her lord and master. . . ." "That why you joined the Stern Gang?" "I used to be close to the Canaanites as well." "For the same reason then, apparently." She felt like telling him about Yehuda Dolav, him, too, in the nationalist underground, her first love, and here in Jerusalem, in this very neighborhood, Kerem Avraham, with its prim houses, chaste green shutters on rusting iron hinges, but she checked herself. He was talking in the abstract, without warmth, and she resented him. Stupid idea, she fumed at herself, this trip to Jerusalem, and now all this aimless trudging. The spoiled boy detests responsibility and you are asking him to lead you through his town, lead you to your fulfillment—what wonder he refuses! "Where *are* we going, as a matter of fact?" she stood still. "To Abu Tor, didn't we say?" "Why Abu Tor?" "For a view of Silwan, remember?" Elisheva smiled, mollified. The tranquil charm of his eyes in the Jerusalem twilight. The Biblical waters of Silwan "that go softly." *You* lead him to the dark caverns of the city's womb. "I'll have to find a place to sleep," she said softly, at peace now. "Help you?" She studied his eyes again. No, no hint of depravity in them, not a touch of ambiguity. "I'll just make a call. Wait for me."

Dialing in a nearby shop she again felt a moment of dizziness, like last night, when he said that about showing her "nooks and crannies." At the Scottish Hospice they gave you a key to the front door and you could let yourself in at any hour of the night without anyone being the wiser. And the building stood apart, sunk in darkness and enveloped in a fierce scent of pines. When the familiar woman's voice said she had a room available, on the second floor at the end of the corridor, and she could come whenever it suited her as the front door would be left unlocked, a pulse throbbed in her temples. Dangerous, dangerous, and'll end in disaster, she told herself. Utter madness.

"I didn't even take a nightgown," she said when she returned to him. "I came as I am, with just this handbag."

"Found a place?"

"At the Scottish Hospice. They know me there. It's where I always stay when I'm in Jerusalem."

"In a church, of all places?"

"Why not? The pastor and his wife are pleasant, broad-minded people, there aren't any idols or saints or anything, and besides . . . I'm no rabbi's daughter. . . ."

"A whiff of faraway Scotland . . ."

"Not really. What you see from the second floor is a view of the Old City, the Wall. . . . I might be able to make out the house you were born in . . . if you showed me. . . ."

"There's not a stone of it standing. . . . Mind if I call in on my mother for a few minutes? Tell her I'm here."

"I'll wait for you at some café nearby."

"Come along and meet her."

She looked at him, uncertain. "Are you offering me both city and mother?"

"Faded gold, both of them," he said.

Dusk had already descended on the Bukharan Quarter and a smell of pita bread and pepper and damp laundry came from its paved courtyards. She was listening to his stories again—one about a wealthy Bukharan widow who had secretly married a poor Talmudic scholar from Hungary and kept him locked up in her attic for fear of what her fellow Bukharans would say; one about a Georgian stonecutter who had hidden a treasure of jewels in the cistern in his yard and was buried together with it when the house collapsed; and about a teacher at Lämel School who would make passes at the girls and in the end turned out to have been a missionary. Tales of a Palestine of Turks and Arabs and a tiny Jewish community that roused memories of her own student days on Mount Scopus. His voice was confident and, now and then, as he spoke, held an exciting note of sensuality.

When they reached the deserted alleys of Beit-Yisrael and his nearness in the dark, the seclusion, was making her flesh ache, she told herself he was tormenting her deliberately, yes, deliberately, never even touching her hand. And if it wasn't deliberate then he was simply obtuse and didn't deserve another thought. "Listen, *must* you go to your mother?" She stood still. "I'm going to sleep there and I can't just surprise her in the middle of the night. . . ." "M'm, I see." She walked on. How reasonable! "Why?" he asked. She glanced at him and said with a smile, "I thought perhaps we could go up to Mount Scopus. . . ." Brosh laughed. "We'd end up on the Mount of Olives," he said.*

Brosh knocked at the door and a small woman, her soft gray hair covered with a black veil, opened and looked surprised at the sight of her son.

"This is Elisheva, Mother. She teaches at Tel Aviv University. . . ."

"Elisheva what?" Inspecting her face.

"Tal-Blumfeld."

"Both Tal and Blumfeld?" With a smile. Her face had a peaceful, gentle look.

"Tal is my husband's last name."

"Come in, come in." Seating them by the table in her cramped, spotless room.

---

*Between 1948 and 1967, Mount Scopus and the Mount of Olives were Jordanian territory. The Mount of Olives, one slope of which is a Jewish cemetery, has become synonymous with "cemetery."—TRANS.

"Jews often have names like Moshe-Haim or Avraham-Baruch, but last ones . . . Tal is a beautiful name!" Her voice was mild, Elisheva noted.

"Too short for a university teacher," Brosh joked.

"Modern ways," said Elisheva. "Women want to show they're independent."

"Yes, yes, I know. . . . Remember that English lady from the Scottish hospital, Amnon?"

"Bruce-Collins."

"Yes, Bruce-Collins, and she was *not* married. A very agreeable, cultured woman. Not Jewish though. . . . And you teach what?"

"Literature."

"And that's how you met my son. I see. I didn't know they had a university in Tel Aviv!" Turning to Amnon as though in reproach.

"It's very new," said Elisheva, "just a few years."

"I knew the Jerusalem university when it was on Mount Scopus. I don't know where it is now. I'm told it exists—I believe them. Where is it, this new place?" Turning to her son.

"You know, Mother, you know quite well." Laughing.

"The Terra Sancta building?"

"You know. I showed you!"

"I don't remember." Shrugging. "Will you have tea?"

Elisheva declined, and the old lady did not urge her.

"Born here?" she asked.

"Yes. Nes-Ziona."

"Myself I must have been seven or eight when I saw Nes-Ziona for the first time. Before they built the railway that was. There used to be a coachman in Jaffa, Gissin was his name, who'd drive you to Rishon, and then you had to walk the rest of the way on foot, through the dunes. Hot it was, and no shadow. But I was a little girl."

"With your father?"

"Father, blessed be his memory, was an agent for Singer machines and he often used to take me with him. That's how I came to know the country thereabouts, the villages, and Ramleh, Lydda, as far down as Gaza we used to go. But it's many years since I've been to Nes-Ziona. Not since the wedding of Batya

Katz, who is a relative of ours on her mother's side. Her mother is a niece of Mordechai Leherer's, him who bought up all the Wadi Chanin land. Are there any of the Leherers left?"

"Grandchildren."

"And Tal, your husband, he from Nes-Ziona as well?"

"Tolkovsky they used to be called. They came later." She felt a sudden chill. For the first time since leaving Tel Aviv she remembered that tonight, at this very moment, old Tolkovsky was getting married.

"Tolkovsky the bookbinder?"

"No, he was a veterinarian."

"We used to have a bookbinder by name of Tolkovsky in the Old City. You remember him, Amnon, next to the Beit-Yoseph yeshiva he lived. A great scoundrel. And when he moved to the Plain we all breathed easier. Not least Moshe Salomon, who was his competitor." Laughing. "So if you teach literature you must have read my son's stories."

"Certainly!"

"And what do you think of them?"

"She's a severe critic, Mother."

"I think they are good," said Elisheva.

"Myself I don't read them. My legs are too old."

"Your legs?"

"It's like walking over rocks. Walking and stumbling, walking and stumbling. Why write such difficult language?"

"These here are also written in a difficult language." Elisheva turned her eyes to the large bookcase taking up one wall with row upon row of Talmud volumes.

"Sacred literature is for studying, not reading," Amnon's mother said unperturbed. "But stories? Our Jewish stories are written very simply, anybody can understand them. But his . . . No, I can't read him."

"Yet you did, for all that," Amnon chuckled.

"Did I?" Wondering.

"You even offered me some comment. Quite right you were, too. About the dog."

"What dog?"

"You said no Arab in the Negev would ever fetch a pail of water for a dog who belonged to someone else. Remember?"

"You really made a mistake there! And you made others, too. The ravens! Who said there are no ravens in the Negev? I once went to Hebron with your father of blessed memory, before the great massacre that was, and we saw ravens, plenty of ravens all the way there!"

"Hebron isn't the Negev," Elisheva remarked.

"You don't think the ravens stop dead on the roof of the Machpela Cave, do you? If they come to Hebron they'll fly on to the Negev as well! You get ravens everywhere! The Prophet Elijah, when he dwelt in the desert . . . But why do I stick my old nose in? If you say it's a good story, and you teach literature at the university, then I'm sure it's so. Myself I don't read it. No. And your husband, what does he do?"

"He's an insurance salesman." Taking cigarettes out of her handbag.

"Insurance. That's good. A steady income, I'm told."

"He's even managed to insure me," Amnon laughed.

"You? What do you want insurance for? You have no wife, no children," she said unhappily.

"I have a mother!"

"God have mercy!" In shocked alarm. "For me? That if maybe, God forbid, God forbid . . . No, no. You signed already?"

"It's like a kind of saving, Mother."

"Saving? If you've money to spare then put it in the bank, buy papers, but insurance? For my sake? Father, bless his memory, when they came to him with insurance . . ."

Elisheva observed the harmony that reigned between mother and son, both tacitly complying with the rules of a game of verbal ping-pong: he knows all about her tongue-in-cheek innocence, her feigned ingenuousness, and accepts them, and she knows he knows, and knows he loves it; he adores her equable sagacity and she basks in his adoration. And she noted the facial likeness between the two: the light, sea-gray eyes, the sheer transparency of the temples, and above all the mouth—thin, taut upper lip over full, fleshy, well-defined lower lip. And when they smiled, it would be frugally—the smile confined to the corners of the mouth. Their whole character, she thought, was expressed in those lips: a combination of intellectual tension, strong-willed and with a touch of malice, with an impetuous, pleasure-principled sensuality. When her glance rested on his mouth, she could imagine herself biting the underlip and tasting its blood, could imagine a grappling, a throwing him down on a carpet of pine needles in a wood. A flush covered her face: as though the scene were enacted before the mother's eyes.

A full moon, red Jericho pomegranate, gazed down upon the streets of Meah, She'arim, poured its filmy light over paved courtyards, deserted balconies, stone gates, religious interdicts stuck up on walls. Brosh knew each house, its inhabitants, its history. Here, he told her, lived one Silberschlag who in forty-seven had refused to leave the defeated Jewish Quarter come what may and had to be dragged out by force; here—one of the Bratzlayer Hasids who wrote amulets and spells and magic cures; here—the mad bagel woman who had allegedly mixed poison in the dough . . .

Yes, Mister Guide, thought Elisheva, I am inexpressibly grateful for these instructive bits of Jerusalem lore. In just this tone of voice, evincing relish in the telling and unconcern with the listener, you might be spinning them to no-matter-who, man or woman. Why not admit you are running on like that just to avoid a coming face-to-face with me, a personal intercourse of whatever kind, whatever degree of intimacy, not to mention physical contact, perish the thought. Because as a matter of fact you are afraid of me. I mean scared out of your wits by the idea of being alone with me, in a situation that might make a demand upon your manhood. Is it due to a lack of self-confidence? Or is the lack of self-confidence due to the fact that I am older than you, more experienced, married? Or maybe—

Maybe I do not exist as an erotic object at all as far as you are concerned, but only as an intellectual lady with whom it is agreeable—or not so agreeable—to discuss occasionally Pinter, Sartre, Steiger, classical and nonclassical openings of stories.

If that's the case we may as well part company right now, and I'll leave you to this romantic setting of stars and stone fortresses and moonstruck valley which—yes, I admit, make me feel a bit light in the head—

"I suppose you lived in a ghetto till you were actually quite grown-up . . ." she broke in.

"Yes, practically speaking, yes. First in the Old City and later in a religious neighborhood. . . ."

"With all the bans and prohibitions and taboos. . . ."

"Quite."

"And God help you if you so much as looked at a woman!"

"Looked?" he laughed. "When I was sixteen we had a Sephardi washerwoman . . ."

And all of a sudden she felt relieved. Like that time when he had brought the book and everything had turned easy and simple. He told her about the washerwoman and how she would squat in the yard with the laundry tub between her plump knees, giving him an occasional tantalizing glimpse of her thighs accompanied by inviting leers. Sometimes she would ask his help with shifting the tub or hanging up laundry, and would press her thighs or breasts against him. When he had refused her advances time and again, she accused him of having stolen money from her purse, set up a hue and cry, and since no one believed her she cleared out of the house and was never seen again.

"The righteous Joseph!" Elisheva laughed.

"Not all that righteous after all. For weeks afterward I was consumed with remorse. . . ."

"For harboring sinful thoughts . . ."

"For not seizing my chance!"

"For that!" She burst out laughing. "So why didn't you, then?"

"Because I didn't have enough imagination."

"To foresee the pleasure involved?"

"To see that this pleasure was actually attainable. I just couldn't believe it!"

"The Gates of Repentance are ever open!"

"Not hers! . . ."

"Poor Amnon." Linking her arm in his and rubbing her head against his shoulder. "When was the first time you did sleep with a woman?" Whispering, her face raised at his.

"Twenty-two, three. . . ."

"When you got married?"

"Oh, no, long before that!"

"In spite of the bans and taboos . . ."

"Ah, yes, the flesh is weak. . . ." Sighing.

"My poor saint. . . . Was it at Gethsemane?"

"Not far from there."

"Do you know I had my first great love here in Jerusalem?"

"Tell me about it."

In front of them, past the twisting alleys of Sham'ah, the Old City wall appeared luminous in the moonlight, and beyond it the white chalk rock of Mount Zion, a few shrubs, rooftops glimmering through a cluster of pines. A little farther on, proud in its loneliness, stood the Scottish Church, its tower crowned by a halo.

Speech was growing difficult, and between sentences she made an effort to silence her breathing. You ought to be ashamed of yourself, she thought, panting like a bitch in heat. And at the same time: Yes, like a bitch, why not? To be abandoned, cheap, whorish, why not? I'll abandon myself tonight—come what may!

Where the street ended in a stretch of barren field strewn with shrubs and boulders, she stopped with her back against a wall, and taking his hand pulled him to her and gave him a fierce look that said: I shall kill you tonight! Brosh smiled and bent his head toward her as if to kiss her hair, but she laid her hand over his mouth and pushed his head away and whispered, breathing hard, "You've no idea how . . ." and added to herself, "vulgar I am." She looked away toward the tower of the Scottish Church from which only a short walk separated them now. It stood there as a silent promise of bliss, and it would be a waste to nibble at it and leave yourself half hungry. "Come, come," she said, drawing his arm around her waist, and after a few steps, laughing: "Literature and criticism walking hand in hand . . ."

"And to the church, what's more!" Joining in her laughter.

Two dew-decked cars were parked on the gravel of the yard and the pine trees were shedding a shower of needles upon them. Soft, careful rays of moonlight crept tentatively over the walls of the building, the tower, the slumbering windows. Softly, carefully, Elisheva opened the door and led him by the hand through the entrance hall, through the light from one window, through the sweet scent of prayer books and ancient furniture; on tiptoe up the marble staircase to the second floor, along the passage, to the last room. She opened the door, closed it behind them, and with her hand still on the knob she pulled his face close and crushed her lips to his. Under the veil of moonlight she whispered to herself with closed eyes: You are caught, my poor saint, caught, caught! Her bag slipped from her hand to the floor.

"I'd no idea you . . ." he whispered to the hot breath of her mouth when she undid the buttons of his shirt with impatient fingers.

"I know." Sealing his lips. I know, know, know. Don't talk now. I am savage, abandoned, cheap, the joy of it, of your tongue in my mouth, mine in yours, yes yes yes, you are as hot as I am, as eager, just wait, wait, I'll get out of these, not like that, the zipper, yes, just one button, yes, free, oh, your marvelous hands, caressing, carousing, on fire, and now I am all, and you all, I go mad when you squeeze my breasts against your hard chest and the honey flows from me, pours from me, where were you all these nights when I was sick with longing to melt beneath these fingers playing on my flesh, come now, come, not here, there, on the bed, yes, on the bedspread, yes, no matter, yes, now, pierce me, prick me, yes, like that, yes, that, you are a god, a giant, a rearing giant, you never knew what a slut I was, yes, a common slut spreading her legs, her womb, toward this giant, this rash, rushing, oh, heaven, toward this torch, more, more, more, how big and wonderful you are, I am mad, melting, gone, oh, god!

"A classic opening," she laughed afterward, burying her face against his chest, appeased, curled up against him.

"And the rhythm, too," kissing her ear, "so personal. . . ."

"You can boast to yourself that . . ." Her giggle trailed off against his throat.

"That what?"

"That . . . you've fixed literary criticism." Hiding her laughing face in his arms.

"Or vice versa?" He laughed.

"I don't care, my Ulysses." With a kiss on his underlip.

"Homer?"

"Joyce, Joyce." Wrapping her leg around his thigh.

"**Y**ES, I see him occasionally."

"Well, and?"

"And what?"

"And what's he like?" Dinah's winsome, innocent curiosity on the other side of the line.

"H'm ... rather unstable, I'd say."

"In what way?"

"Hard to explain. . . . What are you doing at the moment?"

"Nothing special."

"Feel like going out a bit? To the beach?"

"Lovely!"

"Hop into a swimsuit, sun ourselves."

Lying in a deck chair, exposed to the sun and breeze, she wanted to rebuke Dinah for neglecting herself: the pink freckled shoulders had grown a bit too chubby, and so had her legs and her bosom. Village girl, wild growth. Comparing her own figure to Dinah's, she seemed the younger of the two: the narrow waist, the thighs ... Contentedly she felt the sun seeping into her body, her body storing up heat, for the whole day, the night.

"Cynara?" She lowered her shoulder straps, baring her breasts to below the cleft.

"Oh, you know the kind!" Dinah said spiritedly, "Sort of tall, bushy thistle with fuzzy bloom. . . . You grew up in a village, didn't you?"

"I never knew names of plants. Blue?"

"No, not a globe thistle, bigger than that, branching out. . . . Anyway, they grow all along the edge of our field right up to the railway tracks. So on Sunday the two of us, my brother and I, took scythes and went to mow down the cynara. They fall with a huge crash, you know, like trees! Like that 'how are the mighty'! And the kid makes fun of me all the time because I'm so out of practice. . . . See these scratches? The thistles kept falling on top of me. But what a marvelous feeling! You know what the air in Jezreel is like: about ten you get this hot scorching wind with a smell of dry hay, flaming in your face, swaddling you sort of, and you feel as if you're ... land-sick, yes, land-sick. . . ."

"And, uh ... did you work all those days?" Elisheva looked at her affectionately.

· 165 ·

And felt she had grown away from Dinah in the last three weeks. Hard to believe how much.

"It was marvelous! We made bonfires to burn the thistles. . . . And for two whole days we did nothing but weed nettles. The place is teeming with them, always has been ever since I can remember, and we always used to weed and weed and we haven't managed to get rid of them yet. Kind of stubborn growth, you know, with immense vitality, and doing a terrible lot of harm. Well, so me in sandals, and the kid in his bare feet, but whose feet would get stung? Only mine, of course, city girl that I am! . . . Yes, and one day we climbed Giv'at Hamoreh. . . . I only stayed five days altogether, but what worlds apart! . . . I come to the village and it is all like of old, I start taking care of the milking, the feeding troughs, collecting the eggs . . . and it's all so natural. . . . When I got back to town, you know, I asked myself what in fact am I doing. . . . I missed the feel of soil under my feet, those little crumbly clods. . . . And the space and stillness sort of buzzing through the thistle stalks. . . . But after a week or two I get used to the city again and forget and walk the pavements like a proper urbanite, looking at the shop windows . . . too soon. . . ." She gave a little rueful laugh.

"Yes . . ." Elisheva glanced at her absentmindedly.

"Oh, and listen: we have some olive trees in our yard, you know, so in one of them, in a little crevice in the trunk, we found the nest of a titmouse. You know the kind—that cute little bird with the crest and the yellow underside? Well, when I came, the female was brooding, and we used to go and watch the male bring her insects, worms, and feed them to her with his beak. Then one morning we saw the male was gone and the hen was sitting on the eggs and uttering heartbreaking little cheeps of despair. . . . So what did my brother do? He took a long piece of wire and stuck a worm on the end, like a fish bait, you know, and dangled it over the nest. . . ."

Just don't let him play me the same trick he did last week, Elisheva thought, staring out to sea, when he left me pacing the pavement in front of his house like a streetwalker, up and down, forty minutes on the clock, before he had the goodness to show up. And the big idea: an editorial meeting. Ha! Who ever heard of an editorial meeting in the evening? A flimsy excuse which argues a measure of naïveté. But you forgive him, in the end you forgive, and you will again tonight if he keeps you waiting like that, please God that he won't. Of course I'll forgive, of course, how can I fail to, the way he plays your body like an instrument even before everything, before, when you sit on his knees in the armchair and his fingers only just brush against your nipples through the thin silky dress, idly as it were, acting as if he couldn't care and saying things of grave import about Cabala and the mysteries and God knows what while you are quivering inside, you and your nerves on edge, pretending to listen to him and all of you ravaged, swamped, aching for him to, for you to be grabbed and letting go and losing yourself, and you squint at that narrow bed in the bachelor's den of this ascetic, wild and tumbled room, books and books all anyhow, Hebrew and English, Petronius and Donne, and Dylan Thomas, and anthropology, and mythology, wonder if he's read them all. His insight deeper than yours anyway, *his* intuitive. Bring flowers tonight, add a female touch to male domain. Buy a Chinese vase, like the one you saw in that boutique, and a picture to put on the wall instead of that awful Rodin—incredible lack of taste for a person like him—and change that cheap curtain, too, and a new bedspread, Persian or Bukharan embroidery, a red lilac, exotic, over the bed so narrow there is only place for two astraddle, and rolling to the floor, like then, the second or third night, when we imagined we'd woken up the whole house. Wonder what he thinks, that man next door who's seen me twice already, bad luck, a doctor or something, German anyway, seen me leaving at one or two after midnight. Smiled at me though. Who cares? Yes, for a four poster I'd change it, sumptuous, with heavy drapes and high cushions, like at Windsor or Fontainebleau, like Marie Antoinette or Maria Theresa, and me in a green silk flowing gown crouching like a tigress—

"A real domestic tragedy: Father titmouse vanished without a trace, and then the mother as well. And the fledglings, three in all, were only beginning to come out of the eggs, scratching and picking at the shell, and unless they were fed they were going to die within hours. So we fetched bread crumbs from the kitchen dipped in milk, and my brother climbed up the tree with the crumbs in one hand. . . ."

Or last Friday, when at eleven, even before we'd got anywhere, he packed me off home. You've got to go, Elisheva, as if he were anxious for my domestic peace, for my worried husband who might be standing by the window keeping vigil. Such moral rectitude! Fake, really. I wonder whether right in the midst he isn't maybe being alive to my husband's supposedly sitting up to await the wife of his bosom? Moral cowardice, rather, not rectitude. The constant fear of getting involved, God forbid he should get involved. Wants to go scot-free. Or maybe he identifies with him, who knows? Betrayer with betrayed. Who maybe himself was the betrayed once. Male solidarity. Perfectly ridiculous *he* should worry, not me. And why should I, when Shuka never asks about my coming or going, never where, how, when, always trusting, never occurs to him I'm capable, the cuckold. Wonder where the expression comes from, Artemis, isn't it, who turned somebody into a horned ram when she went bathing nude in the river. To capture her lover's heart. Artemis? Anyway, it's not my fault if he doesn't ask where are you going and where have you been? And maybe he senses something after all, like the other Friday when I wouldn't let him and afterward he didn't say a word all next day. Of course I will, will let him, of course, but not the same night! Not whenever it pleases him! When it pleased me; no, I'm not indifferent, no, but not in the same way. Something different, blind. Stop it, Doctor, will you, stop comparing!

"Like a return to childhood, sort of. And getting back to town it's as though at a stroke, hey, presto I'm a grown-up once more. Like Alice and her magic bottle. Like a biological experience or something. Haven't you ever felt like that?"

"Like what?"

"As if suddenly finding yourself in a different incarnation of yourself and not knowing exactly . . ."

"Yes. . . ."

You know you wouldn't do it. You'd never leave him.

"And maybe it's good after all. I hoard, like a pond hoarding sun—and afterward I sit here in my room in town and produce little scribbles on paper and the images float to the surface like bubbles of childhood. . . . But I run on and on. . . . Now you tell."

"What about?"

"It's ages since we saw each other. . . . You were going to tell me something about Amnon Brosh."

"Nothing important really. . . ."

"I met him a few days ago."

"You did?" Feeling the crimson flush and trying to check it.

"On Dizengoff, about noon. I'd never have dared go over, you know, I never go near those literary hangouts anyway, but Avishag Rochel was sitting there and called me, so I joined them, and I'm glad I did. He's always made me wonder about him, that man."

"As a writer . . ."

"Not only. No. Or maybe it *is* the same thing in his case. He's so much *there* in his stories, his personality positively shines out of them. . . ."

Elisheva felt a twinge of envy: another partner, even if only passive, to share in what must be hers alone. Who'd invited *her* in?

"And did he come up to expectation?"

"Oh, he did! Just as I'd imagined him. And it made me so glad inside. . . . The sort of glad feeling, you know, that here life was sparing you at least one disappointment. . . . Because it happens so rarely. Life's so liberal with them. . . ."

"What did you talk about?"

"He didn't say much. A word now and then. But even a few words can make you sense the fullness within, you know, so calm on the outside and with such a restlessness underneath, something always stirring and seething. . . . Sort of like this landscape, you know, trembling with unrest beneath the apparently warm and serene air. . . ."

This honest peasant girl was beginning to annoy her with her talk. Who wanted her butting in anyway?

"He thinks a lot of you. . . ."

"Of me?" A startled laugh escaping her.

"I mentioned you in connection with that article. He praised it highly. Said it's a pity you don't write regularly. About Hebrew literature."

"How perfectly ridiculous!" she exclaimed and felt the crimson betraying her outright now.

"Why?"

"Because he's lying in his teeth! He didn't like the piece at all. Said it was difficult, and involved, and scholarly . . ." Her voice sounding much too loud in her ears.

"No, no, he speaks of you with real respect."

"Speaks of me!" With a loud snort. How dare he! she fumed, in public. Flaunting all the night secrets in broad daylight. And with *respect!*

"Don't you believe him?"

"Oh, I told you, he's unstable"—lifting handfuls of sand and heaping it on her feet—"quite unstable."

"I didn't notice . . ." Dinah said doubtfully.

"He comes of a religious family, you know." Pouring a thin trickle of sand over her ankle.

"Yes, born in the Old City, wasn't he?"

"M'm, rabbi's son."

"Mother still living, I think."

"You know he used to be married."

"Yes, I told you myself."

"That's right, so you did."

"But I don't know anything about his wife. Do you?"

"Me!" Smiling. "How should I?" And picked up another handful and watched the sand spill in a thin flow against her bronzed thigh, trace a rivulet across the curve, through the golden down, and slither off.

"Think he's got any interest in women at all?" said Dinah uncertainly.

"Why do you ask?" Elisheva smiled at her.

"He looks so sort of diffident, detached, withdrawn. . . ."

"Oh, never trust their looks." Quickly brushing the sand off her thigh. "Let's take a dip, h'm?"

Waves trip rippling in the sun. The vast space. How swift she is, that peasant girl, rising way ahead, diving, rising, diving, gaining distance like a streaking seal. To lie like this, flat on your back, face the sun with closed eyes, arms and legs barely pad-

· 170 ·

dling, locked in light, rocked by water, and you welter-swelter in an enormous hammock, boundless sea sheet, God holding the edges. You cradled, no land, no skyline, light splashing your eyelids and day shall not wane into evening. Whatever you are, whatever may be, he is yours. Yours and not. A wave. Dipping, may be gone suddenly. Won't see him. Oh, I'd die then, die. Don't think. Wave. Dip. I'd curse the day I saw. Heard. His name. Yes, even then, before I saw, only heard his name, heart skipped. I remember. Fate. Fate hell. Shouldn't. Have. Started. End hard. Inevitable. Man proposes. Wave. How much longer you give it? A month, two, three, but the end is bound to come, bound to, how will you bear it? I will. Unless. Yes. Unless. No choice. Why not? Flash of bird. Not hawk, not vulture, maybe gull. Hovering high, wheeling. Where are you, Dinah, to give it name? My golden peacock flew away o where my golden peacock. Even if you'd ended, even if left, even if run away, he wouldn't have stayed with you. You force him, trap, violate. As he said: For the first time in my life I'm not giving account to myself, bow to necessity. Can interpret that two ways. Try not calling him, ten days, not a chance you'll hear of him. He'd be only too glad, relieved. Don't think, don't. One night you enter his room, announce: I'm through with my husband for good. Oh, God, he'd freeze with horror, have a fit! Can see his white face, the shock, the dismay, he'd run to the end of the world to escape you. Not his conscience, no, abject fear. To bear the responsibility, the guilt, all that rubbish. Better stop. At once. I couldn't. Rather die. Wave dipping. Wheel, no turning back. Oh, these notions, about the point of relationships. Their point. What point except happiness? Moment by moment. Stolen by day, stolen by night. Day by day, night by night, maybe for years, maybe forever. This very night to go to his room, sun all of me, salt, scalding. Burning night, night divine. Drowning. Where am I, where is the shore? Round and round the sun turns sun burns. Don't think. Come what may. Just don't leave me suddenly, not unawares, warn me beforehand. I beseech you. Rapture to lie like this flat on back, eyes closed leaf on water, no north no south no past no morrow no ravens no books no sorrow no cloud to shroud sun only radiance blessing caressing your body, this body that tonight, this very night, yes, Dr. Blumfeld, yes.

"**F**OR you." Elisheva handed the receiver to Shuka hurrying in from the kitchen, and went back to combing her hair before the mirror.

His heart froze: the nasal drawl, the sensual voice here in the bedroom, under his wife's eyes! "Gogo?" His breath choking him he blurted, "Sorry," slammed the receiver.

"Who was it?" Elisheva glanced at him from the mirror.

"Wrong number, I guess," he said and turned to go back to the kitchen.

"She asked for Tal! *Mister* Tal!"

"Don't know her." In a hot haste to leave, hide, disappear.

And sitting at the kitchen table, face flaming: a trap, a plot.

And decided to drive over to her place at once, to warn, tell her to never dare . . . But at that instant the telephone rang again.

"Mr. Tal!" Elisheva called, the receiver high over her head.

"Your girlfriend," she whispered, handing him the receiver.

"Yes?" he breathed out of the burning. And heard the honeyed, cajoling voice: "What's the matter with you, Gogo, not to even . . ."

"Oblige me by calling at the office during office hours." And he hung up.

"The girlfriend?"

"Sure, sure!" With a hollow laugh.

"Still?"

"Some pain in the neck." Turning to go.

"Why did you get all red then?"

"Me?" Laughing.

"You're a bad liar, Shuka. Look at the mess you made of it in just three minutes: first you hung up and said it was a wrong number. Then you said you didn't know her, even though she asked for you by name. Then you told her to call you up at the office, which means you *do* know her. And now you tell me she's a pain in the neck, which means you've been talking to her before."

"I wanted to get rid of her, can't you see?" he cried with an exaggerated show of annoyance, and comforted himself with the thought that now his blush might be attributed to anger. "She's a client with a claim for damages, and every single day . . ."

"All right! I don't care the least who she is. . . . I just wanted to point out that even if she *were* someone who's stuck on you . . ."

"Oh, sure!"

"You don't have to get so rattled. It isn't the end of the world."

"On the contrary!" Laughing.

"She's got an interesting voice, anyhow, this client of yours. Very sexy!" She smiled at him while applying lipstick.

"I hadn't noticed." Returning to the kitchen.

She might call again, the bloody fool! he thought, pouring the rest of the soup from his plate into the sink. In a minute, in an hour, even in the middle of the night. Suddenly, wake us all up: "Gogo?"

He was thinking how to forestall her: leave the receiver off maybe, cut the wires. Else it might end in disaster. Utter ruin.

Or some evening when he'd be out she'd ring up and tell Elisheva: I'm sure you know that your husband . . .

They're capable of anything, her sort.

Must salvage. At once. Go to her, tonight, tell her in so many words: It's all over. And what happened was only an accident, won't happen again.

And make no mistake: I love my wife and she loves me. We have a happy family life and I'll be much obliged if you . . .

She'll only laugh of course: I know, Gogo! All I want is . . .

And she won't let go. Just to spite!

Capable of anything, her sort.

"I'm off, Shuka." Elisheva standing by the kitchen door in her purple dress with the shoulder straps. "Be back about eleven, twelve." Her eyes stayed on his face for a moment, smiling, as though searching it for what had happened before, then she came and kissed his cheek. "So long, Shuka."

Shuka was surprised: a kiss, tonight of all things? After that phone call? To console him?

But was relieved to hear the door close behind her.

He wiped the table, piled the dishes into the sink, listening: the telephone was silent. Not a sound out of it. The silence was comforting, cheering. He went to the bedroom, stopped in the doorway, and looked at the instrument, reassuring himself: yes, silent, not a sound out of it.

He knocked lightly on Avigayil's door.

He found her on the bed, curled up on her side, an open book at her elbow.

"What are you reading?"

Avigayil tilted the front cover to show him: *Dream Threshold—Poems,* Dinah Lev.

"Dinah Lev! Where'd you get that?"

"Mother."

"Good?"

He saw the answer in her shining eyes.

He picked up the book, leafed through it. "Understand them?"

"Why not?"

He paused at a page, read. "Interesting?"

"Sad."

"Dinah Lev? Such a . . . sunny girl!"

"Very lonely, it seems." Swinging her legs to the floor and sitting up.

"Yes . . . maybe. . . ."

"Want to read it?"

"I'll try. . . ." Shuka smiled at her affectionately. "But why are *you* sad?"

Avigayil shrugged her shoulders. Tears welled up in her eyes.

"What is it, Gilly? Anything wrong?" he said gently.

"No . . . nothing . . . the poems . . ."

"That much?"

Her wet eyes open on him, she said:

"Do you know what it means when someone writes about death . . . as though it meant happiness? . . ." She buried her face in her hands.

He was shaken: her shoulders twitched. She was crying.

Then she stood up and wiped her eyes. "Don't know what got into me all of a sudden." She smiled through her tears and went out of the room.

Helplessly he followed her, found her in the study, standing in front of the bookcase, her finger trailing across a row of books. For a long moment he hesitated, then said:

"Look, Gilly, you're on holiday now, why don't you go away for a bit?"

He waited for her to say something, his eyes taking in the bright hair coming down to her shoulders, the slender back. He asked himself what it was that troubled her.

"You might go and stay with Grandfather for a week or two . . . or you might go to that girl in Netanya . . . or even to Eilat. You could stay in a hotel there, go swimming. I could easily spare you a hundred and fifty, two hundred pounds . . ."

Tough nut. May stay silent like that for hours, won't answer you, won't turn her back, sealed, keeping you out.

The light of the foaming wave tops, of the glittering sand, struck at his eyes. Drops of sweat stuck to his lashes and he had difficulty spotting the dingy stand perched at the foot of the dunes. He wiped his forehead, his neck, halted at some distance, watching. Through the rows of deck chairs, the greased faces of women, the piles of colorful clothing, the damp, slippery infants scurrying about, the balls ping-ponging in rhythm with the waves, he saw that the rickety wooden platform in front of the stand would never for a moment be deserted: a child with a popsicle, two children with popsicles, a woman with a glass of lemonade, a potbellied man wolfing a doughnut, an athletic young man glued to a transistor radio . . . and saw her hand going out to serve and retrieve. If she had been alone he would have gone over, ordered a glass of lemonade, said lightly, offhandedly: What's up, Jeanette, you phoning me at home? And if she would smother him with endearments as usual, he would reply, Oh, you know, it wasn't serious . . . you've plenty of handsome young fellows . . . you never thought that I, a married man . . .

A tennis ball struck his leg and he bent, wanted to hurl it in a wide arc, high and far; but its owner, black-haired and agile, forestalled him with a long arm, snatched it and ran back to his place. With an admiring gaze Tal followed the ball flying back and forth between the rackets with hard rhythmic thuds, never missing its aim, driven by strong, light, graceful arm-sweeps, this side and that, from the arm of the slim, black-eyed boy to that of the long-legged, wet-haired girl; back and forth, back and forth, beating out endless time, drawing bowstrings against an endless ocean. Beautiful. Young.

He was thirsty and bought a bottle of lemonade from a passing vendor. Drinking, he saw again that the front of the stand was never for an instant empty. People coming and going, coming and going. This isn't the place, isn't the time, he thought. And meanwhile the day was frittering away. A weekday. Clients phoning the office and Ziona answering with devastating indifference: The boss ain't in. Won't be. Dunno.

No choice but to return tonight. To her place. At an early hour, not give her a chance to repeat her tricks. And not linger, not succumb.

The tide splintered against the mossy reefs and showered them with spray. Sweep of transparent blue. Summer radiance. Ball thudding. Dizzying. You could merge in this lightness of water and sand, melt in it. Like water in sand. Be free of time, of care. Forget, dream, be here for hours, hours, the sun drifting slowly across the sky, and you stretched under it and knowing splendor everlasting behind closed eyes.

About death—he recalled—yes, about death, and in happiness!

Quite thinkable.

A bunch of young men were standing beside the stand, jabbering, snickering, and a moment later he saw Jeanette, in an open blue dress, storming out of the back entrance and brandishing a broom over the head of one of them, who ducked swiftly to avoid the blow. Loudly cheered by the others, she pursued him over the strip of damp sand till he leaped into the water, waded in, and was swallowed by the waves. Heaping abuse upon the youngsters, chasing them off with the broom, she returned to her post behind the counter.

Common slut, he grimaced, and wondered at himself how—

And turned, trudging through the deep sand, up the dunes and toward the car.

The gate hinges produced a hoarse squeak, warning of the approach of a stranger. When the door opened he started, recoiled as though someone had pushed him off the doorstep: the bewhiskered, gleaming face was absolutely familiar, though he couldn't remember where from.

"Come in, come in. Guess it's Mrs. Levy you want."

"Not in?"

"She'll be in in a moment. Take a seat, take a seat."

As though avoiding a minefield he skirted the table and sat on the sofa.

"The name's Albert," with a polite smile. "I'm a cousin of hers."

"Have we met?" he asked tremulously.

"The fire. Giv'at Herzl. You're the insurance fellow. Tal, right?"

"Yes." It was coming back to him like a bad dream of long ago.

"Remember? Me telling you it was done deliberate. The way I figured it, I mean. And you . . ."

"Yes, there was a big crowd there, was hard to hear. . . ." He remembered in consternation how rudely he had repulsed him.

"Yeah, I know. What happened in the end? Cops come up with anything?"

"Short circuit. Thing like that happens."

"Some half a million, no less."

"Happens. Especially at these old carpentries."

"They get a fire that place every couple of weeks. Bad business for insurance companies." He grinned and offered his cigarette case.

"No, thanks. I don't smoke."

The child came in, dark and hairy, dragging his legs in their braces.

"Know the gentleman, Shlomo?"

The child nodded, approached the table, leaned against its edge and stared at Shuka with big blank eyes.

"How are you?" Shuka forced a smile.

"Poor kid, them legs," said Albert. "Needs new irons."

"Too short?" Shuka looked at the child.

"Shlomo's a big boy, though, eh, Shlomo?" Albert gave the child's arm a sound thump and, turning to Shuka, whispered, "Jeanette's told me you've been a big help. We're all sure obliged to you, we sure are."

"Oh . . ." Shuka spread his hands.

"The concession stand and all, put her on her feet. You know the state she was in. Didn't have nothing. Nothing!" He flung an arm across the back of the sofa as though taking Shuka under his patronage.

"I hope she's got enough to keep her now. . . ."

"Yeah, she's okay"—tipping the ash into the tray—"more or less, summers specially. It's just"—lowering his voice confidentially—"spot of trouble just now. She got to place the kid in an institution, see, and . . . She don't know where it's going to come from. Tough."

All of a sudden Shuka felt trapped, caught in a den of thieves. The arm above his shoulders going to drop like an ax.

The phone call. The frame-up. Blackmail.

"An institution?" Bracing himself.

"It ain't just the legs," Albert whispered, "it's . . ." Touching his forehead. "There's a connection, see? . . . The doctor explained it to her: it's nerves. If the nerves in the legs don't work proper then the brain don't work proper either. Kind of like a short circuit. . . ." Grinning.

Shuka looked into the child's eyes and felt the impulse to run.

"He's a bright little fellow. . . ."

"Soft in the head," Albert hissed in Shuka's ear. "A softy."

Shuka went on staring at the child's eyes, big black eyes topped by hairy brows that grew together over the nose. He wanted to get up, escape from the vise of that arm.

"Tough," sighed Albert, bending toward the ashtray, "woman all on her own, you know, with a sick kid. . . . I try to help out a bit, do what I can but . . . I got a little vegetable shop at Abu-Kabir, got an old father laid up sick in bed. . . ."

Shuka recalled how two months back a motorcyclist had extorted 10 pounds from him: he had been driving in his car along Allenby Road, Saturday afternoon and traffic scarce, when all of a sudden a motorbike had shot past him, then made a sharp right turn into Geulah, virtually under his front wheels. A hairbreadth or he'd run into him. Fellow hadn't been hurt, just knocked over with his bike. With a dirty look in his eyes he had opened the car, got in, and commanded: To the police station! and had groaned, seizing his knee: My leg! You smashed up my leg! And next moment two others had appeared out of nowhere and under threats ordered him out of the car. And the ignominy of how he had given in to them and emptied his wallet of all it contained—10 pounds.

"The concession stand saved her, sure. She'll be thanking you for that all her life. But between you and me," crushing out the cigarette in the tray, "it's hardly enough for bread."

"Mr. Tal." Jeanette entering in a thin yellow housedress, all wet hair and rosy lips. "Sorry to've kept you waiting. . . ."

"I should have let you know I was coming. . . ." Shuka rose to his feet, and Albert followed suit.

"Always happy to see you!" Jeanette flashed him a look, washed and sparkling.

"You'll pardon me, I got to go now," said Albert, squeezing his way between sofa and table. "See you tomorrow." Planting a kiss on Jeanette's cheek. "Glad to've met you, Mr. Tal." Shaking Shuka's hand. "Hope we're gonna see some more of you." And rumpling the child's hair, sending a congratulatory smile to the happy couple, he walked to the door and went out.

"Bed, Shlomo!" Jeanette smacked the child's behind lightly and propelled him toward the door.

"Been a long time!" She seated herself close to Shuka and took his hand in both of hers. "Where've you kept yourself such a long time?"

Shuka pulled his hand away, said sternly, "What did you mean, calling me up like that last night?"

"I got worried! Didn't know what'd happened to you!" Opening her eyes at him in wide innocence.

"But at home?!"

"What could I do? I'm at the stand all day, and by the time I'm through you aren't in your office anymore!"

"But at home?!" he repeated crossly.

"But your wife don't know a thing!"

Shuka couldn't make up his mind whether she was naive, as indicated by the wide eyes of the little girl afraid she'll be punished for a little accident, or trying to put something over on him.

"You haven't told her, have you?"

"No, I haven't," he said shortly, grudgingly.

And was promptly annoyed with himself for having been forced into a conspiracy against his wife. And with whom!

"So why didn't you answer? Why did you just hang up on me like you didn't know me, like . . ." she said with a little whine of reproach in her voice.

"What did you expect me to say?" grinning wryly.

"You could've said you'd been busy, that you'd see me tomorrow, next week . . . dunno . . . something!'

Again Shuka wondered: Did she really fail to see what might have happened, or was she only putting on an act?

"I been missing you so . . ." she lisped, breathing against his cheek, taking his hand to rub it along her thigh.

Shuka pulled his hand back and moved away from her.

"Do you know why I've come tonight?" he said.

"To see me!' Searching his eyes.

He was briefly silent, trying to recapture the speech he had rehearsed, but in vain.

"I came to tell you," he said, "that things can't go on like this. . . ."

"What things?" Gazing into his eyes.

"Between us . . . all this. . . ."

"Mean you won't come to see me anymore?" A startled look in her eyes.

"Yes," he made himself say.

"Why, Gogo?" Pressing herself against him, placing a hand on his knee.

"Hard to explain."

"But if no one don't know, then why can't you come to see me?"

"I just can't." Avoiding her eyes.

"Look at me." She put out a hand, turned his face toward her, and peered intently into his eyes. "You scared? Tell me honest!"

"Scared?" he snickered. "What of?"

"Dunno. Your wife maybe." Keeping her eyes fixed on his face.

"I told you, she doesn't know!"

"Then what? I want to understand," she demanded.

He remembered how he had been going to say: Look, me and my wife . . .

Ridiculous, absolutely ridiculous. Who was she, after all?

"You wouldn't understand."

"I'm not that dim. What happened? Wasn't I good for you?"

A fatuous smile spread over his face.

"Go on! Tell me, tell me"—pinching his middle—"wasn't I good?"

"It's not that."

"Then what? Tell! Aren't I supposed to know?" And backing off a little she grew serious and examined his face. "Maybe there's somebody else. . . ."

Shuka looked at her and the thought struck him: an honorable way out! Somebody else. Young. Intelligent . . .

And the name Dinah, Dinah Lev, rang in his head.

A possibility, why not?

Not unthinkable anyway.

"It's complicated, Jeanette . . ." he said.

"So there *is!*"

"Very complicated. . . ." Cagily.

"I see," she said. She rose, moved prim and upright to the buffet, took a cigarette from a pack, strode to the kitchen, struck a match, and returned to the room blowing smoke up in the air.

Through the transparent dress Shuka caught sight of the black brassiere, the red lace-edged panties.

"I hope you're not sore . . ." he said, getting up.

Jeanette watched him from a distance, her eyes squinting, against the smoke or in hostility against him.

"Tell you the truth, Mr. Tal," she said, "I took you for a different sort of person."

"In what way?" He gave a crooked smile and felt suddenly oppressed.

"A bit more honest, Mr. Tal."

Shuka looked at her, reflected whether he ought not put her straight, explain it wasn't dishonesty that made him act this way but quite the contrary. . . .

Even though, he thought, if you are deceiving your wife with someone else, with Dinah say, then she'd be right after all.

And either way you'll come out the loser. Cutting a figure, in fact, and she'll have the best of it.

"Anyhow, if you ever need help . . ."

"Thanks, Mr. Tal, I got the number."

"Hope we'll meet again sometime . . ." he said, opening the door.

"Either we will or we won't." Shutting the door behind him.

Walking through the darkness to his car, he felt humiliated and unclean. And a sense of foreboding caught him: the affair wasn't over yet, it was just starting: the phone call, Albert. The child's institution. The deception. The double deception.

What the devil had put the name Dinah into his head?

K ANTEROWITZ, he read in the documents. But he was quite unable to concentrate.

The complicated case of Kanterowitz: the main of the apartment on the top floor had sprung a leak, and the water had seeped through to the apartment below, that of the client Kanterowitz, and produced a damp patch over all of the bathroom and half the living-room ceiling. It had also caused a short circuit and ruined the heater. The insurance company of the top apartment repudiates its liability, claiming it rests with the company that insured the building. The latter in turn claims that the burst main is a result of repairs carried out by the tenant of the upper apartment on his floor tiles, and the party accountable are the insurers of the household contents. Kanterowitz's claim for damages, amounting to IL. 800—

But he was unable to concentrate. He recalled the dream he had woken up from that morning in a cold sweat: the child. Hiding in a tangle of undergrowth. There had been a swamp there, somewhat like the one near the Rubin River. Spotting him, the child had tried to run, hobbling on his braces. He had wanted to shout a warning, tell him he might fall into the swamp, drown—

He had had only one brace on, he recalled. That's why he was limping so curiously, with a kind of twist. The other was lying near a bush.

And that girl, stuck in the swamp up to her middle. In a black bra, and her stomach smeared with mud. . . .

Not Jeanette.

Not Elisheva.

And then! The child stopping, aiming the brace at him—a gun. And staring at him with big eyes—

The horror!

Kanterowitz—he brought back his mind to the papers in front of him. And realized once more that Kanterowitz's policy did not cover damage incurred through a third party.

Now it came back to him: it had been yesterday's girl on the beach, in a tight bikini, with straight supple legs, feet thudding against the damp sand.

"Get me Migdal," he told Ziona, "I want Shmueli."

And thumbing the documents, Jeanette's final words rang in his ears, the words with which she had shut the door on him: "Either we will or we won't." Not so much the words themselves as the chill implied by them, in which now he could detect a threatening note. And he reflected how if he had been a bit subtler he could have gone about it quite differently—peaceably, amiably, in kindness, in a light spirit, maybe even, as a parting token—

"Shmueli? About this Kanterowitz business. I've got his policy here before me . . ."

Shmueli submitted that the case was plain: obviously the top-floor tenant must pay for the damage as a first step. As far as insurance coverage was concerned, we'd see later. A legal problem? Perhaps. Let them fight it out in court between them.

And the moment he hung up, the blood rushed to his face recalling suddenly how Jeanette had said, "I got the number." Which number? She's got two! And my home phone. Yes, not here but home, at any hour of the day or night. Might even have phoned this morning very likely, an hour ago, five minutes after he'd left for the office.

Or Albert: It's about your husband . . . I can tell you, if you don't know . . .

He picked up the receiver and dialed his home number, heard the rings echo through the bedroom. Five, six, an empty echo.

Could be Elisheva's on her way here already. To have it out.

In the ominous silence of the office, Tal tried to arrange his thoughts and distinguish between the plausible and the far-fetched: Albert *may* phone, but not home. He won't because there'd be nothing in it for him. He may phone the office and say: Look, Mr. Tal, placing the kid is a matter of no more than four hundred pounds a month. You don't *have* to, of course, but I'd cough up if I were you . . . for your own good. . . .

And if he'd refuse, thought Tal, what could he do? Threaten to tell Elisheva? Rubbish, because not enough of a threat. An everyday occurrence in five out of ten families. Why five? Seven. Nine.

And nothing to feed a public scandal on either, if that's the way Albert's mind works. No paper would print a headline: "Insurance Man Tal Deceiving His Wife," or: "Domestic Trouble for University Lecturer." Absolute rubbish.

Next possibility: that Jeanette may phone home, night after night, and ask for him.

In that case he'd tell Elisheva that she's someone trying to squeeze some damages out of him to which she isn't entitled. That she's out of her mind. Elisheva'll believe him, won't start imagining things.

On top of which one might call in the police, complain of annoyance, threats.

Might call in the police in either case.

And after all you haven't committed any crime, dammit. So what are you so scared of anyway?

Crime . . . he grinned, remembering—and was amazed at himself how he could have forgotten while arguing with himself and his persecutors all this time—how he used to walk his legs off to get her a permit for her beach stand. How he used to bring toys for the kid, presents for her, without asking for anything in return. . . . A crime indeed. . . .

If worse came to worst he'd call in the police, he decided.

And with that shoved the Kanterowitz papers aside and applied himself to a circular about a marine insurance seminar to be held in Haifa in January, participation fee: IL. 150.

But reading the words "war damage claims in theory and in practice," a new possibility struck him: She might phone Elisheva while he was out and ask to meet her. Elisheva would agree, no reason why she shouldn't. And face-to-face in some café she'd spill it all, the full story, blow by blow—

For all he knew she already *had*. And that's why Elisheva

wasn't at home. Because where would she have gone to at such an hour? Summer vacation.

The sweat broke out on his forehead.

The agony. Tal felt utterly convinced that he deserved it, in punishment. And only wondered why it had been so late in coming. Why hadn't these feelings of guilt and remorse—as he called them—troubled him before; why only now, just when he'd put an end to this wretched affair—and of his own free will, without any pressure from outside? Why were they only now overwhelming him with such a rush? Like certain diseases, he told himself, which lurk inside you for a long time without you being aware of them and then suddenly they erupt like a rash: blisters, pox, pimples.

Actually, he reflected, to be straight with himself, he ought to confess to Elisheva.

And the moment the idea occurred to him he felt somewhat relieved. A way out. A kind of purging of sins. He'd make a clean breast of it, however hard that would be. She'd understand, forgive. And he himself'd be a different person, purer.

If she were at home now he would phone to say he was coming, and set out at once. It's not the kind of thing you put off.

But Elisheva was not at home, and Tal felt badly alone with his guilt and remorse, as he called them, which hadn't been cleansed yet. The more when thinking how he had added to the burden on his conscience by those hints to Jeanette about having another affair. Another deception.

Dinah. How absurd!

If at least he could call Dinah, exchange a few friendly words with her, to make his lie less blatant.

But he didn't know Dinah's number, and couldn't find it in the book, because she was boarding with some family whose name he didn't know.

He picked up the receiver and dialed his mother's number at the perfumery.

"Hang on a minute, Shuka." He could hear her, busy with a customer apparently. And while waiting he recalled how one evening, lying in Jeanette's arms, on the sofa, he had heard the child's voice calling from the next room, Mamma, Mamma, and had wanted to pull away from her, but she had whispered no, Gogo, don't mind him, he'll soon hush up, and it had seemed as if the child's cries had only excited her the more. Horrible! How could he! He felt sick at himself, full of shame. "Yes, Shuka, what is it?"

"Just to hear how you are."

"Hear? Come and see!"

"I will, Saturday. So how's everything?"

"Fine. I'm always fine. And you?"

"All right."

"Sure?"

"Yes, why?"

"Because if you call me up I guess something's *not* all right!"

"You're wrong. . . ."

"Oh, well. You wouldn't tell me anyway. How's Avigayil?"

"Off on a trip with a friend. . . ."

"I can't hear you!"

"I say she went to Jerusalem, with a girlfriend. . . ."

"Are you hoarse or something?"

"Me?"

"The way you sound, so faint, as if . . . Why to Jerusalem all of a sudden?"

"Why not? School starts in a week."

"She spends the whole holiday at home and only now at the last minute . . . ?"

"You know her, moods. . . . How's your health?"

"Fine. Sacha's a bit ill, lying down."

Tal swallowed, paused.

"What's wrong with him?"

"It's his back. Took him all of a sudden. He's getting injections but they aren't much help. He may go to Tiberias after the High Holidays, try the hot springs. We'll see. Meanwhile there's nobody to take care of him at home. . . ."

"Can't he get up?"

"Dreadful pains! At that age, you know. . . ."

Ziona came in and made a sign that someone was waiting on the line.

"Got to call off now, Mother. . . ."

"Take care of yourself. And don't forget, Saturday."

Tal replaced the receiver with a sigh and picked it up again. Shimon Avrech. Truck smashed into him at the Elite crossing. Can he come at once?

Tal collected papers, dispensed instructions to Ziona. How old would he be, dear old Sasha? Sixty-six? Seven?

Approaching the intersection, he saw the familiar bustle from afar: the police car with two wheels on the curb, two policemen holding a tape and measuring distances, a bunch of idlers surveying the damage, the abandoned truck—reef in the stream of traffic—splintered glass in the road.

The brow of the Peugeot wore a deep gash across its right side. Eye torn out. Brain monstrously crushed.

Avrech was leaning against the brick fence, white as a sheet.

"How did it happen?"

Avrech pointed a lifeless hand at the wreck. "Look . . ." Unable to speak.

"You didn't see him?"

"Lunatic . . ." he mumbled with trembling lips.

"It's not his fault." A dark-skinned boy, eager to volunteer his account. "I saw what happened. The truck was coming up from here, see, and the light was on red, and he went through like a shot, and crashed into . . ."

"Lunatic! Through a red light!" said Avrech, still shaking.

"Main thing is you came out of it alive." Then he asked, "How about the other fellow?"

"Ambulance took him away." The boy again. "Nothing very bad though. Broke a leg is all. It was *his* fault. I can give evidence in court if you want me to."

"New car," mumbled Avrech. "Three months, hardly."

"Happens. What can you do? Main thing you came out alive."

"Your engine." A bystander strolled over. "When a job like that knocks into you, you've had it!"

"Can change it." Another bystander. "New engine, welding, how much d'you figure? Two thousand maybe, two and a half."

"Insurance'll pay . . ." The first, with a snigger.

Tal walked around the Peugeot, peered at the engine under the crumpled hood, and came back to Avrech.

"Ruin your life, those," whispered Avrech.

"There's worse things," Tal smiled, then soothingly matter-of-fact: "Look, you give the particulars to the police, I'll phone for a tow truck, we'll get her to the garage, call in the assessor, and we'll see what can be done. Come and see me at the office this afternoon. Main thing is you're alive. Know where I can make a phone call hereabouts?"

Avrech indicated the nearby filling station.

Moving away, Tal was thinking how a traffic accident was something that might happen to Albert as well. Crossing the road, say, at Herzl. A narrow, busy street. Or a vegetable truck backing up at his shop, and knocking him flat against the wall. The rate of fatal accidents in this country is the highest in the world, something like one to twenty thousand. According to the law of probability . . .

Then he told himself that when you wish bad luck on some-body, that is precisely when . . . And decided to leave the matter to Providence, to fate.

He recalled how a few months ago he had wished bad luck on Dushkin. Had prayed. Not an accident. Natural death. Nothing had happened. Though come to think, this business with his back. And just when he'd dropped the whole idea.

He entered the gas station, crossed to the telephone, dialed the first two digits of the assessors, and paused. Then he dialed his home number.

"Yes, Shuka?"

And the voice was clear, lively, as always.

"I phoned you before but you weren't in."

"Uh-huh, had to go out. Did you want something?"

"Look, Eli," and for an instant, feeling nothing but relief, he forgot what he had meant to say. He'd tell her how much he loved her, he thought. "Is there a letter from Gilly?"

"No, why? Are you worried about her?"

"A bit. She didn't leave any address."

"Why'd she write anyway? She's coming back Sunday. What's making you worry?"

"Nothing, I thought . . . Everything all right?"

"Of course! . . . What's on your mind, Shuka?"

"Nothing special. . . . I'm talking from the Elite crossing. There's been an accident here."

"Anything serious?"

"Not really. One driver a bit injured."

"And you're upset."

"A bit. . . . Ah, there *was* something: have you got Dinah Lev's phone number?"

"Of course. . . . You want to talk to her?"

"No. . . . I mean, somebody's been asking me about her book. . . ."

"Well?"

"I thought I'd ask her. Where to get hold of it I mean. . . ."

"At any bookstore! . . . I don't see . . ."

"It's nothing"—laughing—"I just thought I'd ask her to let me have it. I'd pay for it, of course. To give to this fellow . . . I owe him . . ."

"I don't get it but never mind. You want to talk to her—do. She'll only be too glad. She's very fond of you."

Shuka took the number. He picked up the receiver and let it rest in his hand for a long moment.

Then he dialed the assessors.

Was she aware that the time was 1:00 A.M.?

Yes she was and was nevertheless reluctant to get out of bed.

Was it because she intended to stay in it till morning and not return home?

No. Because of indolence. Because of a desire to taste to the full the warm pleasure lingering between the bedclothes after a gratifying intercourse.

Was she afflicted by pangs of conscience?

Languorous, the sweetness stilling in her womb, spreading through her limbs, trickling to her toes, shoulders, arms, Elisheva lay waiting, wide-eyed into the darkness and the faint square of light from the glass-topped door, for the return of Amnon from the bathroom. But basking voluptuously in the familiar lassitude lapping in the body after the peak, she was also aware of the *less* familiar lassitude, not of sweetness but of blight, which is a distinct symptom. Listening to the splash of water beyond the wall, first in a steady flow from the tap and then in a stinging downpour from the shower, she wondered for the thousandth time whether to tell or not to tell. And knew she wouldn't, not tonight, not tomorrow, no, nor in a month. And if, to be sure, this was it—dark horror or radiant joy?—then time alone would swell what it would, spawn what it might. Hearing beyond the wall the click of metal on enamel, a swish of curtain, a tap of foot, she tried to distract her mind from her own flesh and blood and concentrate on tomorrow's lecture. Chapter 17 of *Ulysses,* "Ithaca": 7 Eccles Street, the kitchen, the cocoa sipping, the comparison of the Irish and Hebrew languages—*Kolod balej-waw pnimah*—the catechismal method borrowed from the *Summa Theologica.* But her thoughts spiraled back to herself:

Was she afflicted by pangs of conscience?

No. Because she held that she did not cause suffering to one who was ignorant of the facts. And she did not believe in a sin committed by violating abstract moral principles imposed by a so-called Omnipotence.

Would she have been afflicted by pangs of conscience were she to know that suffering *was* caused to another person?

She would not have called them by that name, but by some other such as pity or a sense of responsibility, and would have weighed the amount of suffering caused to herself as a result of renouncing the gratification of her desire, against the amount of suffering caused to the other as a result of her yielding to it.

Would she have renounced it if she knew that the first alternative tipped the balance?

One wonders. The flesh is stronger.

What else troubled her, lying upon the narrow bed, waiting for the return of her companion from the bathroom?

Remembering full well that the date was October 16, 1966, and her period six days late.

Had no such delay ever occurred before?

Not in all the seventeen years since the birth of her daughter.

Would she consider it a fearful disaster were her suspicion confirmed?

No.

An inextricable mess?

The threshold of a new life, filled with pain but rich in pungent emotions and in spiritual uplift.

What attracted her attention in the darkness?

A bird's egg, or a pigeon's, or a snake's, lying to the right of the thick volume of *Mishnat Ha-Zohar*, Isaiah Tishbi edition, Mosad Bialik, Jerusalem, which lay on the table near the bed beside the empty flower vase.

Why did it attract her attention?

Because she fancied having seen this egg before and did not remember where, or rather—it reminded her of something and she could not remember of what.

Was the memory pleasant? Unpleasant?

She made an effort to drive it out of her mind and concentrate on tomorrow's lesson.

With what success?

None, because her mind returned to herself and she wondered what kind of person she was, whether of the element of earth, water, air, or fire, emotional or intellectual, or emotional-intellectual, or amoral-emotional, or amoral-intellectual, or perhaps a husk, because she recalled a passage Amnon Brosh had quoted to her out of a book called *Valley of the King* by Naphtali Ben Ya'acov Elhanan, which says that until the hour of the midnight cock's crow the husks drift about the world, and she thought how midnight had passed and the cock had crowed and she was still drifting in the air.

Amnon's vest glimmered white in the dim room. "Turn on the light?" he asked, his finger on the switch.

"No, don't," she said, and jumped out of bed, grabbed her clothes from the chair, and dashed into the bathroom.

A cool smell of almond soap. Gillette razor blades. Palmolive shaving cream. Bachelor's cosmetics. Hairs in the basin. Coarse white toilet paper. Ascetic. His hard manhood. Your beautiful body that is waxed young, is grown sweet, grown filled. With his.

What affinities did Bloom find between the moon and woman?

Her antiquity in preceding and surviving successive tellurian generations; her nocturnal predominance: her satellitic dependence: her luminary reflection: her constancy under all her phases . . . her splendor, when visible: her attraction, when invisible. . . .

Her waning and waxing. Full. Pregnant. Birth of new moon. Pregnancy. Birth.

She picked up the shaving brush and breathed in its smell. Manhood in its singleness, independent, unattached, self-sufficient, existing as an absolute entity. Strong.

Afterward, rinsing her crotch, she checked to see whether anything had appeared to signify. A miracle? Disappointment?

The Laws of Impurity at Meah She'arim. In the Old City.

Stoning for the wife who has trespassed. The bitter water.

And wiping her thighs and lips with his towel she enfolded herself in his being.

Dressing, her clothes took her back to the civilized world: wife, mother, university lecturer. In a strange man's bathroom, after midnight, dressed you really look the deceiver, she told herself in the mirror. But naked you are true. The naked truth. Lying naked you aren't lying, she smiled, then thought: But when are you—you? Naked, a bitch in heat? Or in these husks of civilization? The blessing on "Him who clothes the naked"—recalling an interpretation Julius had told her of: Him who covers the lower world against the husks attaching themselves to it. The lower limbs, that is. . . .

"Light?" Her finger on the switch.

"No, better like this."

His cigarette a glowing point from the depths of the armchair. The white soles of his feet. This fear of the light. Who was it said that lovers are embarrassed at the beginning of love and at its end?

She sat in the other armchair, facing him, searched the table, found cigarettes, matches, lighted one.

Capable of sitting like that for hours without opening his lips.

"When do we talk?" she said, straining to keep her voice steady.

"What about?"

One side of his face like a mask in the flicker of his cigarette as he inhaled.

"Us."

He won't talk. He'll temporize, hem and haw, shun. The truth.

"Go ahead," he said.

His voice deterring, distant. This remorseless distance, only moments after the hot panting of bodies joined and locked!

"Do you despise me?"

"What for?"

"For being . . . unfaithful?"

Saying nothing, nothing. Silence implies consent.

"If that's what it is, I have a part in it myself," he said. She noticed the thin smile on his lips.

"Maybe you despise yourself as well. . . ."

Silence again. Implies admission.

"Tell me: am I imposing myself on you?"

"Imposing?"

How like him: no direct answers. Rhetorical questions, parrying, evading.

"I'm afraid that if I should let you go . . . you'd never take the initiative. . . ."

"You're a married woman . . ." he said.

The technical excuse.

"Tell me the truth: does your conscience bother you?"

"My conscience?" he laughed briefly. "No, I'm not that ethical. Though I admit that . . . no, it's hard to put it into words."

She waited, on edge. At last he said:

"A question of self-respect."

And after another silence:

"Loyalty is a question of self-respect. Like telling the truth."

The bitter water: the trespassing wife to be stoned. The guilt all mine. The lying, the deceit. But you, why didn't you say so at the start? Why not before you made love to me? Don't you realize that if that's how you feel it is *you* who have degraded *me,* and that you've no right to flaunt your moral principles in my face?

"What do you suggest I do?" she asked in a harsh voice.

"Suggest?"

But as though himself flinching from his evasiveness, he said:

"You're a proud woman. I'm certain you won't do anything that might debase you in your own eyes. . . ."

Debase! she jeered, looking at him. The falsity of it, the

untruth! Someone who loves truly doesn't preach like that. Not even to himself. He's beyond choice. He's not debased in his own eyes even when he's forced to lie, to "deceive"! A phrase of Simone Weil's popped into her head: "His love is violent but base—a possible sentence. His love is deep but base—an impossible one."

"Do you love me, Amnon?" She heard her own voice in the darkness—submissive, pleading.

The die cast. No return.

Brosh put out his cigarette in the ashtray. Then he took her hand, pulled her toward him, kissed her. A long, chivalrous kiss.

She felt a chill loneliness, despondency. Hemmed in by the streets of the dark city beyond the window. And a high, starry, cold sky. And the worst of it that you can't force an emotion on anyone, by any means. You can enforce your presence in one room, your body in one bed, your lively mind in conversation, but not love. No. You may scream, hit him, tear him to shreds, but not love. And there is no bridge across this abyss. Oh, the saddest of all in this short life of ours is that you cannot force love on one who will not love!

She pulled her hand out of his, and turning her glance to the bedside table asked, "What's that egg? A snake?"

"A snake?" he chuckled. "No. A bird. Someone gave it to me."

"At the paper?"

"Yes."

"One of your fans?"

"Fans?" Laughing. "If one's an editor in addition to being a writer, one never knows just where that sort of thing ends and flattery begins."

"Or bribery?"

"Perhaps . . ."

His full life, without you, twenty-four hours a day in which you have no share, no access, no claim. Friends, fans, his reflections, his writing. From the moment you leave. And tomorrow, a new day, a long morning, noon, evening, without you, your existence.

She wanted to kneel at his feet, put her head in his lap and cry.

"Done anything on your story?"

"A bit . . . a page or two . . ."

"Read me some."

"Now? It's half past one!"

"Don't worry."

Brosh hesitated, looked at her.

With pity?

"All right."

The tears welled up in her, welled up despite herself and overflowed into her eyes as he read. She knew how good the story was, and how profound, this story about the sect of early Christians retiring into the Judean desert. The allusive language. The monotonous cadences, like the monotony of the hot desert wind . . . With envy in her heart and the sadness of parting, she knew how good and how profound this story was.

Yes, to part from this, too. From the creative mind, from the soul filled with yearning. And you will go back to your teaching, apply your analytical faculties to literary texts. His, too, someday. A writer by the name of Amnon Brosh. As though it had never been, this night. The nights.

Silently he walked with her to the nearby taxi stand, and when he opened the taxi door for her she swayed and collapsed on his shoulder.

"It'll pass, it's nothing," she replied shakily to his alarmed stutters.

"Can I get you anything . . ." Supporting her.

"No . . . just give me a minute . . ." Burying her face against his chest.

"I'll come with you."

"No, no need. Better already. I'm sorry." Listening to his heartbeats, signals in the dark of a sailing boat, sailing away, away.

Parting? Forever?

Oh, I'll never endure it! she sighed in the taxi.

The bleary lights of deserted cafés. The darting lights of headlights. The stragglers on the abandoned banks of the road. The ignominy of your weakness. The husks of fireflies flitting through the air. Angular houses, staring, wrapped in pale shrouds. Trees slumbering in courtyards acrawl with vermin. You into exile.

Lying beside Shuka's scrappy breathing, she told herself that if this was indeed it—and that fainting fit was added proof—she would not dispel it. She would carry the child of the desert recluse, give birth to his spirit, bring up a son in his image. And never disturb his peace, never place any burden on him. In four or five months, her condition obvious, she would tell him about it and say: You owe me nothing. You do not even have to see me. Nor keep faith. It is the fruit of my sin and I shall bear it. I am a proud woman, as you said.

And when she imagined herself in her pregnancy, big of belly and breasts, proudly carrying the fruit of her womb, she felt cleansed, and envisaged days of happiness.

For a year, two years, she would not go to the university, would devote herself to the child. Uri? Jochanan? Jonathan? The Holy Family . . .

Ah, were it not here, not now, were it other times, in another country! In the household of Clive and Vanessa Bell at Gordon Square, with the Bloomsbury group, with Leonard and Virginia Woolf, with Carrington married to Ralph Partridge and in love with Lytton Strachey, and the three of them living together, a spiritual-erotic communion, one big literary family, in which the family consecrated in wedlock is assimilated. Or floats hither and thither, each a cell unto itself. A cell becomes attracted to another, parts from it, returns, with multi-intellectual, multisexual stimuli, in the common search for beauty and truth, the common repudiation of conventions, the raging arguments on Fabianism, art, style, without cant, without all those sanctimonious, mean, pious, petit bourgeois, petit-everything falsehoods about moral purity and the sanctity of family life—a proper little love nest, safe and sheltered, with a proper little housewife in whom "the heart of her husband doth safely trust." Or like George Eliot, who after Lewes's death married their friend—Ross? Cross?—younger than herself by how much? By over twenty years! And the difference between us? Seven years, eight. Yes, were it not now and not here, in this small and shut-in country, tormented, sun-scorched, bleeding, bullets whizzing in its air, and those trapped inside it scurrying like rats and each man clinging to his wife, to hold, not to let go, before he falls on the battlefield. Were it in another time, another country—

A literary pregnancy, she laughed to herself, remembering the first night in Jerusalem.

O N Friday, the twentieth of October, in the middle of her lecture about *Dead Souls,* after a delay of ten days, and after having already resigned herself to the fact and sheathed it in a cocoon of dreams—Dr. Tal-Blumfeld received her menstrual period. Expatiating upon the surrealistic elements inherent in this Russian *poème* she said: "The tendency of the collective-provincial mind to see in Chichikov a masquerading Napoleon Bonaparte fled from the Island of St. Helena, like its tendency to see Akaki Akakyevich as a reincarnation of Ferdinand VIII, is evidence of its unwillingness to acquiesce in . . ." And at this point, in the middle of the sentence, she felt the warm flow escape from her womb, and the slight moistness at its issue. For an instant she swayed and a mist clouded her eyes. She laid a hand on her forehead and resumed: ". . . in a situation where the foolish hero himself befools . . ." And thereafter the sentences stumbled against one another as the cars of a derailed train, and it was all she could do to stop them from overturning.

Hadassah Hermon, whose eyes did not leave her teacher's face for a moment, and who was, as always, sensitive to its most fleeting expression, noted with consternation the crimson flush covering it for an instant, and the pallor immediately after; and noted, of course, the disruption of the sentences in the resumed lecture, which seemed to have got completely out of hand: something about Belinski and satire, then suddenly Pushkin's view of the Russian's melancholic disposition, and without any bearing on it—about the tragedy of Madame Bovary . . . Right after the lecture she went over to her and said:

"You look pale, Doctor. Are you unwell?"

"No . . . nothing much . . ." Elisheva gathered her papers, and raising her eyes at her said, "Do you remember the motto of *Anna Karenina?*"

Hadassah Hermon pondered for a moment.

" 'Vengeance is mine, I will repay,' isn't it?" she said.

"Is there any logical connection between it and the novel? Between it and Anna's love for Vronski?"

Hadassah fixed her eyes on Elisheva's as though to probe them for a clue.

"Think about it." Elisheva cast a smile at her student and left the room.

For one moment Hadassah stayed where she was, trying to find an answer to the question, but the next she was struck by the question itself, which did not bear the slightest relation to the lecture about the Fantastic in Gogol's *Dead Souls,* and she wondered if anything had happened to her teacher to throw her completely off balance. Also, there had been that queer glint in her eyes when she had smiled at her and rapped out—"Think about it."

In the corridor Dr. Warshavsky, on the way to his office, stopped before Elisheva. "Do you know an individual by name of Yoram Hagorni?" he asked belligerently.

She stood still, willy-nilly, fearing that before long a pool of blood would collect at her feet.

"Being elevated from the ranks and dropped on Tel Aviv," he said, his bald, white-fringed crown silvery in the light from the wide windows. "If you haven't heard the news yet, let me have the honor: this bottom of Jerusalem's barrel is scraped up for our benefit, presumably with the idea that what is one man's poison is another's professor. That he does not have an M.A., I know; whether he does have a B.A., I do not, but here at any rate he is going to function as senior lecturer. It seems that a little learning in Jerusalem is a dangerous thing—for us! And you haven't yet heard . . ."

"No, I haven't, I'm sorry, I'm in a great hurry," and she left him.

Reaching her own office she locked the door and confirmed the presence of blood. Like a fatality, a dead birth, a dashed dream, a love bubble burst and draining away. Her blood guilt. She buried her face in her hands and the images spun before her closed eyes: the desk lamp in his room, with its green transparent shade; her brassiere limp over the back of a chair; his brittle voice talking to her as he poured black coffee into tiny cups; the reproduction of Cezanne's *Card-Players* on the wall; the olive trees of Abu Tor, the moonlight pouring over Jerusalem stone, threading through pine needles, and luminous in a room simmering with desire; the staircase to his apartment on the second floor, night after night in the stolen hours, and the nameplates of the other tenants—Dr. Wiesner, Rachel and Alfred Tuchner, Ari Barnea; Ari Barnea from the Chamber Theatre, who bumps into her leaving the apartment after midnight and greets her with a conspiratorial smile that promises discretion; the furtive homecoming, in the dark, on tiptoe. . . . Once she had found Avigayil in the kitchen, having tea. "You've become a fly-by-night lately," Avigayil had said. "M'm, conferences, talk-talk." And told herself it was only half a lie, because half the time they *would* spend talking. "Thought maybe you had a lover," said Avigayil. "Me? At my age?" she had laughed and turned away. The madness of it, all these months, without sense of time, or place; and the spun-out trance of the past ten days, as during an illness, walking about on air, nursing a crazy make-believe of a pregnancy in secret, a birth by fraud, a child growing up in your husband's home which he will think his to the end of his days! All flown. Dissolved in blood. Nevermore. And nevermore the downy birthmark on his left arm, and she smiled to herself while the tears burned her lashes, remembering the round birthmark, the size of a coin, which she would finger and toy with sitting on his knees. And the dimple in his firm chin, cradle of voluptuous mouth. And his voice, low and vibrant, when he told her the story of the bewitched maiden of Damascus and the holy candles. Or when he would say, so quietly, image of upright manhood— "It's late, Elisheva, you must go." Elisheva. And now an end to all that. An end?

Her thoughts went back to the day her mother died. She had been nine then, and when everybody returned from the graveyard, in the afternoon—a hot summer day and gnats flitting among the dusty bougainvillaea leaves—and the whole family, supplemented by the foreman who drove the big Chevrolet, Rabinowitz, were seated in the salon, on the sofas, the armchairs, in a ring around the huge vase on the table filled with faded white roses—she had demanded that Aunt Rivkah leave the house, go back to Hadera. Because she was ugly, short, high-shouldered, and she hated her. Daddy has tried to soothe her, but she had cried and stamped her feet and screamed, and when her wish wasn't obeyed she had stormed out of the house and thrown herself flat on her face on the grass in the orange grove behind the house, and lying there had felt ants squirming over her neck, her cheeks, crawling into her ears, and had jumped up in fright and threshed about and hit out wildly at herself to shake them off, and had been sure that from now on she would be ugly forever and ever because her face would be spotty all over and all the family would disown her because of what had happened and nobody would love her any longer, and her only comfort had been that Ishaia Gefen the math teacher would love her still, and go on loving her more than ever now after her mother's death.

Opening her eyes, she told herself: this is reality—the noon light, the sun, the walls of this building, the watch on your wrist. Nothing has changed, everything is as before. And he exists, and you, and you'll go on meeting him and loving in joy and in torment. All the rest is nightmare. Sick fancies. And this moment now is the point of division between fantasy and reality. And she recalled the thesis she had begun writing years ago— about reality and fantasy—and which she had never found the time to complete. And thought how the process she was undergoing was the reverse of the way it worked in literature: instead of a soaring to the heights of fancy—a coming down to earth. And the notion flashed through her mind: perhaps literature becomes inverted in me, like a mirror image?

She decided to phone Amnon and tell him she would come tonight. And say nothing of what she had gone through these past few days.

When she asked to speak to Amnon Brosh she was told he wasn't in, and when she inquired when he would be, she was passed on to the editorial secretary. The secretary said he had gone on leave. "But that's impossible!" Elisheva exclaimed. "It's still the case, madam," the secretary said in an ironic voice (an old hand at protecting the writer-editor against adoring females out to make a nuisance of themselves—the thought crossed her mind). "Do you want to talk to his substitute?" "How long is he going to be away?" "A month, two months, I don't know exactly"—the secretary, maddeningly. "But he must have left notice when he'd be back!" "I'm sorry, madam, I've told you what I know," and hung up on her.

For a moment she remained stunned, shocked: He'd run for it! Like a thief! A coward! And her mind started roving all over town, all over the country, pursuing him—

But in the next moment she took herself in hand.

And ordered a taxi. Urgent.

Like a whirlwind she swept past Julius without greeting him, past the hostile stare of Miss Bloch, through the knots of students looking up at the running clatter of her heels, headlong down the staircase and across the square, hailing the taxi before it could stop.

The streets reeled by, warped by the midsky sun. She made the driver wait beside a drugstore, supplied herself with the necessary, and told him to drive on, through Dizengoff, to his place. Her eyes scurried among the crowds sitting in cafés, strolling along the pavements, searched, in vain. The flower shop. The clinic. The hairdresser's. "Electrician all jobs executed." The empty lot. She stopped the taxi in front of his house, paid, flew up the stairs.

Her ring produced a hollow echo. Again and again and again.

She was about to turn back but checked herself, rang at the next-door apartment, Barnea's. "Yes," she heard a sleep-husky voice, "just a mo." Presently he appeared in the half-open door, bare-chested and with rumpled hair: "Oh, it's you. What can I do for you? Come in?" "Sorry to bother . . . I just wanted to ask if you happen to know whether Brosh is away, and where one could find him. . . ." Barnea gave her a speculative look, part leer, part mockery. "I'm sorry, I'd be delighted to help but I haven't the faintest. Came home at three last night myself. . . ." "He's needed urgently and nobody knows exactly . . ." "I'm really sorry . . ."

She came out into the street—and to hell with dignity when your heart lies fluttering!—and hurried toward Dizengoff. She made a tour of the cafés, entering, winding her way between tables, ostentatiously the bearer of an urgent message, her glance taking in the pavement sitters. At Kasit she made straight for the bar, bought cigarettes, and asked the barman whether he had seen Brosh. The man announced his name, once and again, but no one looked up or responded.

And from there she went home in a stupor.

Shuka hadn't come back yet, Avigayil was out. She dropped beside the telephone and put her hand on the receiver. Where to call? Once he had talked of going to Eilat. There were over a dozen hotels in Eilat. His mother in Jerusalem? But his mother had no phone. His brother in Upper Nazareth.

She searched the directory. No Brosh in Upper Nazareth.

He might be anywhere in the country, gone to the four winds.

Or gone abroad! Her heart sank at the sudden thought.

And she saw him at the airport, boarding a plane. Plane taking off. Touching down. Rome, Zurich, Paris?

She dialed the paper's number, asked for Brosh's replacement.

"This is Dr. Tal-Blumfeld speaking. From the university. I believe you are filling in for Amnon Brosh. I'm sorry to bother you but he's wanted urgently and we would like to know where we can get hold of him."

"Yes . . ." a placid drawl, "trouble is I don't know either. . . ."

"Didn't he leave any address? Phone number?"

"Quite, that's what I'd like to know myself. . . ."

"Didn't you see him before he left? Sorry to bother you, but . . ."

"You'd be surprised, no . . ."

"Funny . . ."

"I couldn't agree more . . . I'm here just by accident . . . I'm a rewrite man, and only day before yesterday they told me . . ."

"And didn't he leave any notice when he'd be back?"

"Very wrong of him, I guess. . . . But you know what writers are . . . All of a sudden he informs the chief that he's going, and he ups . . . So I fill in for him, and I don't even know for how long. . . . Not my thing, literature and all, actually. . . ."

The thing was becoming serious. Sinister.

Or maybe not. Maybe he had just gone away to be by himself, to finish his story.

Eilat. Sodom. Ein-Gedi. The Kinneret. Hanita. And suddenly it occurred to her that Dinah might know, might have come across him at a café, in the street, at the paper.

Her landlady answered the phone, said that Dinah had gone away, two days ago, hadn't said where, or when she'd be back.

The blood rushed to her face. Like the stab of a knife the thought of the two of them having gone away together struck her. Eloped. Betrayed her. Both of them.

The bird's egg in his room.

Hers. From the nest in her parents' yard.

To his room. At night. The *other* nights. In the selfsame bed.

And the more she turned it over in her mind—black thoughts of revenge racing, raging—the more convincing it seemed. Borne out by the facts:

That Dinah hadn't got in touch with her for several weeks.

And how she had pumped her, slyly, sneakily, questioning her about him the other day at the beach, the artless little peasant girl, the soulful poetess.

And he, too. The reluctance to discuss Dinah, when she had mentioned her name, asked him what he thought of her poetry.

I've very little grasp of poetry, he had said.

Literary editor and all.

And once, she now recalled, he had said how he envied people who had grown up in a village, in the bosom of nature.

The bosom of nature all right.

Bird's egg, love nest.

She wrenched her mind to conjure up the image: the two of them making love. In a grove. Her firm breasts, brown arms, warm laughter.

Warm bosom of nature's daughter.

The black blood thirsting for revenge, clouding the mind, raging.

And in the fraction of a lucid interval, the thought: birds of a feather, really. Writer and poetess. Their ages, inclinations, tempers. Conversations about birds, beasts, flowers.

When Shuka came home from the office toward evening, she said:

"I'd like you to take me for a drive tomorrow."

"Take you where?"

"To Merhavia."

"Merhavia?" With an astonished look.

"I'm worried about Dinah."

"What's happened?"

Her white face shook him.

"I'm afraid something must have."

And she told him about Dinah not having got in touch for weeks, and suddenly leaving without saying where, or when she'd be back.

Shuka's mind turned to suicide.

"Noticed anything unusual . . . lately? . . ."

"She's always rather unusual."

Shuka treated her anxiety with silent respect. He remembered that Dinah had been married and then divorced. So young, too. Trouble sure to follow when a family breaks up.

"Of course we'll go," he said.

And was even looking forward to it. Such a long time since they had gone on a real trip together.

B EYOND the Shefayim junction, the houses petered out, to be replaced by rolling green farm country darkened here and there by patches of cloud sailing overhead. Shuka whistled, "Oh, pioneer / With steady ha-and / Pave the way / Build the la-and . . ." over and over.

"I know I'm off tune," he smiled as they crossed the bridge over the Poleg, "but that song's stuck in my head and I can't get rid of it. Never thought of it for years, and all of a sudden . . ."

"I don't mind," said Elisheva.

Shuka shot her a glance, and seeing her hard stare, intent on the ribbon of road unfurling backward, he patted her knee and said:

"Don't worry so, Eli. I bet everything's all right, nothing's happened to her."

He had gone over the various possibilities last night and realized how absurd it was to think anything bad could have happened. They'd have been bound to hear. She had gone to see her parents, no doubt, or if not—to some other place.

At the Netanya intersection he slowed down to pick up soldiers thumbing a ride.

"Do me a favor, Shuka, not today." Elisheva put her hand on his arm.

He drove on unhappily, wanting to reproach her: Have a heart, Saturday, maybe their first day off in a month, must reach camp, God knows where, three empty places in back, always easy to find an excuse not to ... But on second thought he found justification for her: the worry, the fretting—

And after all, when once in a blue moon they went on a trip together ...

"Next year—Avigayil ..." he said a mile or two farther on.

Elisheva came out of her reveries.

"What?"

"To the army. Next year."

"Unless she gets married before."

"Married?" he grinned. "Not likely."

"How do you know?"

"I may be wrong, but I've a feeling things aren't quite smooth between them. Now she sees him, now she doesn't ..."

"A year and a half, and I've never even had a look at him."

"Me—once. Came home late, found them having tea in the kitchen."

"What's he like?"

"Bit phlegmatic. Got to drag the words out of him."

"You mean you talked?"

"A bit ... Dreamy type. Writes poetry."

"Oh, no!"

"No what?"

"I wouldn't wish her a poet, or a writer, or an artist."

"And that from you?"

"Unstable characters. Nothing but trouble."

"Who'd you want her to marry then—a dentist? A building contractor?"

Elisheva kept silent.

"An insurance agent?"

"Someone like you. Reliable. And honest."

"Ho-ho!" He gave a big laugh.

"I consider you an ideal husband."

"When did you arrive at that conclusion?"

"I've always thought so."

Shuka accelerated on the heels of a white car speeding in front.

"See that Simca?" he said. "Been trying to overtake me since the roadside inn and I didn't let her. Caught me off guard for a moment and slipped past, the little devil."

"No races, Shuka!"

"Don't you figure it's nervy?"

"I'd rather you didn't."

Two children kneeling on the back seat of the Simca jeered at him through the window and egged their father on.

"No use, kids!" Shuka grinned at the children who were jumping up and down on the seat and cheering the contenders.

The distance shrank and Shuka pulled out to the left, overtook, drove a short space side by side with his challenger, sent him a gracious smile, passed, and drove on ahead, king of the road.

"Happy?" said Elisheva.

"Saved the Fiat's reputation," Shuka laughed.

A light breeze blew up puffs of sand from the dunes. The screech of crows dropped from the oak tops, tumbled backward as under a scythe.

"So you think I'm an honest person," Shuka grinned.

"What?" Rallying.

"You said I'm an honest person."

"Aren't you?"

"Not quite."

"Don't go coy on me."

"You don't know what I'm capable of."

"Such as?"

"Lying, cheating, betraying confidence . . ."

"The Day of Atonement is two months past, Shuka."

"You don't believe me!"

"I'd have found out sometime in the last twenty years."

"What do you know of what I do at the office, on the road, paying calls . . ."

"You'd never be able to hide it from me."

"I wipe out the traces!"

"You're not cunning enough for that."

"And if you ever get to hear . . ."

"I won't believe it."

At the Hadera intersection there were more arm-waving soldiers, and again his heart grieved at having to drive past them. But later, along the Wadi Ara road, when traffic grew sparse and two lone soldiers appeared in view at the turnoff into a stony Arab village, their hands pining for the approaching car, Elisheva said, "Oh, well, take them, otherwise they may stand here for hours," and with a sense of relief Shuka stopped and took them in.

"Where do you have to get to?" he asked, driving on.

"Kiryat Shmonah."

"Only as far as Afula, I'm afraid."

"Never mind, we've got all day."

Shuka questioned them about the situation on the Syrian border following the incident in which four Border Police were killed when their jeep hit a mine. "Happens every day now," one of the soldiers said, "Sha'ar Hagolan, Almagor, Ashmora . . . Day before yesterday they got as far as Ma'ayan-Baruch. Booby trap. They slip across at night, plant them in fields or mud tracks, hard to detect." "They've stopped their Jordan-diversion games though, after the blow they got." Shuka communicating by means of his rearview mirror. "They still tried to carry on, south of Almagor, with equipment from their engineering corps, so they got the stuff dropped on them from the air." "I read in the paper that at that meeting of theirs in Damascus they decided to start again." "See 'em try. They won't live to regret it." "Could blow up into a real war, no?" "Not likely. They're dug in good, but it's a defensive formation. Soon as they stick out a nose—they get it." "What's all that from Beirut about Syrian forces moving on the border?" "Could be. We didn't notice." "And Nasser warning he'll join in." "Talks about us and means it for Hussein." "Figures we're scheming with Hussein to topple the regime in Syria, eh?" "That's what the Russians tell him." "Yeah. Read what *Pravda* said? General Rabin brandishing his sword!" "Poppycock. Like at the Security Council. What's his name, their delegate?" "Petrov." "Eshkol got scared all the same. Called in the ambassadors of the Four Powers." "We ought to cross the border, blow up a few villages like we did at Hirbet and Rif'at, shut 'em up for a bit." "Not that easy, I'd say, with all those entrenchments—Tel-Azaziyat, Tel-Hamra, the Banyas. They've got a hell of a topographical advantage over us there." "Not easy, sure, but you can avoid them. Like Banyas you can get to from behind. Just let 'em give us the green light!" "Eshkol's scared." "Let him put Rabin in charge!" "The way the Arabs have it, eh?" "In security matters, why not? Eshkol can manage the budget and leave the fighting to Rabin!" "Think again." "When you got them sitting there on top of you, once is enough!"

Shuka was seized with a fit of homesickness for his camp, for a stint of Reserve duty; for the backslapping encounter with old acquaintances gathering from far and wide as to a class reunion; to his quartermaster's counter over which he hands out shiny greased guns, munition belts, blankets reeking of grease, uniforms reeking of disinfectant; to that whole noisy, bustling traffic with its cheerful exchange of profanities, with soldiers coming and going, collecting and depositing, signing receipts, being checked off on lists, being scolded and giving back as good; to the sweaty hullabaloo of the mess, the din of plates, the jugs of watery compote, the soup bowls, the jokes flying across tables, the easy flirtation with girl secretaries; to the iron beds with the straw pallets, the dusty concrete floors, the stag-party atmosphere of after-duty discussions. He wondered when his call-up would come.

"Either of you know Major Gilead?"

"Uh-huh, from the commando."

"How's he doing?"

"Okay. Wife had a baby couple of weeks back. Girl."

"Great! His fourth. Give him regards from Shuka. Shuka Tal."

"Golani reserves?"

"Southern Command. Old friends. Since schooldays. Remember Raphi?" Turning to Elisheva.

"Which Raphi?"

"Steinberg. The one whose people lived next door to the Local Council."

"What about him?"

"Signed on for the Regular Army ten, twelve years back. Already had three kids then. Changed his last name to Gilead. I told you about meeting him at Rafiah during the Sinai Campaign. . . ."

On the outskirts of Afula he followed a car into a filling station, stopped beside it, asked the driver for his destination, and when he was told "Tiberias," transferred the two soldiers to it. "Don't forget: Major Gilead. From Shuka Tal. Nes-Ziona," he said in parting.

A tense autumn hush lay over the fields on the way to the village. Tall, brittle thorn-stalks trembled in the nagging wind. Gray birds trailed low over the stubble and perched swaying on bushes. "Sparrows?" Shuka sent a look after them. Elisheva shrugged. "Sparrows," he said.

"Smell of chicken runs," he said as they entered the village street. "Chicken manure." Then he stopped to inquire for the Lev home.

The front of the house looked peaceful enough, with nothing to indicate anxiety or sorrow. Under a hibiscus flowering among the Persian lilac, a cat was grubbing the soil with its hind legs, and from a corner of the yard came the drowsy mutter of hens. Shuka stopped at the gate and picked up a handful of soil, smoothed it in his palm, and said, "See? Basalt."

Dinah wasn't there. Her mother, a buxom, healthy-looking, effusive woman, was *so* glad to meet Elisheva, of whom she'd been hearing *so* much from her daughter. The father, thin, with a shriveled face and a dry smile, said little. Both were surprised to be told by Elisheva that their daughter had been away from Tel Aviv for several days, but Shuka took note of the fact that it did not seem to worry them overmuch. "She'll have gone to visit Shoshana," the father surmised, explaining that Shoshana Ulitzki was a childhood friend at present living at Kibbutz Ayelet Hashahar, and that Dinah went there often. "She'd have written to say, Avraham," the mother objected. "She doesn't tell us everything"—the father, with a smile at Shuka. "She'll be *so* sorry to have missed you"—the mother. "She's got such a high opinion of you"—the father flatteringly to Elisheva.

Hava Lev pressed them to stay to dinner, but they declined, saying they had only looked in for a few minutes and ought to be on their way. Hava drew near Elisheva and asked her to sit down at the table a minute, presumably for a little confidential chat.

When they were seated the father took possession of Shuka and led him out through the back door to show him the farm.

Pausing to inspect the green fodder, Shuka inquired about the percentage of lime in the soil, the amount of drainage, whether sulfuric fertilizer was used, and so on. When Avraham showed surprise at his familiarity with matters agricultural, he explained that he had grown up in a village, that his father had been a vet and that he himself had always been fond of the country. "There used to be a time when I thought of becoming a beekeeper." With a deprecating smile. "Afraid you'd get stung, so you turned insurance agent," Lev joked. "In the insurance business you get stung worse than a beehive, believe me," Shuka replied. "I'm sure it's no bed of roses," said Lev. "You can bet," said Shuka. "More nearly a bed of nails, sometimes." But wishing to get the conversation away from himself he asked to what extent the austerity was felt at the farm. "It's hard, of course," said Lev. "Outlay on supplies has gone up, production costs have gone up, but we've got to take it, like it or not. In the long run their policy is correct. A lot more goes to export now. Most of our eggs are sent to Europe." "Yes, the government needs money," said Shuka. "The security budget alone comes to four hundred fifty million dollars!" And as they passed on to the situation on the Syrian border, Shuka recalled his talk with the soldiers and said that what ought to be done was raid a few villages across the border to teach the Syrians a lesson. When Lev voiced his doubts, considering the danger involved in such an operation, Shuka said, "There's ways. They got all those strongholds, true, but you can avoid them, get there from behind."

The two women rose when they came in. Hava Lev looked flushed and as though suppressing some emotion, and Elisheva did not appear quite calm either. Presently the hosts saw their visitors out, and Hava Lev kept waving after the moving car.

"Home?" asked Shuka, stopping where the road joined the highway.

Elisheva was gazing straight ahead as though turning things over in her mind.

"Home?" he repeated.

"Would you mind going on up north?" she asked, a little uncertainly.

"Up north where?"

"I thought we might look in at Ayelet Hashahar. Maybe she's there, at her friend's."

Shuka scanned her face: something wrong with her, and she won't tell.

"Her parents aren't worried, so why should you be?"

"Please, if it's not too far," she said, dejected.

Something wrong with her. Even if you'd ask she wouldn't say.

"To Ayelet Hashahar!" he announced, a general sounding the charge, and with that put the car into gear and turned north.

Approaching Kfar-Yehezkel, he asked:

"What did she talk to you about, her mother?"

"Three guesses," said Elisheva with a sad smile.

"But she's not worried."

"Badly worried."

"What about?"

"Her condition, her future, everything," she said nervously. "I told you she's in a bad state emotionally."

"She never impressed me that way at all. Quite the contrary, I always thought—serene . . . I'd almost say happy."

"That's what you think. It's just on the outside."

Shuka remembered about her poetry, about what Avigayil had said. A person's face tells you very little of what goes on inside him, he told himself.

"One thing I'm sure of anyway," he said, "is that she hasn't done anything silly."

The sky was growing lighter the farther they went, and the Jordan Valley lay in a gentle springlike warmth. The plain and the hills to the east were a soft pearly white that filled his eyes. Roads lined with olive trees, banana plantations, clusters of white houses, banks of rushes, grapefruit orchards, wide stretches of green and gold. "What a beautiful land!" he marveled. "What a beautiful land!" Elisheva turned her glance to the east, to the hills. "And so peaceful! Idyllic!" Sweeping the whole plain with his arm. "Why don't you say anything?" He slapped her knee. "I admire in silence," she smiled. "Sing me something." He nudged her with his elbow. "Have you ever heard me sing?" "But here, in all this! . . . If I were a poet I'd make you a poem!" "Try!"

Arriving close to Deganya, he said:

"All right, here goes—first stanza: 'By the Hills of Gilead/ White as a pearl/I love you, my darling/My innocent girl." How's that, Doctor?"

Elisheva looked at him affectionately and her eyes filled with tears.

"What is it, Eli?" he said wretchedly. "What's making you so unhappy?"

Elisheva pulled a handkerchief out of her bag and blew her nose.

"Memories? Regrets?"

"No, nothing . . ."

"Look at the Kinneret!" Trying to cheer her up as they drove along the lake. "Isn't she a beauty?" Then he said, "Let's stop at Tiberias and I'll buy you a splendid fish dinner."

The water swished rhythmically against the quay where they ate. The cloud on Elisheva's face darkened his brow. "Don't you like it?" he said disappointed, watching her pick without relish at the fried fish. "I'm not hungry," she said. He tried to get her to talk but did not manage to win a single smile out of her. When he had finished his food he tore the leftover bread to pieces, threw them in the water, and watched the tiny fishes shoot up to the surface, nibble at the bread, fan out and away and back again to nibble. The sight did not make him glad. His eyelids drooped and he did not know whether with tiredness or grief. With tiredness, he told himself, remembering that he hadn't had more than four or five hours' sleep last night. Elisheva got up and went to the washrooms and he paid the waiter and stood looking at two bronzed and slippery boys who were leaping into the water, diving, bouncing up, and leaping in again. He wondered how they stood the cold.

"Shall we go on?" he said when she came back.

"Lot of blood," she said.

"Where?" he asked in alarm.

"Got my period yesterday," she said.

He was puzzled. It didn't fit his count.

"So late?"

"Uh-huh. I didn't know what to make of it either. Was getting worried already."

When they were under way again he told himself that that explained why she was so jumpy, so tense. The usual biological business: alternate waves of depression and hysteria. The blood draining out of the body, and the spirit troubled. A bundle of nerves. He made another count and found she was ten days late. Unusual. First sign of the coming menopause?

He felt a heavy fatigue in all his limbs.

At Ein-Tabha he turned off the highway and started toward the lake.

"Where are you going?" she asked, surprised.

"*Must* have a break," he said.

And drove along the narrow twisting road up to the grove at the water's edge.

Druse women in long dresses, bright yellow and blue, lilac, scarlet, were paddling in the lake up to their knees, whooping and giggling and squealing, a flight of exotic birds rending the peace of Eden.

Shuka lay down at the foot of a large eucalyptus tree, his head against its roots, his feet touching the shingle. "Just fifteen minutes to stretch my legs," he said to Elisheva who was sitting with her back against another tree, and closed his eyes.

He woke up in a sweat, recalling his dream:

Jeanette worked at a cold-drinks factory, operating a capping machine. The bottles turned on a round metal disc and an arm of the machine pressed the tin caps down on them as they passed. He stood by her side and told her he had invented some device to improve the process and do away with the earsplitting rattle.

He couldn't think what the device had been like now.

When the foreman moved away he told her to come with him. They left the factory and climbed the path up the hill. There was a tool shed halfway up, and he suggested they go in and lie there. She agreed and whispered joyfully: At last, at last! But when they entered they saw there was nowhere to lie down, for the shed was filled with rakes and plows. When he pulled up her dress she said, Not here, Yehoshua, not here, let's go outside, on the grass. They went out and continued up the path, and when they reached the top of the hill Elisheva appeared before them. He was overwhelmed by a terrible feeling of shame and by a sense of finality, of death. He wanted to swear to her that nothing had happened between them but knew she wouldn't believe him.

"How long have I slept?" he asked.

"Five minutes, six . . . Go on, sleep, sleep a bit longer."

Shuka shifted himself over to her and put his head in her lap.

"It seemed like an hour."

"What made you groan like that?" Stroking his hair. "Had a dream?"

"Guess so, don't remember."

"Close your eyes, sleep."

He lay still a moment longer, nestled in her lap, taking comfort from her touch after the horror of the dream. Then he shook himself and got to his feet. "Let's go," he said.

They arrived at Kibbutz Ayelet Hashahar toward dusk. They parked in the square in front of the dining hall, and Elisheva suggested that he wait till she found Shoshana Ulitzki. If Dinah was there she would come for him, if not—they'd turn back at once.

Shuka inspected the square, wandered across the lawns, climbed a hillock and surveyed the kibbutz, the plain to the north, the grizzly Hermon. He could make out the buildings of Kibbutz Hulata in the distance and, vaguely, the main street of Yesod-Hama'ala marked by a row of trees, some patches of reed. It must be ten or twelve years since he'd been here last. The landscape had stayed the same, but the kibbutz itself had changed out of all recognition. He remembered old yellowing houses, cracked and crumbling concrete paths, wispy apple trees and overgrown yards. Now he found a splendid park, fountains, a sizable swimming pool, trim houses, and on the edge of the settlement the modern constructions of a luxurious guesthouse. He stood and looked at this, hands in pockets, like a man checking over property in which he has a share. He speculated on its profitability: 32 rooms, he believed. Could put up 64 guests in peak season. Say 60. At 25 pounds a day that would come to 1500 gross. The number of personnel would be 30 at most. Assuming an outlay per person of even 10 pounds a day, they'd be left with a net profit of 900. Divide by 30 personnel, you'd get 30 pounds for a workday. Not bad for wages. Though not all that high either—

He walked back to the car, and not finding Elisheva turned to explore in another direction. He spotted the dairy where cows stood trampling the mud and dung, and drew near the gate. Enclosed in its pen stood the bull, black, white browed, the tuft of its male organ limp, its testicles dangling heavy between the short thick legs. As a boy of eight, he remembered, in the summer vacation, he had accompanied his father on his calls, and it was then he had seen the act of copulation for the first time. How the bull, its shaft red and long and slender as a lance, had leaped with its forelegs on top of the cow as if to overpower her, and his father had taken hold of the trembling moist organ with his own hands and guided it at the vulva. And he himself with his own eyes had seen the lust of the bull when thrusting toward the uterine passage, and the shiver of pleasure passing through the cow's back, and his father had pummeled her spine with a stick from neck down to tail, he hadn't known why. His own little organ had stiffened too, embarrassingly, and he had blushed and shuffled his feet pretending to scrape at clods of soil with his shoes. Presently he had seen the bull's shaft, tip dripping, contract and return to its sheath, and he had marveled at such a long staff vanishing inside it. A scene of much violence and wonder, kind of a revelation of nature's elements, and it had stayed in his mind for days, years.

Now, when he heard the cows' mournful lowing, his mind went back wistfully to those times with his father, making the rounds of stables—to the odor of Lysol at periodical foot-and-mouth epidemics, to the serum injected by flashlight between the ribs of cows with inflammation of the udder; to their pitifully shrunken, wrinkled udders. Mastitis, he remembered. That's what it was called. And brucellosis was the one that caused abortions. Or could that have been the name of the virus? The serum? And then there was rinderpest, and pneumonic fever, and bovine tuberculosis, and there had been quarantine, and the blood and milk testing, and the vac . . . vaccination.

One cow reared up over the hindquarters of another as if to mount it. "Randy," he remembered, and turned in his tracks.

Elisheva stood waiting by the car.

"Didn't find her, of course," he said taking the keys out of his pocket.

"No."

"Honestly now, wasn't it pointless to come all this way to Ayelet Hashahar just because . . . Surely if something had really happened . . ." Opening the car door and getting in.

Elisheva got in on her side without replying.

"They'd have informed her parents, announced it on the radio . . . nobody can disappear just like that . . ." Turning the key in the ignition.

But the engine didn't start. The indicator lights were on and the engine didn't start.

"What's wrong?"

"I don't know. Maybe she's overheated from the long drive." He made several more attempts but produced no sound except for a squeal from the switch.

He got out, raised the hood, tugged at a wire here and there, knowing it was useless. He was gripped by dismay: here, at the other end of the country, a five hours' drive from home, and on a Saturday. Stuck. And what for?

Two boys came by and he asked them to push him downhill. Maybe a miracle would happen, like that other time.

Elisheva got out and helped with the pushing. At the bottom of the slope he let out the clutch but the engine didn't even splutter.

The boys offered explanations: the battery empty, the dynamo gone, the starter overheated and burned.

"Know of any garage open around here?"

"Saturday. Everything closed. Stay the night at the guest-house, you'll get somebody to fix it tomorrow morning." They stayed awhile, commiserating, then went off.

"What are we going to do?" Elisheva looking to him for succor.

"We'll stay. Nothing in for it."

· 216 ·

"I'm not going to spend the night here," she said resolutely, "not under any condition."

"What do you want us to do then?"

"Anything except stay here. I'll walk down to the highway and thumb a lift. I'll get home somehow."

"By yourself?"

"I can't stay! Don't you see? I can't!" she cried out passionately.

Shuka looked at her and again he thought: something's happened to her, something that's thrown her completely off balance. No, it couldn't be just her period.

"I'm sorry, Shuka," she said in a low voice, "but I'm in a bad state. Believe me—bad. I know it's my fault. I shouldn't have dragged you all this way. No point at all. But I'll go out of my mind if I have to stay here a whole night. You can't leave the car so I'll go back alone. See you tomorrow."

And she turned and walked rapidly down in the direction of the highway.

Shuka got into the car and applied himself to the key. Angry and hurt, he was praying for the miracle to happen now, for the engine to come alive: he'd drive off, pass her without stopping, and leave her stranded on the road.

He turned the key hard, again and again, in first gear, in second, in reverse, with the brakes engaged, released.

Emerging from the car, despondent and bitter, he saw Elisheva coming back.

"Let's go over to the guesthouse then," she said.

"I'm sorry," she said when they got there.

The room was stuffy and smelled of disinfectant and new furniture. As soon as they turned the lights off they heard the drone of a mosquito, reeling from wall to wall, landing somewhere for a moment's suspense, and striking out again with a thin persistent whine. Shuka hit out a few times at his cheeks, his arms, to crush it, but the drone resumed, ominous and shattering. He got out of bed, turned on the light, found DDT in the wall cupboard, shut the window, and sprayed thick clouds of it in all directions, on the walls, the furniture, the ceiling. Afterward, lying in the dark, a heavy silence in the drugged air, he heard the lowing of cows from afar.

He heard Elisheva's breathing, her tossing and turning in the bed. After a long time, an hour or two, he heard her get up, go to the bathroom, take a shower, come back and lie down. He heard her lying still for a while, and then growing restless again, and in the dark he saw her pulling the blanket up over her head, then kicking it off, then rolling over on her stomach, then flat on her back again, hands under head.

"Why aren't you sleeping?"

"I can't. Why aren't you?"

"Try not to think. Close your eyes and don't think."

"I tried. It's no use. I'd as soon get up and start walking, all the way to Tel Aviv."

"Are you too hot?"

"Not, it's not that. Go to sleep, Shuka, don't take any notice of me. You needn't stay awake because of me."

He was moved, filled with tenderness, wanted to take her in his arms, comfort her, lull her to sleep under his wing, but did not dare cross the distance between the two beds. He sensed she was keeping something from him, something that put a barrier between them. He thought of what she had said about his being "honest" and told himself that now was the time to unbosom himself to her, here, in the dark, in this room, because if not now . . . And at the same time he knew: a dangerous step, fateful, fraught with disaster.

After a prolonged agony of indecision he braced himself and took the leap in the dark:

"I've got a confession to make to you."

And felt as if he were dropping from a great height, and only a miracle could save him from being shattered to bits.

He waited for her to say something, but she kept silent.

Then he said, heavily:

"I know that what I'm going to say now . . . may finish everything between us. But . . . I must. Owe it to myself, if not to you."

Elisheva lay motionless, her face intent on the ceiling.

"It's a thing of the past. Something that was. Not anymore. But I've got to tell. Must be no lies. Just *because* you trust me. As you said."

Her silence heavy as a millstone.

"I could just as well have kept it. Guess you'd never have found out."

He fell silent. Frightening abyss. And the words he'd say— more sinful than the deed.

When the silence dragged on, she said in a dry voice, "Tell me."

"I expect you can guess."

"No."

He held back still, as though waiting for an angel to deflect his knife-holding hand from the altar. Then he took a deep breath:

"I've been involved. With a woman. Not long. Few months ago."

And felt dizzy, as though falling, a long drop, with the bed, the floor, the entire room. And did not dare turn his head to look at her.

"Now you want to leave me," he said.

Elisheva heaved herself up, her back against the wall, hands hugging knees. The silence hung heavy in the room.

"What's her name?" she said at last.

He was stunned. Her being able to ask, to speak at all.

"You don't know her."

"Still?"

He felt dizzy again, overwhelmed by shame. After a moment he said: "Annabel."

"Annabel what?"

He did not answer, felt trapped, sullied. Instead of the cleansing truth—another lie.

"You can tell. You know I'd consider it beneath me to go and search for her."

For a brief moment he could tell himself it made no difference, it might just as well have been Annabel. But against his will he lied again.

"Liebermann," he said.

"Pretty name, Annabel," she said.

"It all happened a long time ago."

"How long?"

"Six, seven months."

"And since then . . ."

"Nothing."

The darkness hid his flaming face.

"How many times?"

"What?"

"Did you sleep with her."

His heart froze. The bald phrase, which he had never spelled out even to himself. Exposed in all its vulgarity. And what was meant to be a cleansing confession turned into a humiliating inquest.

"I don't remember."

"Twenty? Thirty?"

He felt strangled. On the rack. The more he'd answer the more she'd ask, probe. The deeper in he'd get.

"I don't remember." Mutinously.

"Still?"

"I don't remember. I told you: It's a thing of the past. Nothing now, as though it never happened."

"What made you give it up?"

"I felt I didn't want it."

"Afraid I'd find out?"

"No." Then added, "You never seemed to care what I did with my evenings anyway."

"Nor you . . ." But she stopped and pulled the blanket over her legs.

"What about me?"

"Forget it."

A vague suspicion floated into his mind, but he pushed it away.

"Pretty?" she asked.

"Who?"

"Her. Isabelle, Annabel . . ."

"Yes." Matter-of-factly.

"Married."

"Yes."

"And her husband . . ."

"Never saw him."

"Where did you use to meet? Her place?"

"What difference does that make now?"

"If it makes no difference you can tell me."

"Yes, at her place."

"When the husband was out."

He said nothing.

"How old?"

"Don't know. Thirty-two, three."

"A blond?" With a little laugh.

"Yes."

Elisheva closed her eyes, her head thrown back at the ceiling as though in immense weariness.

A chill went through him. Everything was finished. He pictured the hopeless parting tomorrow: he'd have the car fixed, and then there'd be the long trip, the tormenting silence all the way to Tel Aviv. And when they'd come home she'd pack her things and move out. He'd be left with Avigayil. Left with the office, Ziona. Life insurance.

And all for one moment of folly, when he'd made the blunder of opening his big mouth. If he hadn't, everything would have stayed the same. Forever. One moment of folly, and no turning back.

A single spark of hope: on the way, the long way home, four or five hours, he might yet be able to explain. Explain himself. The circumstances. That it had been of no account, that nothing had really changed. Maybe she'd understand and forgive.

Suddenly he heard her voice:

"That evening of the party, when you left all of a sudden and no one knew what had become of you . . . was it to her you went?"

Shame welled up in him again, burning shame not to be redeemed by a lie. To be paid for.

"Yes," he admitted.

"To celebrate your birthday in her bed?"

"You'll have to leave me," he said, utterly crushed.

"Oh, you fool!" She buried her face in her hands and laughed.

Her laughter shook him, the sound of it bubbling into her hands, spluttering. It took a moment before he realized the laughter had turned into a sob, stifled sobs trickling in tears down her face.

She got out of bed, rummaged in her handbag, found a handkerchief, and lay down again, turned her back to him and covered herself with the blanket.

He swung his legs to the floor, looked at her, then crossed the distance and knelt by her bed.

"Eli." Touching her arm.

"Leave me alone." Flinching as though he were filth.

"Eli," he tried again.

Silence. Then, without turning her face to him:

"You might at least have waited till after my period." In a hoarse voice, muffled with tears.

When the windows paled with dawn he felt a bitter hurt, bitterer than all the night's offenses, when he saw how she had fallen asleep, was sleeping profoundly, with light peaceful breaths drifting on the morning air.

"OF course the story really begins only in the second chapter," Elisheva was telling some thirty students gathered in the spacious room, which was cut in half by a shaft of noon light slanting in through the wide window. "We recognize it in the 'frontal' opening that takes up right away both to the narrational sensation and to the hero who is its object: 'That morning Collegiate Assessor Kovalev had awakened rather early . . .' and in the third sentence we are already told that, looking in the mirror, 'he was bewildered to find that instead of his nose there was nothing but a bare smooth surface.' He jumps out of bed, shakes himself—no nose. And next moment he rushes off to the police station to report the theft. Note how the narrational flow is at once broken off in the next passage by a typical Gogol interjection that has its precise parallel in the opening of 'The Overcoat.' The parenthetical passage contains a satirical observation about the bureaucratic hierarchy under the czarist regime—the titles, the ranks, the status of collegiate assessors, corresponding to the aside about 'departments' in 'The Overcoat.' Remarks like these are scat-

tered throughout the story and achieve a peak of comic tren-
chancy in the depiction of Kovalev's boastfulness whenever he
finds himself in the presence of the state counsellor's wife and the
senior officer's widow. We are therefore bound to conclude that
this matter of rank and social status forms an integral compo-
nent of the overall meaning . . ."

But the name Annabel rang incessantly through her mind,
and side by side with the shadowy figures of the assessor Kovalev
and the barber Yakovlevich, her eyes beheld the image of a
gorgeous blonde, now with long flowing locks, now with short
dancing curls, always with the eyes of a huntress in pursuit of
quarry.

"In this work, just as in the Slavonic folklore which served
Gogol as a source of inspiration, we find a mixture of the real
and the fantastic—in our case, a piece of hocus-pocus: the
mysterious disappearance of the nose and its transformation
into a person wearing the outfit of a state councilor. However,
the surrealistic element does not, as with Kafka, constitute a
sealed world, independent and self-contained and with its own
set of rules. In this connection, it is interesting to note the
writer's own attitude toward the element of the fantastic of his
own creation, an attitude which, as we shall see in a moment, he
voices at several points in the story. At the end of the first, the
introductory chapter . . ."

Elisheva opened the book lying on the desk before her, but as
she turned its pages to find the relevant quotations she found
leaping out of the pages instead the nude, the completely nude
body of the gorgeous blonde sprawled on a bed, spreading her
legs with a whorish leer at the figure crouching over her.

"Yes," she said, closing the book, "three times the author
interrupts his narrative to remark on its supernatural aspect: a
kind of irony doubling up on itself. He concludes the first
chapter with the words: '. . . But here the incident becomes
befogged and it is completely unknown what happened after
this point.' At the end of the second chapter he describes the
superstitions that were rife among the people at that time, such

as a belief in magnetism, witchcraft, and the like. And at the end of the story he himself treats the whole of it as a thing in the middle somewhere between fable and farce. . . ."

"As literary fancy," a student put in from his place in the third row.

"Yes, quite"

"As a kind of thing he pretends to be amazed authors choose to write about, as he says," the same student added, encouraged by her assent.

"And demanding a suspension of belief." With a smile at him. "A piece of irony within irony."

And saying it she paused. For an instant, as though in flash of eerie light, everything, everything seemed like a piece of irony within irony to her: all that had happened in the past few months, all the coincidences, her standing here now lecturing on Gogol while somewhere there existed one Annabel, and somewhere else—heaven knew where—a writer called Brosh and all this life, rent, riven—

"Let us return to the business of the nose, however," she resumed. "The deformation of a bodily organ is, of course, quite an old ironic device. Think of fairy tales, or of Ovid's *Metamorphoses*. Man is turned into an animal, a plant, a stone; one of man's organs, standing for a certain quality in him, is cut off, vanishes, or, on the contrary, assumes abnormal proportions, or adopts a bestial guise. Think of Bottom in *Midsummer Night's Dream* or, to switch for a moment to contemporary literature, Ionesco's *Rhinoceros*. The nose in Gogol's story is a symbol of overweening pride, of presumptuous ambition. Just as it does miraculously vanish and turn into a silly official strutting along the Nevski Prospect; just as it is found at last by the inspector and returned to its owner, who has difficulty sticking it back on his face again . . ." For a moment she lost the thread, hesitated.

"The physician suggests he keep the nose in a jar of methylated spirits." The student sprang jauntily into the breach.

"Yes, to preserve it . . . And just as it vanishes one morning for no good reason, so it reappears again one morning in its proper place between the two cheeks, again for no good reason. Gogol's innovation, however, does not lie in the use of this literary gimmick, but in his introducing it into the social context of his period. The point is that he uses it to ruffle, however briefly, the social stagnation in which his characters are wallowing. It's as though he had cast a pebble into a muddy pool and created a tiny ripple. . . . The ripple will dissolve soon enough, of course, and everything will be smooth again. . . . But the pebble has been cast, and it has been cast in the form of a joke, and the entire social fabric is suddenly revealed in an ironic light. . . ."

Annabel! A bitter smile rose to her lips as she dropped into the chair at her office and cast her books on the desk. Not Sarah, not Leah, not Yocheved—Annabel. Annabel Lee in a kingdom by the sea. How unutterably romantic. Or maybe—a little bourgeois bitch in a boudoir. Or even less—a common hussy. Her name like one of those lists of glamour beside a row of lighted doorbells in Soho doorways: Violet, Diane, Laura, Annette, Jeanette. Annabel. Third landing. Cheap perfume and brief red panties. Mind it? Yes. Frankly, yes. The irony of fate: while your sick imagination is furiously plotting how to find, foil . . . suddenly, a dull blow on the head: Annabel. Fleeing lover and faithless husband. *Quid pro quo* of a Molière comedy of cuckolds. A fool's revenge on the subtly cunning mind. *Sancta simplicitas.* Yes, my dear Julius, there's another one for your Praise of Folly. Fools rushing in all right.

A moral query, Doctor: When a person is being paid back in his own coin, measure for adulterous measure, what right has he to feel injured?

Because Pascal: The heart has its reasons which reason does not know.

A psychological query, Doctor: If just punishment for sin is supposed to cleanse the heart of guilt, why then does it fill *your* heart with a thirst for revenge?

Because the heart's reasons are not subject to laws of morality either.

A *theo*-logical query, Doctor: Hell—and I am referring to the fire of jealousy and the brimstone of vindictive fantasies—is it a punishment sent by God or a game thought up by the devil?

Purely rhetorical: you believe in neither.

Is there an All-Seeing Eye? Sin and retribution? Eye for eye?

The telephone, she recalled. That evening, when he had gone pink, grown confused, floundered, lost his wits. Hadn't been an Annabel sort of voice, though, not blond. Oriental, rather. Or maybe there'd been more than one. Two, four, twenty. Insurance salesman going from door to door, and sin lieth at every door. Holes invite rats in. Husbands not home and free play. And a lot of them go for that big, jolly, bear-hugging type. When had it been, that phone call? August. Hadn't been seeing her for six-seven months, had he? The liar.

Must be an all-seeing, all-hearing something after all, and all your deeds in the open ledger: Brosh on the one hand and Tal on the other, in a league to apply the bitter water.

Quid pro quo.

She made an effort to collect her thoughts for her next lecture. The substantive difference between the opening of "The Nose" and that of "Metamorphosis," she rehearsed to herself. The assessor Kovalev and Gregor Samsa. Kafka creates a hermetically sealed universe and leaves it to its own laws without interfering, qua narrator, even once. Whereas Gogol . . . While in both cases—the deformation of organs . . . Hocus-pocus, organ vanishes, puff . . .

Might put Shuka's organ in a jar for preservation, she giggled to herself suddenly.

Kind of like a bird, black, long-necked, plucked bird in a jar on a shelf.

The idea sent the blood to her cheeks and she started toying with it. Make a nice story, a la Gogol, opening:

"Insurance salesman Yehoshua Tal awakened early that morning, got out of bed, and, stepping out of his pajama pants discovered with astonishment that the shaft of his manhood, the apple of his pie . . ."

The thing was making her laugh, was fun, and she continued to embroider on it:

". . . that his shaft, the precious tool that had served him so well all these years—was gone! He couldn't believe his eyes: How? When? Where had it gone? What a hideous disaster! . . ."

She had the entire story framed in her head, from start to finish, complete, perfect, very funny. She pulled a blank sheet of paper from the tray on her desk, wrote the first sentences she had composed in her mind, and continued:

"In a panic he pulled at the sheet, ransacked his half of the bed—the other half being occupied by the still sleeping Annabel—and found nothing. He scrabbled about the floor by the bed—could it have dropped between his knees when he sat up?—peered inside his shoes, between the chair legs, under the bedside table—gone without a trace. Impossible! he told himself, groping for his crotch and convincing himself anew that alas—oh, horror!—instead of his sweet sugarplum there was a smooth patch of fur. Sick at heart he stood facing the bed, nothing but the pajama tops to his body, and felt the world go black. This is worse than death, he mumbled, worse than death.

" 'Annabel,' he whispered softly, trying to awaken his bed-mate.

"Annabel was lying on her side, wrapped in her sheet, the gold-yellow hair falling over the pillow.

" 'Annabel,' in a broken but slightly louder voice.

"Annabel opened her eyes and saw a curious sight, the significance of which didn't penetrate her sleep-dazed mind: the big awkward hulk of a man was standing before her in a queer pose, his legs apart, his broad face straining to keep back the tears, and one hand pulling at a corner of his jacket to hide his private parts.

" 'Look what's happened,' he said and raised the jacket an inch or so.

"She could make nothing of it at first, but when after rubbing the cobwebs out of her eyes she spotted the vacancy, she clapped her hand over her mouth to hold back a scream.

" 'But it can't be!' she exclaimed, sitting up with a jerk. 'We had it with us all night, didn't we!'

" 'Yes,' Yehoshua Tal agreed balefully.

"She refused to believe it. She stared at the furry patch down his voluminous belly, seeking to find what ought so naturally to be there, and was horrified when the truth stared her full in the face at last: the bird had flown out of its bush! It can't be—she put her hands to her cheeks—it's unheard of! Impossible! 'Could it have . . . slipped . . . fallen? . . .' Gazing at him bleakly.

" 'I looked . . .' he said in a wretched voice.

"With a resolute gesture she flung off the sheet and started hunting frantically through the bed, under the pillows, in the folds of the bedclothes, poking the mattress in case it had got stuck somewhere, then going down on all fours, peering under the bed, delving as far as her hands would reach.

"Yehoshua Tal stook with his eyes lowered, blinking down the slope of his belly. He felt like crying to see himself unhinged, robbed of his heraldic sword, the staff of his life. Gone. And instead—"

Briefly Elisheva paused. The scene stood out vividly before her eyes, and she relished her racy description, the fluent, lucid phrases, with the kind of relish obtained from scratching at itch. She tried to imagine how he would in fact behave if it *really* happened to him, and presently she continued:

"Then he shook his head and started to dress.

" 'What're you doing?' cried Annabel.

" 'Twenty to eight,' he muttered. 'Got to go to work.'

" 'Work!' she gasped.

"Yehoshua Tal hadn't missed a day's work for the past fifteen years, rain or shine. At eight o'clock in the morning he would show up at the office, spend a few hours at his desk, then go out to run about town in his car, capturing new clients, hurrying to the scene of an accident, collecting premiums, and, in case of a death, appearing solicitously in the house of mourning to console the family and settle their affairs. He had witnessed plenty of disasters in his life, and now—such a disaster! And not even insured.

" 'Have you looked in the bathroom?' asked Annabel, looking at him with commiseration.

" 'In the bathroom . . .' He emitted a dismal snort. 'You figure it's a mouse or something running from one hole to another?'

"Nevertheless, going to wash and shave, he surveyed the bathroom floor from wall to wall and even bent down to glance under the washing machine. For an instant the suspicion flashed through his mind that Annabel's husband, Mr. Liebermann, had returned from his trip sometime during the night, crept into the house, stolen his treasure—tit for tat—and run off with it. But he drove the thought away at once: How could the man have known he had spent the night with his wife?

"Annabel came to him, kissed his mouth, and whispered, 'Coming tonight?'

"Tal was about to nod his head in assent when it struck him, a piercing arrow: He'd come, would he? How? What for, dismembered as he was? Ruined!

"And now a worse thought struck him: When he got home, what would his wife say when she discovered his undoing?"

She paused again and suddenly all the fun had gone out of it and only left a bitter taste in her mouth. She thought how for months on end, for nights without number, she had been living under a deception. A great drama had raged, rampant with dark violent passions, and she had known nothing of it. She had been fooled, cheated, conspired against, and it was no comfort at all to know that at the very same time she herself had been taken up with a drama of her own, equally passionate and dark. Neither comfort nor cause for forgiveness. She took up her pen to go on with the story, but her heart was no longer in it:

"Throwing her arms about his neck, Annabel raised her eyes at him and murmured, 'Don't worry, darling . . . it'll be all right. . . . I'm sure it will. . . . It'll come back suddenly just like it went, and everything'll be . . .'

"But in that instant she saw Tal's eyes, which were fixed at a point on the floor behind her back, open wide in ghastly fear, and when she turned to see what had happened she gave a shrill scream and jumped up on the bed.

" 'Kill it!' she shouted. 'Kill it!'

"Tal stood there petrified, unable to move a limb. A strange reptilian thing was creeping over the floor, a thing like a long-necked, shieldless tortoise. It was making for the bed, its revolting head shaking to and fro.

" 'Kill it! What are you standing there for!' wailed Annabel, dancing on the bed in her nightgown.

"But frozen with terror Tal made no move. He had recognized it at once for what it was—"

Elisheva read over what she had written, and when she came

to the end blurted out: Pastiche! and folded the three written pages, tore them up, and dropped the scraps in the wastebasket.

"**L**OOK, if it happend once," Ziona was saying, "but this is like the *fifth* time, and I simply can't look this old man, this Yermilowitz, in the eyes anymore. Hardly drags himself up the steps and all, and comes in here panting till I'm just about fit to cry, and every day I got to tell him: Tal's out, Tal won't be in, dunno when and all that, when all the time I know he's absolutely *right,* he's got a *claim* on them, the company's *got* to pay him. And it's not as if Tal denies it either, I saw all the papers, it all goes through me, right? So he comes, poor man, says what's gonna happen and all, and I just don't know *what* to tell him. Because my dear boss isn't even good enough to let me know where he's going and when he'll be back, just pops in for a couple of minutes in the morning, goes through the mail and buzzes off again, and that's the last I see of him all day. . . You there?"

After a moment she heard Rachel Molesco's voice at the other end of the line: "Just took a bite out of my sandwich. Go on."

"Thought you'd gone off."

"So why should you care though?" Rachel asked wearily.

"What?"

"I say what do you care? It just means less work for you."

"Sure, but it makes a girl feel bad all the same. Not just like this old man. People calling up and all and I just don't know what to tell them. I say he'll be in in the afternoon, and then sometimes he doesn't show up in the afternoon either, and kill me if I know where he's knocking about. . . ."

"A woman, I bet," said Rachel Molesco.

"Him? Don't make me laugh! He's scared of 'em!"

"Of you too?"

"Me? Hardly knows I exist. Try and ask him what color my hair is. Wouldn't surprise me if he were scared of his own wife."

"What's she like?"

"Search me. Never set eyes on her in my life. Brainy dame,

you know, professor at the university. With spectacles, I bet, and bats in the belfry."

"Nice voice?"

"On the phone, you mean? Hardly get a chance to find out. Phones him maybe once a month."

"Me, I could tell *you* everything that goes on between my boss and his wife."

"Listening in . . . ."

"Why not? A secretary's got to know everything."

"Interesting?"

"There's times I feel like I want to stick in a word, like telling her: Don't you see he's lying to you, Mrs. Rephaeli? Only just manage to keep my mouth shut."

"Mean he's got somebody on the side?"

"One? A proper Casanova!"

"With you, too, I guess. . . ."

"Fat chance he has!"

"That's what I keep telling you, like how I'm bored stiff in this place."

"Hold on a sec, somebody's come in. Don't hang up."

Rachel Molesco was employed by the lawyers' firm of Rephaeli and Shochat. The two girls would occasionally meet over lunch at the nearby café. Of late Ziona, out of sheer idleness, had taken to gossip with her for hours on the phone.

"Some goof," Rachel's voice came back. "I tell him Rephaeli's in court all day Wednesday, but he won't take no for an answer. Says he's going to stick around waiting for him. . . . So what were you saying? Ah, how you're bored stiff."

"I'm not complaining, but a girl wants a bit of fun sometimes, if you know what I mean. Eight hours is no joke, 'specially when you're all by yourself in the office nearly all day. And just now this place is a proper graveyard. . . . Something's got into him, into my boss, you mark my words. There's times I feel like he doesn't understand what people are saying to him. . . ."

"Like how?"

"Like— Look, I tell him I had a call from Hasneh and they're asking for the papers of one Perlmutter, so he gapes at me like I'd been talking Chinese or something, and then he says to me in such a voice, you know, like he didn't give a damn, he says, 'Can wait.' Can wait? I say, but the man's *died,* and his people need the money and all. . . . He doesn't care. And him so correct and businesslike always, too much even."

"Yeah, you told me."

"He's got me worried, I tell you. If I knew his wife I'd call her and tell her to look after her husband a bit, get him to see a doctor or something. . . ."

"Better keep out of it. You still seeing Gaby?"

"Mean I didn't tell you he called yesterday?"

"He did, did he?"

"I went all over queer when I heard his voice."

"Well, and?"

"Let him wait! I told him I hadn't got a single night free all week. Baby, he says to me flirty-like, Baby, you know I hate to hear you talk like that. . . ."

"They're all the same. Did he at least tell you where *he's* been hanging out all this time?"

"You don't think I'd ask, do you? A girl's got to have some pride. Oh, that reminds me," lowering her voice to a near whisper, "remember me telling you about Alice Markowsky?"

"That singer?"

"Yeah, from the Butterflies Duo. So she got pregnant, and then about a month ago she went and got rid of it."

"She didn't!"

"You heard me."

"And you telling me how she's a virgin and all."

"*Was,* my dear, *was.* So listen, so I meet her at the movies with Dan, and she doesn't *know* me. Fancy that. Haven't you two met? says Dan. So then at last she gives me a nod, all la-di-da, you know, doing things with her eyes. And then it so happens that we're sitting right behind them, Ziva Levy and me. So the picture starts and the lights go down . . ."

T HERE was a weight pressing against Tal's head, a hard, heavy weight, blunting vision. Like a stone. Mornings at the office he couldn't concentrate. If I talked to Annabel Shofman, he thought, the weight would lift, melt, and my sight clear up. A number of times—virtually every morning, in fact, as soon as he sat down at his desk—he had tried calling her, and every time he had drawn back. All he meant to say was but a word or so about the third installment of the annual premium being due, but as soon as he touched the instrument his hand would sag. Once he had gone as far as dialing the first four figures, though not before rehearsing the exact words he would say, in a fairly cool voice, not entirely cool but fairly cool. But when he got to the fifth figure he withdrew his finger from the dial and replaced the receiver. And again, concentrate on his work he could not.

If he could only just see her, he thought, meet her, just once, and on absolutely *neutral* ground. Say hello with a no-more-than-polite smile, remind her casually, as though quite by the way, of the outstanding debt, and that's all. Come across her accidentally, in the street, or some shop, or queuing up at the movies, or at a gas station. How are you, Mrs. Shofman, everything fine? Yes, me, I'm fine, thank you, working as usual, good-bye.

Once, over a year ago, she had said to him: You may call me Annabel. With a seductive smile.

Annabel nothing. Mrs. Shofman.

"What'll I say if people ask, Mr. Tal?" said Ziona when he passed her on his way out.

"Tell them I'll be back this afternoon."

"This old man, Yermilowitz, I expect he'll come in again today. Anything I should tell him?"

"I'm not in."

And he went down to the car. And drove northward, out of town.

The Shofman villa stood by itself on a narrow road running down to the beach, surrounded by its expanse of shrub-dotted lawn. He parked well out of sight, near a curve at the edge of a thin tamarisk copse, two wheels on the road and two in the sand. He got out, crossed the few steps to the copse, and obtained a view of the house: red-tiled sloping roof like some European country-residence; the blinds closed over the intimate secrets within; the massive door with its brass knocker keeping out strangers; the imperturbable peace of the lawns, the shrubs, the flagged path, as though all sunk in slumber. In front of the open brick garage—not inside it—stood the blue convertible. Hers.

Tal directed his steps toward the beach. If, as he passed the house, she should come out, he would say, Hello, Mrs. Shofman, and if she asked what had brought him here at such a time of day he would say: My morning exercise, to keep in shape. That's right, like Ben-Gurion. The waistline. Getting a day older, too. And if she invited him in he'd refuse. He'd casually mention the matter of the money and refuse to come in. No hurry, Mrs. Shofman, I know I can trust you. You can mail the check. Discount Bank, isn't it? That's right, I've got a memory for that kind of thing. Good-bye.

He'd feel relieved. Of this pressure at least.

Annabel did not come out. The house was quiet, as though asleep, and he walked on seaward.

Standing atop the dune, looking out to the sea which was murky and frothing after last night's rain, a shudder went through him: Everything had changed, everything, since that night at Ayelet Hashahar. The house seemed empty, cold. Even the white of the walls had turned a bleak white. You were aware of the sound of your own footsteps. And nobody to talk to. If at least she'd burst out at him. Or on the contrary, cut him dead. But no, she speaks when occasion calls for. There's some meat for you in the fridge. Avigayil asked if you could leave her five pounds before you go. I'll be a bit late today, sixish. Shmueli called, asked you to call back.

No sulking, no. On the contrary, softly, very softly, you could say gently even.

Twice he had tried to broach the subject, had wished to explain, had even considered confessing—a second confession—to reveal that the whole Annabel business had never been, that he had made it up. The first time she had announced: I don't want to hear. The second time she had got up and left the room.

Everything's gone to pieces, he told himself.

The sea was turbulent and murky and was whipping row upon row of waves toward the beach. A lone woman with a leather handbag dangling from her hand and with nothing but a faded dress to her body was trudging along the strip of damp sand below. She was moving curiously, staggering now and then, lurching drunkenly. Occasionally she would stoop, pick up something from the sand, shell or pebble, put it in her bag, and stagger on. A madwoman, he thought.

Suddenly he whirled around as if stung and rushed back. The notion had struck him that at this very moment someone was trying to break into his car and steal it. He crossed the distance between the dunes and the copse at a near run, and only calmed down when he saw her, meek and loyal pet sitting quietly under the trees.

Turning his head for a last glance at the house he suddenly caught sight of Annabel. She was coming out of the house dressed in a pair of tight brown slacks topped by a blazer, her hair tied up in a soft green scarf, and a gaily flowered bag in her hand. She strode briskly to the car, got in, started, backed out through the gate, made a swift sharp turn on the road, and drove off. As the car passed him he caught a flash of her profile—a blue glint of hair flowing out of the scarf; the sharp outline of brow, nose, chin, long throat; the slanting eye with its bright, mocking sparkle. He stood quite still, wondering, awed: The entire scene, from the moment she left the house till she swished out of sight, had had a sort of lyrical charm: the sportive-sophisticated clothes upon her stately figure, the way she swung the keys of her car as she crossed the path, a gesture of such feminine grace and yet of utter self-confidence; the elegance and sure skill of her driving . . . everything bespoke self-possession, self-assurance, beauty . . .

There never was anything between us, he told himself. Never. And getting into the car he felt the weight pressing against his head again.

A strange thing happened next time: He walked along the road, past the house, as far as the beach, turned in his tracks— the house peaceful, closed and shuttered, her car in its place before the open garage door—and reaching the copse he did not find his car where he had left it but some twenty or thirty paces farther on, and facing the other way. He was stunned: He did not doubt having parked it at the curve, *and* facing north, since he had come from the south! But on the other hand he could hardly imagine someone entering the car—how?—moving her a few paces and turning her around just to play him a trick. Then what *had* happened? Could he have turned her around himself before parking and forgotten it?

This pressure, he thought. Blunting, clouding the mind.

Some days later, on an overcast morning, he drove to the main street of her suburb, entered a café, sat on the high terrace overlooking the street, and ordered coffee. From this vantage point he could observe the passing cars, the shop doors. If he saw her in the blue convertible, pulling up at one of the shops and going in, he would follow her inside, to buy cigarettes. Hello, Mrs. Shofman. Just happened to pass. Everything all right? Yes, a fairly small sum, if you remember you might send a check.

And that would be all.

Tal drank his coffee and watched the occasional car entering the street from this or that direction. Ragged clouds drifted low across the sky. The ficus leaves shone wet, tipped by trembling raindrops. A delivery truck stopped in front of a grocery store and the driver began unloading crates of cauliflower. Crisp, chunky cauliflower heads, crinkly white, fringed with green.

Tal's mind went back to the village. A mistake maybe, he thought, maybe I should have stayed there, not moved to town. Have finished agricultural school and become an agronomist, or a farmer. A dense tropical plantation, beehives. He thought of Ella, Furman's girl, who had worked as a typist at the Local Council when he was a teller at the bank, and with whom he would spend summer evenings on benches in the park. Cold lips she had, and soft damp limbs. Thrusting his hand into her bra would feel like dipping it in water. The nipple would give between his fingers as though dissolving into the flesh of her breast. And before kissing she would carefully smooth back her hair behind her ears. "Bad boy, Shuka." Kissing the tip of his nose and at the same time expelling the hand that crept up under her skirt. They had nearly become engaged, and Furman had already assigned him a position in his warehouse, except that just then Elisheva had appeared on the scene like a scorching breeze—

He got up, paid, and left. Walking to the car he asked himself what he meant coming here, what did he chase this woman Annabel for, and what was the point of all this madness anyway? Seventy to eighty percent of all married men deceive their wives at some time or other, at least once in their marriage, and nothing happens. No one makes a fuss, because they do it on the quiet. Because they aren't fool enough to blab about it to their wives and get themselves into trouble. Because they use their wits. And only you, bloody fool that you are, must bloody well confess and give yourself away, and what's more—about something that *never even happened!*

Seventy to eighty percent! he repeated to himself, getting in behind the wheel. And not just the husbands, the wives too!

But saying that he felt a needle stab his brain, right through the top of his skull:

How do you know Elisheva hasn't?

How *do* you know?

Because *she* would obviously not be so stupid as to tell *you,* confess to *you!* Not her!

And in a flash the image of Julius Gertner appeared before his eyes.

And he recalled coming to her office and finding them in there together, and how taken aback she had been at the sight of him, as though caught red-handed, and how furious with him afterward. Why had she been so furious? In fact, for no apparent reason.

And the glances that had passed between them at that party—it was all coming back to him now, driving south, back to town—the stolen glances. And the way she'd sat anxiously watching every word he let fall. And her flushed face, the state she'd been in.

And the many evenings, the countless evenings that she had gone out and come home after midnight. Gone where? How many conferences do professors have and how late do they last?

All those evenings! All those nights!—he cried out to himself—till after midnight!

Tears pricked his eyes.

To catch her at her office right now—he thought—take hold of her and shout in her face: And you? With that tricky old bastard Gertner, just philosophical chitchat? All those long evenings? Nights?

And reaching the Ramat-Aviv intersection he did not continue on south but took a sharp left turn and drove toward the university.

The lecherous old bastard! he thought. Every single day! In her office!

To show up unexpectedly, catch them at it, in the very act, at the scene of the crime, heaven and earth to witness.

Medieval philosophy, he snorted, Praise of Folly!

Eleven o'clock. She'd be finishing a lecture now. Or if not now then in ten minutes. He didn't care if it took an hour. He'd lie in wait. Pounce.

He turned in at the parking lot, stopped, got out, walked toward the large humanities building, up the broad steps.

And through the door, inside, the corridor.

Wide, empty, shining corridor, like a ski slope.

A student, briefcase in hand and coat over arm, passed him at a run, sliding, nearly bumping into him.

For a moment he felt lost in the wide shining corridor.

If she's not there I'll wait for her by the entrance, he decided, and turned to her office.

Halfway there he stopped.

Better wait for the intermission, he thought.

And turned right, to the men's room.

Empty. No one. Smell of bleach. Water dripping into a urinal. A sudden gush and gurgle.

He entered a cubicle and locked himself in. Clean.

On the seat, he pictured himself entering her office, finding her alone.

Entering, finding her with a student.

Finding her talking with that fellow Gertner.

And maybe it was all rubbish, nothing between them.

And after all she's got as much right as you.

If only *you* had kept your mouth shut.

One chain of errors, your whole life.

He remembered how at school, in the eighth grade, he'd once hit another boy for calling him names. A sound thrashing.

Afterward, that evening, he'd gone to the boy's parents to apologize.

Fool to have beaten him and fool to have apologized for it. One error begets another.

Or the dried flowers he'd sent Rachel Yaffeh. Anonymously. Wonder how she'd found out it was him. Good joke for the whole class to get merry over.

And those nocturnal raiding parties on orchards, filching plums.

Errors.

He stood, pulled his trousers up. A man ought to be able to respect himself, he recalled his father's words, whatever you do, so long as it's nothing you have to be ashamed of.

When he came out, the corridor was filled with students swarming back and forth.

He dodged through and went out to the noon sky, hurried to the parking lot.

The car wasn't there. Gone.

The blood rushed to his face: dozens of cars, row upon row, side by side. Not his.

He passed between the rows, up and down, back and front, inspected them from above. Not there.

He wanted to run to the office, call the police, charge the management with responsibility for—

Only when he looked around at the building did he realize his mistake: it wasn't this parking lot but another, on the other side of the building.

The pressure on his head, he said as he got into the car, blurring.

On his way to the office he decided to call on his mother. She might be in for the noon break.

Dushkin opened the door.

"What a surprise!" he said in a rasping, smoked-up voice. "Come in, come in."

The morning paper lay spread out on the table.

"Sit down," said Dushkin and seated himself across from him at the table. "Seen that?"

Shuka glanced at the headline:

ZA'IN: WILL TURN
ISRAEL'S BORDER SETTLEMENTS
INTO GRAVEYARD

And under that in fat print:

Syrian Premier Announces Support for
Fedayeen Terrorists, Promises Military Aid

Rubbish, thought Shuka. This whole Gertner thing. Just poppycock.

"Just threats," he said disparagingly.

Dushkin looked at him with a wry smile.

"That's what they said about Hitler too. No one believed him!"

"Who's Za'in? Some little pipsqueak."

Dushkin lighted a half-smoked cigarette and peered at him with dull eyes as though his glasses had hazed over.

"Ought to take a look at history," he said. "All the evils have always come upon us from the north. All the conquerors. Tiglath-pileser, Sennacherib, Nebuchadnezzar, Titus, Vespasian, the Crusaders, the Mamelukes, the Turks—all of them came from the Syrian side."

Shuka was trying to concentrate. Only about philosophy, medieval literature? he thought. In that small room, evenings? And he isn't that old!

"The British came from the south," he said.

"The British gave us the Balfour Declaration," said Dushkin, "and they cleared out after thirty years in any case. Mark the historical difference: those who came from the north laid the country waste, those who came from the south either settled down here, or else only stayed for a short time. We ourselves came from the south—the Exodus. The Nabataeans, the Arabs —settled down. The Pharaohs made brief raiding excursions and cleared out, and one of them married his daughter off to Solomon. The Ptolemies brought prosperity to the country. So mark my words: the danger is from the north! King David knew what he was about when he conquered the Syrians of Zobah and Damascus!"

"You want us to take Damascus?" Shuka grinned.

"A pipe dream, you think? Absurd?"

"I'm just not interested."

Dushkin's look was a mixture of pity and contempt.

"Know why you're not interested? Because you, along with everybody else in this country today, have got the mentality of shopkeepers. Recession! That's what you've got on your banner. That's the great vision. That's what's left of all the grand dreams from the pioneering days—recession! The ugliest symbol of retail trade, petite bourgeoisie, narrow-mindedness. What's everybody talking about these days—the price of a new fridge, the best kind of hair dryer to be got in Cyprus, how to go about obtaining a visa for Canada. They've taken away beauty, honor, national pride."

Shuka recalled the Betar demonstration in the village. His father. Maybe she'd done well to remarry.

"You want war?"

"I want a homeland. Not just a state—a homeland. And I want it to be big and secure, and safe from mobs yelling for our blood. I was in Jaffa during the twenty-one riots, and in Jerusalem in twenty-nine, and I remember. And today's Arabs are no better than that lot—they're worse. And instead of bowie knives they've got machine guns. In twenty-nine, when I was working at the Jerusalem Electric Corporation, I was told by an Arab engineer—an educated, intelligent man, mind you—'If you won't get out of here yourselves' . . . and made a gesture like cutting his throat. And today Yussuf Za'in says: a graveyard. Same mentality, but coupled with Russian arms. And we complain to the UN like good little children running to teacher. . . ."

The blood rushed to his head remembering the wedding, Elisheva's absence, her trip to Jerusalem. Where had she spent the night?

"You won't be fighting anyway . . ." he said, rising.

For a moment Dushkin remained at a loss for words.

"That answer's too easy." Rising in turn, his hand pressed against his side.

Poppycock! thought Shuka. Can you really for a moment imagine it, her with . . .

"Your back's still bad, I see. How are you otherwise?"

"I won't be fighting anymore anyway, as you say."

"We'll neither of us fight, I hope." Shuka's lips curled in a bitter smile. "How's Mother?"

"Complains she never sees you."

"Yes, I've been busy." Shuka wandered through the room, glanced at the pictures, the antique silver carriage, the crystal goblets. He picked up a book lying on the sideboard and opened it: *Herzog*. By Saul Bellow. Maybe she'd done well to marry, Mother.

"Read it. A good book," said Dushkin. "All the jitteriness, the sickness, the anomaly of the Jewish people."

"Preachy?" said Shuka, thumbing the book. "Zionism and all that?"

"No," Dushkin smiled. "But the depiction of a single character sometimes reflects the destiny of an entire nation. American Jews today are just where our Russian intelligentsia was eighty years back. The same sense of rootlessness, the same insecurity, and the same bewilderment verging on madness. Like the stories of Berdichevsky, Gnessin . . ."

"I'll return it." Shuka took the book.

Leaving, he felt the weight pressing against his head again.

"ALONE?" said Elisheva in a detached voice. Detachment was an effort because of the hot wave that beat up her body to her face.

"Not all alone, of course. I've a childhood friend there, a Merhavia girl."

Dinah's voice on the telephone was warm, open, faintly drawling, as always, but Elisheva would not trust it.

"Had a good time?" she said coldly.

"Lovely! Too short though. Three weeks . . ."

"When did you get back?"

"Last night. I found a letter from my parents. Such a pity I wasn't there when you came! . . ."

"M'm, we were just passing . . . You going to stay in town now?"

"So hard to get used to it. You wake up to such an entirely different world. It's full summer there now, you know."

Elisheva hardened herself not to respond to the open, intimate tone. And the suspicion and mystery persisted, rankling.

"Right, then . . ." Suppressing her curiosity. "We'll see each other sometime. . . ."

"I guess so . . . I suppose you're busy, as usual. . . ."

The chill that had come into Dinah's voice showed she had taken offense. The urgent need to know, to find out the whole truth, proved stronger in the end than the resolve to maintain a distance.

"What are you doing tonight?" Elisheva said, once more detached.

"Nothing special . . ."

"We could meet then . . ."

"I'd love to. Shall I come over?"

"No, not here!" Elisheva said quickly.

"Some café?"

"All right. Where?"

"Café Shor?"

"Fine. Say in half an hour? An hour?"

Replacing the receiver, she shut her eyes. She saw the oasis of Ein-Gedi: palm trees, oleander, bubbling brook, the waterfall overhung with maidenhair . . . the scene all set for a romantic affair, a passionate affair, a sex affair. Had they? Behind her back? Dinah's manner bespoke nothing but frankness, honesty, and yet . . . the something something who "win us with honest trifles, to betray us / In deeper consequence" . . .

She got up with a sigh: Café Shor. An open wound, still smarting.

They arrived together and met at the entrance. "What a tan!" Elisheva smiled at her.

"Ages since we met. I've missed you."

Inside, the only unoccupied table was the same one as before. In the corner, under the red lampshade.

"So you were at Ein-Gedi, h'm . . .?" Elisheva put her handbag on the table.

Dinah's story drew on a wealth of exciting impressions: the working at the vegetable patch, the getting up before dawn and the sun rising over the Hills of Moab, the sunsets crimson on the Dead Sea, the swims in the brook, the trips to the waterfall at dusk, the plants, the birds . . .

"How romantic," said Elisheva.

"Ye-es . . . Yes and no. Romantic and unreal. It's like a walk on the moon. You sort of lose your sense of weight. You float . . . That white glitter all around you, the salt . . . Like before Creation, sort of. . . . And on the other hand . . ." Pausing.

"On the other hand, what?"

"I don't know . . . On the other hand you get, in that same place, people, radio, gossip, the noisy conversations in the communal shower, the dining hall . . . the practical everyday business of living . . . such a contrast . . ."

"You enjoyed it though. . . ."

"Oh, yes! A different world . . . And I didn't know whether I was running away from myself or coming back to myself. . . ."

Elisheva examined her face. Suspicion dissolved at the open expression, the unreserved speech. And yet . . .

"Any adventures?" Smiling.

"No!" With a laugh, then adding, "That is, there nearly was something."

"Nearly?" Elisheva reddened.

"You know how it is at a kibbutz. A girl appears from outside, unmarried, they know she writes poetry . . . so naturally they go for her . . . And I was sort of in the mood for it too. . . . And besides, when you're at such a . . . romantic place as you say, you feel like letting go a bit, and in a strange place you feel sort of less accountable for your actions anyway. . . . Not seriously, not . . ."

"Yes . . . quite."

Dinah laughed. "But they make such heavy going of it, that crowd. Big clumsy kids. So there was this fellow, the typical sturdy kibbutznik to look at him—mustache, lots of hair on his chest, bit of a joker and all. . . . We worked together a few days picking tomatoes, and I really liked him a lot. . . . Oh, what am I telling you all this for . . ." she interrupted herself.

"No, go on. . . ." Elisheva felt ancient in the face of such glowing youth and vitality and warmth.

"We went hiking together a lot," Dinah continued. "One day I suggested we go to the waterfall for a dip. When we got there I undressed, not thinking twice, you know, the way we always used to back home when we'd go bathing at the Harod Spring, and I stood under the water. . . . He was so embarrassed he didn't even dare look at me! . . . Afterward, that evening, in my room, he was miserable, depressed, gave me a long spiel about his unhappy childhood and all . . . I just didn't feel up to it."

Elisheva smiled, somewhat relieved.

"Think he was in love with you?"

"I don't know. Maybe. There's some flaw about this so-called manly, forthright kibbutz type: they lack both the simplicity of the country-bred and the sophistication of the townsman, and that's what makes them so awkward, so inhibited. . . . How's Shuka?"

"All right. . . . So you're going to stay in town now . . ."

"Yes . . . Hard to adjust again . . . and yet, when I walked through the streets today I discovered that in spite of everything I do love Tel Aviv. I really do. It's pretty, and it has an air that's both festive and everydayish at the same time. Something open, democratic. Life itself is sort of without illusions here . . . sort of optimistic, you know, taking things as they come with a sort of faith, without doubts and quibbles: that's how it is, that's how it ought to be. The business of living itself. Don't you agree?"

"Depends on my mood. Sometimes I feel like you do, sometimes not . . ."

"You working hard these days . . ." Dinah looked at her.

"Not particularly. Start of a new year always means work." Then, braving it: "Have you seen Brosh lately?"

"No, have you? How's he really?" Dinah said animatedly.

"I was supposed to let him have some article, and they told me at the paper he'd gone on leave."

"Annual?"

"Extended, they said."

"Gone to write, I suppose. . . ." Dinah said.

"Maybe . . ."

"I'm quite curious about him. . . . I'm dying to know what his next book's going to be."

"His book?" Elisheva smiled.

"Aren't you?"

"Yes . . . in a way . . ." And with a straight look into Dinah's face: "You two would make a perfect couple."

"Me and him?" Dinah laughed hard and a fierce crimson covered her face. "What on earth makes you say that?"

"It's what I think," said Elisheva with a smug feeling of having caught her bird.

"But it's quite ridiculous, Elisheva!" Dinah exclaimed in rather too high a voice.

Then what are you getting all hot about? Elisheva said to herself, watching the culprit who had all unwittingly confessed.

"You're really suited to each other, you know."

"But what put that into your head!" The blush spreading to her throat, her ears.

"You *are* a little bit in love with him, aren't you?" Elisheva said with a stiff little smile.

"It's silly . . . it's just . . ."

"You needn't hide it from *me*. . . ." Elisheva assuming the manner of a teacher exhorting her pupil to hold nothing back, to put her faith completely in an older woman.

"But it's ridiculous. . . . There's nothing to hide. . . . It's true there was a time when I *thought, thought* I was in love with him. . . ."

"See? . . ."

"But that was a long time ago . . . and it only lasted a few days anyhow. . . ."

"When?"

"Two or three months ago, when I used to meet him at the café sometimes. . . . I was quite dazzled by him, I admit. . . . There's something very fascinating about him, you know, sort of enigmatic. . . ."

"Enigmatic?" Elisheva gave a skeptical smile.

"Well, maybe not quite that . . . I don't know what to call it . . . A kind of reticence which makes you feel there's a whole world of secrets and mystery behind . . . Very intriguing anyway. But I came to my senses. Quite soon, too."

Elisheva watched her, aching with memories. The nights in his room. Jerusalem. The reticence an impenetrable armor.

"What cured you?"

"Sheer instinct of self-preservation, I'd say. I saw myself living with him, the two of us in a room, morning, noon . . ."

"Saw youself *living* with him?" Elisheva laughed. The cheek, to actualize such a possibility, even if only in thought. It made her blood boil.

"I really set my imagination to work at times like that. I'm not so romantic when it comes to that. . . . What I picture to myself isn't the night, but the morning *after*. . . ."

"*Was* there such a night?" A twisted smile appeared on Elisheva's burning face. She was afraid she'd lose control.

"Oh, nonsense! But there *might* have been . . ."

"As far as you are concerned, you mean . . ."

"D'you know something, I have a sort of naive faith, sheer superstition maybe, that if I should want something very much, really very much, willing it to happen and seeing it happening in my mind, then it really would. . . ."

Elisheva felt an obscure resentment starting to gnaw at her.

"Never mind the other person's will . . ."

"Sort of against his will . . ." Dinah laughed a little.

"You're very sure of yourself, aren't you!"

"Oh, you know I'm not. . . . But when it comes to personal, emotional ties . . . Once, you know, as a child, I decided I'd 'hypnotize' my history teacher. I was dying for her to like me. I used to stare at her in class without taking my eyes off for a second. . . . But I'm boring you . . ."

"No . . . What made you think he'd be susceptible though?"

"Oh, little things, you know, a glance, a gesture, a smile. . . ."

Dinah stopped. Under her frosty smile, Elisheva's hostility was very near the surface now.

"You think this is all just wishful thinking, don't you?" she said.

"No . . . I'm only struck with admiration at your self-assurance!" She emitted a short laugh. "Well, what cured you, then?"

Dinah paused, reflected, then said:

"A trifle, really. One night he offered to see me home. We walked, miles and miles, till two or something."

"Home?"

"We didn't go up. I wasn't sleepy, so we just went on till we got to the Yarkon, and walked along its bank . . ."

"Don't tell me you took off your clothes and went swimming?" Elisheva grimaced.

"In the *Yarkon?*" Dinah laughed, scanned Elisheva's face,

resumed: "Anyway, I was quite enjoying it. There was a moon, and the trees, those thick eucalyptuses there with their bare roots groping for the river . . ."

Dinah interrupted herself again and looked at Elisheva.

"Go on." Elisheva shook a cigarette out of her pack and lit it.

"Yes . . . so we talked a lot, and he told me things and I told . . ."

"Interesting?"

"The things he told? Yes. About his childhood, and about Jerusalem, and about Cabalists in the Old City, and stories about people in Meah She'arim. . . ."

Again Dinah paused. "Are you angry with me?" she asked.

"Me? At you? Why on earth? Go on . . ."

"I thought . . ."

"Oh! Do go on . . ."

After a moment she did: "All of a sudden he fell silent, and that was that. Didn't say another word. We turned back, and all the way, for maybe a full hour—not a word. Just kept silent. Stubbornly. Even rudely, I'd say. As though I didn't exist. At my door I said good-bye, and afterward I though how terrible it would be to live with such a person for twenty-four hours a day."

"Just because he kept silent?"

"Yes! He treats you as if you were air. Not a scrap of consideration for you. You're at the mercy of his whims. And me I've got quite enough whims of my own to be able to live with a person who makes *his* whims dominate the entire relationship."

"And that's what made you come to your senses? . . ."

"Does it surprise you?"

"I find it a bit strange that such dispassionate considerations —about what may or may not happen in the future, in a future family life—should be able to cool off, or should even completely quench, such a powerful emotion as being in love . . . with a girl like you especially . . . a poetess . . ."

Dinah's eyes stayed on her for a long moment, as though she had discovered a new aspect of Elisheva's personality and was reluctant to acknowledge it.

"I've been burned before, Elisheva. More than once," she said in a voice heavy with experience.

Elisheva stabbed out her cigarette and flattened the ash with it, rubbing it across and across the ashtray.

"Do we really ever learn from experience?" Raising her eyes.

"Learn? No. But our instincts grow sharper, warier of illusions. Know what I'd wish myself today? A little security. A man in whose arms I could close my eyes and trust him forever after. Not a very romantic wish, is it?"

Elisheva looked at her, smiling.

"Is there such a man?"

"There is," she said, and added after a moment, "Shuka, for instance."

"Perhaps . . . But still, Dinah, still, you must admit that if you'd gone on seeing him . . ."

"You're wrong," she said with finality. "No."

"Even if you'd discover that on his part . . . ?"

"That wouldn't happen!" Dinah was blushing again. "Never!"

"Why not?"

"Because . . . I don't think he's capable of it, falling in love, I mean. Truly in love. Falling in love demands a readiness to let go, open yourself . . . a certain generosity, tolerance . . . while he . . . you know him."

"Very little," said Elisheva.

A long silence followed, and then she picked up her cigarettes and lighter and said, "Shall we go?"

"You're angry with me," said Dinah.

"Oh, what put that into your head? I'm tired, that's all. Just tired."

Afterward, at the door, after paying the waiter, she said, "If I were your age today I'd have fallen in love with him."

"Something like that occurred to me while we were talking," Dinah said outside in the street. "Only I didn't dare say so."

"And I wouldn't have come to my senses either," Elisheva said with a parting smile.

T AL left home in the morning to go to the office. But at the point where he should have turned left, his mind forming a picture of the room, the documents, Ziona's face, he said to hell with it all and drove on.

He passed the crowded thoroughfares, turned east, and when

he reached the broad highway and was carried along on the swift flow of southbound traffic, he told himself: Drive where you will, wherever the car takes you, never stopping, to the end of the world.

The air was pure after the early-morning rain. White clouds snowballed in the sky, coiling and cleaving and drifting apart to leave wide patches of cold and intense blue ocean between them, and the rain-flattened sand smelled fresh and good.

A flock of soldiers, hands pleading, stood by the shelter on the coastal road, but he did not stop or slow down. You can't carry the burden of the whole world on your back, he said. Leave something to others.

And as he drove on a sense of boundless freedom seized him. Like escaping a bottleneck for open space. For horizons leaping ahead and retreating, leaping and retreating. Who's to stop you?

He steered with one hand, one elbow resting comfortably on the window ledge. Trucks piled high with boxes, sacks, timber, iron girders, came toward him, wheezing and snorting uphill, and he smiled to himself: The world struggles, toils and struggles, bears and suffers. And all for what?

Glowing colors, at their most vivid! He marveled at the sight of the broom shrubs, the tamarisks, the eucalpytus trees, the white-and-gray roof tiles on both sides of the road. Then came the citrus groves—thousands of grapefruits peering through the heavy foliage, light-green, radiant-green, round, oval, pearly with raindrops. Good harvest this year, he said. But when he thought of all the drudgery involved in their cultivation the year round—the irrigation, the hoeing, the spraying, the scurrying back and forth between trees, the gathering bent-backed from morning to night among the low scratching branches, straining up to the high ones, climbing ladders, fetching and carrying packing cases, loading on trays, trolleys, trucks, the calling, the shouting, the truck drivers' snarls, the shrill bargaining—he decided it was an evil thing under the sun. What for? And the endless calculations. So-and-so much investment per acre, so-and-so much the fetching price, and the deductions, for the marketing companies, for income tax—the endless calculations—how do people have the strength to put up with it all?

For a moment, approaching Nes-Ziona, he considered turning off, driving into the village, taking a look at the old courtyard—the quince trees, the row of tall, upright Persian lilacs, the hibiscus shrubs, the tangle of weeds shooting up wild about the dripping taps and at the base of walls—

But on second thought he decided—no. Definitely. And continued southward.

The cackle of hens came from the faded, rickety coops on both sides of the road.

His mind went back to his mother. Russian princess captured among the fences of a village in Palestine, with the lowing of the cows, the cackling of hens, maize and millet seeds trodden into the hard dust, cow pats aswarm with glittering drowsy flies . . . Surrounded by peasant poverty, she had tried to preserve a memory of bright salons: silver teaspoons, crystal goblets, green velvet tablecloth. The delicate silver carriage.

And bleached her hair a flaxen yellow.

Even today—cooped in among the perfume bottles—still young. Capable of doing a waltz with all the bounce of a ballet girl.

With Dushkin, he grinned.

Rubbish, doesn't exist, away, behind your back! Stepping on the accelerator.

Heavy trucks were rumbling in a busy flow from the direction of Ashdod Harbor. New apartment buildings going up over there, stuck in the sand, flighty, wide open to wind and sea, blank faces turned to the electricity poles shouldering the burden of long lines, the length of the land.

Housing for immigrants, Algerians, Moroccans.

Albert, he thought.

Albert may still phone, with a snort. Just let him try.

Talk to me with flowers, my love.

Jeanette's face, with her coaxing, seductive smile floated before his eyes, and he felt no remorse. For the first time he felt no remorse. Not a twinge. It's all happened for the best, he said. All for the best. Experience gained. Who's to tell me do or don't.

He thought of Dinah Lev. Once, at home alone, he had asked her what she was doing and she had laughed and said: I sleep. I love sleeping so much. I'd like to sleep without end, without responsibility and without guilty feelings . . . We'd all like to be God's little children, not answerable for our deeds. . . .

God's little children. His heart warmed at the thought of Dinah. A true friend.

And in a flash it struck him that all his life he was surrounded by women: his mother, Elisheva, Avigayil, Jeanette Levy, Dinah—

Annabel?

Ziona at the office. Dinah.

A true friend, Dinah. A pity to leave.

There were plowed fields on both sides of the road now, with clotty, crumbly, shiny furrows. Beyond them clumps of houses sheltered by trees. And after the plowed fields, green pasture of new wet grass, luscious grazing land. Goosefoot and quills and chickweed and shepherd's purse and dyer's-weed and foxtail and rain flowers. A lush plenty to squat over as in childhood. Thou visitest the earth . . . makest it soft with showers . . . and the little hills rejoice . . . with flocks . . . Been years since we've read any Bible.

Villages, development towns, agricultural machine workshops, enormous concrete pipes, the two-story Arab house at the crossroads. Before Ashkelon he turned left to the Beer Sheva highway.

A cart heaped with manure stood in the middle of a plowed field and two slight men with straggly black beards were unloading it in broad sweeps of pitchfork and scattering it over the field.

When they straightened up briefly and sent a glance at the highway, his heart filled with compassion for the whole world.

Aching world, he thought. People slaving away at backbreaking jobs. Working from morning to night, then coming home to a dark pitiful place, eating a mush of millet and eggplant and green pepper and wiping their plate with hunks of bread. A wretched life.

Or suddenly the head of the household, the provider, receives a summons for Reserve duty. *Force majeure.* He leaves his home and is taken to some godforsaken nameless nowhere, to crouch in the dust of some emplacement with a machine gun knocking against his ribs. Yes, sir, no, sir, rushing about obeying orders, from here to there and back, and between a here and a there haunted by visions of home, the kids—

And if it isn't Reserve duty it's the price of kerosene going up, or bus fares, or the cow getting sick, or the long line to the sick-fund doctor in the middle of the day, or—

The world needs remaking, he thought. Because in spite of progress, technology, communication, planning, the welfare state—the amount of suffering doesn't diminish. There must be a cycle of suffering in the world, he mused, like the cycle of matter in nature, the blood circulation. Suffering changes shape but its amount stays constant. It's part of the makeup of the universe, like a chemical substance.

If it isn't suffering hunger, it's a thing like red tape, for instance. Think of the agonies of some poor sucker who lives in an outlying settlement, doesn't know the country at all and the language haltingly, who sits in a waiting room at some office to obtain the signature of some clerk—on a note for sick leave, or exemption from some tax or other, or the right to benefit from some social insurance dole—and there's the delay, and the insolence of the clerk who sends him on to another clerk, who sends him to a third, and he rushes about looking for an address on a scrap of paper which he can't read, and misses a day's work, something like twenty pounds maybe, and the anxiety, the bitterness, the distress—

The world needs remaking.

That a man be free of cares. Be free to sleep as much as he wants, like Dinah said. Sleep in the morning, too, rest, dream. Not scatter manure in fields, not need the services of officials. Be lazy, be idle, and be none the worse for it.

Take this man you're approaching now, who is standing under the tin shelter by the side of the road waiting for a bus, him and his basket of radishes, neatly done up in bunches, green and red, from his own garden. Who knows how long he's going to wait like that, an hour, two hours, and by the time he reaches Beer Sheva it'll be noon and the radishes will have wilted, and if he *does* sell part of them—how much, and how much will he earn, if you figure that he's had to pay the bus fare there and back, and a whole day gone, and the amount of work that he's put into growing those radishes, and rooting them up, and washing them, and tying them up—

You could have given him a lift, come to think of it.

But does that remake the world? The social order?

For a moment he considered stopping, turning, going back to pick up the lone figure standing there with eyes screwed up for a bus to appear. But in the meantime he had driven some distance, and it would be ridiculous to go all the way back to pick up some stranger.

So now I am suffering, too, he told himself, suffering because of having failed to take the man. I mean, my good intentions didn't subtract anything from the amount of suffering in the world. And if I'd *have* carried out my intention and taken him, even then—maybe I'd have suffered from his company, so then again—

A white plain, pockmarked and stone-ragged, stretched out before him, and in the distance of shimmering skyline Beer Sheva loomed like a mirage: tall horizontals trembling on a water-blue background. The trembling stopped and steadied and assumed the shape of buildings, building projects, the plain at their feet a carpet leading to a royal town.

Only when he entered it did the town shrink to his eyes. It was hot and the streets were close and yellow and dry with loamy dust. Hikers in Arab keffiyehs, with canteens, knapsacks, crowds of them hugging café walls, cabdrivers clamoring for passengers as though plying their wares, a donkey with a load of firewood stopping in the middle of the road and obstructing traffic, its owner urging it on and the donkey refusing to budge. A fat, red-faced girl with an enormous knapsack on her back was trudging along the pavement as though climbing a hill.

Tal stopped, parked the car in the street, and went in search of a cold drink. A big headline leaped to his eyes from the string of newspapers at the stand:

MURDEROUS ATTACK
FROM TEL-AZAZIYAT:
TRACTORIST GRAVELY INJURED

There's going to be a war, he said, drinking.

Maybe even today, general mobilization.

They'll call at home and I won't be there.

There'll be radio announcements. Remember your code: Songbird.

A wave of warmth swept through him: general mobilization. All the patterns to change. The whole country to be on the move as a huge swarm of ants. Families breaking up. All the men leaving home, going on the roads, flowing toward camps, borders, lines. The barracks to fill up, swell, the roar of tanks making the earth tremble, half-tracks loaded with soldiers rolling in all directions, as marked on the maps, each man to his post, swift and smooth and accurate and clicking into place.

And you will be among men, he laughed to himself.

Be or not be.

He turned and strolled along the street, pausing at shop windows. Toys. Toy cars. Game called Going Places. Doll Carriage. Marbles. With colored spirals inside, colors like Hanukkah candles.

Lead marbles, he recalled. Shot with a snap of fingers at little hollows dug in the dry soil. You used to be good at that, even standing up and aiming along one arm, let alone lying flat on your belly, one eye shut.

There's going to be a war, he thought.

Men's shirts at IL. 25, at IL. 17, a suit at 78, very cheap. Ties at 3, 5, 6.95, who can afford that, 6.95. Light-blue dress on a dummy at 49.90. Old-fashioned. Provincial place, Beer Sheva. Third-rate stuff. Black brassieres, red brassieres, flesh-colored, meshed, transparent. Silk panties, or nylon, pink, red, tiny, no bigger than your hand, a handful. Elisheva's white. University lecturer.

He turned away from the window and bought a bagful of chick-peas from a street vendor, strolled on munching. Great thing, idleness. Who's to tell you do or don't?

Colorful populace, mixed: Oriental youths, long-haired tramps, kibbutzniks, Bedouin, old-time pioneers, soldiers—

His mind went back to the ravaged waste of the town in forty-eight, right after its conquest: all of it one rambling Arab desert inn. Shattered windowpanes, and shutters torn off their hinges, and pitted walls, and its single road holed and rutted, and a dribble of sewage coursing through the trash and the ruins to the dry pebbly riverbed.

War.

And maybe there won't be, he thought.

He bought an ice-cream cone and paused before the clothier's display again.

Odd how far away the Tel Aviv days are, he thought as he got into the car.

Your finest hour, he said when he was back on the open road. Free to go, wherever, forever, without count or account.

The elementary right of every man is to resign, he told himself. Resign his job, his duties, resign as a husband, a father. It's one of the basic principles of a free society.

Range after range of hills, cropped bare, shorn as camel hides, raked here and there by wooden plows, dotted with sparse bushes. Desolate goats roaming hillsides, grazing dust. A sheep dog loping for the horizon. Islands of green in the distance—a settlement, squares of grass, whirling sprinklers. Then the yellow again. Yellow waste. Lone tents, figures huddled in black cloaks—

The light wind was making him sleepy. He nearly dozed off, except that his clients appeared now, claiming their due. I'm on leave, he shooed them off, you mind? But Yermilowitz refused to give him peace. Parched plains and jagged hillsides stretched out on both sides of the road as far as the sky, but Yermilowitz's heavy head remained stuck before him. He saw him climb the stairs to the office, enter, sit, mutely beseeching, subduing his protests and waiting. Two thousand pounds, the premium of his burgled jewelry. A sick old man.

Ought to have left instructions with Ziona. At least that.

Could make a short stop at the next place, buy a postcard and mail it off:

"Dear Ziona, Had to go out of town unexpectedly on personal business. Please get in touch with Hasneh and remind them of that debt to Yermilowitz. I promised him I'd settle it within a week. Apologize for me next time he comes. All the rest can wait. If people ask tell them I'll be back. Soon. Regards."

Another postcard, to Elisheva:

"I've gone away. Don't know when I'll be back. Feel I must be by myself for a while. Hope you'll understand. Yours."

Or:

"I've gone away. I don't know where I'll be yet. I felt I needed to leave home in order to throw off the depression of the past few weeks. I'm not blaming you. I must take the consequences of my actions. Give Avigayil my love and tell her not to worry. In case the bank sends the bill, please settle it. Yours."

No, wrong. Another way:

"Dear Eli, You must be surprised at my irresponsible conduct—going away without notice or explanation and leaving everything behind. But I hope that you, of all people, will understand that there are moments in a man's life when he takes stock of all he has done, of all his past, sees all the mistakes he has made—"

Rubbish.

A postcard to Dinah:

"I thought of you in the Negev wilderness and decided to write a few words. I am traveling by myself along the road, with nothing anywhere but hills of lime, deep wadis, here and there an acacia, and some shrubs whose name I don't know—and am amazed at not feeling lonely at all. On the contrary, though I'm far from people or towns or anything, I don't feel lonely at all, just free. Free of all responsibility, of the need to give an account to anyone or to explain myself. I've always found it hard to explain myself, or put things into words. I remembered how you said to me once that in this big harsh world a person may sometimes be allowed to let go and not be responsible for anything. You said—to sleep, to sleep without end. I find that to travel, travel without end—is more liberating. You sort of scatter yourself to the wind . . . become part of the open spaces . . . of the infinite . . ."

Letters to everyone under the sun, he grinned to himself, like that crazy guy Herzog:

"Dear Prime Minister, Allow me to draw your attention to the problems of the man in the street. I realize that your time is taken up with much more important matters than the one I wish to bring up in my letter, especially what with the security situation so grave just now and a war liable to break out any day, but I am sure you will agree with me that when all is said, the welfare of every citizen is the welfare of the State. Mr. Prime Minister, I have been an insurance agent for the past fifteen years. I think I can say in all modesty that I have served my clients in good faith, and have at the same time fulfilled my civil obligations: I have done Reserve duty every year, paid my income tax, etc. Owing to the pressure of work I have never in all these years taken a holiday even once. Following a crisis in my private life (whose circumstances this is not the place to relate), I was forced to leave home today (I am married and have a daughter of 17), leave the town where I live and abandon my work. This may appear as an irresponsible act, a shirking of the elementary obligation of every citizen to contribute according to his powers and abilities to the general welfare, to the national produce, and to the public services, of which insurance is one. In view of the fact that I am a self-employed person, with no higher authority to turn to in this matter, I consider it my duty to explain it to you, sir, as follows: As long as I (Y. Tal, born in Nes-Ziona) can remember, we have been living in a continuous state of tension—of work, security, immigrant absorption, etc. This tension has a grave effect on the character of this country's citizens, making them prone to irritability, aggressiveness, impatience, imbalance. It seems to me that the time has come to pay some thought to the question of how to relieve this tension, how to enable the man in the street to obtain some peace of mind, how to give him an opportunity to now and then enjoy life *without* work, *without* care, *without* the burden of responsibility. To be free sometimes to do as the fancy takes him. I dare to suggest, Mr. Prime Minister, that if this opportunity were granted him, our society and our State would take on a totally different appearance. I do of course realize that the state of tension we live under is not due to ourselves alone, but is a result of the relations between us and the neighboring Arab countries, of the need to absorb immigrants, build the country, etc.

Nevertheless, allow me to suggest that if the relief of tension were one of the aims we were striving for, if the State realized that the citizen is not just a creature with national obligations, but that he is a person with weaknesses, breakdowns, fears, regrets, mistakes, mistakes, mistakes—"

He reached Mitzpeh-Ramon at half past one. He stopped at the gas station and filled his tank, then walked up to the restaurant on the cliff overlooking the crater, took a table outside, and ordered a stew and a bottle of beer.

Looking into the abyss below made his head swim. The colors stood out bright and vivid, veins of red and orange and purple and mustard yellow, circling the large crater around and around, undulating in whole or in broken waves as though traced by some prehistoric ocean, and he imagined he could see castles in the distance and ancient cities, ruined temples, giant fossilized beasts. And the long deep ravines emerging from the crater with zigzags of green at their base seemed to be leading to other cities still, timeless and unknown cities on some plain beyond the mountains. The huge cliffs crouching at the heart of the crater—as though an avalanche had come crashing down from the mountaintops and frozen there in an instant when the earthquake stilled—seemed to be moving now. And seeing the silver ribbon of road snaking down into the crater, crossing it and becoming lost somewhere in the range of hills at the other end, he was gripped by a fear of plunging headlong down the sheer slope into the abyss and being shattered there, at a precise point between two stark cliffs.

He fixed his eyes on the appointed spot and kept staring at it as though hypnotized. He had a vivid image of himself reaching a bend halfway down the slope, losing control of the wheel, turning over several times with a slide of rocks in his wake, and the splintered and crushed car coming to rest against the cliffs with his torn body inside it, lifeless.

He felt sorry about the car, which had served him faithfully and had been a kind of home away from home, even a refuge sometimes. And when he visualized his home without himself the tears sprang to his eyes. He saw Avigayil shutting herself up in her room, burying her face in a pillow to stifle the sobs, saw

Elisheva, stunned at the news, the hushed confabulation of the neighbors collecting on the staircase. Azulai, Mrs. Hurwitz from the ground floor, old Malkin of the delicatessen across the street. A house struck by death—

He remembered that he was insured for 50,000.

Elisheva wouldn't even know how to cash the money, whom to apply to, how to cope. She'd always been helpless where money affairs were concerned.

The restaurant owner put a plate with meat, potatoes, and green peas before him and asked if he would like a pickled cucumber as well. Tal looked at him blankly, then said, "No, thanks."

He saw the people gathered around the black-draped coffin. The neighbors. A couple of insurance agents. Old family acquaintances from Nes-Ziona. His old teacher Ze'ira maybe, if the news had reached him. Gilead from the army, if he'd be able to get off that day. His former partner, Yehieli.

With a pang of conscience he thought of all the things he had left unfinished, Yermilowitz's insurance money among them.

Who else will be there? he thought. Except for his mother, Dushkin, Elisheva's father—

Jeanette! With a flutter of alarm.

And felt at once he had to warn her somehow not to dare—

No, he reassured himself, she'd never even know. She doesn't read newspapers.

And Ziona, of course. Crying hard. A good girl, after all, doing her job, and she'd feel very lonely staying in an empty office with her boss gone beyond recall and papers lying on his desk unsigned—

And Dinah, yes, Dinah. A true friend.

Through the faint sighs of the wind gathering thistles before it he heard the voice of the cantor—high and sad and heartrending, in the prayer for the dead—God abounding in mercy, who dwells on high . . . and the tears choked him. He wanted to hug Avigayil, standing there proud and erect with a handkerchief at her eyes, wanted to tell her: You're a big brave girl and I can rely on you, and you'll grow up, and you and Mother will have each other, and you'll see it's not as bad as you think—

The wild crater stirred before his eyes, valley of doom, abyss yawning wide to disaster, to the fatal accident that would soon befall. And when he turned his eyes back to the restaurant, it, too, seemed to be marked by the calamity that had come to pass, or was about to pass: the place was empty and the owner was standing alone behind the counter with a frozen expression on his face. The air itself was frozen. And all around—a hush. And the small defenseless village beyond—empty and frozen, too. Was all the world asleep? He wanted to go to the restaurant owner and say: Look, I'm going to drive down into the crater. I may have an accident. There's a possibility I may, at any rate. Look out. If you hear a sound of stones slipping, or the noise of a crash, you'll know it's me. Here's my address, my phone number. No, better notify the police first. Or no, call up the office, my secretary.

"Any news on the radio?" he asked going over to pay.

"Didn't listen, why?"

"Saw in the paper this morning there'd been another Syrian attack."

"Nuts . . ."

"Nobody coming in here today," said Tal.

"Weak," said the man, "off-season."

He was very careful driving down the steep twisting road. He drove in low gear and kept his foot on the brake and slowed down to inch the car around each hairpin bend. The chains of mountain wound around and around him, now to his right, now to his left, and he took care not to look down into the mesmerizing chasm. He hugged the wall of rock, nearly grazing it to keep from slipping. Gradually the depth diminished.

When he reached the bottom of the slope and saw the two high pillars of cliff to his right—much taller now than they had appeared from the top, tall and sheer and overshadowing—he was astounded to find at their feet, and in the narrow pass between them, nothing but a few clumps of thistle, their dry stalks rustling in the light breeze. He stopped the car, got out, crossed the few steps to the cliff, and inspected the ground about them. When he looked up to measure the height he had come he was seized by dizziness again and his sight blurred. Rings spun and flickered, green and orange and yellow reels. Could it be the sun? he thought. But the sun is behind me! And when he turned to look behind him the crater itself seemed to go around before his eyes. It's the reaction, he told himself, the sudden relief from fear. It's like what happens when you ease a heavy sack off your shoulders, and when you straighten up—dizziness, and rings going around. Sit down, grip onto something solid and it'll pass, he said. And went back to the car.

But as he drove on, the same thing happened. The chains of mountain spun, not swiftly as before, but in a wide circle moving slowly from west to east—the castles, the temples, the rock pillars, the giant sphinxes—and though he didn't for an instant stray off the road crossing the valley, he felt as if he were losing direction, as if he were in fact moving without any direction at all. Moreover—he was hearing voices. Was it the wind whispering in the thistles? Or a wind forcing its passage through the mouth of the valley, rasping at the rock face and twirling dust? And from time to time a kind of drawn-out wail, rising and fading. Your imagination, he told himself, playing you tricks. Due to the strong light you aren't used to, and the colors, and being alone in all this wide space. Just let your mind take grip of something real, solid—

And he tried to think of Yermilowitz. Yermilowitz had insured his apartment, the contents of the apartment, that is, for IL.20,000, and paid an annual premium of IL.160. The value of his burgled jewels was IL.3000, in spite of which the company would reimburse him only 2000, since the relative proportion of the household contents as a whole and the lost articles . . . But thinking of it, he didn't see Yermilowitz sitting across from him at the office but standing with lowered head and white face among the mourners gathered round the coffin. And right away he saw the rest of them standing there once more: Elisheva, Avigayil, his mother, Blumfeld, Mrs. Hurwitz, Azulai—

Elisheva's colleagues from the university would come, too, he thought.

Professor Gertner.

Rubbish, that suspicion. A respectable man, well on in years.

Her students. Avigayil's friends. Dinah. The writer Amnon Brosh.

Altogether quite a crowd when you count them one by one.

It's only when you think of your death that you realize your friends are not so few.

A distinguished gathering: Professor Gertner, other professors, the poetess Dinah Lev, the writer Amnon Brosh—

And thinking of Brosh he thought of his novel.

And discovered all of a sudden that he was covering the same ground as the hero of that novel—Jonathan or Jochanan—and that he was now among just the same scenery described in it. Amazing coincidence. Briefly the notion flashed through his mind, ridiculously, amusingly, that he was imitating Brosh's story.

And maybe all life was an imitation of some story?

He shot a glance at both sides of the road and was amazed to see that the crater had vanished. That is, he had left it behind. How come he hadn't noticed? He was driving through a white billowing plain now, rough with limestone, a desert waste.

I couldn't be going to that place where Brosh's hero lived anyway, he told himself. The whole point of that story was about the road being shifted to bypass that gas station, and I am traveling along the *new* road!

The white light reflected by the plain beat against his eyes and he felt dizzy again and thought he had lost the way.

Take grip, he said, and when he took grip lists of figures from insurance sheets danced before his eyes: a list of ages, a list of sums, a list of policies, of premiums. He tried to calculate: Age forty-five, medical category A, all-risk life insurance at a sum of IL. 50,000 index-linked—but the figures became mixed up in his head. Elisheva laughed: You've been at it all those years and you can't figure out the premium for a man of forty-five, medical category A? He grew angry with her and said he had never made a mistake in his figures and only now, because of this blinding light, and the desert, and the emptiness . . . Because of that? she said. Yes, because of that! he answered crossly, for you'll admit that at least in these matters . . .

And felt a dull ache starting in his head.

He stopped and got out to relieve himself. He took a few steps toward a lone prickly bush, undid his trouser buttons, and watered it. Far away to the west he saw a pointed mountain range and a few acacias scattered on its slope.

Turning back he was stunned:

The blue car wasn't where he had left it but far ahead. It was traveling on its own, yes, on its own, because there was no one behind the wheel. Sailing along the straight strip of road, heading south, amazingly steady, soundless, still, reaching the distant horizon and disappearing beyond.

Could it be, he thought, or am I seeing things?

It's a fact, he answered. It's a fact you're left without it, alone.

And for some reason it didn't only seem natural, but as though somehow foreseen.

A fact, he repeated, and did up the last button in his trousers.

"I'M thinking."

"What about?"

"Guess."

"Whisper."

"About how in half a year."

"In half a year what?"

"We won't be lying in the dark like this, whispering, you and me alone together."

"We'll be alone together wherever we are."

"Lonely-alone."

"Soldiers get leave, Gilly."

"Not often."

"No."

"Are you scared?"

"Of being lonely?"

"Being in the army."

"You can only be scared in a silence. Armor's too noisy to think."

"Sure armor's what you want?"

"I want to be inside a machine."

"Prosaic."

"What isn't?"

"Paratroops. Aircraft. Flying in the sky like a bird. Floating down like in a dream."

"You've been reading Saint-Exupéry."

"Not from him."

"What I want is the grayest, the earthliest, just that."

"Just to show to yourself."

"Maybe."

"Think you'll stand it?"

"I'm thin, but I'm tough."

"Yes, you're tough."

"You? Scared?"

"Of the hard bed in camp, the army blanket, the sheet. Rough on a woman to lie on a hard bed."

"Of straw."

"And all alone. Alonest thing for a girl, to lie in a room with ten other girls."

"I'll come to see you. Stealthily. Under cover of night. Sometimes."

"Always stealthily—us."

"Lovers under covers."

"Uh-huh."

"You're stolen fruit. Sweet."

"And you."

"Cherries."

"Now now, love, your parents'll be back."

"They won't come in here."

"They'll hear."

"Whispery, kisspery."

"I must go. It's after one."

"The night's still young."

"My father'll be angry. Don't want to upset him."

"Don't get up yet."

"All right, just for a little."

"You said you'd introduce me to your mother."

"I hardly see her myself."

"Think she has someone?"

"No. No."

"You said so once."

"I thought she had. Was wrong."

"Keeps to her room."

"Yes."

"And he?"

"Same. Hardly see him either."

"Out of town."

"Whole days. Today, too."

"They haven't made up."

"No. They hardly talk."

"Miserable?"

"Me? Sorry. For both of them."

"Any idea what it's about?"

"Their age, I guess."

"Their rage?"

"Age. Middle age."

"Their change of life."

"Their faith."

"Their faith what?"

"Lost, I think."

"In each other?"

"Each in himself. Therefore in each other."

"Won't happen to us."

"Won't."

"Not even after twenty years."

"No."

"Never."

"No. Never."

"Every night like the first."

"Young and warm."

"Very. Very-very."

"No, sweet. Keep still."

"Don't want?"

"Mustn't."

"Lovely warm. Two birds in a barn. Come to no harm."

"Someone's come in, I think."

"No."

"I heard a key."

"Only the neighbors."

"Look at the shadows on the ceiling. Floating."

"A reflection."

"Like in a lake, a pond."

"Sink in."

"Stop."

"Avigayil, Avigilly. Floating as a water lily."
"Please. Not now."
"With her soldier dallydilly."
"Pink rhymes."
"Like rest on breast, mouth on mouth."
"I'm getting up. Got to."
"Just a bit longer."
"Can't."
"Why?"
"Not free."
"With me?"
"Now."
"One more kiss."
"Just one."
"Long kiss."
"Sweet."
"Bliss."
"Lovely, feeling you."
"You."
"I'm a crazy girl."
"No."
"To give in like that."
"Yes."
"Don't know why."
"Because of us."
"Yes."
"Together."
"So much. Just be careful."
"Yes."
"Ah—"

REALITY and fantasy in literature.
But though the structure of her treatise was more or less framed in her mind, Elisheva was still only at the first chapter, which itself had already come to forty-eight pages in crowded handwriting, buttressed by dozens of footnotes; and on this

evening, after months in which she hadn't touched it, she decided to try and take it up again. A few hours before, when standing before a roomful of students, she had faltered briefly in her lecture (about the disintegration of the narrative sequence in Flaubert's *Saint-Antoine*), because the image of Amnon Brosh had passed like a fleeting shadow before her eyes again and brought on a moment of heart-sinking—she had told herself: Take yourself in hand! You've got to make an end of all this! And, back in her office, she had repeated to herself that it was absolutely imperative that she put a period to this whole stupid affair; that she had wasted far too much time (five months, counting them) on romantic fancies which had been futile and pointless from first to last, including this endless brooding over Shuka's "infidelity" (what nonsense! So what if he had hopped into some Annabel's bed a few times? The more so as he was suffering hell for his sins, while if you were honest with yourself you'd put him out of his agony!), and that she must—at once, today!—get back on course and start working. She reached home at four, and as a first step applied herself promptly to tidying the house and cooking supper for three—a proper hot meal—which was something she hadn't done for the past six months or so. When Shuka still hadn't come at seven she began to get worried. "Maybe we'd better call the office," she said to Avigayil. "The office is closed after five, for your information," said Avigayil. "You can call Grandmother though." Elisheva smiled. "Grandmother will be happy enough to hear your voice," she said. "Not about such a matter," said Avigayil. When they had finished supper, Avigayil said, "He'll come back, don't worry, he always does," and left the house, as on nearly every other evening.

At half past eight Elisheva went to the study and sat down to work. She opened the drawer and took out the thick file which bore the inscription, "Reality and Fantasy in Literature"—

That, however, was not the title she had in mind for her thesis, but rather: "The Ass and Rosinante," or, "The Gold-Loaded Ass"; or—which might be apter as far as a Hebrew reader was concerned—"Balaam's Ass." She had several reasons for wishing to wreathe her heavy and rather cumbersome chains of literary and scholarly pearls around the neck of such a lowly animal:

firstly, because it figured in so many works of fiction presenting reality and fantasy juxtaposed, as well as in countless fables, parables, and folktales, one of the earliest examples of the latter being, of course, the story of Balaam's ass; secondly, because the opening chapter of her work consisted of a meticulous analysis of Apuleius's *Golden Ass;* and thirdly, because she intended to establish her main argument on an exhaustive study of *Don Quixote.*

Dr. Tal-Blumfeld's main premise—developed in her mind over many years, supported by evidence from the literature of all times, and the basic assumption underlying her lectures at the university—was this:

For a literary work to assume the right to be called by its genuine title, namely, an "independent literary entity," it must conform to the laws of reality—only to release itself from their restraint. Both conditions of the formula—conformation *and* release—must be shown to exist in it at the same time. Conformation by itself may result in nothing but an imitation of reality, that is, in a work lacking any dimension beyond what exists in the actual world (and she intended to prove this assumption by invalidating the theories of Aristotle, Pope, Matthew Arnold, Benedetto Croce, and others); release by itself—that is, *complete* departure from reality—produces works whose effect is purely entertaining or didactic (whence she denied the artistic value of satires universally accepted as classics of their kind, such as *Gargantua and Pantagruel, Candide,* or, nearer home, Mendele's *My Horse*). The ideal relationship between reality and fantasy is the father-son, Daedalus-Icarus one, where a precise, geometrical-architectonic recording of detail subject to the laws of reality (Daedalus), begets the means to cut loose from it, the wings on which the work of art soars toward the sun, as it were (Icarus). Or another mythological metaphor that might fit this literary ideal: Pegasus. (It always amazed her anew how just those two, horse and ass, such earthly creatures with four feet planted firmly on the ground, figured so large in mythology and other imaginative literature complying with the principle of her basic assumption. She used to toy with the notion sometimes that in modern mythology, if there were such a thing, the appropriate symbol would be not a winged *horse* but a winged *car. . . .*)

In order to illustrate her premise she meant, then, to deal exhaustively with *Don Quixote*. Cervantes had at first intended to write a parody of the morality play and story of his time, depicting a madman bent on emulating the knights of the ballads, for example, Baldwin, and ending up convinced he *is* that knight. If Cervantes had really followed this line—beyond the first seven chapters—he would have achieved nothing but yet one more didactic, mediocre piece of satire to add to the many written by his contemporaries. But by elevating Sancho—just Sancho, on his ass, the epitome of down-to-earth realism—to the position of a hero, Cervantes had supplied the wings to make his creation "fly." It is Sancho to whom the mad, starry-eyed, self-styled knight replies when he says: "I know who I am, and I know too that I am capable of being not only Baldwin or Abindarraez, but all the Twelve Peers of France, and all the Nine Worthies as well, for my deeds are greater than any of theirs"; whereupon he must set out to prove his greatness in face of all the powers of reality." From being victim he turns into a visionary who leaves reality and soars beyond it, in the process managing to inspire the people around him with his visions and transport them from the world of here and now to more exalted spheres. The two opposites are attracted and cleave: Quixote is inseparable from Sancho with his peasant's common sense, and in consequence his flights of fancy have their roots in the soil; Sancho himself, on the other hand, occasionally achieves, under the influence of his master, veritable *tours de force,* spinning imaginative tales, for example, about Dulcinea or about Rosinante, or as ruler of the island. When at last Quixote is defeated by the Knight of the White Moon we stand by him against all the powers of reason and sanity. There is no longer a burlesque of the ideal knight of ballads like Malory's *Morte d'Arthur,* but a perfect fusion of the real and unreal, plumbing the profoundest depths of human experience and exposing whole layers of social and psychological conduct. It is as if the ass had given wings to the horse. A study of the various parts of the novel will shed light upon this reciprocal relationship—the fundamental relationship in any great literary work. Hence the motto she had adopted for her treatise, taken from *Don Quixote:* "An ass loaded with gold goes lightly up a mountain."

Concurrently with her main premise, Elisheva intended to advance a second—and one she considered an authentic discovery of her own—which was designed to illuminate the mythos-ethos relation in literature, that is, the motif of sin and retribution. While perusing the vast material required to substantiate her basic premise, she had noticed that the transition from reality to fantasy was invariably accompanied by the consciousness of sin. The point appeared most obvious and explicit in Ovid's *Metamorphoses,* where the transformation of humans into objects, plants, and animals is an outright punishment for sin; or in the Balaam story, where the ass opens its mouth to speak in consequence of its master's sin. Yet the same thing turns up, if in a rather more disguised manner, in all the later works from *Midsummer Night's Dream* to Gogol's "Overcoat" and "Nose," Kafka's *Trial* and *Castle,* Ionesco's *Rhinoceros* and *Amedée,* and so forth. Again, with writers such as Proust, Joyce, Virginia Woolf, where the departure from reality takes the form of a disruption of syntactic norms—the stream of consciousness, interior monologue, the disintegration of language, the fragmentation of scene and event—it too derives from a consciousness of sin and from a desire to revoke the connection between it and retribution. It is as though by disrupting the realistic, "natural" order the writer meant to disrupt the "divine" order of sin-retribution and create a new paramoralistic harmony. And this, in turn, had suggested to Elisheva the hypothesis (still requiring corroborative evidence) that the departure from realism in modern literature might be bound up with a cosmic sense of guilt, that is to say, a feeling that man's very existence is sinful. On the aesthetic plane, this sense of the moral meaninglessness of human existence might be traced through to the grotesque, the tragic irony, the absurd.

Now, seated at her desk, she took out of a second drawer the two cartons of index cards, one arranged by subject, the other by author's name, and set them down before her. Then she pulled at the ribbon of the file containing her manuscript, and a scattering of notes slipped out, scraps of paper with references, remarks, and annotations jotted down perfunctorily; and glancing over them she realized the wrong she had done herself by neglecting her work for so long, since it would take twice the trouble to decipher all those notes now and call to mind all the material alluded to. Two days of work for every one of neglect—and she'd have her work cut out for her, long evenings of rereading material which before had been fresh in her mind. "Life, charmed by its reflection in art, imitates art far more than art imitates life." Oscar Wilde, she remembered. But in connection with what? "The conflict between stasis and kinesis." Joyce, of course. "Cyril and Vivian at the library, their talk about art v. nature. p. 147." But it didn't say in what book. "The only beautiful things are the things that do not concern us"—a reflection of your own? A quotation? "Robbe-Grillet ab. *Last Year at Marienbad:* "The events taking place in a perpetual present, a world without past, closed in on itself, barring escape into memory." In what connection? "T. S. Eliot's fatal error re critic's emotionality." "Is a work of art nothing but a collection of symbols whose laws we must discover, completely ignoring its 'message'?" Ronald Barthes, she remembered. A theory to be refuted. "Racine is Racine, Proust is Proust." "Latin poetry— beaten copper." Lovely. Whose? "At Dangoor College Greek was taught in the 11th Century." "The unity of ethics and aesthetics ac. Belinski. Comp. w. Chernyshevski." And in English—"poor little rich girl." D. H. Lawrence maybe, or just a phrase that had struck her. A dentist's receipt for IL. 15. Which you forgot to give Shuka. Odd all the same he isn't back yet. Think he drinks sometimes? No, you'd know if he did. And a whole closely written page, in pencil: "I'm alone in a field, lying down among marigolds or dandelions. Pretend I'm sleeping but I'm not. I hear steps and say, Oh, that must be Julius. Tell myself that if it's him I'll reel off a Rabbi Nachman of Bratzlav story without slipping up once. I lift my head and see it isn't Julius but a bull with enormous horns, like an antelope's. Somehow I'm not afraid but wonder how come it's a bull when he has such a heavy udder. Daddy's chauffeur Rabinowitz appears in the uniform of a Russian general and says severely: Come home, hurry up, they're calling you. I want to shout at him, tell him to go away, and wake up. A feeling of irreparable loss." A dream from about a year ago or more. Before the "affair." A sigh escaped her.

When she began to read the first chapter, which had lain untouched for so many months, she realized what an amount of work she had put into it: looking up dozens of references, rare texts, old periodicals, encyclopedias. And was amazed she had had it in her, the zeal and perseverance, and the courage to take the plunge and wade through all this stuff! The reasoning was sound, built up like a kind of intricate defense case, with arguments tested and proved and following coherently from each other. She found hardly a need to correct, insert, or erase anything. But the reading took a long time, because every page put her in mind of the circumstances of its writing, or of the reading required for its writing, and the memories went far and wide. A quotation from I. A. Richards set her thinking of the *Odyssey*, of Telemachus, of Stephen Dedalus, of Dublin . . . And recalling Dublin and "The Dead" and the moving scene between Gabriel Conroy and his wife Gretta in the hotel early in the morning, she recalled Patrick O'Donovan of London University, and the first night with him, in his room, at the little hotel in Tavistock Square, her first man, and in the morning when she had seen the blood on the sheet she had felt so solemn, as though she had offered a sacrifice to the gods; and she remembered washing the sheet in the morning, so sort of festive, with such a stolen-happiness and threshold-of-new-era-in-life feeling, so full of hope, of great expectations; and how when she was hanging the sheet to dry before the shilling-fed gas fire, Patrick had said, "A shilling's-worth penance for sin. Where I come from they'd bury you in the Bog of Leighlin—unhallowed ground!"—and she had come back at him with a verse from Isaiah: "If thy sins be as scarlet . . ." Then she remembered their arguments about the IRA and the IZL, which reminded her of Yehuda Dolav, and of Jerusalem under the British, with the rolls of barbed wire, the Russian Compound, Government House on the hill, the Greek Church in the old City . . . again a sigh escaped her when she thought of Amnon Brosh.

When she had finished the chapter she was startled to see the time: a quarter past eleven, and Shuka not back yet. Her worry turned into anxiety granted even that he'd gone on a round of out-of-town clients, as Avigayil had suggested earlier in the evening, it couldn't be till all hours, and without letting her know. Or hadn't he let you know on purpose, let you worry as punishment?

She returned to the notes again: a string of quotations from the *Poetics;* an exhaustive summary of *Satyricon* for purposes of comparison with Apuleius. The next slip of paper made her smile: Tchernichovsky's "Three Asses"—the whole poem copied out. She remembered it had been when Avigayil was having it at school, and she herself had considered using it, as evidence. Evidence for what? Asses as a subject for allegory, as a symbol? And a new title for the entire treatise occurred to her: "The Asses and the Kingdom": a writer going like Saul in search of asses and finding a kingdom, through elevating the earthy and material to a level of apotheosis.

The final sentence on the final page, page 48 of her manuscript, read: "It follows that a writer is arbitrarily forcing his will over events set in train by motivations whose significance is beyond him," and she was already formulating the next three or four sentences she would write. But when she took up her pen she found herself listening to the voices and sounds from outside, waiting to pick out the sound of footsteps crossing the yard. The worry tugged at her heart: an accident maybe, a crash. Ought to call up the police maybe, the hospitals.

But if an accident, God forbid, they'd have let you know at once. He carries his papers on him. Always.

She flushed at the sudden notion that he might have gone to that woman Annabel. That he might be with her now, in her room, in her bed, at this very moment—

Out of vindictiveness.

She got up, hurried to the living room, picked up the phone book and searched through it, found some dozen Liebermanns in a row.

And the name listed would be the husband's anyway.

And even if you found hers?

An idle suspicion, she told herself, resuming her seat at the desk. Not after that "confession." Not now, when he's torturing himself sick.

"Comp. Petronius–Proust *A la Recherche.* Comp. Trimalchio's Banquet, *Satyricon*—'Circle' episode, *Ulysses.* Flow of events in opposite directions."

You never know the surprises you're in for from another person, even after living with him for twenty years under one roof, in one bed. Would you ever have thought him capable of starting an *affaire* like that? Him? Honest, faithful him?

"Order Steimatzky: R. W. Kenner and *Here Comes Everybody,*' Burgess. Look up library: *Kenyon Review* 1956."

Unpredictable thing, human nature. Complex mechanism, won't function according to fixed rules. Psychology not much help, not an exact science. Gropes in the dark, more hit and miss than anything. Like astrology. Ever expected things to work out the way they did with Amnon? Dinah? And with you yourself?

"Joyce's development from *Dubliners* to *Ulysses* like Picasso's from naturalistic academic drawing to Cubism. Artist must plumb reality before taking the big leap beyond."

Read the stars, see if you can't catch one falling.

Steps on the pavement, drawing nearer, nearer. Man's.

Going past, retreating, fading somewhere at the end of the night-black street.

If Avigayil were at home she'd call her grandmother. Something's happened. Something bad.

Leaves falling. Wind whispering.

"Correspondence between *The Dead* and Agnon's *The Doctor's Divorce:* in both stories—hotel setting, young husband jealous of memory of wife's first lover. In both—mortification at realizing the lover of inferior status. Both—the unbridgeable abyss. Think Agnon read Joyce?"

Only when you imagine disaster you realize how attached to him. The sense of security he gives you, no escapade a substitute for that. Only when you have it, truly only when you have it, you permit yourself such forages, knowing you always have the safe protection of the cave to fall back on.

After twelve.

Maybe the police after all.

Or gone out of town: Netanya, Hadera, Gedera, Ashkelon. Two hours there, two back, four hours just the trip.

Go to bed, sleep, in the morning you'll find him beside you.

The sheets were cold and lonely-feeling. A square of light was vaguely outlined on the ceiling and in it what looked like tadpoles flickering through water.

Yes, Dinah, after all—no, not after all but in fact—a happy life. Comparatively, like what's not. His very being. The blunt masculine honesty, inspiring trust and confidence. The warm, glowing him. Complementing opposites, as you said. Twenty years!

And musing on the "crisis" that had suddenly rocked the bottom of their life (it had all started at that party, she observed to herself—it had all started with Dinah mentioning *Ravens There Were None*), and going in her mind over all that had happened since, a time of six months, openly and in secret, and with all its odd and unexpected repercussions, its amazing intricacies—she thought it ought to be put into writing, and how it ought to make an interesting novel, exciting, rich in psychological, erotic, social undercurrents. Five characters, at least, and so unalike—yourself, Shuka, Brosh, Dinah, that Annabel (who's she? where's she? like some fairy tale), the tangle of relations between them, most of which the actors in the drama are unconscious of, and only the author's eye seeing it whole. The author remaining, "like the God of creation, beyond or above his handiwork, invisible, refined out of existence, indifferent, paring his finger-nails." *Integritas, consonantia, claritas.* But who is the author? What is the point of view? The style is the man, but the style is also a consequence of period, of subject material, of setting. And the setting of this particular novel—Tel Aviv, the Mediterranean, the unconsolidated mixture of Eastern and Western cultures, the mid-sixties, a time of lull between storms, a kind of low tide, and the ebbing water collecting in puddles all over town, at cafés, offices, homes, bedrooms, lecture halls, and weary, limp seaweed drifting back and forth, back and forth, meeting, retreating, until the next flood tide—

And as she tried to visualize the shape of this novel—even just to formulate an opening sentence—she found different styles clashing in her mind irreconcilably. On the face of it—following the sequence of the plot, a romantic plot of love and infidelity—a realistic, conventional novel would be called for, something in the manner of *Madame Bovary* or *Anna Karenina* which you might open with a sentence like, "One evening when insurance sales-man Yehoshua Tal came home from his office, he found that the regular order of life had been disturbed: supper wasn't ready, his wife, a literature lecturer, was out and had failed to leave any word about where she had gone, his daughter Avigayil . . ." Yet

· 276 ·

on the other hand, how could such a style do justice to all the nuances of thought, of emotion, hidden passion, to the invisible currents of the unconscious? And how would it comply with the principle of conformation to the laws of reality in order to cast them off? Didn't precisely this material, with its relationships so involved and the protagonists so unaware of them, demand the use of interior monologue, the disruption of external narrational sequence, the multiplication of time levels, the endowing of each separate moment with its full significance while stressing its inner, autonomic law?

How now at this moment, with you lying awake in the darkness, like Molly Bloom in 7 Eccles Street, listening to the sounds in the hushed street, the stairway, to the sighing of leaves in the branches of the Persian lilac through the window, please let him come, let nothing have happened, let the heavy steps be heard climbing the stairs, and the creak of key in lock, click of metal against metal, and the soft scrape of his shoes in the dark, and the rustle of clothes being shed, and his big body stretching beside you, and you rolling against him wordless and eager, wildly athrob, and he sweeping you up like then, ah, God, twenty years! like then, that walk among the orange groves, with the maddening smell of the acacia in bloom, and the sand seeping into your sandals and wriggling between your toes, and the distant water pump pounding pounding through the limpid night, and your arm around his broad waist under the wing of his strong and wary arm, too wary to cup the hankering breast, and he telling you in his warm whisper how in the eighth grade, yes, even then, he would weave spells and find omens in anagrams of your name, all that childish silliness of loves me loves me not loves me which you are capable of even today with all your great grown-up learning, like that time with Amnon when you tied knots in your hankie to charm the spirits or when the mirror broke and you thought that now, don't remind me don't break my heart with that madness that isn't wasn't won't ever, over and done with forever and ever, only him for you one and only, where was I, yes, the orange grove, when we passed Bockser's packinghouse, was it Bockser or Stamper I don't remember, and you told yourself he'll be mine tonight and all the days after and always, haven to flee from all storms, your head on his shoulder safe and secure as Dinah says rightly, and you drew him toward the trees, toward the close growth humming thronging with crickets and croakings and winds caressing or bat beating startled wings, and you said to him here on the dew-damp sand I don't care where don't care at all because you were so longing yes so very long longing who knows what time it is quarter past one or half past someone's crunching steps in the yard maybe Avigayil no not Avigayil either the cheek to come home so late every night after night me at her age never dared not a minute after midnight running home like Cinderella be a fool to believe she's a virgin still of course not who knows what's good what bad unbearable to think godforbid an accident god-forbid or who-knows-what better not think not tempt the devil tried and tested way to ward off evil eye to lie still not move eyes closed and in a minute or two three four you will hear the steps on the pavement and soft on the stairs and creak the key and grunt the door open and shut and thudthud on tiptoe close closer the bed and shudder the springs when he throws himself beside you and sweeps you in his arms like then on the dew-damp sand when he took you with his sure manhood hard and hot and fierce piercing till your breath going out in a cry ah to live life all over again young like then—